OFFICER
DOWN

ALSO BY MICHAEL GRANT

LINE OF DUTY

OFFICER
DOWN
MICHAEL GRANT

DOUBLEDAY

NEW YORK LONDON TORONTO

SYDNEY AUCKLAND

PUBLISHED BY DOUBLEDAY a division of Bantam Doubleday Dell Publishing
Group, Inc., 1540 Broadway, New York, New York 10036 • DOUBLEDAY and the
portrayal of an anchor with a dolphin are trademarks of Doubleday, a division of
Bantam Doubleday Dell Publishing Group, Inc. • All of the characters in this
book are fictitious, and any resemblance to actual persons, living or dead, is
purely coincidental. • Book design by Terry Karydes • Library of Congress
Cataloging-in-Publication Data: Grant, Michael, 1940 Dec. 21–   Officer
down / Michael Grant. — 1st ed. p. cm. I. Title.
PS3557.R2674033 1993 813'.54—dc20 92-37205 CIP •
ISBN 0-385-41968-6 • Copyright © 1993 by Michael Grant All Rights
Reserved Printed in the United States of America July 1993 First Edition
                1   3   5   7   9   10   8   6   4   2

Dedication

This book is dedicated to my mother, Anne Grant Mackin,
whose all too short life exemplified dignity and grace.
Among other things, she taught me how to think
and how to laugh.

Acknowledgments

Thanks to my wife, Barbara, and my daughters, Jennifer and Amy, for the time, ideas, and encouragement they gave me while reading the many drafts of this novel.

Thanks to David Gernert for his vigilance in keeping me, and the novel, on track.

Thanks to Steve Rubin and Judy Kern for taking time out of their busy schedules to read the manuscript and offer their valuable advice.

Thanks to Natalie Bowen. Her astonishing attention to detail helped me say what I thought I'd said.

And a special thanks, as always, to Kathy Robbins for her advice, encouragement, and wisdom.

Chapter
1

4:00 A.M. MONDAY, MARCH 11, 1991 • Police Officer George Wagner, assigned to the late-tour security detail at One Police Plaza, looked at his watch and yawned. It was time to make another sweep of the building. Following department procedures, he dutifully wrote in the log book with a large, sprawling hand: *0400 hrs. P. O. Wagner to inspect the perimeter of OPP.*

He drew a line underneath the entry and tossed the ruler aside in disgust. A cop for less than two years, he still bridled at the department's penchant for putting everything on paper. He zipped up his jacket and stepped out of the heated guard booth into the cold March air.

Officer Fred Renker, who'd been guarding the entrance to the building's garage, slipped into the protective warmth of the small enclosure. "Man," he said, slapping his gloved hands together, "I'm freezing my ass off."

"And I'm dying of boredom," Wagner said.

Renker, a twenty-seven-year veteran, nodded his head knowingly. "All you rookies are the same. You're a hard charger now, but wait a few years. You'll be begging for a detail like this."

Wagner grinned. "Not me. Effective sixteen hundred hours today, I'm outta here."

Renker's eyebrows went up. "Full duty?"

"Yeah. I saw the surgeon this afternoon. He's sending me back to my old command."

A blast of wind forced Renker to take a step back into the heated guard booth. "I gotta admit *this* detail sucks. But I got a friend works security in Central Repair. His biggest headache is keeping the coffeepot full. I'm cultivating a hook to get me transferred there."

Wagner made a face. "Screw that. I wanna get back on the street and start making some more collars. I ain't going to the bureau guarding a fucking building." He nudged his jacket zipper up another inch. "And speaking of guarding buildings, I'd better check the perimeter before the sergeant shows up."

"Take your time," Renker said, sliding the door shut.

Wagner climbed the stairs leading to the promenade that linked One Police Plaza and the Municipal Building. He stopped for a moment to let his eyes grow accustomed to the reduced light. Even in the gloom, the hulking, rusting sculpture squatting between the two buildings loomed massive and ugly.

At this hour a handful of bums were usually sleeping on the benches, but not tonight. A biting March wind had chased the homeless indoors. Stifling a yawn, Wagner continued his tour around the

MICHAEL GRANT

perimeter of the building, occasionally shining his flashlight into darkened recesses looking for—what? Since he'd been on this lousy detail he'd done nothing but chase winos.

For as long as he could remember, he'd been fascinated by the stories told by his uncle, a detective in the 44th Precinct. From the moment he'd heard his first "war story" he knew what he wanted to be: a detective in the New York City Police Department. And the day he'd graduated from the Police Academy, his uncle had given him the prescription for entry into the coveted Detective Bureau. "Georgie," he'd said, "go out there and make all the collars you can."

His fiancée, Angela, didn't like the uncle's advice. Fearful for George's safety, she was forever begging him to stop making so many arrests. But with the bravado of a young cop, he assured her he could take care of himself. Then, to appease her he'd remind her how much easier it would be saving for a house on a detective's salary.

When he'd been assigned to the headquarters security detail after his radio car accident six weeks earlier, he'd done his best to turn a lemon assignment into lemonade. In the beginning he'd worked straight-eights, patrolling the recesses of the building and surrounding areas looking for drug dealers and muggers. But after a couple of fruitless weeks, he realized there was little in the way of criminal activity within the shadows of police headquarters.

Yawning, Wagner approached an alcove, favored by bums because it protected them from the biting wind, and played his flashlight into the dark empty space. He was about to move on when he noticed a large shopping bag. Curious to see what the winos were drinking this week, he poked the bag open with his nightstick and shone the light inside. Involuntarily, he sucked in his breath. Illuminated in the beam were several sticks of dynamite wrapped with electric tape.

Instinctively, he backed away and reached for his radio. Then he remembered what he'd been taught in the Academy: never transmit near explosives; the signal could set off the detonator. He considered running back to the guard booth to get Renker, but what if a bum should come by and pick up the bag? Then he saw the blackened fuse tip; it had been lit, but had gone out. What the hell, he thought,

**Officer
DOWN**

it wasn't a felony arrest, but discovering a bomb at One Police Plaza couldn't hurt his career. With an audible sigh of relief he reached down to pick up the package.

The ensuing explosion blew out a dozen windows in the federal prison across the street and rattled windows in City Hall two hundred yards away. In the Wall Street area, less than a mile from Police Headquarters, the rumble reverberated and echoed through the deserted streets like a distant thunderstorm.

Chapter

2

5:15 P.M. MONDAY, MARCH 18 • A week after the headquarters bombing, New York City Police Commissioner Thomas Cassidy sat in the back of a taxi and ignored his wild ride through Washington's chaotic traffic circles. His mind was preoccupied by the strange, abbreviated conversation he'd had less than fifteen minutes earlier with the assistant director of the FBI.

The police commissioner had been summoned to testify before a congressional subcommittee about upcoming legislation having to do with federal aid for narcotics enforcement. It was a routine bill and he was irritated that they'd asked him to come. His testimony hardly seemed necessary and he had better things to do than entertain a group of bored congressmen with tales of crime in the Big Apple. After reading a statement prepared for him by his legal staff, and answering the obligatory questions—"Yes, Congressman Ball, the city would welcome the much needed federal funds." "No, Congressman Mark, there are no easy solutions to the drug problem"—he was excused.

The assistant director, a dour man not given to idle conversation, was waiting for Cassidy in the corridor outside the committee meeting room. He slipped Cassidy a piece of paper with an address on it. "The Director would like to meet with you at this location," he whispered. He saw the puzzled look on Cassidy's face and added, "The Director will explain."

The taxi pulled up in front of a twelve-story building not unlike thousands of other office complexes that housed the armies of consultants, lawyers, and lobbyists who gravitated to the nation's capital to tend to the special interests of powerful men.

Cassidy got off the elevator on the eighth floor and found a door with the name Lawson Enterprises printed on it. There was nothing unusual about the interior of the office—except for the man seated at the reception desk. There was no mistaking the clean-cut looks of an FBI agent.

The man pointed at a door. "Go right in, sir. The Director's expecting you."

The sparsely furnished room contained a conference table and six chairs. At the far end of the highly polished table sat Richard "Skip" Coffey, a former federal judge, who had presided over the affairs of the Federal Bureau of Investigation for the better part of the last decade.

Skip Coffey, the son of an ex-senator from Texas, had spent most of his adult life in politics. The fact that he was the personal friend of the president may have given him the fortitude to develop his reputation for hard-driving pugnaciousness. Under his tutelage the FBI had become a more efficient and effective agency. But his proactive aggressiveness had ruffled more than a few feathers on the Hill and in the Justice Department.

Coffey, a short man with a tight-skinned face that made him look younger than his sixty years, rose and grasped Cassidy's hand. "Tom, good to see you again. Thanks for coming. I must apologize for this cloak-and-dagger routine but you'll understand why in a couple of minutes."

Coffey, sensing Cassidy's puzzlement, motioned the commissioner to sit down. "This office," he said by way of explanation, "belongs to the Bureau. In a nosy town like Washington, it helps to have someplace to go where one is not constantly dodging reporters. Imagine"—he chuckled mirthlessly—"needing to have a safe house in the nation's capital." He opened his briefcase and took out a leather-bound folder.

Cassidy, who'd long ago learned to read upside down, read the words stamped on the cover—FOR THE DIRECTOR'S EYES ONLY—and was suddenly reminded of the vast difference between him and Coffey. Even though Thomas Cassidy presided over thirty thousand police officers and was responsible for the safety of more than eight million inhabitants with their diverse needs and problems, he was still a local police administrator with parochial concerns and limited resources.

Skip Coffey on the other hand ran an organization of only ten thousand agents, but the Bureau's jurisdiction was worldwide. The Director of the FBI had access to the CIA, the Defense intelligence agency, as well as local law enforcement agencies throughout the country. Traditionally, the FBI expended a great deal of time and energy gathering intelligence, but they were often parsimonious in sharing what they knew.

Now, sitting opposite Skip Coffey, the most powerful law enforcement official in the country, Cassidy wondered what kind of secrets the FBI Director had to share. And, more important, why he wanted to share them.

"I'm afraid your unnecessary appearance before that subcommittee today was my idea," Coffey said. "It gave me an excuse to get you down here. I hope you don't mind." Without waiting for a response, he continued. "Tom, what does narco-terrorism mean to you?"

Cassidy was of course familiar with the term, but he didn't know a great deal about it. "Terrorist groups banding together with drug traffickers?"

"Exactly. The perfect merger. The drug lords provide the money and the terrorists provide the muscle. In the past, lack of financing has kept the terrorist elements in check. Now drug dealers, who have tremendous financial resources at their disposal, have begun to use terrorists as hired guns and they've developed a deadly partnership. Narco-terrorism is rapidly becoming a major concern in the international community and, I might add, a matter of national security in this country as well."

Cassidy stole a glance at his watch and wondered what time the last shuttle left for New York. "Skip, I know you didn't invite me here for a history lesson," he said as tactfully as he could. "Does this have anything to do with the New York City Police Department?"

Coffey's easy smile faded. "What you're going to hear now," he cautioned, "must never be spoken of to anyone outside this room without my permission. Is that understood?"

Cassidy nodded. The somber look on the FBI Director's face banished all thought of the shuttle from his mind.

For only the second time in his life, Thomas Cassidy ordered a drink on a plane. He was just finishing it when the FASTEN SEAT BELT sign came on. He glanced out his window, just forward of the left wing. The plane, making its final approach to LaGuardia, was passing over the southern tip of Manhattan and the skyscrapers, dominated by the huge Twin Towers, were ablaze with lights. Even though he had been born and raised in New York City, he still gawked like a tourist at the breathtaking aerial view of the city at night. But tonight he saw his city in a different light. Down there in those buildings and on those lighted ribbons of streets were more than eight million people and he, Thomas P. Cassidy, had sworn to protect each and everyone of them. But now, for the first time in his five years as

MICHAEL GRANT

police commissioner, he had serious doubts whether he'd be able to carry out that oath.

He forced his eyes away from the window and back to the pad on which he'd written the names of several ranking police officers. Since the plane had taken off, he'd been trying to come up with a suitable candidate for the unusual project Coffey had proposed. There were dozens of ranking officers in the department who had considerable knowledge of terrorism. But some were too young, others were too old, while still others lacked the seasoning for such a delicate assignment. He needed a self-starter, someone with street smarts *and* the ability to get along with other federal agencies. He stared glumly at his list and drew a line through another name. This wasn't going to be easy.

It was after ten by the time he climbed into the back seat of the black Oldsmobile waiting for him outside the shuttle terminal. He'd been on the go since six this morning and he was exhausted. His sixty-year-old body wanted nothing more than to go home, take a hot bath, and go to bed. But he knew there was a pile of paper waiting for him back at the office. He instructed his driver to take him to One Police Plaza.

In the darkened car he loosened his tie and once again thought of his impending retirement. He hadn't told the mayor yet, but he'd made up his mind to pack it in at the end of the year—his fortieth anniversary in the department. Forty years—the last five as the police commissioner—was enough. And after what he'd been told this afternoon, the rest of the year looked like a lifetime.

Ray Fleming and a fellow jazz fan, Manny Botnick, had just come from the Blue Note in the Village. They'd left after two sets and stopped in a smoke-filled bar on Seventh Avenue where the bleary-eyed clientele was more interested in a tape-delayed hockey game than the two jazz tunes Botnick had found on the decrepit jukebox.

The two young men, who'd known each other for three months, had met at Blockmann's Pistol and Rifle Club. In addition to their mutual love of guns, they'd discovered they both liked jazz and in the course of attending a few concerts and haunting every jazz club in the city, they'd become friends.

Physically, the two couldn't be more dissimilar. Fleming, an expert marksman, stood a shade over six feet and had the black-Irish curly dark hair and blue eyes that caused girls' heads to turn. He also possessed an easygoing nature that allowed him to tolerate a very insecure and often abrasive Manny Botnick. Few others could.

Botnick, almost a foot shorter than Fleming, had a sad, droopy face that made him look as though he had the weight of the world on his shoulders. In a desperate attempt to give his face more character, he'd grown a mustache. But it was no help. The sparse, uneven appendage slid down both sides of his mouth, giving him a permanent pout. A professional student and part-time musician, he played guitar in pickup bands around the city. He wasn't good enough to play jazz professionally, so he had to settle for playing weddings and schlock society band gigs.

As Fleming was ordering two more Heinekens, a man wearing dusty jeans and mud-covered work boots stumbled away from the bar and pulled the plug on the jukebox. "I can't hear the game with all that fucking noise," he muttered to his two friends.

Botnick turned on his stool. "Hey, pal, I'm listening to that."

The drunk, over six feet tall and weighing more than 250 pounds —most of it in his bulging stomach and neck—glared at Botnick with small bloodshot eyes. "Hey, little man," he said. "Don't let nothing but fear stop you from plugging it back in."

Botnick jumped off his stool. "Just watch me, fat ass."

As Botnick walked toward the jukebox, the man threw a sucker punch. Fleming saw it coming and yelled a warning. Botnick ducked, but he caught a glancing blow off the back of his head and crashed into the jukebox.

Fleming came off his stool, spun the man around, and drove two hard rights into his big belly. Whooshing like a deflating balloon, the drunk's knees buckled. Fleming's uppercut caught the man flush on the nose. Gushing blood, the man fell backward, overturning two bar stools.

The bartender, brandishing a sawed-off baseball bat, hurdled the bar and stood between Fleming and the fallen man. "That's it," he said. "No one's gonna bust up my place. You wanna fight? Take it outside."

Fleming looked down at the man on the floor, who was now vomiting up beer and half-digested peanuts, and put up his hands in supplication. "I don't want a fight," he said to the bartender. "I just came in to have a beer and listen to the jukebox."

The scowling bartender turned to the man's two friends. "You guys get him the hell out of here. Look at the mess he's making."

The two men, seeing how quickly Fleming had dispatched their buddy, prudently decided not to pursue the matter further. They dragged their friend off the floor and stumbled out the door.

Botnick climbed back onto his stool. "What'd you butt in for? I could have taken him."

Fleming grinned at his pugnacious friend. "You get ten points for balls, zero for brains. He'd have killed you, Manny."

Botnick's scowl turned to a sheepish smile. "Yeah, I guess you're right. Jesus, where'd you learn to fight like that?"

"Sunnyside. When I was growing up if someone didn't like the color of your tie, you had a fight on your hands."

Botnick rubbed the back of his stinging head. "Damn, that guy can throw a punch."

"Naw, he's a big patsy. Like most bar fighters, he's a head hunter. But nobody outside the ring ever won a fight going for the head."

"So how come you busted him in the nose?"

Fleming reached for his bottle. " 'Cause there's another rule in street fighting: Always leave a mark. Make sure the other guy knows he lost the fight."

Botnick, who came from a background where most disputes were settled by words, looked at his friend with newfound admiration. "Ray, this is a side of you I haven't seen before. You're a fucking animal."

Fleming grinned. "Naw. I never started a fight in my life, but I never walked away from one, either. Besides, I don't like big guys picking on little guys."

Normally, Botnick, who was sensitive about his height, would have

Officer DOWN

fired back a caustic rejoinder, but considering Fleming had practically saved his life, he let the remark slide. "Hey, Ray," he said, moving on to his favorite topic, "I picked up the Omega yesterday from the gun shop. What a beauty! It has three interchangeable barrels—thirty-eight super, forty-five, and ten-millimeter. It's got a removable front sight and adjustable rear sights."

Fleming smiled at his friend's enthusiasm. He'd never met anyone more interested in guns who was such a lousy shot. Botnick was forever buying the latest hot gun, and when it failed to improve his shooting, he'd toss it aside, and buy something else.

"Manny, another gun? You've got more guns than most third-world armies."

Botnick picked at his mustache. "You sound like my old man. 'Malcham,'" Botnick said, imitating his father's thick accent, "'when are you going to get a real job and stop playing with those meshuga guns?'" Botnick shook his head. "He's such a pain in the ass. Last summer he got the bright idea I should work in his Brooklyn laundry plant. Experience the business from the ground up. Fuck that. I didn't last till noon the first day. By eleven the temperature was over a hundred ten degrees. I told him to shove it and spent the rest of the summer in the Hamptons. I figured if I'm going to be hot, I might as well get a tan. Anyway, this Omega should improve my shooting." He looked at Fleming in awe. "I don't get it, Ray. You've been using the same old piece of shit since I've known you, but you always punch the hell out of the X-ring."

Fleming grinned. "My Colt Gold Cup National isn't exactly a Saturday night special. Besides, it's more in the genes than in the gun. You can't teach yourself to have a standing pulse rate of forty and twenty-ten vision."

Botnick toyed with his bottle. "Hey, you know the way you're always talking about ways to make a quick buck?"

"Yeah."

"Well, I think I have the answer."

"What?"

"Not what, who. A friend of mine named Lyle Petry. Ray, you gotta meet this guy. I met him at a gun club on the Island a couple of months ago. He's one hell of a shot."

Fleming's head snapped up. "Better than me?" Although he'd never admit it to Botnick, he didn't think there was anyone who was better with a pistol than he was.

"I don't know if he's *better*. But he's really good."

Fleming was suddenly curious. "Why do you want me to meet him?"

"You guys could make a few bucks together."

"How?"

"Money matches."

Fleming made a face. "Manny, I can shoot the balls off a butterfly at twenty-five yards, but I don't have the bucks to be a match hustler."

"I know, I know. I told Lyle. He wants to see you shoot anyway. If he thinks you're good, he'll put up the money."

Fleming was doubtful. Manny was always coming up with schemes that sounded good in the beginning, but fell flat when it came time to deliver. "Why would he risk his money on me?"

"How the hell do I know? I guess good shooters are scarce. Besides, Lyle can afford to lose it."

"What's he do for a living?"

"I don't know, but he's always got money. Ray, when are you going to the range next?"

"Wednesday night. I gotta fine-tune myself for that match in Westchester next week."

Botnick perked up. "Hey, is that state trooper going to be shooting?"

"Yeah."

"This I gotta see. He almost outshot you the last time."

Fleming remembered. He'd gotten off to a shaky start and just managed to squeak past the sharpshooting cop in the last ten rounds. "It's not even going to be close this time," he said. "I'm going to blow the son of a bitch out of the water. After this match he'll probably take up bowling."

Botnick chuckled. "Modesty ain't one of your strong suits, but I hope you're right. I didn't like that bastard. In fact I don't like cops period." Manny yawned and pushed his half-finished bottle away. "I'm beat. I'll see you at Blockmann's on Wednesday. I'll see if I can get Lyle to stop by."

"Okay." Fleming feigned indifference, but he was curious about the man Manny had described. Aggressive by nature, he enjoyed a challenge and was already looking forward to shooting against someone who was "almost as good" as he was.

Chapter
3

11:10 P.M. TUESDAY, MARCH 19 • The Midtown South Precinct boundaries encompass a major chunk of West Side Manhattan real estate from Fifth Avenue to the Hudson River. An eclectic area, it includes the best the city has to offer—the Empire State Building, Rockefeller Center, Madison Square Garden, Macy's, a host of glittering hotels— and the worst—the Port Authority Bus Terminal, run-down Eighth Avenue hotels that charge by the hour, and Times Square: a four-square-block zone festering with runaways, junkies, and prostitutes of all ages and sexes.

It was just after eleven when Deputy Inspector Dan Morgan, arriving early for the beginning of a late tour, walked through the station house's glass doors into barely controlled pandemonium. Outside the complaint room a never-ending line of victims—some bloodied, some crying, others sullen—patiently queued up to file their grievances, while a steady stream of manacled prisoners in the firm grasp of their arresting officers flowed up the stairs to the second floor to begin the initial stage of the arrest process. Above the noise of ringing telephones and squawking police radios, the desk officer shouted out post changes and reassignments to cops passing in front of him.

Morgan came behind the desk and nodded to Lieutenant Rudy Sloan, who was talking to Joan, the precinct's resident psycho. The desk officer, oblivious to the bedlam surrounding him, rested his head in his hands and listened to the heavyset woman describe her latest ordeal.

"I'm telling you they're giving me AIDS by laser injection," she whined. "You gotta do something."

"Joan, did you do what I told you to do last time?"

She straightened her old-fashioned straw hat, piled high with plastic flowers and cherries. "It didn't do no good."

"What'd ya use?"

"The stuff you told me to use," she said evasively.

His eyebrows went up. "Did you use Saran Wrap? Yes or no."

"No," she mumbled. "There was a sale on another brand, so I bought that instead."

The lieutenant turned to Morgan with a look of helpless resignation. "Inspector, I do my best, but no one listens to me." He glared at the woman over his glasses. "I've warned ya before, Joan. This is important stuff. You can't use any old brand-X crap and expect it to ward off laser beams. Ya gotta go top shelf. It's ya life we're talking here."

She looked suitably chastised. "All right, Lieutenant. I'm gonna go out right now and buy the Saran Wrap. Tell me again, how do I do it?"

"Refresh me. Where are the lasers coming from?"

"Saturn."

Morgan, who'd heard this story before, looked up from the roll call. "I thought it was Mars, Joan."

"It was, Inspector, but once they found out I knew where they were, they moved their location. They're smart, these bastards." She nodded her head vigorously and the hat slipped in front of her eyes.

"That's good news for you," the lieutenant said.

Joan, readjusting the unruly hat, looked at him warily. "Yeah? How come?"

"Saturn is farther away. The lasers aren't as powerful. What time do they zap you?"

"Usually around nine."

"Okay, now pay attention. First you take a bath—everyone knows dirt attracts laser beams. Then you face south—"

"Which way is south?"

"Downtown, toward the Battery. Now you wrap your whole body in Saran Wrap. Make sure you can breathe," he cautioned. "It wouldn't do for you to die of suffocation trying to ward off laser beams now, would it? Then you turn three times—is it to the right or the left, Inspector?"

Morgan studied the wide-eyed woman whose bizarre makeup made her look like a clown. She had painstakingly painted two perfect circles of rouge on her cheeks, and her eyebrows, pencil-thin half-moons, completed the image. Joan, he knew, wasn't afraid of laser beams; she was afraid of being alone. At least three times a week the unhappy woman came in with stories of aliens and demons. It gave her an excuse to talk to cops, the only friends she had. Hers wasn't an unusual case. Men and women, claiming to be pursued by everything from the CIA to extraterrestrials, haunted station houses throughout the city. "Right, then left," Morgan said.

The lieutenant repeated the instructions. "Okay. Turn to the right three times, and then three times to the left."

"That's it?"

"Yep. It will make you invisible to them. They won't be able to see you anymore and they'll have to look for someone else to bombard."

"Are you sure, Lieutenant?"

"Hey, I was right about the talcum powder, wasn't I?"

"That's true. I haven't been bothered by the voices since I started spreading it around my bed."

Morgan watched Joan shuffle out the door and said to his lieutenant, "Rudy, you should have stock in Saran Wrap."

"I know. It's good shit. It's the only kind I recommend for laser beams."

Morgan flipped through the pages of the command log, the large green book used by the desk officer to record the minute-by-minute events—ranging from homicides to lost property—that occurred during the tour. "What's happening, Rudy? Anything I should know about?" He had a desk full of paperwork waiting for him and he was hoping for a quiet night.

"The usual shit, boss. A night filled with those events that alter and illuminate our time, and—"

"Rudy, cut the Walter Cronkite routine."

The lieutenant smiled, gratified that the inspector knew whom he was imitating. Sloan had tried that line on several of the younger cops, but most of them had never heard of Walter Cronkite.

Rudy Sloan had been a desk officer long enough to know that when a CO asked what was happening he really wanted to hear that everything was under control. But Inspector Morgan was a hands-on boss who wasn't afraid to hear the usual litany of problems that occurred on an average four-to-twelve in Midtown South.

"It's early yet, Inspector, but I already have a dozen ladies of the evening in the back. I'm waiting for the wagon to take them to court. Sector Adam is out of service. Kirby was bitten by a psycho. He's at Bellevue. His partner, Barry, took the collar. We're sitting on two DOAs—the ME is backed up again—and we just came off a radio backlog alert. Other than that, everything's fine."

Morgan slid the log back to Sloan. "Just another routine night?"

"Ya got it, boss."

The hectic but highly visible precinct was a steppingstone in the department's career path for commanding officers with the talent and luck to survive its many pitfalls. In the year that Dan Morgan had been here, he'd managed to correct some of the problems that had caused his predecessor to be transferred in disgrace. If he could keep himself and the two hundred cops who worked for him out of trouble for one more year, he'd make full Inspector.

Some of his less career-oriented peers looked upon his assignment in horror. But Morgan relished the excitement, the pressure, and even the mountains of paperwork that kept him busy for twelve hours a day. Now that he was separated from his wife, he had plenty of time on his hands and he preferred spending it in the station house than in his cramped apartment in Chelsea. Fortunately, his hard work had not gone unnoticed. The Borough commander had ranked him first among all the precinct commanders in Manhattan South.

A young female officer, who was so short the lieutenant had to lean forward to see her, approached the desk. "Loo, I'm back from the DOA on Thirty-eighth Street." She brushed the bangs out of her eyes. "I didn't have a meal yet."

The desk officer made an entry on his roll call. "Okay, Hauser, go eat. When you come back relieve Colello. He's sitting on a DOA at 419 Thirty-first."

She rolled her eyes, but knew better than to complain to the unsympathetic lieutenant about the unfairness of sitting on *two* DOAs in one night.

"How's the new baby, Joyce?" Morgan asked.

Officer Hauser's face lit up in a wide grin. "She's beautiful, Inspector. Wanna see a picture?" She held out her service cap.

Morgan nodded and took the hat. On the inside, protected by a plastic holder, was a photo of a plump, smiling baby girl with wide brown eyes. "She is beautiful, Joyce. Looks just like you."

The young woman blushed. "Yeah. That's what everyone says."

"Female cops," the lieutenant mumbled after she'd left. "It just ain't right, boss. She oughta be home playing with her baby. Not playing cops and robbers out here with the big guys."

Morgan said nothing. He knew the department's position on women and should have challenged the sexist remark, but the truth was he agreed with his lieutenant. In spite of all the rhetoric about women's rights and equality, he, too, was convinced that women didn't belong in police work.

Sloan scratched his chin sheepishly. "I'm not breaking her chops with the two DOAs, boss. This is her first tour back from maternity leave. I figure she can't get into any trouble baby-sitting a couple of stiffs."

Suddenly the glass doors banged open and a cop, gripping a prisoner by the lapel of his leather overcoat, dragged him through the doors.

"Well, well," Sloan said gleefully. "Sanchez got the President."

"The President" was a well-known pimp who ran a stable of girls on 42nd Street from Eighth Avenue to the river. The cops in the precinct had tagged him with that nickname because of his real name: Cleveland Lincoln Jefferson. Besides dressing outrageously— even by pimp standards—the President was famous for his penchant for cop fighting.

Sanchez stopped in front of the desk and hauled the prisoner to his feet. Jefferson towered a full foot over the diminutive police officer. Sloan stood up to better appreciate the full impact of Jefferson's latest ensemble. Under an ankle-length leather overcoat he was wearing an iridescent purple suit, emerald green shirt, and for contrast a cherry red tie and yellow suede boots. The green silk shirt was open to the navel, revealing a half-dozen gold chains and medallions around his neck. Six diamond-studded earrings ran up the side of his left ear.

Sloan shook his head. "For chrissake, Jefferson, you look like an extra from *The Wizard of Oz.*" The lieutenant turned to Morgan. "Get a load of the overcoat," he said out of the side of his mouth. "For what that costs I could do Disney with the wife and kids for a week."

He turned his attention to Sanchez. "What've you got?"

"One for assault on a police officer, Loo."

"He's a *lying* motherfucker," Jefferson yelled.

Sloan waved a quieting hand at him. "Where?"

"Eighth and four-two."

MICHAEL GRANT

"I got a motherfuckin' *right* to stand on that corner. This is a motherfuckin' free *country*!"

The lieutenant paid no attention to him. "What happened, Sanchez?"

"He was punching out one of his girls. I told him to knock it off and he tried to hit me with this." Sanchez held up a "slapper"—a twelve-inch length of leather with an ounce of lead sewn inside.

"So what'd you do?"

Sanchez tried unsuccessfully to suppress a grin. "I subdued the miscreant."

Sloan gave Morgan a baleful look. "Boss, do you hear what they teach these kids in the Academy?"

"He's a motherfuckin' *liar*," Jefferson howled in his defense. "That ain't *mine*. It's *his*. And he hit me in my *face* with dat thing."

Sloan squinted at the gash over Jefferson's left eye, which was still dripping blood on the expensive overcoat. "Naw, a slapper didn't do that. Sanchez, what'd you hit him with?"

"My fist, sir."

Sloan grinned. "I know you fought in the Golden Gloves, but what'd you do, stand on a fire plug?"

"I got a good reach for a guy my size, Loo. It surprised a lot of guys in the ring."

"I'll bet. Okay, take him in the back and get him ready for Central Booking."

"I wanna see my motherfuckin' *lawyer*," Jefferson shouted.

"Has your motherfuckin' lawyer been notified of your incarceration?" Sloan deadpanned.

"Damn *straight*. He be here in a minute."

As if on cue, a short, shabbily dressed man with kinky gray hair came rushing through the doors. Sloan and Sanchez let out a collective groan. Benny "Sue 'em all" Kane was on the case.

He spotted his manacled client and immediately launched into his act. *"Release* that man," he bellowed. "This is an *outrage*!"

He looked up at the desk officer. "Who's in charge here?"

"I am," Morgan said. Until now he'd been content to let Sloan handle the arrest, but he knew Kane's reputation and thought it best to intervene before the loudmouthed lawyer got out of hand.

Sloan's head swiveled in surprise. By tradition it was the unfortunate job of the desk officer to stand in harm's way when the shit hit the fan in the station house. Most commanding officers made themselves scarce when they saw a sticky situation begin to develop because later, if there was an internal investigation, they could truthfully say they knew nothing about it. It wasn't fair, but it was a smart move, especially when someone like Kane was involved. It was a certainty that every cop within earshot of this arrest would be named in one of Kane's famous civilian complaints.

Kane eyed Morgan. "Who are you?"

"Deputy Inspector Daniel Morgan, the commanding officer of this precinct."

"Inspector," Kane brayed, "*you,* and every officer involved in this travesty of justice, are in a lot of trouble. I intend to file a complaint with the Civilian Complaint Review Board *and* a federal suit under the 1984 statute."

"What can I do for you?" Morgan said in a deliberately low voice.

Kane poked Sanchez's chest with a stubby forefinger. "I want *this* man suspended immediately."

Morgan slowly walked around from behind the desk. Cops coming into the sitting room for the beginning of the late tour stopped their idle conversation to watch how their CO was going to handle "Sue 'em all" Kane. Dan Morgan had developed a reputation as a boss who wasn't afraid to use his hands. The precinct cops still talked about the night a fight broke out in the sitting room between two guys who had stolen a brand new Corvette and the owner and his three brothers. The arresting officer, the only one in the room at the time, tried to break up the fight, but he was getting the worst from all sides until Morgan, hearing the altercation, vaulted over the desk and dove into the melee. He took a knife off one of the brothers and cold-cocked another one before additional help arrived.

Someone turned the squawking radio down and the room grew silent with expectation. Even prisoners stopped protesting their innocence to watch the showdown.

MICHAEL GRANT

Morgan stopped in front of the little man and looked down at him. "First of all, Counselor," he said in a voice barely above a whisper, "stop yelling."

Kane blinked rapidly. No cop, not even a deputy inspector, had ever challenged him before. "I want this man suspended," Kane repeated. He hated talking softly. Without the volume his voice lacked authority.

"Not only won't Officer Sanchez be suspended, but if you put another finger on him, I'll have *you* arrested."

A few *"All rights!"* escaped from the cops in the sitting room.

"You can't do that," Kane sputtered. "I'm an *attorney*. I know the law."

"Counselor, you're a piece of maggot shit who makes money defending pimps. Now get out of my station house."

"I want to talk to my client." In spite of his effort to sound forceful the sentence came out like a whine.

"See him at arraignment."

Kane couldn't believe this was happening. He looked into the tall inspector's face trying to decide if he was bluffing or plain crazy. He *knew* he had a right to talk to his client and this meshuga inspector couldn't stop him. But Kane, who'd made a name intimidating cops, wasn't a fool. There was no point in putting his hard-earned reputation on the line for an imbecile like Jefferson. He looked past Morgan at his client. "I'm going directly to court, Mr. Jefferson. By the time you get there, I'll have all the necessary papers drawn up. You'll be out in an hour."

He looked at Morgan, who, it seemed to Kane, hadn't blinked in the last ten minutes. "As for you, Inspector, I won't forget this."

Morgan's expression didn't change. "Does this mean I shouldn't call you to do my will?"

With as much dignity as the short, ruffled man could muster, Kane turned on his heel and, ignoring the snickering and catcalls from the cops in the sitting room, marched out of the station house.

Sloan turned the desk radio back up to its normal ear-shattering level. "Okay, show's over. Everybody back to work." In an instant the precinct resumed its normal rhythm.

Sloan leaned over the top of the desk. "That was ballsy, Inspector, but take it from an old-timer. Watch out for Kane. He's a treacherous bastard. He can hurt you in this job."

Morgan knew all too well what someone like Kane could do to his career. His eyes wandered to the cops in the sitting room preparing for the late tour. Most of them were young—older cops with more seniority usually transferred to quieter precincts in Queens and Brooklyn. Some read WANTED posters, others discussed the latest hockey scores, and a few sat alone, idly thumbing through the early edition of the *Daily News*. "Rudy," he said, "I turn these guys out at roll call and tell them to get the pimps and pros off the streets. It's my job to back them up when they do their job."

Sloan, surveying the cops in the sitting room, grew serious. "It's getting harder and harder to do the job out there, isn't it? That poor kid down at headquarters last week—"

Morgan scooped his mail out of the box and started toward his office. "I have a lot of paperwork," he said abruptly. Then, over his shoulder he added, "Let's hope the rest of the night is quiet."

Lieutenant Sloan watched his commanding officer walk toward his office and wished the department had a hundred more COs like him.

Chapter
4

8:35 P.M. WEDNESDAY, MARCH 20 • Blockmann's Pistol and Rifle Club, located in the basement of a building on Thomas Street in lower Manhattan, lacked the plush carpeting, well-lighted locker rooms, and other amenities of the wealthier, genteel gun clubs in the suburbs. There were exposed pipes, peeling paint, chronic cockroach infestation, and a wheezy ventilation system that gave out occasionally. But it was *because* of its location and relatively low overhead that it could afford to keep the membership and range fees within the reach of ordinary people—taxi drivers, teachers, and women from all walks of life who, living alone in a hostile city, felt a compelling need to develop their marksmanship. And it was also a convenient place where people who shared the same passion could meet to shoot and compare notes about the latest in firearm technology.

Ray Fleming, enveloped in his own private cocoon of concentration, stretched his right arm forward and sighted along the barrel. For him the act of firing a pistol was akin to a mystical experience. He'd been hooked on shooting since the very first time he'd picked up a revolver and discovered that he had the ability to hit a small target many yards away. Some people spend their entire lives looking for the experience that defines their existence. Fleming had found it five years ago as a sixteen-year-old high school student the day he tried out for the pistol team.

He adjusted his grip and the front sight post nestled in the slot of the rear sight. Then he raised the gun until the sights were aligned with the bottom of the black bull's-eye twenty-five yards downrange. Satisfied he was on target, he shifted his focus from the bull's-eye to the gun. The sights came into sharp relief as the black bull's-eye blurred, as it should. Proper alignment of the gun sights was more important than the target.

The gun sights, swaying ever so slightly in his hand, drifted in front of the target, but the movement didn't bother Fleming. Inexperienced shooters, disturbed by lack of steadiness, always tried to overcompensate, but only succeeded in making it worse. Fleming knew some movement was inevitable, but it didn't matter. As long as he maintained proper sight alignment, the bullet would strike the bull's-eye.

His concentration filtered out all sound around him. He didn't hear the sporadic, staccato gunfire from others on the firing line. He didn't hear the idle conversation of shooters behind him awaiting their turn. Nothing existed except him and the target. The gun had become an extension of his right arm. Even though the target was twenty-five yards away, Fleming felt he could almost reach out and touch it. He inhaled, let some breath out, and holding the rest, squeezed the trigger with a slow, steady pressure. The gun jumped in his hand as the round exploded from the muzzle.

Behind him, Manny Botnick, sighting on the target with a scope, whistled. "Beauty, Ray. Four o'clock in the X-ring."

Unhurried, Fleming repeated the procedure five more times. Then he pressed a button and the target, attached to a cable, jumped toward him. As it came closer he was pleased to see six holes in a less than one-inch diameter.

Botnick snatched the target from the retaining clips. "Jesus, Ray, what a shot group!"

A voice behind them said, "It looks like you fired it from a bench-rest position."

Fleming turned toward the owner of the voice, a lean man about his height with close-cropped blond hair.

Botnick held up the target. "Hey, Lyle, was I exaggerating or what?"

The man examined the shot group with professional interest. "Real tight group."

Lyle Petry's piercing pale green eyes fixed on Fleming, but he spoke to Botnick. "You were right, Manny. This guy is a hell of a shot." He held out his hand. "Lyle Petry. It's a pleasure to meet someone who knows how to shoot."

"Thanks. From what Manny tells me, you're pretty good yourself."

Petry shrugged self-deprecatingly. "I try."

"Try, my ass," Botnick interjected. "Ray, this guy could live off the money he makes from money matches with rich dudes."

"Now, Manny, you make it sound like I'm stealing."

"You are. Practically. I've seen some of these shoot-outs. Most of those old bastards couldn't hit a bull in the ass with a howitzer." He nudged Fleming. "You should see the equipment these guys have, Ray. The latest in hot guns. Everything customized. And they *still* can't hit shit."

Ray Fleming and Lyle Petry shared a bemused look that said they were thinking the same thing: Manny Botnick could have been talking about himself.

Botnick spotted Petry's gun case. "Hey, Lyle, why don't you and Ray have a little shoot-off?"

"That's what I came for."

Fleming had been looking forward to the opportunity to test his skills against this stranger, but looking at Petry's expensive leather jacket and gold watch, he suspected a hustle. "Wait a minute guys, I'm broke. I can't shoot for money."

Botnick pulled a wad of bills from his pocket. "Don't worry, I'll back you."

"Manny, I don't want—"

Petry put his hand on Botnick's arm. "Put your money away. This will be a friendly match. Ray, what do you say to loser buys beers?"

Fleming grinned. "What the hell. I guess I can afford that."

"Damn it, Ray," Botnick chided. "Think positive. *Lyle's* gonna buy the beers."

As word quickly spread that there was going to be a match, shooting stopped and one by one people gathered around Fleming's shooting point.

"How do you want to do it?" Fleming asked.

"Fifty rounds unsupported. How does five-yard increments from five to twenty-five sound?"

"It's a little unusual, but it's okay with me."

Petry took a customized 9mm Smith & Wesson from his gun bag and wiped it with a rag.

"What model?" Fleming asked.

"Six-nine-oh-six."

"Kind of a short barrel for target shooting, isn't it?"

Petry smiled. "I do all right with it. Go ahead, Ray," he said. "Why don't you lead off?"

At five yards, Fleming shredded the center of the X-ring and Petry did the same. As the target was moved farther away, the shot groups widened, but both shooters stayed within, or close to, the X-ring. After forty-five rounds they were even. The match had come down to the final five rounds at twenty-five yards.

Fleming stepped up to the firing line. Except for the soft metallic clicking as he fed bullets into the magazine, and the wheezing of the ancient ventilation system, there was total silence. An experienced competition shooter, he was used to the tension and pressure of a match. But for some reason Petry had unnerved him. Maybe it was that disconcerting half smile that was both friendly and sardonic in turn, or those icy pale green eyes, which at this moment he felt boring into the back of his skull.

Fleming was suddenly conscious of his breathing; it was too fast. He took a deep breath and felt his heart rate slow. Downrange the target looked smaller than usual. He adjusted his protective glasses and forced all extraneous thoughts from his mind. He brought the gun up to eye level and his mind went on automatic pilot. Sights aligned, he squeezed the trigger and the muzzle flash obliterated the target for an instant.

Botnick trained his scope on the target. "Ten," he whispered hoarsely.

Fleming muttered a curse. He'd let his concentration wander. Three more times Fleming squeezed the trigger, and three times Botnick, his voice rising with excitement, called out, "X!"

Fleming carefully laid his pistol on the shelf in front of him and wiped his sweaty palm on his shirt. The last round. One more X and Petry would have to shoot a perfect five-X to beat him. He picked up the gun, which seemed heavier than usual, and carefully aligned the sights on the bottom of the black circle. Blotting out everything but the weapon in his hand and the target downrange, he squeezed the trigger.

"X!" Botnick shouted.

Fleming, drained, stepped away from the firing line. For the first time he was conscious of his shirt sticking to his sweaty back.

Petry stepped up to the line and squinted at Fleming with that disturbing half smile. "I'm glad we're only shooting for beers."

All eyes focused on Petry. With his left hand casually resting in his trouser pocket, he raised his pistol and fired his first round.

"X," Botnick called out.

Petry fired two more Xs. The match had come down to the last two rounds.

Fleming anxiously drummed his fingers on the arm of his chair.

There was nothing at stake in this match, but the outcome suddenly took on great importance to him. He studied his opponent's stance. Perfectly balanced and relaxed with his right hand stretched toward the target, Lyle Petry looked as though he'd been carved from granite.

Petry fired.

"Ten," Botnick whispered.

Fleming exhaled softly. Petry couldn't win, but he could tie, and Fleming wasn't looking forward to firing another fifty rounds. As Petry prepared to fire his last round, Fleming squinted at the target to see where the last shot would go, but it was no use. The target was too far away.

The final shot exploded from the muzzle and Botnick fell back against his chair. "Ten," he said incredulously. "No X!"

A collective groan swept the room, then everyone converged on Fleming to congratulate him. Petry, standing at the edge of the crowd still wore the half smile. "I guess I'm buying."

They went to a bar down the street from Blockmann's. Petry returned to the table with three Heinekens and slid into a chair across from Fleming. "Where did you learn to shoot like that?"

Fleming, still on an adrenaline high from the close win, picked at the label on the bottle. "High school," he said. "Until then I'd never fired a gun in my life. A buddy of mine wanted to try out for our high school team and he dragged me along. I took to it like a duck to water."

"Are you as good with a rifle?"

"Yeah, but I like pistol shooting best."

Botnick butted in. "What he's not telling you, Lyle, is that he was the high school state champion for three years running."

Petry looked genuinely impressed. "I was watching you, Ray. You're a natural. How old are you?"

"Twenty-one."

"You have a real steady hand that generally comes only with age and experience. You ever shoot for money?"

"No."

"Why not?"

MICHAEL GRANT

"I can't afford to. Besides, I just like shooting for the sport."

"Why not do both? Enjoy it and make money at the same time."

Botnick, sensing a deal in the making, spoke up. "What are you offering, Lyle?"

Petry's eyes, flashing momentary annoyance, pinned Botnick. "Are you his agent?" he asked softly.

With considerable difficulty Botnick broke eye contact and self-consciously tugged at his mustache. "Yeah. I get fifteen percent of everything he makes."

The eyes swung back to Fleming. "What do you do for a living, Ray?"

"I drive a cab." Fleming glanced at Petry's gold Rolex and felt compelled to add, "It's only temporary."

"Hey, I got a good buddy drives a hack. Where do you work?"

"Docker's Taxi in Long Island City."

"Naw, he works for an outfit in the Bronx. Anyway, about that match. It won't cost you a thing. I put up all the money. All you have to do is shoot and share in the profits."

"It seems like a lot of trouble for a few bucks. I think I'll pass."

Botnick choked on his beer. "A few bucks? Don't go by the nickel and dime crap you see at Blockmann's. Lyle is talking big money matches at private clubs.

Petry leaned forward. "Ray, I have a doubles match Friday night and I need a partner."

"I don't know—"

"For chrissake, what have you got to lose?" Botnick blurted out. "If I could shoot like you, I'd do it in a minute."

Fleming met Petry's level gaze. Manny had been right about Petry. He was an excellent shot. Together they'd make an unbeatable team. "All right," he said aloud. "Why not?"

Chapter
5

7:35 A.M. THURSDAY, MARCH 21 • Lyle Petry, sitting in a parked car on a deserted road on eastern Long Island, watched intently through his rearview mirror as the car approached him. The vehicle pulled up alongside and the passenger, a tanned man with short-cropped black hair, said, "Excuse me, sir, could you tell me how to get to—" Suddenly a gun appeared in his hand. He pointed it at Petry and pulled the trigger. The slide mechanism of the 9mm automatic slammed forward with a heart-stopping metal click. The man's smile was wintry. "Bang, bang, Lyle, you're dead."

Lyle Petry turned to the man sitting next to him. "See any problem with that, Alvaro?"

The man picked at his salt and pepper beard nervously. "I don't like people pointing guns at me, even if they are unloaded." Then he added grudgingly, "It looked all right to me."

Petry yanked the door open. "Then it's a good thing *I'm* running this operation and not you. It's no good, guys," he said to the two men in the car. "Switch places."

The driver, a muscular black man with rusty red hair, leaned across the seat. "What's the problem, Lyle? I'm the better wheel man and Jimmy's the better shooter."

"But Jimmy isn't left-handed and you are."

Both men in the car exchanged puzzled glances.

"So?"

Petry stepped back from the car window. "Jimmy, point the gun at me again." The man did as he was told. "See a problem?"

Jimmy shrugged. "It's a little awkward, but—"

"A *little* awkward? You have to turn forty-five degrees to get the gun up to the window."

"It only takes a second—"

"And in that second you telegraph your move."

"He won't have time to react."

Petry leaned close to Jimmy and pinned the man with pale green eyes that had turned to ice. "The first rule is: Always remember *who* your target is. He's not going to be civilian this time. He's going to be a cop and you have to assume that he'll react." Petry tapped the roof of the car. "Okay, switch places. Let's try it again."

Glen, coming around to the other side, chuckled. "This reminds me of when I was a kid. I always got to play first base because I was left-handed."

Petry put his arm around the stocky man's shoulder. "It's a good thing you shoot better than you play baseball. By the way, what weapon will you use?"

"A MAC-ten. It's a good squirt gun and I can fire—"

"No, you don't need a lot of firepower, just accuracy."

"How about a twenty-two with high-velocity rounds?"

"Why?"

"Lightweight gun, low noise."

Petry shook his head. "Negative. You'll be using a silencer, so the noise won't matter. Besides, the twenty-two isn't powerful enough."

"Lyle, it's more than enough for a head shot."

"What if he ducks?"

"Huh?"

"What if he sees the hit coming and he dives across the front seat?"

"I shoot through the door."

"With a twenty-two?"

For the first time Glen seemed uncertain about his decision. "The high-velocity rounds should penetrate the door."

"Unless the rounds hit a steel strut or a bolt."

The man's face broke into a wide grin. "What the hell am I arguing with you for? What am I gonna use?"

Petry playfully tapped the man's cheek. "A nine with hollow-point steel-jacketed bullets. If the target tries to evade, empty the clip into the door."

"A nine-millimeter it is, Lyle."

With Jimmy behind the wheel and Glen in the passenger seat, they backed down the road and repeated the procedure. On the first runthrough Petry, always the perfectionist, saw a problem. "You didn't pull up far enough," he said. "Look at the angle. The door center post could deflect the bullet." On the second attempt he saw something else. "You're coming up too fast, Jimmy. Nice and easy, you don't want to spook him."

When they got it right on the third try, Glen said in a British accent, "By George, I think we've got it."

Petry smiled, but there was no humor in it. "*I'll* tell you when you've got it."

Jimmy and Glen exchanged looks of resignation. They knew from past experience that there was no use in arguing with him. He'd keep them here until *he* was satisfied.

MICHAEL GRANT

Petry looked at his watch. "Okay, let's do it again." Jimmy slammed the car into reverse and, crunching gravel and dirt, roared back up the road in reverse leaving a cloud of dust in his wake.

Alvaro, who had been a silent observer during all this, said, "Lyle, when are you going to do this?"

Petry squinted up the road at the vehicle slowly approaching. "Tonight. If these two ever get it right."

Alvaro laughed. "Everything you do must be worked out to the finest detail."

Petry climbed back into the car and fixed Alvaro with those green eyes. "I don't run a goatscrew operation," he said evenly.

Alvaro smiled for the first time. "That, my friend, is why I hired you."

Lyle Petry looked at his watch. It was almost eleven P.M. For almost an hour the three men in the maroon Mustang had been crisscrossing the West Side streets of Manhattan looking for a suitable target. Finally, Lyle Petry, sitting in the back seat, broke the silence. "There." He pointed over Jimmy's shoulder. "A police car just made a right onto Forty-fifth. I think he's riding solo."

Jimmy accelerated and turned into the block about two hundred feet behind the police car. In silence they followed the radio car as it meandered through the streets of the West Side.

Jimmy glanced at his watch. "It's almost eleven-thirty. We've been following this son of a bitch for almost a half-hour. What the fuck is he doing?"

Petry, his eyes intent on the radio car in front of them, patted Jimmy's shoulder. "Patience. We'll follow him all night if we have to."

A few minutes later, the radio car turned off Tenth Avenue onto 43rd Street. Halfway down the dimly lit street, the blue-and-white pulled in behind a panel truck. Jimmy, using an unattended trailer truck as cover, quickly pulled in behind it.

Glen, who was sitting in the front passenger seat, turned to Petry. "I can't see him. What's he doing?"

Petry rolled his window down and carefully stuck his head out. The police officer got out of the car. "It's a broad," Petry whispered. "She's writing a ticket on that panel truck."

Glen grunted. "A woman. That make a difference, Lyle?"

"No," Petry said without hesitation. Then he smiled. "In fact it's even better."

Jimmy drummed his fingertips on the steering wheel. "Well, is it a go?"

Petry looked up and down the block. Except for a few parked cars and trucks, the street was deserted. He watched the police officer slip the ticket under the windshield and return to her car. The interior light came on.

"Looks like she's gonna do some paperwork." He took another look up and down the block. "Street's quiet; she's parked on the right side of the street. Okay, it's a go."

Glen slipped the nine-millimeter out of a shoulder holster and screwed the silencer into the end of the barrel as Jimmy eased away from the curb.

Petry issued last-minute instructions. "Remember, Jimmy, nice and easy. You cover a hundred and eighty degrees in front of you. You see anyone, sing out. I'll handle the rear one-eighty. Glen, you concentrate on the target."

As they pulled up alongside the radio car, the officer's head was down and she didn't see them approaching. Jimmy tapped the horn.

Police Officer Joyce Hauser, looking up from her memo book, pushed the unruly bangs out of her eyes and rolled her window down. "Yes, sir?"

This, thought Glen, was even easier than they'd anticipated. The police car's engine was out of gear, the window was down, and from the expression on her face, she suspected nothing. He didn't even feel the need to say anything. Smiling broadly, he brought the weapon up and squeezed off a round. The gun made no more than a quiet *psst*, but the impact of the bullet exploded her head in a cloud of red and pink froth and threw her violently across the front seat.

Glen raised himself off his seat and looked into the police car.

MICHAEL GRANT

When he saw the condition of the body, he knew there was no need for a second shot. "It's done," he said evenly. "Let's go."

Two blocks away, at the corner of Eleventh Avenue and 41st Street, police officers Tony Amonti and Nelson Lopez were sitting in a parked radio car. As the Mustang went by, Amonti slapped his partner's knee. "Hey, Nelse, you see that Mustang?"

"Yeah."

"He had no license plate light. Let's go."

Lopez made a face. "No license plate light? Come on, Tony, that's a real bullshit summons. Give him a break."

"Fuck 'em. The sergeant's on my case about low summons activity. If I don't hang some paper tonight, he'll be all over my ass at return roll call. Let's go."

Reluctantly, Lopez slapped the car in gear and stomped down on the gas pedal. As Lopez closed the distance between the vehicles, Amonti leaned forward and squinted. "Check the guy in the rear window, Nelse. He keeps looking back this way. I got a feeling about this one." He keyed the mike. "Sector John to Central . . . We're following a nineteen ninety Mustang . . . color maroon . . . Request a ten-fifteen on New York license plate number . . . 483TNG."

Nelson looked at the speedometer and increased the pressure on the accelerator. "He's speeding up, Tony."

Amonti tossed the mike on the seat and buckled his seat belt. "That Mustang's five-point-oh-liter engine will eat up this bucket of shit. Let's take him now before he gets too much of a lead."

Just as Nelson put his foot to the floor, the dispatcher came back on the air: *"Sector John . . . you have a ten-sixteen on New York registration 483TNG."*

"Goddamn!" Amonti shouted. "Screw the summons. I got a grand larceny auto!"

Nelson flipped on the roof lights and siren. "Let's take 'em, amigo."

As soon as the lights and siren came on, the Mustang leapt forward with squealing tires and a thin cloud of burning rubber.

Amonti grabbed the mike. "Sector John to Central . . . We're in pursuit of that maroon Mustang. Heading south on Eleventh at Thirty-third."

Immediately other cars came on the air: *"Sector Boy heading west on Thirty-third . . . Sector Adam going north on Tenth."*

Nelson, with his hands locked on the wheel, riveted his attention on the Mustang weaving in and out of traffic in front of him. "Jesus, Tony, that son of a bitch can drive."

Amonti, broadcasting the progress of the chase, had been watching with dismay as the Mustang increased the distance between them. *"Marone!"* he yelled over the sound of the siren and whining engine. "He's getting away. Step on it, Nelse."

The more powerful Mustang was steadily pulling away from the slower radio car. Suddenly, with tires squealing, the car made a sharp turn into 25th Street.

"The Mustang just made a right," Amonti shouted into the mike. "Heading west on Twenty-fifth."

"Now's our chance," Nelson said. "That turn will slow him down." Nelson approached the corner at full speed. He braked just before he started his turn, cut the wheel to the right, and stomped on the accelerator as they roared into 25th Street.

Amonti was the first to yell, but Nelson saw it at the same time. Just around the corner, the Mustang was parked at an angle, blocking the street. The three men, standing behind the vehicle, opened fire. Nelson yanked the wheel to the left. The violent motion, throwing both men to the side and below the windshield, saved their lives as the windshield shattered from a well-aimed fusillade. The car, out of control, mounted the sidewalk and crashed into a fire hydrant.

Dazed, Amonti tried to see through the demolished windshield, but a column of water from the ruptured fire hydrant obscured his vision. He turned toward his partner who was holding his hand to his forehead. Blood trickled between his fingers. *"Nelse!* Are you okay?"

"Yeah . . . I banged my fucking head on the steering wheel. Where are they?"

MICHAEL GRANT

"I don't know, partner, but we're sitting ducks in here." Amonti pulled his revolver. "Ready?"

Nelson drew his gun. "Now."

Both men opened the doors and dove out of the car. Amonti rolled through a puddle and came up pointing his gun at—nothing.

Panting for breath, he slowly rose to his feet. The Mustang, engine still running, was still in the middle of the street, but the three men were gone. For a fleeting moment Amonti almost thought he'd imagined the entire event, but then he turned and stared slack-jawed at a bizarre scene. Droplets of water, backlit by the radio car's headlights, drifted in the air like silver beads and the column of water cascading down on the wrecked vehicle reflected the radio car's red dome lights, giving the scene an eerie, almost festive look. Draped over the roof, Nelson Lopez held a red-stained handkerchief to his head.

Suddenly, an uncontrollable shaking began in Tony Amonti's legs and hands. He stumbled back to the car and, ignoring the spraying water, the soaking wet seat and bits of shattered windshield, sat down heavily in the front seat.

Nelson Lopez, his eyes wide with fright, leaned into the car. "You and your fucking summons—"

The crackling radio interrupted his tirade. *"Report of ten-thirteen in the Midtown South precinct . . . Officer shot . . . Forty-first between Ninth and Tenth. What units responding?"*

At about the same time Amonti spotted the vehicle, Deputy Inspector Dan Morgan was sitting in his office discussing the latest crisis—prostitution in midtown Manhattan—with his street-conditions sergeant. The prostitutes had become a thorn in Police Commissioner Cassidy's side ever since a visiting Episcopal bishop had been attacked by a drug-crazed pross outside his midtown hotel three months earlier. Since that celebrated incident the commissioner had been besieged by an army of religious and public-interest groups, demanding an end to the growing invasion of ladies of the evening on the streets of midtown Manhattan. The "pross war," as the press was fond of calling it, had become a major public relations concern for the commissioner, eclipsing momentarily the out-of-control drug war that raged in the streets of New York.

As the commanding officer of the largest precinct in midtown, Morgan had been charged with formulating a plan to get the prostitutes off the streets—no easy task given the volume of prostitution in the area. With fewer than two hundred cops to cover all the posts and sectors, he was stretched thin. It required a lot of imagination and a little sleight of hand with his manpower deployment, but Morgan had managed to put together a successful program. It was just this sort of diversity that Morgan loved. He relished coming to work and solving the bewildering assortment of problems that crossed a precinct commanding officer's desk daily.

Morgan pried the lid of his coffee container. "How's it going, Sarge?" he asked.

"It's a real logjam in court, boss. They ain't got enough cells to hold them and some of the judges are cuttin' the girls loose in groups."

Morgan sipped the steaming black coffee. "That's what I told the PC. The courts are the perennial choke point in the criminal justice system. If he can't get the judges to cooperate we're—"

Lieutenant Sloan ducked his head into the office. "Thought you should know, boss, Sector John is in a chase."

Forgetting the prostitute problem for the moment Morgan and the sergeant ran out to the desk. Another sergeant was adjusting the volume on the radio. "It's a stolen car, boss."

"Who's in Sector John?" Morgan asked Sloan.

The lieutenant scanned the roll call. "Lopez and Amonti."

"Who's driving?"

"Lopez."

If Amonti, one of his young bulls, had been driving, Morgan would have called the chase off immediately. But Lopez, an older man, was more stable and less likely to take unnecessary risks. Nevertheless, Morgan stood by the radio and held the mike, prepared to call off the chase if it got too dangerous or turned east into the more populated part of the precinct. No stolen car was worth the lives of cops or innocent civilians.

After Amonti's last transmission about the car heading west on Twenty-fifth Street, the radio became so quiet that Morgan turned the volume up. After several tense moments of silence, the radio blared: *"Report of ten-thirteen in the Midtown South precinct . . . Officer shot . . . Forty-third between Tenth and Eleventh. What units responding?"*

Morgan turned to Sloan. "Who do we have over there?"

Sloan flipped through the roll call. "No one on foot."

Agonizing moments later, the shrill voice of the first cop to arrive at the scene screamed, *"Officer shot . . . Have surgeons at Cabrini standing by . . . We're coming in."*

Another voice on the radio asked the question that was on everybody's mind. *"Billy . . . who is it?"*

The distraught voice came back: *"Hauser . . . she's been shot bad."*

Sloan, turning stark white, fell back into his seat. "Mother of God," he whispered. "I gave her the summons car to keep her out of trouble."

But Morgan didn't hear. He was running toward the front door.

The first step in the gut-wrenching process of overseeing the investigation of a police officer shooting is a trip to the hospital. In the emergency room Morgan pushed his way through a chaotic crowd of cops, doctors, and nurses. He grabbed the first cop he saw. "Gaffney, reporters will be coming in soon. Get outside and keep them the hell away from the emergency room." Morgan had been through this before. A collision of pushy reporters and angry cops were sure to exacerbate an already tinderbox situation.

"Who the hell's in charge here?" he shouted above the din of voices.

"I am."

Morgan, forcing himself not to look at the doctor's bloodstained green scrubs, focused on the face of the young, sallow-faced man with thick glasses. "How's she doing, Doc?"

The doctor shook his head. "She was dead as soon as the bullet hit her. Massive brain damage. There was absolutely no chance for survival."

The ringing in Morgan's ears was so loud, he hardly heard himself mumble a thanks. As he turned away he spotted a blood-splattered police cap on the floor. He picked it up and angrily shoved it into the hands of a nearby sergeant. "Goddammit, Flynn," he said through clenched teeth, "this is Officer Hauser's property. Protect it."

Another sergeant tapped him on the shoulder. "Inspector, Amonti and Lopez have recovered a stolen Mustang from that chase. We think it's connected to this."

"Any arrests?"

"No, but three guys in the Mustang fired shots at them."

"Good Christ Almighty! Are they okay?"

"Yeah, but the perps got away."

"Where's the car?"

"Twenty-fifth Street."

"Let's go."

On the way out he grabbed Sergeant Flynn. "What's been done so far?"

Flynn, overweight and gray-haired, read from his clipboard. "I just notified the chaplain's office. A priest is on his way out to Long Island to tell the husband. Operations, the borough, the squad, and Forensic have been notified."

Morgan nodded. "Good, get the paperwork started. I'll be right back." He put his hand on Flynn's arm. "Woody, I'm sorry I jumped on you a minute ago."

The sergeant waved off Morgan's apology. "My mistake. Don't worry, boss. I'll take care of her property."

On their way to the scene, the sergeant filled Morgan in on the chase and subsequent crash. When they turned into 25th Street, the fountain of water from the ruptured fire hydrant was still flowing unabated. On the other side of the street two nonplused men from the Water Department pored over outdated blueprints, trying to determine the location of the shut-off valve.

As Morgan came out of the radio car, his attention locked on the Mustang. Ignoring the deep puddles, he slowly walked toward the vehicle, which was still parked diagonally across the street. The hair on the back of his neck rose. "Is this where the car was?"

The sergeant nodded. "Amonti said three guys stood behind it and blasted away."

"Son of a bitch," he muttered.

Forensic was arriving as he returned to the radio car and instructed his driver to take him back to the station house. The jovial cop behind the wheel usually had a couple of jokes to tell. But not tonight. They rode in silence for several blocks. Finally, the radio dispatcher broke the silence. *"Is the CO of MTS on the air?"*

Morgan keyed the mike. "This is the CO. Do you have a message for me?"

"Affirmative. Report to the PC's office forthwith."

Dan Morgan looked at his watch. It was going to be a long night.

As the driver snapped a U-turn and headed downtown, Morgan was thinking about the position of the Mustang and a chill ran down his spine. Those three men had deliberately, and professionally, ambushed two police officers.

Chapter

6

12:30 A.M. FRIDAY, MARCH 22 • At this hour, One Police Plaza was usually quiet, but not tonight. The murder of Police Officer Joyce Hauser had set the ponderous machinery of the New York City Police Department in motion and a steady flow of cars streamed into the underground garage. In the building above, lights blazed in dozens of windows as scores of police officers arrived early to begin the task of finding Officer Hauser's murderer.

As Dan Morgan got off the elevator on the fourteenth floor, he recalled the first time he'd been in the police commissioner's office. He'd never forget the rush he'd gotten entering the office of the most important police official in the country. Teddy Roosevelt's old desk, flanked by the American flag and the flag of New York City and the array of photos showing the PC with presidents and heads of state, only added to the historic aura of the room. Many cops harbored a secret fantasy of one day sitting behind that famous desk, but for Dan Morgan it was more than a dream. To him it was an achievable goal, even if the odds were against him. Previous commissioners had been drawn from outside the department, but Tom Cassidy had come up through the ranks. And while it was true that most commissioners were drawn from the superchief ranks, a previous mayor had appointed an ex-lieutenant to the job. The odds were great, he had to admit, but not insurmountable.

But tonight, as he walked into the commissioner's office, there was no room in his troubled mind for such lofty aspirations.

A red-faced Commissioner Cassidy, bellowing into the telephone, motioned Morgan into a chair. While Morgan waited for the commissioner to get off the telephone, he took the opportunity to study his boss. Many in the department were terrified of the blunt, explosive commissioner, but Morgan, who'd worked for Cassidy in a special task force set up to investigate the Black Liberation Army during the turbulent sixties, liked him, perhaps because they were so much alike—both were hard-charging career cops. Still, they'd often clashed on methodology and procedure. Morgan had since learned to curb his temper, but in those days he was an outspoken, aggressive cop. The only two things that kept an exasperated Cassidy from throwing the brash young detective out of his task force was that he knew Morgan had the best interests of the department at heart and he was exceptionally competent.

In all of his twenty-five years, Dan Morgan had never worked for a better boss. Too many of the department's hierarchy had gained their experience from college courses and how-to management books. But Cassidy, who had a hands-on knowledge of the job and a natural instinct for understanding the people who worked for him, had

**Officer
DOWN**

gained most of his experience in the field. Unlike the previous commissioner, who was an outsider, Cassidy was an old warhorse who had worked his way up through the ranks. And unlike many of his predecessors, he hadn't ducked responsibility by hiding out in safe headquarters assignments. He'd earned his promotions commanding a wide variety of difficult assignments in patrol and the Detective Bureau.

Cassidy had a reputation as a cold fish, but he'd been especially solicitous toward Dan Morgan after he'd been shot. Morgan had been back to full duty less than a month when Cassidy promoted him to deputy inspector and gave him the Midtown South Precinct. Morgan had been grateful. But he still wasn't sure if the promotion was the result of good police work or an act of pity.

Cassidy slammed the telephone down and turned his steel gray eyes on Morgan. "Anything so far, Inspector?"

Morgan was baffled by the question. While it was his job to oversee the initial investigation, the precinct detectives were responsible for the case. And as such they, or their boss, were in a much better position to answer questions than he was. He couldn't recall a precinct commander being summoned to the police commissioner's office to deliver a preliminary report in person; even when it involved the shooting of a police officer.

"No, sir. I just came from the scene."

Cassidy leaned forward and clasped his hands in front of him. "And?"

Morgan hesitated. He didn't know if he could—or indeed, should —put his feelings into words. Policemen dealt in facts, not feelings. Nevertheless, he felt so strongly about the impression he'd gotten from seeing the position of the car that he decided to risk the ire of the commissioner.

"There was something about the scene that was really . . . strange," he said.

Cassidy scowled. "How do you mean?"

Morgan struggled to put his half-formed thoughts into words. "The position of the car . . . three men stopping to shoot it out with two police officers; that took a lot of balls and—"

MICHAEL GRANT

"And what?"

"Professional experience, I guess. Sir, these guys set up an ambush. Who the hell stops to shoot it out with a pursuing radio car?"

Cassidy, frowning, sat back in his high-backed leather chair and studied his deputy inspector. Then his eyes roamed to the window, which framed a panoramic view of lower Manhattan. Once again he thought of his eight million charges. "Inspector, I'm going to offer you an assignment. But first, I'm going to tell you something that is not to leave this room. When I'm done you can tell me if you still want it or not. Understood?"

"Yes, sir." Morgan, instantly alert, drove all the disturbing thoughts of this night out of his mind.

"Four days ago, I had a meeting with the Director of the FBI." Cassidy leaned forward and asked the same question Skip Coffey had asked of him. "Dan, what do you know about narco-terrorism?"

Morgan's professional interest was piqued. Before he'd been promoted to captain, he'd been the commanding officer of an antiterrorist squad in the Intelligence Division. He still kept in touch with the squad and was up to date on the domestic terrorist scene, but his knowledge of international terrorism had to be gleaned from newspapers, magazines, and his own informal research. "I know the Medellin cartel has been using terrorist tactics against the Colombian government to stop them from extraditing drug dealers to the U.S. And from what I read they seem to be succeeding. There's talk that the government may drop extradition from their constitution."

"Perhaps, but apparently not fast enough for the Medellin cartel."

"They've already blown up half the country and assassinated everyone who's gotten in their way. What else can they do?"

Cassidy took off his glasses and massaged the bridge of his nose. "They can export terrorism to the U.S."

Morgan suddenly knew why he was here. "New York City?" he asked softly.

Cassidy's grim face reddened. "Yes. The Bureau has been working closely with the CIA on this. For the past four months the CIA has been trying to track down a persistent rumor that a terrorist group calling itself Puño Blanco was planning to launch a terrorist attack in the U.S.; specifically New York City."

"Have they been able to substantiate the rumor?"

"Their operative disappeared three weeks ago, but he was found the day before yesterday. He'd been burned alive. The CIA retrieved a notebook from the body. Less than an hour ago Coffey called me to tell me the FBI lab had just finished reconstructing the documents." Cassidy's steel gray eyes locked on Morgan. "Puño Blanco is no longer a rumor."

"Who are these people?"

Cassidy scowled. "That's part of the problem. Neither the Bureau nor the CIA has much intelligence on them. They do know they're a splinter group of the Medellin cartel."

"I don't get it. Why go to all that trouble? From what I've been reading the government is about ready to capitulate on the extradition issue."

"The Colombian government is leaning that way, but there are a couple of clear-thinking politicians in the Constitutional Assembly who are holding out because they know what we know: if the government caves in to the cartels, there will *be* no government. Apparently, Puño Blanco believes the U.S. is the key. Force our government to drop its demands and the Colombian government will be only too happy to drop the extradition issue. Like it or not, Inspector, the New York City Police Department is smack dab in the middle of this power play."

"Are they in the city yet?"

"It's believed they've already made contact with an unknown American living here."

"Why an American?"

"Colombian drug traffickers are financing the project, but they want Americans to carry out the attacks."

That made sense to Morgan. Americans would know their way around the city and blend in a lot better than Colombian nationals. "What's their game plan?" he asked.

Cassidy winced as a sharp pain coursed through his innards.

"Random assassination of police officers," he said through clenched teeth.

"Holy Christ! That cop who was killed in the headquarters bombing and Joyce Hauser—?"

Cassidy nodded.

Morgan thought about tonight's ambush. "How long do they plan to kill cops?" His voice sounded hollow to his ears.

"Until they think we're demoralized enough. Then they'll launch a spectacular assault on a highly visible target to demonstrate the impotence of the police."

"But what's the point?"

"They hope the resulting chaos will force our government to capitulate on the extradition issue."

"The whole idea is crazy," Morgan said aloud. But to himself he was thinking the unthinkable: *It just might work.*

"You're damn right it's crazy," Cassidy snapped. Then, in a quieter voice he said, "Morgan, I don't have to tell you what these people can do to us. If our cops find out they're the target of assassins, we're—"

"*If* our cops find out?" Morgan blurted. "You're going to tell them, aren't you?"

Cassidy turned away from Morgan's accusing stare. "I can't."

"What about the cops patrolling the streets? They *have* to know—"

Cassidy slammed his hand on the desk. "Goddammit, Morgan, use your head. If our cops find out about Puño Blanco, we'll have anarchy in the department. They may refuse to go on patrol. They'll carry unauthorized weapons—"

"But you *have* to tell them," Morgan shouted. "Look what happened to the cop at One Police Plaza and Joyce Hauser."

An expression of pain and anger flared in Cassidy's eyes and Morgan was suddenly aware that he was going head to head with a commissioner with a reputation for cutting the legs out from under insubordinate deputy inspectors. But he couldn't stop himself. "How else will they be able to protect themselves?" he said evenly.

Cassidy's face was almost purple. "Goddammit, Inspector, don't tell me how to do my job."

"If you don't want my opinion," Morgan snapped, "then what the hell am I doing here?"

There was a moment of tense silence. Then Cassidy's grim face broke into an exasperated smile. "Morgan, you haven't changed. You're still an opinionated, goddamn pain in the ass."

Dan Morgan refused to be seduced by the backhanded compliment, but he did lower his voice. "Commissioner," he said in a more reasonable tone, "you can't let thousands of cops go out on patrol and *not* tell them what they're up against."

Cassidy sighed and sat back heavily. "Dan, put your emotions aside for a moment and think about this logically. What will happen if I announce to the department the existence of Puño Blanco?"

Morgan knew exactly what would happen. He'd experienced first-hand the kind of fear that Cassidy was talking about. During the sixties the Black Liberation Army had assassinated several cops. Working in a radio car at the beginning of those troubled times, he remembered the anxiety he felt riding down a dark Harlem street— wondering if someone was drawing a bead on the back of his head; waiting for the crack of a bullet. It wasn't uncommon for cops to carry unauthorized weapons in those days. Even he had carried a semiautomatic nine-millimeter in an ankle holster.

He also saw the simple logic in Puño Blanco's plan. The New York City Police Department responded to over nine thousand calls for services every day. If the police had to worry about booby traps and snipers, they wouldn't get to half the assignments, and hundreds of calls—many of them time-critical—would go unanswered. The computerized SPRINT system, which routed calls for services, would overload and crash. On top of that the PBA, the powerful police union, would order its men not to respond to a job without a backup unit, and *that* backup unit's call would go unanswered. The public would be up in arms, and the criminal element, once they realized what was happening, would take full advantage of the backlog of jobs to commit even more crime. The city would collapse into a state of anarchy.

"All hell will break loose," Morgan answered finally. "Someone's

MICHAEL GRANT

got to stop Puño Blanco before they get a chance to kill another cop."

Cassidy leaned forward. "That's the job I'm offering you. Find these people before they kill any more police officers."

"What? How the hell am I supposed to find these people when the CIA and the FBI can't figure out who they are? And they've had four months!"

Cassidy's expression didn't change. "Do you want the job, Inspector?"

Morgan fell back into his seat and an image of a dimly lit hallway flashed before his eyes. "I can't do it, sir," he said softly.

Cassidy's bushy eyebrows rose in surprise. "Why not?"

"Because I don't want the responsibility for the lives of every cop in New York City on my shoulders."

"It won't be on your shoulders, Dan. It'll be on mine."

Morgan was struck by the deep anguish he saw in Cassidy's eyes. Despite his anger at the commissioner for his decision not to tell patrol officers about the threat of Puño Blanco, he understood the rationale for it. At this moment he didn't envy the police commissioner his job.

"Dan, I'm asking you to take this assignment because I think you're the best man for the job. But if the answer is no—and I won't hold that against you—I'll find someone else to do it."

"Would I be taking over the Joint Terrorist Task Force?" Morgan asked.

Cassidy scratched the stubble on his chin. "No. Coffey has asked me to form a smaller unit with agents from the FBI and the DEA who will be under the direction of someone from our department."

"Why another unit? We already have the joint task force with New York cops and FBI agents."

"Too many people. Coffey is afraid that a unit that large won't be able to maintain the strict security required for this assignment. We can't risk a leak. Even a hint of a group like this and the city will panic."

"How many people would I have assigned to me?" Morgan asked in exasperation.

Cassidy regarded him with his poker face. "Two."

"*One* from each agency? What good are three people against a group of terrorists?"

That, Cassidy remembered ruefully, was the exact question he'd asked the FBI Director. "At first I told him straight out that there was no way I'd agree to his proposal," he said to Morgan.

"What'd he say?"

Cassidy scowled. "He said the Bureau and the DEA would conduct the investigation without me. There was no way I was going to let a handful of federal agents control the destiny of *my* police department and *my* city."

"So you agreed to a three-man team."

Cassidy struck his chin out defiantly. "Yes, but goddammit, I insisted that we run the show." He studied the man he wanted for the job. "Dan, you'll only be three," he said. "But each of you will possess the required expertise for this assignment. And you won't be working alone. You'll be backed up by the full power and resources of all the agencies represented."

Morgan had had experience with interagency task forces before and knew it wasn't that simple. "Sir," he said evenly, "that's bullshit and you know it."

Dan Morgan had come into the police commissioner's office a suitably subservient deputy inspector, but during the course of this conversation a shift in power had occurred. He and the police commissioner had become equals. He realized there was too much at stake to stand on protocol. If he was going to take this assignment, he wanted the commissioner to know exactly where he stood and what was on his mind.

"We all know the federal agencies are notorious for their lack of cooperation," he continued. "When the joint task force started there were a lot of problems between our guys and the feds."

"And it got straightened out," Cassidy pointed out. If the commissioner had noticed the subtle change in their relationship, he didn't let on. "Besides," he continued, "a unit this small shouldn't have those problems. Coffey has assured me that he'll send only his best."

Cassidy sat back. "Well, Dan, what do you think?"

Morgan didn't know what to think. A risk taker his whole life, he'd trusted his instincts to make the correct choices and he'd usually been right. But since he'd been shot, he'd been weighing decisions carefully—too carefully.

"Do you want to sleep on your decision?" Cassidy asked.

"No," Morgan said abruptly. "That won't be necessary." His dreams were already filled with enough anxiety. "I'll do it."

Cassidy looked relieved. "Good. I'll tell Coffey I have my man."

"When do I start?"

"Coffey said it would take a couple of days. The DEA agent is still in Colombia, digging up additional information and the FBI agent is busy installing computer equipment in a special office you'll be using. You'll be notified as soon as they're ready." Cassidy saw the look in Morgan's face and added, "Dan, I know you're worried about the police officers on the street. So am I. Just before you arrived, I instructed the chief of department to issue an order eliminating solo patrol. And, as you may have heard when you came in, I've given the commanding officer of the Police Academy until sixteen hundred hours tomorrow to come up with in-service programs that will instruct our officers on officer safety, the proper procedures for car stops, and anything else that will protect them from these sons of bitches. Dan, I'll do everything humanly possible to protect our police officers, but I can't tell them about Puño Blanco."

Morgan nodded glumly. He didn't agree with the commissioner's decision, but there was nothing he could do about it. As he stood up, he remembered one more question. "Commissioner, what does Puño Blanco mean?"

The effects of the long day and this new crisis were evident in the commissioner's tired eyes. "White Fist," he answered. "Apparently the fist is an allusion to the power of the terrorist and the white is the cocaine of the narco-trafficker." Cassidy allowed himself a melancholy smile. "Very poetic, these terrorists."

Chapter

7

7:30 P.M. FRIDAY, MARCH 22 • Ray Fleming got off the Long Island Expressway and, as instructed by Lyle Petry, followed a winding tree-lined road through Oak Meadows, an exclusive North Shore community on Long Island. Fifteen minutes from the LIE, he made a left at a sign that said MANOR HALL COUNTRY CLUB.

At the end of the quarter-mile road loomed a stately white-columned mansion. Once the home of a wealthy industrialist, the sprawling estate, like many others on Long Island's North Shore, had been transformed into a country club. Fleming parked his battered 1980 Datsun between two gleaming Mercedeses, climbed the wide marble steps, and entered the world of big money.

A uniformed gray-haired man, sitting at an antique desk in the center of the thickly carpeted great hall, looked up. "Yes, may I help you?" His manner was impeccably polite, but Fleming saw the eyes sweep disapprovingly over his windbreaker and stonewashed jeans.

"Ray Fleming. I'm supposed to meet a Mr. Carl Weston."

The man consulted his guest list. "Yes, of course. Please take the elevator down to the range, Mr. Fleming."

As the tiny oak-and-mirror-paneled elevator made its slow, bumpy descent to the basement, Fleming whistled softly. Shooting in a high-class joint like this was going to be fun. And the best part was, it wasn't going to cost him a cent. In fact, if things went the way Petry claimed, he'd even make a few bucks.

The doors opened and he stepped into a smaller but much more well-appointed version of Blockmann's. Fleming inspected the facility with professional interest and liked what he saw. Behind a floor-to-ceiling glass wall were ten firing positions looking out at a well-lighted fifty-yard range.

Lyle Petry rose from a plush leather couch. "Any trouble finding the place?"

"Nope." Looking at Petry's blue blazer and tan slacks, he suddenly felt seedy. "Hey, Lyle," he whispered, "I don't think I'm dressed for this place."

Petry tapped Fleming's gun case. "As long as you brought that, you're dressed properly. Come on, I'll introduce you to the competition."

Two men, seated at a small, dark-paneled bar, looked up as they approached. "Carl, Lucas, I want you to meet Ray Fleming."

The older of the two, a tall, imposing man in his late fifties, rose. "Carl Weston," he said with a deep resonant voice. "I hope you're not as good as Lyle Petry says you are. And this"—he nodded to a younger man who was sporting the kind of deep tan that comes only from frequent trips to tropical climates—"is my partner for this evening, Lucas Kane."

Kane, whom Fleming judged to be in his early thirties, nodded, but didn't offer to shake Fleming's outstretched hand. Fleming was about to say something about the man's rudeness, but Petry put his arm around him and led him away. "Time is a-wasting, gentlemen," he said over his shoulder. "Shall we get started? How about ten minutes for practice?"

While they were shooting side by side, Fleming took the opportunity to assess his opponents. Both men, he noted, were using expensive customized guns. The older man was good, but erratic. He held most of his rounds within the eight-ring, but his shot groups were inconsistent. Kane, on the other hand, was much better. He fired at a steady rate and his shot groups were tight.

While fresh targets were mounted, Fleming took Petry aside. "These guys look pretty good," he said.

"You got that right. They *look* good, but they don't *shoot* good."

"How about Kane?"

Petry glanced toward Lucas Kane, who was carefully running a bore brush through his barrel. "An asshole bond broker who thinks he's Rambo. A real dickhead. He'll fold when the pressure is on."

Petry turned to the others. "The usual, gentlemen? Fifty rounds at twenty-five yards. Five for the match and a one for Xs."

They nodded, and without another word the match began. Weston and Kane started off well. After the first twenty-five rounds, Kane had all tens and Xs, but Weston had thrown five rounds into the eight- and nine-rings.

His opponents were shooting well, but Fleming's confidence grew as most of his rounds landed in the X-ring. By the end of forty rounds, Fleming had thirty-seven Xs.

Petry had been correct in his assessment of Kane. As the match wore on and the tension built, the young man's shooting became more and more erratic. Incredibly, he'd even thrown a round into the seven-ring. Weston didn't do much better.

As they fired their last five rounds, Fleming glanced at Petry's target and saw that his partner had put two into the eight-ring. He was surprised, but gratified; under match conditions, he *was* better than Lyle Petry.

While a range attendant tallied the score, the four had a drink at the bar. When the attendant was done, he handed the results to Weston. The older man gave the scores a cursory look, and tossed the paper to Kane. "You're the number cruncher. How much do we owe?"

The only outward sign of emotion in Kane was the twitching of his jaw muscles. He crumpled the paper and threw it on the bar. "Including their Xs, sixty-five."

Each man took out an envelope, stuffed additional bills inside, and handed it to Petry.

With that painful business over with, Carl Weston seemed to relax. "Lyle, I think it's customary for the winners to buy drinks?"

Petry slipped the envelopes inside his blazer pocket and motioned to the barman. "It certainly is. What are you gentlemen drinking?"

Kane stood up abruptly, almost knocking his stool over. "Nothing for me. I have an appointment."

Petry, flashing his half smile, blocked Kane's path. "With a firearms instructor?" he said softly.

Weston chuckled as Kane reddened. "I don't need a firearms instructor," the young man said through clenched teeth. "If I'd had a decent shooting partner, we'd have won."

Petry's pale green eyes pinned Kane. "What do you say just you and me shoot someday all alone? Any distance, any price, any rules."

Weston, smarting from Kane's remark, was thoroughly enjoying the young man's discomfort. "Lucas," he said, chuckling, "if you say yes to that proposition, it'll be a worse decision than your Adtex Industries bond debacle."

Kane glared at Weston. "I thought this club was for gentlemen." He brushed past Petry and muttered, "Only members should be allowed to shoot here anyway."

Weston shook his head. "I'll never get used to the new breed, Lyle. They make piles of money on the Street, but they have no class and they never will. Apparently, my hotheaded friend hasn't learned the first rule of gambling: If you can't afford to lose the money, don't gamble. I apologize for his boorish behavior."

"No apologies necessary, Carl. It's a pleasure doing business with you no matter who your partner is."

The older man's laugh was deep and resonant. "Of course. You always win anyway." He looked at Fleming appraisingly. "Maybe I should have this young fellow for a partner next time."

Petry put his arm around Fleming's shoulder. "Nothing doing, Carl. He's my partner. Isn't that right, Ray?"

"Yeah," said Fleming, who was beginning to like the idea, "we're partners."

They had one more drink with Weston before they left. Out in the parking lot, the two stopped by Fleming's car.

"I like the way you handled yourself," Petry said.

"What do you mean?"

"Kane got under your skin, but you didn't let it affect your shooting."

Fleming smiled. "That's because I was planning on meeting him in the parking lot later and punching his fucking lights out."

Petry grinned. "I like your priorities. Business first, then pleasure."

Fleming, who was still ticked at Kane's slight, said, "I don't care how much money he's got. There's no reason to treat me like shit."

Petry studied Fleming in the dim light of the parking lot. "An idealist. You got anything against money?"

"Hell, no. I just wish I had more of it."

Petry became pensive. "Maybe I can do something about that." Then he said lightly, "By the way, that was nice shooting. Almost too good."

"What do you mean?"

"Nothing. I'll tell you later. Listen, there's a bar in Jackson Heights called Chico's. It's at Thirty-seventh Avenue and Junction. I'll meet you there."

Forty minutes later, Fleming pulled up in front of Chico's and thought Petry had made a mistake with the address. Jackson Heights, once filled with Germans and Irish, had slowly but steadily been slipping into a ghetto. All the telltale signs were present—abandoned cars, shuttered stores, and fire-gutted buildings dominated the blighted landscape. The Germans and Irish, who'd made Jackson Heights a neat-as-a-pin middle-class neighborhood, had been replaced by minorities, predominantly Colombians, who, barely able to afford the rents, were in no position to complain about the dirty streets, run-down buildings, and growing street crime. Most of the store names and window signs were in Spanish. In some parts of Jackson Heights, English was a distant second language.

Fleming went through the doors of Chico's and half expected to find a surly group of Anthony Quinn types with bandoleers strung across their chests. Instead, he was pleasantly surprised to find a subdued, tastefully decorated interior. A few people sat at red banquettes lining the wall, but most of the Friday night clientele crowded around the bar.

Petry, who'd gotten there ahead of Fleming, emerged from the crowd with two bottles of beer in his hand. "Come on, Ray. Let's go into the back and settle up business first."

They sat at an unused table and Petry tossed an envelope on the table. "There's your cut, partner. You earned it."

Fleming, surprised at the thickness of the envelope, peered inside and his eyes widened. "How much is here?"

"Thirty-seven hundred."

Fleming dropped the envelope on the table. "Jesus! For what?"

"For outshooting those assholes."

"How much was the match for?"

"Five thousand, and a hundred dollars for Xs."

Fleming's usual cockiness evaporated. He'd shot in plenty of competitions, but except for the occasional five-dollar side bet, never for money. "Lyle, what if I'd had an off night?"

Petry shrugged. "Then we'd have lost. The trick is to have more on nights than off nights."

Visions of doing this with Petry on a regular basis began to fade. "I don't think I can do this anymore. I can't take the chance of losing your money."

"Don't sweat it, Ray. It doesn't bother me. Besides, you have your own money now." Petry slid the envelope toward Fleming. "It's not stolen, for chrissake. It's perfectly legal tender provided by two upstanding citizens of Wall Street."

Fleming fingered the envelope. "Damn, what an easy way to make money."

Petry laughed. "Hey, let's keep it in perspective. You don't always win."

Fleming grinned and the cockiness returned. "But we did tonight."

As he stuffed the envelope into his pocket, the barmaid came back with two more beers. "I figured you guys could use another round."

Ray Fleming, who hadn't noticed her when he'd first come in, looked up into the most exotic face he had ever seen. She brushed her long black hair away from large, dark brown eyes and looked down at him. "Lyle, introduce me to your cute friend."

Petry grabbed her around the waist and pulled her into his lap. "Does this mean you and me are through?"

She smacked him playfully. "You never had a chance."

"In that case, Celeste Escobar, meet my buddy, Ray Fleming."

She reached out and took Fleming's hand. "You look like a nice guy. How'd you ever meet up with someone like Lyle?" She made no attempt to let go of his hand.

"At the range where I shoot," he said.

She jumped up. "Oh, no. Not another shooting nut! *Guns*. That's all you macho guys think of."

"That's not all we think of." Petry grinned as she ran back to the bar, laughing.

Fleming turned to look at her go. "Lyle, are you two—"

"Naw. We had a little something going for a while, but now we're just good friends."

"She with anyone now?"

"I don't think so."

"Damn, she's . . ." He couldn't think of the precise word and his voice drifted off.

"Gorgeous? Yeah, she's that all right. Also smart. Everyone in this joint has the hots for her, but she's very particular. She's the one that makes the choice." He looked at his watch. "I gotta take off."

"I think I'll hang around."

Petry patted the younger man's cheek. "I know what's on your mind."

Fleming grinned. "Why not? I finally got a couple of bucks in my pocket, thanks to you." Fleming suddenly remembered a question he'd been meaning to ask. "Lyle, what did you mean before when you said I shot too good?"

Petry stood in the doorway. "You saw how those two were shooting, but you shot a whole pile of Xs anyway."

"Isn't that the idea?"

"First rule of money shooting: Never humiliate the competition. They won't want to play anymore."

"Oh, I didn't think—"

"No sweat. I didn't tell you before the match because I didn't want you to worry about shaving the score your first time out. Besides, that dickhead Kane needed a lesson."

A disturbing thought suddenly entered Fleming's mind. "Lyle, when we shot the other night at Blockmann's, did you deliberately miss the X-ring on the last round?"

Petry's half smile appeared. "I did the best I could. You just outshot me. Take care, buddy. I'll be in touch."

After Petry left, Fleming remained in the booth to digest everything that had happened to him tonight. Between Lyle Petry, the money, and Celeste, his mind was spinning. After a few minutes, he took three crisp twenties from the envelope and went out to the bar.

Celeste came down to his end. "Another beer, Ray?"

Ray Fleming flashed his best smile. "Yeah, why not?" he said, tossing a twenty on the bar.

Chapter
8

5:30 A.M. SATURDAY, MARCH 23 • The long, dimly lit hallway stretched to infinity. Through the thick fog Dan Morgan could barely make out the shadowy form of detective Larry Fredericks. Damn it! He was too far away to be of any help when Lawrence came out. He tried to call out to Fredericks, but he couldn't speak. He licked his dry lips and flipped open the chamber of his revolver to check for bullets. *Jesus! The gun was empty!* Suddenly the lights went out, plunging the hallway into blackness. For a moment, unable to tell up from down, he experienced a sickening sense of vertigo. He wanted to run away, but he didn't know how to get out. Without warning, the lights came back on, blinding him. The hallway that only moments ago had been as dark as a tomb was now bright as day. Numbly he looked at the bare light bulb hanging from the ceiling. How could such a small bulb create all this light?

Suddenly the hallway was filled with laughing children dressed in the plaid tie and skirted uniform of St. Bridget's, his old grammar school. A door opened and Willie Lawrence stepped into the hallway. Shielded by the bodies of the children surrounding him, he looked directly at Morgan and bared his crooked yellow teeth in a mocking grin.

From the other end of the hallway Fredericks appeared out of the fog and stood just beyond the cluster of children. *Mother of God, he's too close!* Morgan tried to cry out to him to get back, but no sound came from his mouth. Fredericks, confused by the appearance of children in the hallway, looked to Morgan for direction. Feeling as though he were wading through waist-high water, Morgan began moving slowly toward Lawrence.

A gun appeared in Lawrence's hand. Morgan watched in horrified fascination as the barrel of the gun, moving in a graceful arc, swept across the heads of the children and pointed at Fredericks's chest. The children's shrill screams drowned out the sound of the shot, but Morgan saw the gun jump in Lawrence's hand each time he pulled the trigger. He watched in helpless rage as two slugs shredded the front of the cop's blue jacket. The force of the impact spun Fredericks around and slammed him against the wall. The yellow-lettered word POLICE on the back of the jacket was stained crimson. The young cop clutched desperately at the paint-peeled wall—the last fingerhold on the world of the living—and sank slowly to the floor.

Finally, Lawrence was within reach. Morgan closed his hands around the man's throat, exulting in the satisfying feel of sweaty skin, muscle, and cartilage. With all the power he could summon he squeezed, trying to choke the life out of that infuriating grin. But Lawrence, seemingly undisturbed by the pressure Morgan was exerting on his windpipe, raised his gun. Morgan felt the cold, hard muzzle against his cheek, and an unearthly silence fell over the hallway. The screams of the children and the cries of the dying cop were blotted out. The only sound in the whole world, a sound that Morgan heard with every fiber in his body, was the soft metallic click of the firing pin flicking toward the chambered round.

With a yell he bolted upright in bed. He was clutching the pillow so tightly his forearms were cramped. He hurled the pillow to the floor and fell back on the sweat-soaked sheets. He remained that way, motionless, until the trembling ceased and his pounding heart returned to normal. Then he turned his head and looked at the clock. It was five-thirty.

He was exhausted, but he knew from past experience that he would not get back to sleep. Wearily he sat up. On shaky legs he crossed the tiny bedroom in three steps and flipped on the TV. A young Bette Davis was talking to Paul Henreid.

A ringing telephone caused his head to snap up. He didn't know how long he'd been sitting there, but the Bette Davis movie was over and it was light outside.

He picked up the telephone. "Yeah?"

It was Sarah. "Dan, did I wake you?"

"No," he lied. "I just came out of the shower."

"What time are you picking up Danny?"

Morgan glanced at the clock radio on the night table. It was seven A.M. "I'll be there around nine."

"Okay. See you at nine."

She hung up before he had a chance to ask her how she was getting along.

Dan Morgan drove down the familiar tree-lined street in Bellerose, Queens, and pulled up in front of a brick cape cod at exactly nine A.M. Mid-March was too early to tell if the lawn was going to come up lush and green, but the hedges were trimmed and in general the house looked well cared for. He wondered if Sarah was taking care of it herself or hiring someone. Since their separation nine months earlier, he came to the house only to pick up Danny for their weekly outings. Out of habit he reached for the doorknob, but quickly pulled his hand back and rang the bell.

Sarah, the tall, willowy woman he'd been married to for seven years, opened the door. "Danny's not ready yet. There's still some coffee left. Want some?"

The kitchen, both strange and familiar at the same time, was the place where he and Sarah had always done their serious talking. It was here that Sarah had announced she wanted a separation.

She poured two cups and sat down across from him. With her naturally dark eyebrows and eyelashes, she needed little makeup. There weren't many women, Morgan noted with a mixture of pride— and sadness—who looked as good as she did at that hour of the morning.

"You look awful," she said. "Don't you get any sleep?"

"Sure I do," he lied. "It's just that things have been pretty hectic at the precinct for the last couple of weeks." She was wearing faded jeans and an old sweatshirt but, as usual, she looked terrific. "How are you doing," he asked.

Her hazel-brown eyes twinkled. "Compared to you? Great. You still having those dreams?"

"On and off."

"You've lost weight too. God, listen to me. I'm kvetching like an old Jewish grandmother, but I'm not your grandmother, am I? I'm not even your wife."

He tried to read her expression to see if she was mocking him, but he couldn't tell. The subtlety of her droll sense of humor had always eluded his more practical mind.

She brushed her long hair away from her eyes and stood up. Suddenly the twinkle was gone. "You still having the pain?"

Involuntarily, he started to reach for his shoulder, but he quickly pulled his hand back. "No, it's fine."

That wasn't true. Since he'd come out of the hospital he'd been in almost constant pain. At first he'd tried to ignore it, but after several nights of watching him thrash around in bed, Sarah had insisted that he go to the doctor. The doctor gave him a speech about the effects of ballistic insult to the body and wrote him another painkilling prescription. The medicine worked—when he remembered to take it.

Sarah looked down at him. "Dan, I don't know how you became such a good cop, you're such a lousy liar."

"I said it's okay," he snapped.

Her eyes flashed. "That's your answer to everything, isn't it? *Real* cops don't talk about fear or pain or—"

"Sarah, please. I—"

"Let me see what's keeping that kid," she said, turning and walking out of the kitchen.

Morgan went to the stove. He noticed the new coffeepot and wondered, glumly, if there was anything else new in her life. Angry at his behavior, he poured another cup and slammed the pot down on the stove. He'd promised himself he wouldn't get into an argument with her, but he'd done it in less than three minutes.

When he opened the refrigerator to get the milk, he glanced out the back window. The bare rose bushes lining the chain-link fence suddenly reminded him of the wilted flowers on his night table in the hospital.

If the consequences of that night—a little over a year ago—hadn't caused such an upheaval in his life, it might have been funny. A single bullet had turned his body into a human pinball machine. It had entered his left shoulder, caromed off his shoulder blade, turned south severing an artery, veered west puncturing his lung, then south again, nicking a kidney before it spent itself in his small intestine. It took four operations to repair the damage, and it was touch and go for the first seventy-two hours.

One evening, three days after he'd come out of Intensive Care, Sarah came into his room and closed the door behind her. In spite of her skill with makeup, the dark smudges under her eyes from the many sleepless nights were evident. Without saying a word, she busied herself cleaning up his messy night table. With a vehemence that surprised him, she snatched up a bouquet of daisies and flung them into the wastebasket. White petals fluttered to the tiled floor. "Damn, don't these nurses know dead flowers when they see them?" She turned off the TV.

"Hey," he protested. "The Ranger game is coming on."

She sat on the edge of the bed and patted his hand. "I just spoke to the doctor," she said softly. "He says you have the constitution of an elephant and you're going to be just fine."

He didn't feel fine: his body ached all over. "I told you there was nothing to worry about," he said with all the cheerfulness he could muster.

"Dan, you'll be getting out of the job now. Right?"

He looked toward the night table. "Hey, is there anything to drink? My throat's parched. Boy, could I go for a cold—"

"Dan." Her voice was more insistent. "We have to talk about this."

"Not now, babe. When I get home we'll—"

"No." Her voice had gone up an octave. She cleared her throat and regained her composure. "You're well enough to talk about it now." Tears welled up in her eyes. "Dan, I've never been so scared in my life. When I opened the door that night and saw the chaplain and those two police officers—"

He squeezed her hand. "I know. It's been harder on you than it's been on me."

"Dan, I couldn't go through that again."

"Don't worry, it won't happen again."

She slammed her hand on the bed. "You don't *know* that," she shouted.

Startled by her unexpected outburst, he jumped, pulling the stitches in his shoulder.

"You're not a kid anymore. You're a forty-four-year-old man with a wife and a child! You have to think of us."

Morgan rubbed his burning shoulder. "Quiet down, Sarah. This is a hospital."

"I don't care if it's St. Patrick's Cathedral!"

She had a mercurial temper and he knew better than to argue when she was on a roll. Usually he walked away and let her vent her fury in an empty room, but he was flat on his back with tubes running into his arms.

She stood up and busied herself furiously stacking the magazines on his night table. "If my feelings aren't important, think about your son. You have no right to do this to him again. And another thing. You lied to me. You said captains don't get shot."

Morgan squirmed, trying to find a position where his shoulder didn't burn as much. "It's true. Captains don't get shot."

"Then that makes you a real jerk. Of all the captains in the department, *you* had to get shot."

Sarah's tirade had attracted the attention of the surly nurse who woke him every night to ask him if he were sleeping. She stuck her head in the door. "Are we all right in here?" she said in her raspy First Sergeant's voice.

"*We* are fine. *We* are just having a little chat." Sarah pushed the nurse out and slammed the door in her face. In spite of the throbbing shoulder, Morgan chuckled at the nurse's shocked expression.

Sarah turned her attention to him. "What the hell are you laughing at?"

"Nothing. Sarah, calm down. There are sick people around here and I'm one of them."

That seemed to deflate her anger. She sat on the edge of the bed and her chest heaved from the emotion welling up within her. Watching the soft curve of her breasts against her silk blouse, he began to feel aroused. Suddenly, for the second time since he'd been shot, he wanted desperately to make love to her.

The first time occurred the night he was shot. As he lay sprawled on the filthy hallway floor, staring dumbly at the blood oozing between his fingers, he kept thinking of Sarah and Danny. In those hectic seconds before they half carried, half dragged him down the stairs, he recalled the last time he and Sarah had made love. They'd been interrupted by Danny, who'd barged into the room looking for one of his Ninja Turtles. Quickly pulling the covers over them, they'd whooped until there were tears in their eyes, and looking at the perplexed expression on their son's face only made them laugh harder. In their blissful ignorance, they thought there would always be time to make love. But that night, slumped against the wall, and blinking hard to hold back the darkness that threatened to suck him into oblivion, he wanted nothing more than to feel, just one more time, her warm body against his, to feel her nails dig into his back.

MICHAEL GRANT

During the frantic ride to the hospital, he'd blacked out and had the most erotic dream of his life.

She put her hand on his arm and there were tears in her eyes. "Dan. I love you so much. These last few days—"

"I know, honey." He put his hand over hers. "I'm sorry."

"That's not enough. Please, for my sake, for Danny's sake, you've got to leave the job."

She didn't know it, but that was all he'd thought about since the shooting; starting with the wheel-screeching ride to the hospital. Gasping for air, he kept saying to the wide-eyed detective propping him up in the back seat, "I don't need this shit, Frankie. I'm gonna retire."

He still felt the same when he came out of surgery after the operation. Disoriented to the point of nausea, he tried to focus on the blurry green forms hovering over him. "How do you feel?" one of them asked.

"I don't need this shit," he said hoarsely. "I'm gonna retire."

But the night before they moved him out of Intensive Care, most of the medication had worn off, and he was no longer in the twilight world of semistupification. Just before dawn, he'd had the dream for the first time. Larry Fredericks, the young cop who'd died in the hallway, pointed an accusing finger at him. *"You did it,"* he said over and over again, *"you did it . . ."*

Morgan, thrashing about in the sweat-soaked bed, smashed his head against the restraining bar and woke up. As he lay there trying to catch his breath, a terrifying thought occurred to him: *He couldn't retire.* If he quit now, he'd be a haunted man for the rest of his life.

That afternoon, as they were wheeling him out of Intensive Care, one of the nurses asked the question that had become a running gag with the staff: "Captain, are you still going to retire?"

"No," he said, surprising her, "I'm not."

Walter Frawley, the president of the Captains Endowment Association, was his first visitor. The old, gray-haired captain hovered over him like a concerned grandfather. "How are you feeling, Danny?"

"Like I just went fifteen rounds with Mike Tyson."

Frawley pulled up a chair. "Yeah, but you're going to be okay. I talked to the doc. Congratulations, Danny. You're gonna get three-quarters."

Three-Quarters. The elusive holy grail pursued by so many police-men. A medical disability discharge from the department that meant he'd receive three-quarters of his pay, tax free, for the rest of his life, and all he had to do to collect his check was wake up every morning and breathe.

"I'm not getting out, Walter."

Frawley blinked hard. "Danny, I sit on the medical board. I know what it takes to get three-quarters and you got it. According to the doc, your internal plumbing is a mess. It'll be a piece of cake."

"Walter, read my lips. I'm not getting out."

"Dan, I know you've always been gung ho, but you've done your share. Take the pension and run." The old captain, his brow furrowed with concern, stood up and patted Morgan's good shoulder. "Get some rest. We'll talk about it again."

"I can't get out," he said to Sarah.

She gave him the same look of incredulity Frawley had given him. "Why not?"

"It's complicated." He had no intention of telling her about the dream. "I guess it's like a pilot crashing and having to go up right away before he loses his nerve."

She pulled her hand away. "You're such a jerk. My mother was right. She told me a Jewish girl should never marry a mick cop. All balls and no brains—I'm paraphrasing her, but that's what she meant. I should have married a nice Jewish boy who would have the brains and common sense to get out of the way of a bullet. What is this macho thing with you? What are you trying to prove?"

"Sarah, I'm not trying to prove anything." He didn't fully under-stand it himself. How could he explain it to her? "I have to live with myself. When it's time, I'll leave the job. But on my own terms. Besides"—he tried to sound cheerful—"I'm too young to retire. I have a great career in front of me and I intend to make the most of it."

She looked at him with a coldness he'd never seen before. "Even if it kills you?"

He was brought out of his reverie by the sound of Danny stomping down the stairs. "Daddy!" his son yelled as he came running into the kitchen. Dan Morgan turned from the window and scooped up the six-year-old, thankful that Danny was too young to understand what was going on. Unlike his mother, Danny wasn't angry with his father. On the contrary, he enjoyed the undivided attention he got every Saturday.

Danny squirmed out of his father's grasp. His son, Morgan noted sadly, had already learned that men didn't hug other men. Not even when one of them was his father. "Where are we going today, Dad?"

"Full schedule, buddy. Breakfast at your favorite diner, then the Central Park Zoo, and later I'm going to take you to the top of the world."

Danny's eyes widened. "Where's that?"

"The Twin Towers, the tallest buildings in the city. It's a real clear day so we'll be able to see practically the whole world."

Sarah helped Danny into his coat and gave Dan her stern-mother look. "Please. Try not to spoil him. After he got home last week, he refused to eat anything as mundane as chicken and vegetables for three days."

"I don't let him eat junk food," Dan protested. But he was lying. The fact was, he spoiled Danny on these Saturday outings. It was ironic. When he was living at home, *he* was the disciplinarian who insisted that Danny eat the proper foods. Now, he was letting his son eat anything he wanted. Was he in competition with Sarah? He didn't know, but it had to stop. Today, he would limit the junk food intake.

After a breakfast of waffles with ice cream topping and a chocolate shake, they went to the zoo. Then they drove downtown to the Twin Towers. Although it was Saturday, the observation deck wasn't crowded. Dan, with son in hand, leisurely strolled around the four sides of the deck, pointing out the Statue of Liberty, the Empire State Building, and Central Park.

Uninterested in the facts his father was spouting, Danny pressed his nose to the glass and looked down. "Wow! How did King Kong climb all the way to the top?"

For a moment, Morgan was annoyed that his son hadn't been

listening to him, but then he saw the serious expression on the child's face and tousled his curly hair. "He's a big gorilla, son, and big gorillas can do anything."

Still looking down, Danny said, "Dad, how many people live in all the houses?"

Dan's eyes swept the panorama before him, but he saw a very different city than his son and millions of awe-struck tourists saw. With a cop's jaundiced view, he saw people in terms of crime statistics. Of the antlike crowd scurrying below, he knew that almost two thousand of them would be murdered and seven thousand women would be raped before the year was out. He gazed toward Harlem with its row upon row of tenements—looking benign at this distance—and knew that more than a hundred thousand apartments in those buildings, and similar ones in the other boroughs, would be burglarized.

"How many, Dad?" Danny repeated impatiently.

"What? Oh, about eight million." As soon as he said it, it struck him again: how were he and two federal agents going to find Puño Blanco out there in a crowd of *eight million people*?

It was after seven when he returned a sleepy son to his mother. Sarah, wearing slacks and a turtleneck sweater that showed off her figure to great advantage, took one look at the exhausted but happy little boy and sent him off to get ready for bed.

"Did you two have a good time?"

She didn't ask him to sit down and he felt awkward standing in the foyer. "Yeah. It's funny, but I probably wouldn't spend this much time with him if I were still living at home."

"True. But it *is* quality time."

"Bullshit," he snapped. "Quality time is a term guilty parents use. They squeeze their kids in on their appointment calendars and call it quality time. It's not just the *time* you spend with your kid. He needs to know that you're in the next room available to him anytime he needs you."

She looked amused. "Thank you, Dr. Spock."

"What—?"

"I was being facetious." She shook her head. "Dan, when the

doctors cut out some of your internal organs they must have gotten your sense of humor too."

Embarrassed and angered by his outburst, he snapped, "Maybe that's because I don't see anything humorous about this separation."

Her eyes met his. "Neither do I."

"It was you—"

"No, Dan, it was your call."

"I told you why I couldn't get out."

"I can understand you having to prove something to yourself, but that's only half of it. Apparently you need the job more than you need me."

"Sarah, that's bullshit. I—"

She put her hand up. "Dan, I've heard it all. All I wanted was for you to get out."

"That's kind of selfish, don't you think?"

"Isn't your decision to stay in selfish?"

There was no point in arguing with her. She always got in the last jab. "Anything in the house giving you a problem?" he asked, changing the subject.

"No, the plumbing is fine." She touched his arm and her mood changed. "You know you can come to see Danny any time you want." She leaned over and kissed him on the mouth. The taste and feel of her flooded into him, almost making him dizzy.

"Thanks," he mumbled.

She took a step back as though her actions had surprised even her. "Next Sunday is Easter," she said quickly. "You want to come over and help Danny find Easter eggs?"

Morgan looked into Sarah's eyes and tried to fathom his contradictory wife. One minute she was breaking his chops. The next she was the agreeable, wonderful woman he'd married seven years earlier.

Her face reddened as she misread his hesitation. "If you have other plans, I understand. I just thought—"

"No, Sarah, it's not what you think."

He hadn't planned to tell her about his new assignment, but he didn't want her to think he was shacking up with some bimbo on Easter Sunday. "Sarah, I have a new—temporary—assignment," he said tentatively. "I'm just not sure . . . I'll be able to get away next Sunday."

Her eyebrows went up. "You're not in the precinct anymore?"

"No."

Her smile was part humorous, part annoyed. "Is it a big secret or are you going to tell me what it is?"

Morgan ran his fingers through his hair. "It is sort of a secret. It involves a couple of federal agencies . . . no big deal . . ." He trailed off when he saw her frozen smile fade.

"Is it dangerous?"

"No. Absolutely not."

"But you can't tell me what it is and you won't be able to be with your son on Easter Sunday. Is that about it?"

"I said I don't know yet. I'll try to be here."

She yanked the door open. "Don't do me any favors."

In spite of their strained parting, that night, for a change, he didn't have his usual nightmare. Instead, he dreamed he was back home with Sarah and Danny with everything the way it used to be. But the euphoria quickly evaporated when he awoke and found that he was in his tiny apartment. Alone.

Chapter

9

8:10 A.M. SUNDAY, MARCH 24 • Jimmy, dressed as a TV repairman, silently climbed up the last flight of stairs in an apartment building a half block from the intersection of Woodhaven Boulevard and 65th Street. The clean, well-lighted hallway smelled of Sunday morning: fresh coffee and frying bacon.

He reached the roof landing and stopped to listen. It had been decided beforehand that the mission would be aborted if he encountered anyone on his way up the stairs. But he'd passed no one. He bent down to examine the roof door lock and muttered an oath. Yesterday, when they'd made a dry run, he'd easily picked the lock. But in the intervening twenty-four hours, someone had jammed it with gum. He put his lock-picking set back into his pocket and removed a screwdriver from his tool belt. Inserting the screwdriver between the door and the jamb, he popped the door open with a quick sideways twist. He held his breath and listened, but all he heard was the muffled sounds of TVs behind closed doors. Satisfied that no one was coming, he quickly stepped out onto the roof, walked to the edge of the parapet, and wiped his forehead with a white handkerchief—the signal that the mission was still on. Lyle Petry, standing next to a pay telephone six floors below, saw the signal and immediately dialed 911.

Sunday morning is usually the quietest part of the tour for a sector car—especially in the Forest Hills section of Queens. Most of the residents, weary from the week-long subway commute to Manhattan, sleep late or laze away the morning over a leisurely breakfast and the Sunday papers. Later, as the day wears on, calls for service increase as people, getting on with the business of living, discover that crime is a seven-days-a-week, twenty-four-hours-a-day reality.

Police Officers Jeff Golden and Stephanie Hannon, taking advantage of the lull, ate a radio car version of a leisurely Sunday morning breakfast—coffee and a buttered bagel.

They'd been partners for almost a year and in that time they'd gotten along remarkably well—except when it came to baseball.

Golden scanned the sports page. "Hey, Steph," he said with the quiet certainty of a fanatical fan, "the Mets are going all the way this year."

Hannon, looking up from a Macy's ad, grinned maliciously. "Get real. They're going to do what they do every year—choke at the end of the season. Forget it, Jeffrey."

Golden was about to list his reasons why things would be different this year, when the radio crackled: "*Sector George . . . respond to St. John's Cemetery . . . Meet a complainant corner of Woodhaven and Sixty-fifth . . . Vandals overturning headstones.*"

Hannon keyed the mike. "Ten-four."

Golden looked at his watch. "Son of a bitch. It's not even eight-fifteen. Can't those ghouls wait until after breakfast? Screw it. We'll go when we finish our coffee."

Reluctantly Hannon dumped her half-full container out the window. "Come on, Jeff. The boss is working and you know the flack he's been taking from the community council about cemetery vandals. If he shows up before we do, he might cancel my twenty-eight for next Saturday."

Golden saw an opportunity to needle his partner. "So you'd trade your independence for a lousy day off?"

"It's my best friend's wedding and *I'm* the maid of honor."

Golden rolled his window down and dumped the remainder of his coffee. "Stop. You're breaking my heart." He put the car in gear. "Hey, maybe we'll catch a couple of grave robbers and the captain will give us an 'atta boy' day off. I'll go to the wedding with you."

Hannon rolled her eyes.

"Terrific!" Golden muttered as they pulled up to the corner of Woodhaven and 65th Street. "I throw away a full container of coffee and there's not even a complainant on the scene."

Hannon looked at her watch. "Well, as long as we're here, we might as well take a quick turn around the cemetery."

Golden, still muttering about his coffee, pulled away from the curb.

When the radio car pulled up to the intersection, Jimmy was examining a wire connection near the roof's edge. Dropping the wire, he bent down and opened his tool box. Keeping his eye on the radio car below, he lifted the top tray out of the box, and was about to remove something from the bottom, when the police car drove off. Calmly, he placed the top back, walked to the edge of the roof, and peered down. Lyle Petry was already on the telephone. Jimmy went back to his position and resumed his examination of the electrical connection. He knew the radio car would return.

Golden and Hannon drove along the winding cemetery roads looking for overturned stones. Except for a few mourners, the cemetery was deserted, and there was no sign of vandalism.

"See, Steph? It doesn't pay to rush to these jobs. I always—"

He was interrupted by a radio message. *"Sector George, we have a second call on that cemetery job."*

Stephanie Hannon keyed the mike. "Central, that job is unfounded. We're on the scene and we don't see any overturned stones."

"Caller states he's still waiting at Woodhaven and Sixty-fifth," the dispatcher added.

Hannon rolled her eyes. "Ten-four, Central. We'll go back."

Golden made a U-turn and circled back to Woodhaven and 65th Street. They pulled up in front of an elderly man who was sitting on a bench taking in the morning sun. He hadn't been there when they passed by earlier.

Hannon, closest to the man, rolled her window down. "Excuse me, sir, did you call about vandals in the cemetery?"

"No, Officer, I didn't."

"Been here long?"

"I just sat down."

"See any kids running out of the cemetery?" Hannon asked.

The old man shook his head.

She keyed the mike. "Central, that St. John's job is unfounded. We're at the scene. No complainant. Sector George resuming patrol."

Golden spotted a Mets button on the man's jacket and yelled out the window. "Whaddaya think of the Mets chances this year?"

When the radio car reappeared, Jimmy once again removed the top tray from his tool box, uncovering the disassembled parts of an Israeli-made Galil sniper rifle. An efficient killing weapon, the Galil was equipped with a muzzle brake and compensator to reduce jump and permit rapid realignment. But Jimmy had no need for these embellishments. What he had to do would require only one shot.

Quickly and efficiently, he snapped open the folding stock and screwed the cone-shaped silencer onto the end of the barrel. Then, crouching low at a spot he'd carefully selected the day before because it provided concealment from the windows in the apartment building nearby, he braced the rifle's barrel on the edge of the roof's parapet and trained the scope on the radio car below.

Jimmy estimated the distance to be about a hundred meters; an easy shot. The highly accurate weapon was capable of hitting a six-inch circle at three hundred meters. In practice, he'd pulverized a cantaloupe at more than twice that distance. And once, when the wind conditions were right, he'd added another hundred meters to that. With calm deliberation, he manipulated the adjusting screws and sighted in on the rear seat of the radio car. He saw sections of the *Daily News* and a paper bag. He adjusted the magnification and read the words on the bag: Benny's Bagel. Then he aligned the cross hairs on the back of the driver's head and waited patiently for the target to stop bobbing.

The old man winked. "The Mets are going all the way," he said firmly.

Golden poked his partner. "What'd I tell ya? You don't know what the hell you're talking about, Hannon."

Stephanie Hannon leaned out the window and groaned. "Jeez, mister, you don't know what you've done. I gotta ride with this fanatic for the rest of—"

Suddenly, there was a loud explosion and Jeff Golden's body slammed into her back. The force of his weight drove her head into the side of the door, making her ears ring. A spray of fine shimmering red dots appeared on the windshield and dashboard. Stunned and confused, she pushed him away. "Jeff," she said, turning toward him. "Why the hell did you—?"

His bulging, lifeless eyes stared past her and she saw that the back of his head was oddly misshapen—as though someone had mussed his hair. Instinctively she tried to pat down the unruly black hair, but her hand sank into a soft, sticky-warm cavity.

Stephanie Hannon's world went into slow motion.

"Oh, Jeff . . ." With one hand she gently cradled her partner's head, and with the other reached for the radio. She knew she was slipping into shock—her ears were ringing and she had to keep blinking to clear away the black dots that threatened to obscure her vision—but for the moment her senses remained acute. With a curious feeling of detached pride she noted that her hand didn't shake as she held the mike, nor did her voice crack as she spoke. "Ten-thirteen, officer—" It suddenly occurred to her that she didn't know what had happened to Jeff Golden. She blinked the tears away and began again. "Ten-thirteen, my partner is . . . hurt . . . corner of Woodhaven and Sixty-fifth. Please . . . please hurry . . ."

With exaggerated slowness she returned the handset to its cradle and turned to the old man still sitting on the bench. From where he was sitting he hadn't witnessed the carnage that had just occurred inside the radio car. She tried to focus on him, but the small dots were getting larger and her vision was quickly narrowing to a small circle of light. The man was saying something about Doc Gooden, but she couldn't hear him very well because of the increasingly loud rushing sound in her ears. "My partner's been hurt," she heard herself say in a voice that sounded very far away. Then, as she heard the comforting sounds of the police sirens approaching in the distance, the small circle of light closed, enveloping her in total blackness.

Up on the roof, Jimmy quickly but calmly disassembled the rifle and returned it to the tool box. The last thing he did before he left the roof was to bend down and retrieve the one spent brass shell. He never needed more than one.

Dan Morgan, sorting out his laundry on the bed, cursed out loud. A red sock had gotten mixed up with his underwear and had stained all his shorts and T-shirts pink. He was about to call Sarah for advice when the telephone rang. It was the police commissioner. Morgan swept a pile of pink shorts out of the way and grabbed a pencil and pad.

"There was another assassination this morning," the commissioner said.

Morgan had guessed as much from Cassidy's bleak tone.

"Where?"

"The one-twelve. Less than an hour ago."

"Another bomb?"

"A gun. Probably a rifle."

Morgan groaned inwardly. A skilled man with a rifle had the advantage of flexibility and distance. With the number of tall buildings throughout the city, an assassin had plenty of good locations to choose from. Given the topography of the city it would be virtually impossible to defend against someone determined to shoot a police officer.

Cassidy was still talking. ". . . A sector responded to a phony run for vandals in a cemetery. The operator of the RMP took one round to the head. He died instantly."

"How about his partner?"

"She wasn't hit, but she's in the hospital being treated for trauma."

"Witnesses?"

"Just an old man. He was talking to them when it happened but he didn't see or hear anything."

"Didn't *hear* anything. A silencer?"

"Probably."

Morgan glanced at a calendar. This latest assassination, coming only six days after the last one, demanded immediate action. "Sir, we gotta get moving on this. When are the feds going to get here?"

"Tomorrow morning," Cassidy growled. "I just got off the phone with Coffey. I told him to get off his bureaucratic ass and have those agents here before I'm out of bed."

Morgan could imagine the conversation. Cassidy was slow to anger, but when he blew, there was no stopping him. It was a safe bet that the Director of the FBI had never been spoken to like that in his life. "Where do we meet?"

"Ten A.M. My office."

"Sir, do you know anything about the people I'll be working with?"

"The Bureau is sending an agent named Chris Liberti. She's a computer whiz and an expert on terrorist groups."

Morgan almost blurted out *"she?"* but he held his tongue. Angrily, he threw a pile of underwear against the far wall. "Just what I need," he said to himself. "Only two agents and one of them is a *woman!*"

Cassidy was still talking. "Donal Castillo from the DEA is an expert on the Medellin cartel. In fact that's where he is right now. He's flying a red-eye out of Bogotá this afternoon."

Morgan jotted the names down. Later, he'd make some calls to see what he could find out about these two. But that would have to wait. "Sir, I'd like to get over to the one-twelve, but . . ." He hesitated. As the commanding officer of a Manhattan precinct he had no business snooping around a Queens homicide.

Cassidy, sensing the reason for Morgan's hesitancy, said, "Go ahead. I've already had your orders cut. As of five minutes ago, you've been transferred to my office as special liaison. The title's vague enough to let you talk to anyone you deem necessary without raising too many eyebrows."

"Okay," Morgan said, "I'm on my way."

Woodhaven Boulevard, a major artery in Queens, was cordoned off one full block in each direction from the scene. Car horns and angry shouts from motorists pierced the usually placid neighborhood as harried cops rerouted traffic down narrow residential streets.

Morgan held up his shield and was waved through by a pale cop standing behind a barricade. From the young officer's expression Morgan guessed it was his first personal contact with the reality of what he did for a living. Neophyte cops, excited and overwhelmed by the uniform and the gun, seldom pondered what a police officer's job was all about. Some cops even managed to make it through twenty years without having to come to grips with that stark reality. But for others, like that cop behind the barrier, life as a police officer would never be quite the same again. As of an hour ago, that exciting sense of adventure was gone, displaced by the reality that wearing a blue uniform meant you could die at any time, even on a brilliant Sunday morning.

Morgan was relieved to see an old friend on the scene. It would make his presence easier to explain to those who hadn't yet seen the orders. Neil Quigley had come on the job with Morgan and they'd remained friends ever since.

The short, compact squad commander, who hadn't gained an ounce since the Academy, looked up as Morgan approached. "Danny, you in Queens now?"

"Just got transferred to the PC's office this morning. He sent me out to take a look."

Quigley's professional neutral expression didn't reveal what he was thinking. As a squad commander, he was accustomed to assorted brass from the Puzzle Palace looking over his shoulder—especially when it involved a cop homicide. He didn't like it, but lowly lieutenants didn't tell ranking officers to take a hike. At least Dan Morgan knew what the hell he was doing.

The lieutenant, chewing on a toothpick, started walking toward the police car and Morgan followed. "There's not much in the way of evidence, Dan. The preliminary from the ME is a round from a high-powered rifle."

Morgan's eyes locked on the police vehicle, which was cordoned off by yellow crime scene tape. From a distance RMP 3255 looked very much like the hundreds of other radio cars that prowled the streets of New York every day. Like most, the blue-and-white needed to be washed, and there were the usual dents and scratches from trying to squeeze through too many narrow streets too many times. It was only when Morgan got close enough to look inside that he saw what made RMP 3255 unique. The impact of the bullet had exploded Officer Golden's skull, showering the interior with brain, bone, and blood. In the back seat a bag from Benny's Bagel Shop lay half covered by a bloodstained *Daily News*.

Morgan turned away. "Anything yet, Neil?"

**Officer
DOWN**

"Not much. Two phony calls were made to nine-eleven about vandals in the park."

"*Two?* What do you think it means?"

"I dunno. The calls were less than five minutes apart. Could be the sniper wasn't ready the first time the radio car showed up."

"You getting a copy of the nine-eleven tape?"

"Yeah. I sent one of my guys over to pick it up. He called a few minutes ago. He listened to the tape. A nondescript male voice. Nothing unusual."

Quigley turned toward a row of apartment buildings. "From the angle we figure the shooter was somewhere in that direction." The detective lieutenant pointed toward a row of apartment buildings halfway down the block.

Morgan scanned the many windows. "That's a lot of apartments to canvass."

Quigley nodded glumly. "Yeah, but I'll have plenty of help. Cops on their RDOs have been streaming into the station house wanting to help."

Morgan, who'd done it himself on more than one occasion, understood why cops came into work on their day off. It was one way to alleviate the anger and sense of helpless frustration.

"Any motive?" he asked the lieutenant.

"Nothing yet. We're checking Golden's arrest history, but he was only on the job fourteen months. He came here straight from the NSU. Only made a handful of collars. None of them serious enough to provoke a revenge killing."

"How about the girl?"

"She had less time than he did. Same thing. A few collars. Nothing special."

"How's she doing?"

"She's at St. John's being treated for shock." Quigley, watching a Crime Scene photographer taking pictures of the vehicle's interior, spit the chewed-up toothpick out of his mouth. "I'm trying to knock off the coffin nails," he explained.

A short black detective built like a fire plug hurried over. "Hey, Loo. Farrell just called from the roof of that building. He says the

MICHAEL GRANT

door to the roof was forced. He spoke to the super. He says it was locked last night."

Quigley started for the building. "Stay here," he said to the detective. "As soon as Crime Scene is finished here, send them up to the roof. Tell them to bring plenty of powder. I'll want them to dust the entire hallway and roof landing." As an afterthought, he turned to Morgan. "Want to come?"

"Sure, why not." Morgan tried to keep the excitement out of his voice. Maybe the gunman had made a mistake and left a piece of evidence.

A uniformed officer, standing guard at the roof landing, held back a small crowd of curious tenants.

Quigley studied the lock, but was careful not to touch it. "It's a piece of shit. Wouldn't take much to pop it. Fresh tool marks. Looks like a screwdriver."

They stepped out onto the roof and saw four detectives standing at the edge peering down at the radio car. Quigley looked over their shoulders. "Did you guys comb the roof?"

"Yeah, boss," one of them answered. "Nothing. Just a couple of old beer cans and some junk."

"Well, stop standing around, for chrissake," he snapped. "Collect everything that isn't nailed down. The lab will decide what's junk."

As the chastised detectives spread out across the roof to renew their search for evidence, Quigley gazed out over the expanse of St. John's Cemetery. Finally, after a long silence he said, "Look at that grass, Dan. It's getting real green. Golden was a big Mets fan. Yesterday, I heard him telling someone about the great seats he got for next Sunday's game."

Dan Morgan wasn't listening to the squad commander. He was staring down at the radio car, imagining someone focusing cross hairs on the back of Golden's head. It was clearly the work of a pro. Even with a scope, given the distance and angle, it wasn't an easy shot.

He was also thinking what lay ahead of him. The first day into this assignment and three cops were dead. How many more would die before he, and those two agents, found Puño Blanco?

Even in high school, he hadn't liked playing defense. Aggressive and proactive by nature, he preferred the freewheeling, split-second decisions that running backs made on their way to a touchdown. But now he was forced to play defense while Puño Blanco called the shots.

Chapter
10

9:55 A.M. MONDAY, MARCH 25 • Dan Morgan, who'd just gotten off the telephone with Lieutenant Quigley, sat in the police commissioner's conference room waiting for the others to arrive. The squad commander's news wasn't good. The evidence, what little there was, had been processed with negative results. No prints, no shell casing, not even a witness who might have seen the gunman enter or leave the building. Quigley had even thought to check the parking summonses that had been issued in the vicinity since midnight. It had been a parking summons that had led to an arrest in the Son of Sam investigation. But not this time. Only a handful of summonses had been written and all the vehicles and owners had checked out. There was only one stark certainty: an assassin had executed a police officer in broad daylight and disappeared without a trace. Either he was very good or very lucky. Morgan sadly doubted it was the latter.

His thoughts were interrupted by someone opening the door. The man who came in was dark-complexioned, with intense black eyes, shrouded by thick eyebrows. He was almost bald, but Morgan guessed him to be only in his midthirties.

Morgan stood up and put his hand out. "I'm Dan Morgan."

"Donal Castillo, DEA." The deep voice contained a faint hint of a Spanish accent. "So. Those motherfuckers have killed another cop."

Morgan, struck by the depth of intensity in those dark eyes, said, "Yeah. That's why the PC pushed up the time table."

"Got a phone here?"

Morgan pointed to one on the desk. "Dial nine to get out."

Castillo pulled out a small address book and made several calls. He spoke in Spanish, except for the last call, which he made to the New York DEA office.

He hung up and slumped into a blue swivel chair. "Man, I'm bushed," he said, flashing a weary smile. "I've been in the air all night." Castillo patted down his sparse black hair. "I tried to make some calls from Colombia but it's a waste of time. The fucking revolutionaries are always blowing up the switching stations." He looked at his watch. "So? When do we get started?"

"We're waiting for the PC and Chris Liberti."

Castillo snorted. "A *female* FBI agent. Jesus! Talk about two strikes."

Morgan didn't find Castillo's remark encouraging. It was common knowledge that there was no love lost between the DEA and the FBI. He hoped this interagency rivalry wasn't going to create problems. He slid a copy of the Unusual—a twelve-page report summarizing the circumstances of Police Officer Golden's death—across the desk. "This will give you a quick picture of yesterday's murder."

Castillo looked up sharply. "Assassination. These fucks don't murder people, they assassinate them."

With a start Morgan realized the DEA agent was right. The deaths of these police officers were not ordinary murders. They were well-planned and well-executed assassinations.

As Castillo read the report, Morgan took the opportunity to study the agent, who was wearing an ill-fitting sport jacket and a tie that didn't quite meet his open collar. He was trim, with the thick neck of a man in excellent physical condition. When they'd shaken hands, Morgan had felt calluses on Castillo's palm. He guessed the DEA agent pumped iron.

The night before—in the time-honored tradition of New York City cops—Morgan had made an attempt to find out more about Donal Castillo and Chris Liberti. He wasn't interested in the thumbnail sketch Cassidy had given him of their backgrounds. There were more important things to learn: Were they reliable? Street smart? Did they have any quirks that would make them difficult to work with? You didn't get that kind of information from résumés. Only people who worked with them could answer those questions.

First, he'd called his contact in the Bureau, Charlie Eastman, and asked him to check out Liberti. Twenty minutes later, Eastman called back. "The word is she's a real gutsy lady," he said. "In her first year she did an undercover operation involving the Mafia. I don't know the whole story, but I hear she almost got killed when the operation fell apart. She's spent most of the time in antiterrorist work. They say she really knows her stuff. Lectured at the Academy for our agents, the CIA, and the DEA. The Director thinks the world of her."

"Sounds like a candidate for the Mother Teresa Award. Anything on the downside?"

Eastman hesitated. "Well . . . she has a bit of a rep for being a ball-breaker when she thinks she's being treated like a second-class citizen. It rubs some of the guys the wrong way and she's made a few enemies."

Morgan rubbed his temples. He didn't need this. "Thanks, Charlie, I owe you one."

Next, he'd called Hank Staiger, a DEA agent and old friend of ten years. Staiger, who was in the middle of a heavy investigation, said he'd check out Castillo as soon as he could spare a moment. But he hadn't called back yet.

Now, Dan Morgan, studying the DEA agent engrossed in the report, felt uneasy about entering into a working relationship with someone about whom he knew nothing.

Before Castillo finished reading the Unusual, Commissioner Cassidy came in. Morgan introduced him to Castillo. Cassidy glanced at his watch impatiently. "Liberti isn't here yet. I guess she's caught in traffic."

"She's from the Bureau," Castillo said, flashing a broad irreverent smile. "She's probably having trouble finding police headquarters."

A preoccupied Cassidy shot Castillo a withering glance and impatiently glanced at his watch again. "Let's get started. Dan, you can fill Liberti in when she gets here."

Morgan understood the reason for the commissioner's distracted behavior. In less than an hour he was due at the funeral of Police Officer Jeffrey Golden.

Every police officer killed in the line of duty receives an inspector's funeral complete with uniformed pall bearers, flags, and honor guard, and one of the police commissioner's most unpleasant tasks is to attend these funerals. Morgan had planned to go himself, but Cassidy had told him his time could be better spent getting his squad off the ground. He'd accepted Cassidy's tacit order with more relief than he cared to admit—even to himself. It was one more emotionally draining experience Dan Morgan didn't need.

"Gentlemen," Cassidy began, "it was agreed to have the first meeting here. But from now on—"

Suddenly, the door opened and an attractive woman with short brown hair rushed in. A scowling Cassidy glanced at his watch. "Agent Liberti?" he asked.

"Yeah. Sorry I'm late," she said in a voice unmistakably Brooklyn, "but traffic on Flatbush Avenue was *really* screwed up."

Cassidy, regaining his train of thought, continued. "As I was saying, this meeting has been arranged so that you could meet each other. But from now on you'll meet at an office provided by the Bureau. Miss Liberti, I believe you know where it is?"

The door opened and an aide stuck his head in. "Sir, it's time—"

"All right, Frank." He looked at the three people seated around the table and once again felt misgivings about the whole venture. How the hell were these three going to find Puño Blanco? "I don't have to tell you how important and difficult your work is going to be," he began. "I—" He stopped as he realized that there was nothing he could say that they didn't already know. "I'll leave you in the capable hands of Inspector Morgan. Good luck."

After Cassidy left, Morgan stood up and introduced himself to Chris Liberti. "Well," he said, turning away from her striking brown eyes, "let's head over to the new office and get settled in. We've got a lot to do."

At eleven in the morning West 37th Street, the heart of the garment district, was clogged with double-parked trucks disgorging racks of this spring's line of brightly colored dresses, skirts, and tops. In the street, horns blared from impatient trucks and taxicabs, while on the sidewalk pedestrians dodged racks of clothes hastily propelled in and out of buildings by sweating blacks and Hispanics who paid attention to nothing except the music blasting from their Walkman earphones.

Liberti surveyed the street's chaos with obvious satisfaction. "Super place for the office, huh? I selected it myself. During the day, the area's a madhouse, but after six, it's a tomb. Either way, we won't be noticed."

The three of them crowded into the tiny elevator and Liberti's cologne quickly filled the small space. Usually, Morgan was allergic to cologne and perfume, but whatever she was wearing not only smelled good, it didn't make him sneeze.

They got off the elevator on the fourth floor and stopped in front of a door marked YALE IMPORTS. "The school I always wanted to attend," she said, unlocking the door.

"Where did you go?" Morgan asked.

"Brooklyn College." It was the first time Morgan saw her dazzling smile.

The interior was barely large enough to hold a metal desk and a secondhand swivel chair. Morgan looked around the tiny office in dismay. "You gotta be kidding. There isn't enough room for the three of us," he said.

"Not to worry. This is only the outer perimeter. There"—she pointed to another door—"is where the *real* office is."

She stepped up to a wall-mounted metal cabinet and punched in numbers on an electronic keypad. The cabinet door opened, revealing two smaller boxes inside.

Castillo peered over her shoulder. "What's that?"

"A fingerprint reader and eye scanner. Neat, huh? Biometric state of the art security," she said proudly. "The eye scanner system uses an ultralow-intensity light source to scan the retina. Then it creates a digitalized wave form that's relayed to a microprocessor."

Liberti, seeing the puzzled expression on Morgan's face, elaborated. "The system uses the retinal blood vessel pattern for recognition. Blood vessel patterns are as unique as fingerprints."

Castillo looked at the scanner warily. "How long do you have to stick your eye in front of that hole?"

"About three seconds. It's harmless, and if you come in after a night on the town, the scanner will still recognize you, bloodshot eyes and all."

Morgan, who had no experience with security hardware, gingerly stuck his finger in the fingerprint reader. "How's this work?"

"Basically the same way. The system takes a high-resolution electronic picture of your fingerprint and compares it to a digitized template already on file. The system analyzes up to a quarter-million bits of information to arrive at a comparison. Both the eye scanner and the fingerprint reader work in tandem, making the chances of an error virtually zero."

Morgan and Castillo looked at each other and shrugged.

"Before we go inside," she continued, "let me explain the entire security system. The outer door leading to the hallway is the only one that will require a key. Everything else is controlled by PINs and biometrics."

"PINs?" Morgan asked.

Liberti looked at the two men in exasperation. "Personal identification numbers—passwords. Jeez, you guys been living in a cave or what?" Before they could answer she continued. "Later, I'll give each of you your own PIN and enroll you in the biometric systems. But first, let's talk about the security of the office. That door we just came through looks ordinary, but it's solid steel, and the door buck is made with reinforced steel. No ordinary burglar is going to get past that. If he does, an alarm is transmitted via microwave directly to our monitoring station in Federal Plaza. Our operator will immediately call nine-one-one and report a burglary in progress."

Liberti put her eye to the eye piece, and her finger in the slot. The interior door sprang open. "This elaborate system," she said, leading them into the next room, "is protecting *this* little sweetie."

The three stepped into a spacious office and gathered around a computer terminal bristling with wires and cables. Liberti typed a command and the screen flashed status information. "There were a couple of glitches and I was up till four this morning getting the damn thing on line. That's why I was late. I slept in."

"I thought you were late because of traffic on Flatbush Avenue," Castillo said.

She winked at him. "Hey, I couldn't tell the police commissioner I slept in. Right?"

Castillo grunted. "I guess so. I *never* give a boss a straight answer."

Liberti patted the CRT affectionately. "This baby is patched into database computers in each of our respective agencies, plus a handful of other supersecret agencies whose databases may be useful to us. We have the necessary security clearance to retrieve everything they have to offer."

"What about me?" Morgan asked. "I don't think I have—"

"Done. As soon as Coffey gave me your name, I got the paperwork moving. It came through yesterday afternoon."

She thumbed through a thick mound of printouts overflowing in the paper catcher. "It's started already, guys. Last night I started

**Officer
DOWN**

querying the databanks for the names of radicals with any connection to Colombia and South America. The computer will be spitting out names for a week."

Morgan eyed the formidable pile. "It's gonna be a bitch tracking down all those people."

"It's not as bad as it looks. I'll run this list against other files. A lot of these people are dead, in jail, or out of the country."

"There's still gonna be a lot of names left to check out."

"Yeah," Liberti conceded. "But it's the best I can do."

Castillo scowled at the computer. "Hey, babe, I don't know nothing about these things. Don't expect me to use that."

Liberti's right eyebrow arched. "Listen, Castillo," she said evenly, "how about saving the 'babes' for the wife and kiddies?"

There was a moment of tense silence, then Castillo grinned. "My mistake, *Ms.* Liberti."

"No sweat." She patted his cheek. "But can the Ms. I almost always answer to Chris."

Morgan inspected the room. The two windows looking out onto the street were barred from the inside. He couldn't see any wires, but he was certain the windows were alarmed and tied into the rest of the security system. There were three desks equipped with telephones. A photocopier, a FAX machine, and five sturdy filing cabinets with locking bars lined the far wall. Three televisions with accompanying VCRs—presumably to cover the major network news programs— perched on top of the cabinets. A large tin of herbal tea—hers?— stood beside an automatic coffee maker and a small refrigerator. Special Agent Liberti had thought of everything.

Morgan couldn't help comparing the city's way of doing things with the federal government's. Most PD task forces were hastily thrown together, and the hapless men—often treated like unwanted stepchildren—had to beg, borrow, and steal office space, vehicles, and equipment. Morgan, who'd been a member of some of these ad hoc groups, had experienced these problems firsthand. Even as a precinct CO, it had taken him most of last year to get the city to paint the station house. At least heading up this group had one major perk: for the first time in his police career, he was going to have the luxury

MICHAEL GRANT

of working with brand-new equipment. And even better, the feds, who were picking up the tab for this project, always had an open checkbook.

"Well," he said aloud, "we've got a lot to do. Any ideas where to begin?"

Castillo, who was peering into an empty desk drawer, said, "First off, I gotta say this whole three-man"—he looked at Liberti—"and - woman team is a crock. There oughta be more than three of us working on this."

"Yes, but we'll have the full resources and backing of our respective agencies," Liberti said sarcastically.

Morgan grunted. Apparently, Liberti had been given the same rah-rah speech. "I already went through this with the police commissioner," he said. "We're gonna have to make the best of it. So where do we begin?"

Liberti tapped the computer terminal with a long, glossy-red fingernail. "Right here. The computer will get us through the mountains of reports, profiles, and lists of known and suspected terrorists who might be connected to Puño Blanco."

Castillo put a scruffy loafer on the desk. "You've been watching too many *Star Wars* movies. Biometrics, alarms, computers. What the hell do we need all that crap for?"

Liberti's right eyebrow arched. "Because for one thing, Donal, we don't know who we're up against. Puño Blanco may be a well-trained group with the expertise and technology to come after *us.*"

That sobering thought momentarily silenced the DEA agent. It was true they knew very little about Puño Blanco, but they did know one thing: the group had already demonstrated its ability to carry out three successful assassinations. Castillo yanked his tie off and stuffed it in a drawer. "All right, you've got a point, but it's going to take more than technical toys to catch these mothers. This country's got millions of dollars worth of sophisticated technology—satellites that can read the *New York Times* over your shoulder; thermal imaging that can tell you how many people were in a room hours earlier. But none of it's gonna help here. All this *Star Wars* shit isn't going to find a small group embedded in a city of eight million people."

Liberti, stung by Castillo's implied criticism of her technical equipment, snapped. "Then how do *you* propose we find them?"

Castillo smiled, but his eyes were cold. "The low-tech way; hunt, track, stalk. That's how we do it in the DEA."

Liberti, trying unsuccessfully to keep the irritation out of her voice, said, "You're missing half the point. Puño Blanco is made up of drug people, but they've hired professional terrorists. And terrorists are a different breed. The Bureau has spent a lot of time and energy profiling terrorists, professional criminals, ex–military types, and amoral psychotics who will do anything for a buck. And *they* are a hell of a lot more dangerous than drug dealers motivated simply by greed." She turned to Morgan in exasperation. "Dan, what do you think?"

Morgan had been listening to their conversation with mounting impatience. Clearly, Liberti and Castillo were a couple of hard chargers who had come here ready to work. But they hadn't yet accepted the peculiar nature of this assignment. It had taken most of last night and all of this morning for him to realize it himself. "I think you're both missing the point," he said. "This is *not* a DEA operation. It's *not* an FBI operation. It's not even a NYPD operation. The three of us have been picked to form a separate, distinct group with just one goal: find Puño Blanco." He paused to let that sink in. "I've seen interagency rivalries screw up investigations before," he continued, "and it's not going to happen here. Is that clear?"

The silence returned as the two federal agents considered Morgan's words. Liberti turned toward Castillo. "Morgan's right," she said a little sheepishly. "There's too much at stake here. We've gotta put our petty differences aside and work together. Whaddaya say, Donal?"

Castillo, unconsciously smoothing down a few errant strands of hair, shrugged. "I just want to get to these mothers. It doesn't matter to me who has the best ideas on how to do that."

Liberti glanced at her watch. "Good. Now that that's settled, let's get something to eat while we discuss our game plan. There's a joint called the Nosh Shop around the corner. They make the best pastrami in the city."

Five minutes later, they crowded into the tiny restaurant and found an empty table in the rear. The waiter, a heavyset man with an Adolf Hitler mustache, tossed three greasy menus on the table. "Corned beef we don't got," he announced in a heavy Eastern European accent. "Every*ting* else we got."

Chris Liberti ordered a pastrami sandwich and a celery tonic, pointing out that celery tonic was the only civilized beverage to drink with pastrami. Morgan ordered the same, but substituted coffee. The waiter looked down at Castillo with an expression he reserved for drunks and dimwitted children. "Mister, all day I ain't got. Soon the sun will be settin'."

Castillo looked up from the menu. "Is the pastrami really lean?"

The waiter shrugged elaborately. "For pastrami, it's lean."

Castillo grunted. "Give me a burger *well* done. I don't want it raw, I don't want it medium rare—"

"I know already. Well done."

"—no pickles and no onions. What's the soup of the day?"

"Black bean."

"Is it fresh?"

The waiter cocked his head. "Mister, look what the menu says. It says soup of the *day*, not soup of *yesterday*, not soup of last *month*—"

"Gimme a bowl. And coffee."

When the waiter had gone, Liberti poked Castillo in the ribs. "You always break chops like that?"

"I'm not busting chops. I just like to know what I'm ordering, that's all."

Morgan, aware that valuable time was passing said, "Okay, the computer's cooking, but what else can we do in the meantime?"

"You heard me on the phone earlier," Castillo said. "I was setting up interviews with my snitches and my old partner. As soon as we finish here, I'm going uptown."

Morgan nodded. "Good. I'm gonna talk to someone in our Intelligence Division after lunch. I've also made arrangements to get complete files on the three assassinations. They should be here by this afternoon."

"What'll be in it?" Castillo asked.

"All the paperwork connected to the cases. Sixty-ones—"

"Huh—?"

"The initial complaint report made out by the first officer on the scene." He reminded himself to stop using police jargon; he wasn't working with cops now. "Copies of follow-up reports submitted by the investigating detectives, photos, copies of evidence vouchers, the works."

"Any results from the headquarters bombing so far?" Liberti asked.

"Zilch. There are no witnesses and very little left of the bomb device."

"Has that been examined?"

"Yeah. Our lab did the preliminary and forwarded it to your people in Washington for further analysis. The results will be in the file."

The waiter returned with an armful of plates and unceremoniously dropped everything on the table, leaving the three of them to sort out their own orders. Castillo took a sip of his soup and made a face.

"What's the matter?" Liberti asked.

"It's cold. There's nothing I hate more than cold soup." He pushed it away.

"Have the waiter take it back."

"Naw, the hell with it."

"The hell with it nothing." Liberti grabbed the waiter's arm as he was passing and pointed at the soup. "Hey, pal, it's cold."

The waiter shrugged. "Lady, it was hot when I brought it from the kitchen."

"Where's the kitchen? Yonkers?"

The waiter studied the ceiling. "So I'll bring another bowl."

"Never mind, he doesn't want it now. Just take the soup off the check."

When the waiter left, Castillo nudged Liberti. "You always break chops like that?"

"Hey, this is a tough city. You can't let people push you around." She turned to Morgan. "I've done a lot of business with the PD's Arson/Explosion Squad and I know most of the guys there. Why don't I run over when we're finished here and see what they have to say?"

"That won't be necessary. The report will be here this afternoon."

"Dan, the lab reports don't say a hell of a lot. I can get a lot more information by talking to the guys personally."

Morgan regarded the diminutive FBI agent favorably. She had the kind of impatience that makes for a good cop. "Okay, just make sure you don't tell them why—"

"I *know* what to say." Her testy tone belied her sweet smile.

Castillo gingerly picked up a pickle and deposited it in his unwanted soup. "I can't stand the smell of these things," he said. He wiped his hands with a napkin. "I think we should begin by reinvestigating all three cases, right from the getgo."

Morgan stopped spreading mustard on his pastrami. "How?"

"Start with the headquarters bombing. What time did it happen?"

"Four A.M."

"Then tomorrow morning from three until five, I'll be in the area looking for witnesses."

Morgan shook his head. "The bombing took place two weeks ago. A task force canvassed the area for fourteen days and nights and came up with zilch."

Castillo picked up his soggy roll and peeked at the hamburger underneath. It was dripping blood. "That son of a bitch," he muttered, looking for the waiter, who was nowhere in sight. He pushed the bloody hamburger away in disgust. "Hey, what have we got to lose? It's a place to start."

Morgan frowned at the unimaginative reason for beginning an investigation as serious as this, but he couldn't think of a better starting point. Most investigations started with the name of a suspect, or a witness, or a piece of useful evidence. But after one bombing and two shootings, there wasn't a shred of solid evidence. "Okay," he said reluctantly. "It's worth a try. Chris, will you go with him in the morning?"

"No problem." She looked at Castillo's uneaten soup and hamburger. "Jeez, Donal, you're some fussy eater. If you were my kid, I'd cut your throat."

"If I were your kid," Castillo retorted, *"I'd* cut my throat."

Morgan, who wasn't listening to their banter, continued. "Starting tomorrow morning I'd like each of you to contact your agencies daily to get the latest intelligence reports." He wiped his greasy hands with a napkin. "There's something bothering me about this group. The weapon of choice for most terrorists is a bomb. So why are these people shooting cops?"

"There's one possibility." Castillo suspiciously sniffed his black coffee. "Most terrorists don't have the skill—or the balls—to shoot a man in the head from a rooftop."

Morgan stopped wiping his hands and gave voice to the logical conclusion. "And Puño Blanco does."

"I told you these guys are pros," Liberti said. She started to say something else, but stopped to stare aghast at Castillo, who was about to light an enormous cigar. "You're not going to smoke that thing, are you?"

Castillo grinned. "That's the general idea."

"I can't stand smoke," she said evenly. "Especially cigar smoke." She looked at Morgan in despair. "Do you smoke?"

"No."

"Thank God. Hey, fellas, let's make a deal. Two-thirds of us don't smoke, so how about we make it a rule; no smoking in the office. Okay?"

"Bullshit," Castillo said through a cloud of foul black smoke.

She appealed to Morgan. "Dan, you have rights too."

"Smoke doesn't bother me." He was lying. He hated smoke, especially from cigars, but he wasn't about to side with her against Castillo.

The DEA agent stood up and flicked a long ash into his soup. "Time's a-wasting. There's some people I gotta see uptown."

After a five-minute haggle about the check and the quality of service, Liberti and Morgan left the restaurant.

Outside on the street, Morgan looked distracted.

Liberti said, "Hey, Dan, don't mind me. I always hassle rude waiters. They—"

"It's not that. I was thinking we have so little time and so much to do."

"Don't worry. We'll find them," she said with more confidence than she felt.

He looked down at her. "Before another cop is killed?"

She looked into his eyes, trying to decide whether they were green or blue, and saw something else: sadness. "Dan, we all want to find Puño Blanco before they kill another police officer, but let's face it. That might not be possible."

Chapter
11

The Intelligence Division of the New York City Police Department is responsible for many security functions including dignitary protection, monitoring and investigating organized crime, and domestic terrorism. The Undercover Unit, a part of the Intelligence Division, is responsible for infiltrating these known or suspected groups. And the man commanding that unit was Captain John Zakovitch.

Some of his friends called him Zak. Others called him Father

John, a reference to the fact that Captain Zakovitch, a soft-spoken man, neither cussed nor drank. He had only one vice: he was a chain smoker.

An institution in the Intelligence Division, he'd been the commanding officer of the Undercover Unit for the last twenty-six years. With his wife dead for the past ten years and his only son a Maryknoll priest in Guatemala, John Zakovitch focused his full attention on the Police Department, especially the Undercover Unit, which had become his life.

As the one who personally recruited and debriefed every undercover operative during that time, Zakovitch was the most knowledgeable expert on terrorism in the department. Perhaps the country.

Dan Morgan had first met Zakovitch almost twenty years ago when he'd been assigned to the antiterrorist task force. His job was to meet with Zakovitch daily to get the latest intelligence on radical groups operating in the city, and he'd quickly become impressed with the captain's encyclopedic knowledge of terrorism. The chain-smoking captain not only knew the names of every known terrorist in the country, he could recite a full chronology of the group to which he belonged, as well as the times and dates of every criminal event the group had taken part in.

Zakovitch's cover office was located in a tired building on West 18th Street. Morgan opened the door and stepped into a thick cloud of blue smoke. "Zak, when are you going to give up the coffin nails?"

Sitting behind an old varnished-chipped desk, a rail-thin Zakovitch gave the stock answer he'd been giving all his life. "Maybe next week."

The office was simply furnished with two desks, three filing cabinets, and a pile of telephone books stacked on the radiator cover. But it was sufficient for its use as a nonpolice facility where undercover cops could safely come to get debriefed and file observation reports.

Zakovitch's real office was located in the Intelligence Division building downtown on Hudson Street, where banks of filing cabinets were stuffed with dossiers and photos of every known radical and terrorist in the United States.

After catching up on who was transferred where, Morgan steered the conversation around to the reason for his visit. "I've been transferred to the PC's office," he said.

"I know, Inspector. I saw it in the orders."

Even though they'd known each other for almost twenty years, Zakovitch, a stickler for protocol, insisted on calling all superiors above him in rank by their official title.

"It's no big deal." Morgan tried to sound bored. "I'm doing a special hush-hush project for the PC. The State Department has asked police departments in several cities to provide them with intelligence on radicals connected to Colombian guerrilla groups like FARC, the ELN, and M-Nineteen. State is trying to track the radical groups' source of financing and weapons procurement." Morgan wondered if Zakovitch was buying his story, but the leathery face revealed nothing.

Zakovitch lit another cigarette from the butt still between his fingers. "Is this related to the last three cops killed?" he asked.

Morgan feigned surprise. "Not as far as I know." He didn't like lying to Zakovitch, but he hoped he was doing a credible job.

Zakovitch squinted through the smoke. "The answer is no, Inspector. We have a couple of white supremacist groups, and the usual lunatic fringe people under observation right now, but none with ties to Colombia."

"Do you have many undercovers in the field now?"

Zakovitch's silent, squinty stare told Morgan he shouldn't have asked that question. John Zakovitch treated his undercovers as if they were his children, and in fact many weren't much more than that.

Unlike Narcotics and Public Morals, where undercover operations demanded experienced police officers, the Intelligence Division preferred to draw its candidates from the Civil Service list of men and women who had passed the police officers' exam, but who had not yet been sworn in. The types of assignments these undercover operatives were asked to assume required the youth and naiveté that police officers, no matter how good they were, could seldom duplicate. In the kind of circles to which they were exposed, a recognized face, or an inadvertent slip into police jargon, could mean death.

Every time a police candidate list was established, Zakovitch combed it, looking for suitable operatives. Depending on the department's needs at the moment, he'd concentrate on blacks, Hispanics, women and—now that they were beginning to enter the department in larger numbers—Asians.

An acceptable candidate was called in and the assignment, which could last from ten days to ten years, was explained to him or her. If he chose to accept it, he was sworn in on the spot. A police officer in name only, he might not wear a uniform or carry a gun for years. He was expected to infiltrate right-wing, left-wing, and other extremist fringe groups with nothing more to protect him than his wits. And his only link to the police department was John Zakovitch.

The chain smoking captain, who knew best the risks and fears these men and women faced, would willingly surrender his own life before he would intentionally do anything to compromise their cover.

Morgan saw he wasn't going to get anything further from Zakovitch and stood up. "I'm not done making the rounds. Do me a favor, Zak. If you hear of a group with Colombian connections, give me a call."

Zakovitch toyed with a pack of unfiltered Camels. "Sounds important."

"It's not that." Morgan hoped he hadn't come on too strong. "It's just that the PC would be embarrassed if he gave bum information to the feds." Zakovitch's expression didn't change. Morgan tried to change the subject. "Keeping busy?"

"Fair to middling."

Another stock answer. If Zakovitch had been aboard the *Arizona* on December 7th, 1941, he'd no doubt have given the same answer. When the crusty captain climbed into his defensive posture it was like talking to a recorded announcement. It was time to go.

The walls of the cramped, untidy office of the Arson/Explosion Squad were covered with government bulletins describing the latest in explosive ordinance, as well as photos of gutted buildings and raging fires resulting from explosives that weren't defused in time. On a separate wall, apart from the clutter of department orders and newspaper cartoons, hung a row of pictures of Bomb Squad police officers who had died in the line of duty.

"Semtex?" Chris Liberti slid the coffee container and doughnut across the desk to Detective Vinnie Genova.

The heavyset cop pried the lid off the container. "Yeah, the explosive of choice used by terrorists all over the world. We don't get to see much of it in the city."

"Where did it come from?"

He shrugged elaborately. "Who knows? Semtex is made in the Eastern Bohemian Chemical Works in Czechoslovakia. Because it's virtually undetectable by mechanical means, it's easily smuggled from country to country. It could have come from almost anyplace."

"What can you tell me about the device?"

The detective bit into the doughnut and half of it disappeared. "Very sophisticated," he mumbled through a mouthful. "Not your garden variety bomb made by the JDL, or even the FALN. The brisance was tremendous. Blew out windows for hundreds of yards. Semtex is big league stuff, Chris. It has a speed of detonation of over eight thousand meters a second, so it doesn't leave a hell of a lot of evidence."

"Did you find anything?"

"Traces of mercury."

"Meaning?"

"Probably activated by a mercury switch."

"Not a timer?"

"No sign of one."

"Why a mercury switch?"

"It'll go off when it's picked up."

"What did the device look like?"

"It could have looked like anything. Semtex can be formed into many shapes."

"Vinnie, why do you think he picked it up? A cop should know better."

The detective popped the remainder of the doughnut into his mouth and white powder rained down on his shirt. He tried to brush it away, but succeeded only in smearing it on his tie. "Sometimes these devices are very unstable."

He was hedging, and she knew it. Like all police officers, he was reluctant to criticize a dead police officer. "Vinnie, don't pull my chain. You just said it was a very sophisticated device and I know Semtex is stable. It didn't go off accidentally."

The detective rubbed the sugar powder off the desk with the back of his hand. Then his eyes settled on her. "This is off the record, Chris."

"Trust me, Vinnie, I'm with the government."

They both laughed at the reference to the Bureau's disingenuous opening interrogation line.

The detective lowered his voice. "Semtex *is* stable. There's no way it could have gone off accidentally. I think whoever planted the device wanted the cop to find it and pick it up."

"How would they do that?"

"They could have used the same technique the FALN used years ago. They planted sticks of dynamite using a mercury switch to activate the detonator. Any movement, no matter how slight, and—boom, you were gone. Sometimes they attached a burned fuse to one end, hoping a cop would think it was a dud and pick it up."

"Wow! Were they successful?"

"No, thank God. There was so much shit blowing up then that cops knew better than to touch anything that even resembled a bomb. But things have been quiet lately and the guys get . . ." His professional detachment collapsed. "Goddammit! We tell them not to touch the fucking things . . ."

"I know, Vinnie. Who do you think planted it?"

"I don't know. Usually we have a call from someone taking the credit for the bombing before the smoke settles. But in this case we haven't heard a thing. Chris, you don't think there's another group starting up, do you? During the sixties and early seventies, when the FALN and Black September were active, we had devices going off all over this city. We lost one of our guys disarming one. I wouldn't want to see that shit start up again."

Liberti avoided the worried look in his eyes. "Me neither," she said, tossing her empty coffee container in the wastebasket.

The detective walked her to the elevator. She pressed the Down button. "Hey, Vinnie," she said offhandedly. "Do you know an Inspector Dan Morgan?"

"Danny Morgan? Sure. We were cops in the Three-oh. He's good people. You know him?"

"Not really. I met him at a retirement racket last week. He seemed —I don't know, a little . . . uptight."

The fat detective belched. "They say he hasn't been the same since he was shot."

The elevator doors opened in front of her, but she let them close. "Yeah? What happened?"

"Morgan and a couple of sleuths went to serve a warrant. The perp came out shooting. A cop was killed and Morgan was shot. He was in pretty bad shape."

"Is he okay now?"

"Yeah, I guess so."

Liberti heard the evasive tone in his voice. "But?"

The detective picked at a piece of doughnut with his tongue. "The problem with Danny is that he's always had a real concern for his men, even before he was a boss. That's one of the reasons he's so well liked. I hear he took that cop's death pretty hard."

Liberti remembered the sad look she'd seen in Morgan's eyes and the aura of gloom that seemed to surround the police inspector. "Vinnie, did Morgan shoot that cop by mistake?"

Detective Genova pushed the Down button again. "There was an investigation; the whole nine yards. The physical evidence was inconclusive, but the sergeant on the scene testified that the perp shot the cop."

The elevator door opened and Liberti stepped in. "Is there anyone in the department who blames Morgan?"

"If I know Danny, there's only one," he said as the doors closed. "Dan Morgan."

Chapter
12

4:25 A.M. TUESDAY, MARCH 26 • So far during their early morning vigil, Chris Liberti and Donal Castillo had interviewed two Chinese women on their way to work, and three homeless men. But none admitted to being anywhere near One Police Plaza the night of the explosion.

Castillo pulled his collar up to protect himself from the biting wind that was whipping around One Police Plaza and looked at his watch. "Damn, we've been here only two hours, but it seems like all night."

Liberti pulled her ski cap down over her stinging ears. "All those years in Florida and South America have thinned your blood, Donal. But I don't feel sorry for you. This was *your* idea. By the way, where did you ever get a name like Donal?"

"My mother was Irish and my father was Cuban. It was her father's name."

"Donal—"

"I prefer Don."

"Oh, no. Donal has a much more swashbuckling ring to it, don't you think?"

"No. Come on, let's take another turn around the building."

They started down the stairs leading to Centre Street when they saw a large bundle of rags move. A scrawny hand emerged from the pile and pulled the blanket over an exposed opening. Cautiously, they approached the bundle. Castillo nudged the pile with his foot.

"Get the fuck away from me," a muffled voice shouted.

Castillo lifted the blanket, revealing a head with wild, matted hair. The man's eyes darted about and he pulled the blanket around him protectively. "Get away from me before I kill you."

Liberti flashed her credentials. "FBI. We just want to talk to you."

The man squinted at Liberti's badge. "I don't have to talk to you. The American Civil Liberties Union says I got a right to be here."

"True. You have the constitutional right to stay here and freeze to death," Castillo said dryly. "But just answer a couple of questions first."

The man looked up at Castillo and said, "Kiss my ass."

Liberti saw the fire starting in Castillo's eyes and stepped between them. "Remember the bombing here a couple of weeks ago?" she asked.

"Maybe I do and maybe I don't."

"Were you around here that night?"

"I didn't do it. If I was going to bomb anyone it would be my ex-wife." He tried to laugh, but only succeeded in provoking a hacking cough.

Liberti tried to determine the man's age, but under all that matted hair and dirt, it was impossible to tell if he was twenty or sixty.

The bum looked up at Castillo and grinned, revealing a mouthful of broken and missing teeth. "You're looking at my hair, right?"

"What?"

"Guys who are losing their hair always stare at men who have theirs. Pisses you off, don't it."

Involuntarily, Castillo smoothed his sparse hair. "You got a big mouth."

"Touchy too. Hey, man, lighten up. Losing your hair don't rank up there with the big C."

Castillo's eyebrows descended over his smoldering eyes. "Never mind my thinning hair. Were you—"

"*Thinning!*" The man cackled. "If it gets any thinner, you'll look like a goddamned bowling ball."

Liberti tried to divert the man's attention. "The night of the bombing—"

"All bums have hair," he said to Liberti. "Did you know that?"

"What *is* this obsession you have with hair?"

"It's true. I've made a study of it. I've been around bums for ten years. I never seen a bald bum. You?"

"I never noticed."

The man turned his attention to Castillo. "I'll bet you take great care of yours, don't you? Probably wash it every day and use expensive ointments and shit. And for what? You're as bald as a cantaloupe. Bums never wash their hair, we don't eat right, don't get the right vitamins, and we drink too much. But we all got real good hair. Don't that just piss you off?"

Liberti, who couldn't believe she was having this inane conversation at four in the morning, heard strange gurgling noises coming from Castillo's throat. "For chrissake," she said in exasperation, "were you here the night of the bombing? Just answer the question."

"Gimme some money and I'll tell you."

"Don't jerk me off," Castillo said through clenched teeth, "or I'll drop-kick your ass to Canal Street." He looked down at the filthy bum. "Come on, Chris, he wasn't here. He's just looking for a hand-out."

The man scratched his beard. "Now, now. That's no way to treat a prospective witness." He winked at Castillo. "Right, baldy?" He grabbed his matted hair, held it out to the sides, and stuck his tongue out at Castillo. "Maybe I was here and maybe I wasn't. But I'll never tell you, you fucking hard-on."

Castillo made a move to kick him, and the man pulled the blanket over his head to protect himself. The motion of the blanket fanned the air, releasing an eye-watering stench familiar to Liberti. She leaned over and tapped the man's head. "Hey, I think you've got gangrene, pal."

Castillo muttered an oath and stepped back as though it were contagious.

"I got a lot of things," the man said from under the blanket.

"This one's going to kill you if you don't get it taken care of right away. Where is it?"

"Mind your own business."

Liberti pulled the blanket away. The derelict's right trouser leg was wet and stained. She pulled a small pair of scissors out of her handbag and, ignoring the stench and the man's feeble protests, cut away the pants, revealing a leg swollen to twice its size. An ulcerated sore on his shin oozed pus and fluids.

Castillo's eyes widened. "Jesus, Chris, what the hell are you do-ing?"

Ignoring the DEA agent, she spoke to the man. "How long has it been like this?"

"Who knows? A day. A week."

The FBI agent examined the badly infected wound. The skin sur-rounding it had begun to putrefy. "This needs attention right away or you're going to be a one-legged bum right before you die." She took out a clean handkerchief and wiped away some of the pus.

The man winced. "Yeah, but at least I'll have all my hair," he said through clenched teeth.

"They can put that on your tombstone."

"They don't have tombstones in potter's field."

"You're a surly son of a bitch, aren't you?"

"It must be the weather. I'm always cranky when I'm freezing to death."

Liberti saw a tear squeeze out of the corner of the man's eye. "It hurts like hell, doesn't it."

"Naw, I'm into pain."

She turned to Castillo. "Go around to the police booth and ask them to call an ambulance."

"What for?"

"Because he needs one." Liberti's tone left no room for further discussion. Castillo went, leaving them alone.

"You got a name?"

"John Doe."

She held her hand out. "Chris Liberti."

The surprised man wiped his hand on the grimy blanket and shook Liberti's hand. "Dave Keel," he mumbled.

"Where you from, Dave?"

"St. Louis."

"You're a long way from home."

"Not far enough." He looked at Liberti suspiciously. "You're not one of them goddamn missionaries, are you?"

"No. Dave, were you here the night of the bombing?"

"Give me a double sawbuck or you'll never know."

Liberti took a twenty-dollar bill out of her handbag and dropped it on the blanket. The thin hand reached out and clawed the bill out of sight.

"The night of the bombing," she prompted.

"Was as cold as a well-digger's ass. I was coming up these stairs—"

Liberti suppressed her excitement. "What time was that?"

"Bums don't pay a whole lot of attention to the time. Let's see, I was thrown out of the Salvation Army canteen just after midnight, looked for someplace else to stay . . . I guess I got here sometime after three."

"Then what?"

"I was going to bed down in an alcove around the other side of the building. It's a good spot on a windy night. Anyway, this guy's standing at the top of the stairs. At first I thought I was gonna get mugged, but he holds up a ten-spot. 'Here,' he says, 'this is for you. Get yourself something to drink.'"

"What did you do?"

"I went and got myself something to drink."

"Did you come back that night?"

"Yeah, but the place was crawling with cops and fire trucks. I took off."

"Did the police talk to you?"

"Nope. I ain't been back here until tonight."

"What did the man look like?"

"Couldn't see much of him. He had a woolen cap pulled down over his face. I told you it was cold as hell."

"Tall or short?"

"I'm five-ten. Shorter than me."

"How old?"

"Early twenties, I guess."

"Fat or thin?"

"A little chunky."

"White, black, Hispanic?"

"White."

"Distinguishing characteristics? Scars, big ears, small eyes?"

"He had a real rat's-ass mustache. I remember that."

"Was there anyone with him?"

"Didn't see no one."

For a moment Liberti wondered if the bum had made up the story for the money, but she quickly dismissed that idea. His story rang true. A group like Puño Blanco wouldn't make many mistakes. She guessed they were planting the bomb when Keel had stumbled upon them. Amateurs might have killed the wino or run off, but a professional would know that a ten-dollar bill can create a lot of amnesia in a drunk.

"Anything else you can remember about that night?" In the distance she heard the wail of the ambulance. "It's important. A police officer was killed."

"Nope. That's all you get for your twenty."

When the EMS team arrived, they took one look at Keel's leg and loaded him onto the gurney.

"Where are you taking him?" Liberti asked the driver.

"Bellevue."

"Fuck that!" Keel bellowed. "I wanna go to Doctors' Hospital."

After the ambulance had gone, Liberti related Keel's story to Castillo.

"Do you think he saw the bomber?" Castillo asked.

"Either him or his accomplice. When we get done here I'll pick up a photo montage kit from the office and go up to Bellevue. Maybe he can give me a composite photo to work with."

"What if the guy refuses to admit himself? He'll disappear and we'll never find him."

"No chance of that. If he doesn't get immediate attention, he won't last the night."

Castillo looked at her curiously. "How do you know so much about first aid?"

She patted his cheek. "Donal, my friend, there's a lot you don't know about me."

A half-hour later, Chris Liberti, armed with a photo montage identification kit, drove to Bellevue. She was in a good frame of mind. Despite doubts she'd shared with Dan Morgan, the early morning canvass—which Castillo had insisted upon—had yielded a witness. Depending on a witness's ability to recall detail, a composite photo could produce a fairly accurate representation of the suspect. How good a witness Dave Keel would be remained to be seen.

Bellevue is a sprawling medical complex covering several city blocks and Liberti, exhausted from lack of sleep, was beginning to feel she'd covered every square inch of it. She'd gone to the Emergency Room first, but was referred to Admissions. From there she'd been directed to several wards, but Keel wasn't to be found in any of them. Finally, she was sent to a special ward where the army of New York's homeless, who'd become victims of crime, accidents, and benign neglect, were warehoused.

The powerful scent of disinfectant wasn't enough to mask the sour odors emanating from the patients inhabiting the overcrowded ward. Liberti flashed her credentials at a roly-poly black nurse. The shiny brass name tag pinned to her ample breast indicated she was the ward supervisor.

"Do you have a patient named Dave Keel?" Liberti asked.

The woman's surly look said she had more important things to do than talk to nosy cops, but between answering the telephone and scratching notations on a stack of charts, she thumbed through the patient roster. "He ain't here."

For a moment Liberti wondered if Castillo had been right. Maybe Keel did sign himself out. Then she remembered the condition of the leg; there was no way he could have walked out of the hospital. Risking the nurse's further ire, Liberti said, "He was brought in last night. He has to be here. He has a gangrenous leg."

The supervisor mumbled under her breath and turned to another nurse, who was getting ready to go off duty. "Betty, you know anything about a David Peel?"

"Keel," Liberti corrected gently.

The other nurse slipped on her coat. "Yeah, he was brought in late last night, but I was on another ward most of the night." Frowning, she pulled the fat supervisor aside and Liberti heard her whisper: "He was CTD. Check the list."

Liberti's heart sank. She knew what the cruel initials stood for. CTD—circling the drain—was a term used by some doctors and nurses to describe a dying patient.

The supervisor ran her chubby finger down the morgue roster. "You're too late." She tossed the list on the desk. "Died seven-thirty this morning. I don't suppose you know who the next of kin is?"

Liberti shook her head.

"Didn't think so. These damn street people must shoot straight out of the sewer full growed."

"How old was he?" Liberti asked.

The nurse looked at the list. "Thirty-two."

A discouraged Liberti walked to the elevator bank. Keel, the only one who had seen someone from Puño Blanco, was dead. As she waited for the elevator, she idly watched a porter push a hamper filled with the remnants of clothing and blankets down the corridor and wondered if they belonged to David Keel.

Chapter
13

Don Castillo leaned up against the schoolyard's chain-link fence and watched the players warming up. A big-bellied man with "Julio's Restaurante" emblazoned on the back of his green and yellow uniform shirt was smacking fly balls into the outfield. Three fielders, all wearing the same green and yellow uniforms, took turns gracefully gliding across the asphalt outfield to shag the high-fly balls.

The schoolyard on East 116th Street was quickly filling in anticipation of the first game of the season. It was that time of the year when dozens of young and not so young men suited up for Spanish Harlem's highly competitive softball league. The players and their fans took these schoolyard softball games just as seriously as the games played in Yankee and Shea Stadiums.

Castillo's eyes, constantly sweeping the growing crowd for a familiar face, finally found one: Freddy Posada. Posada was Castillo's most interesting, if most pathetic, snitch. He was barely twenty-eight, but his drug habit had added at least ten years to his earnest-looking face.

Fighting the odds, Posada had managed to pull himself out of the gravitational pull of the black hole of Spanish Harlem. He'd gotten an education, become a schoolteacher, and married a pretty third-grade teacher. With a modest house in Queens, and two daughters, Freddy had made it. Almost. He was caught shooting up heroin in his own faculty lounge. In rapid succession he lost his job, his teaching license, his house, and finally his wife and daughters.

Castillo had busted him two years later for possession of three grams with intent to sell. When Castillo discovered that Posada was an intelligent and articulate young man who knew a lot about what was going on in the street and was willing to talk about it, he brokered a deal with the federal prosecutor. Freddy Posada copped a plea and served eighteen months. The day he was released from prison Castillo was waiting for him. In the intervening two years Freddy Posada had become one of Castillo's most productive snitches.

Castillo bought a can of Coors from a man illegally selling beer out of an Igloo cooler and made his way across the schoolyard. He slipped up behind Posada. "How's it going, Freddy?"

Posada jumped at the sound of the voice. "Wow, man, you gave me a scare. Hey, Donny, how're you doing, man?"

Castillo looked into the dark eyes, now watery and yellowed, and knew Posada was still hooked. "Can't get the gorilla off your back, huh, Freddy?"

Posada scratched his scraggly beard. "I tried man, I tried. But," he shrugged, "you know how it is."

"Yeah, I know. Come on, let's take a walk."

Posada's eyes narrowed. "Donny, I'm clean, man. I got nothing on me. I swear to God."

Castillo knew that his snitch, like all junkies, was a chronic liar. He was sure Posada was dirty, but he answered, "I know. I just want to talk."

Posada followed Castillo out of the schoolyard and across the street to the stoop of an abandoned building. Castillo sat on the top step where he had a clear view of the street, while Posada, anxiously tugging at his beard, remained standing at the bottom of the steps.

"I've been away, Freddy. What's been happening?"

"Nothing, Donny. Same old shit."

The ritual had begun. Snitches were reluctant to give up information quickly for a couple of reasons. The first was money. They figured if they held out, they could drive up the price. But there was another reason: even snitches didn't like being rats. By allowing Posada to ramble on with useless information, Castillo permitted the sensitive ex-schoolteacher to maintain some semblance of dignity. For the next ten minutes Posada babbled on about mutual friends and enemies, most of whom were either dead or in jail.

When Castillo judged that they'd played the game long enough, he got to the point. "Freddy, who's running the street now?"

"Mr. Arberlaez."

"Hector Arberlaez?"

"Yeah."

"What happened to Endara?"

"He had a disagreement with someone. A few weeks ago he got blown away eating a pepperoni pizza in Ramon's."

"So Hector Arberlaez is the boss man now," Castillo said more to himself than Posada.

"You know him, Donny?"

"Yeah, I know him."

Three years earlier a joint operation between the NYPD and the DEA had resulted in the arrest of ten men involved in an elaborate distribution network. Hector Arberlaez was the only one to beat a conviction because a key witness recanted his testimony. Castillo would never forget the smug look on Arberlaez's face as he walked out of the courtroom with his arm around his attorney. That smug look had put Arberlaez on Castillo's personal target list. One day, he promised himself, he'd get another shot at Hector Arberlaez.

"He's probably gonna be here later. That's his team." Posada nodded toward the Julio's Restaurante bench.

"Civic-minded, too." Castillo said. "What a guy."

Posada saw the look on Castillo's face and said, "He's a bad dude. Don't fuck with him, Donny."

Castillo's smile was cold. "I'm a bad dude, too."

Just then there was a ripple of excitement as a customized black Lincoln Continental with smoke-tinted windows pulled up in front of the schoolyard. The driver, a thick-set man wearing an ill-fitting suit that emphasized the bulge of a gun, got out and ran around to the other side of the car. At the same time, another man, wearing dark glasses, got out of the front passenger seat and scrutinized the crowd that had begun to collect.

Castillo grinned. "These guys have been watching too much TV, Freddy. They think they're the fucking Secret Service."

"They're bad dudes. That's all I know."

Castillo knew that Posada had reason to be afraid. If anyone in that car recognized Castillo as a DEA agent, Freddy Posada was dead meat.

Castillo stood up. "Hey, Freddy, good to see you again." He shook the man's hand and pressed a twenty-dollar bill into his sweaty palm.

"Thanks, Donny. Hey. I gotta split."

As Castillo watched him scurry down the block, he wondered if he'd ever see him alive again. A twenty-eight-year-old full-blown junkie like Freddy Posada was living on borrowed time.

Castillo stopped in front of a man selling shaved ice. As he studied the half-dozen colorful bottles, purporting to be fruit juice, he wondered what was really in those bottles. But Castillo had long since given up worrying about the quality and sanitary conditions of the dozens of street vendors he'd frequented over the years. Stoically, he'd come to believe that if he hadn't died of food poisoning by now, he never would.

"Hey, pop," he said. "Gimme a raspberry."

The old man wiped his filthy hands on a dirty towel and shaved some ice into a paper cone. Then he poured the red liquid over the ice and handed it to Castillo.

Castillo gave him a buck. "Keep the change."

The old man's eyes lit up. If today was like most days, he was bound to get ripped off by a couple of kids who ordered an ice and then ran away without paying. A dollar would help offset the loss. "Thank you, *señor*."

"A bit early to be selling ice, isn't it?"

"*Si,* but"—he nodded to the crowd—"there are plenty of customers."

Castillo looked across the street at the black Lincoln. The rear door opened and Hector Arberlaez stepped out. He was dressed in a well-tailored light gray suit, but he still looked like the street hood Castillo remembered.

"Who's gonna win?" he asked, still staring at Arberlaez.

"Julio's. They have the best team."

"The best that money can buy?"

The ice man flinched. "I do not know about such things," he said, pushing his wooden cart away from the black Lincoln.

Hector Arberlaez, looking like the mayor of Spanish Harlem, waved to people on the street and walked toward the schoolyard. The crowd parted like the Red Sea.

The driver got back into the car and lit a cigarette. Obviously, he planned to remain parked in front of the schoolyard entrance, but a radio car pulled alongside him. Both officers got out. One cop, with his hand on his revolver, scanned the rooftops while the other approached the Lincoln. Castillo, with his hand on the gun in his pocket, backed into a doorway and watched the rooftops on the other side of the street. He was close enough to hear the exchange between the cop and the driver.

The cop, a middle-aged black, pushed his hat to the back of his head and said, "License and registration."

The driver gave the cop a surly look.

"Hey, your ears don't flop over, scumbag. Give me your license and registration."

Castillo chuckled as he realized what was going on. The cops knew who owned the car. As uniformed officers they realized they'd never find grounds to arrest someone like Hector Arberlaez, but they could harass him and his people.

The driver produced the papers and the cop started back to the radio car. "Hey," the driver shouted. "Whaddaya gonna do?"

"Give you a summons." He pointed to a traffic sign. "You can't park in front of a schoolyard."

"For chrissake, I'll move the fucking car."

"Sure you will. As soon as I finish writing the summons."

A few minutes later, he returned and handed the driver the papers. The driver, with a great display of bravado, ripped up the summons and tossed it out the window.

The officer grinned and took out his summons book again. "That's gonna cost you another summons, shit-for-brains."

The enraged driver banged on the steering wheel. "For what?"

"Littering," the cop said, deadpan. "We all gotta do our best to keep New York City clean."

After issuing the driver the second summons, the officer was walking toward his car when the man yelled out the window. "You cops are a fucking joke."

The officer pivoted. "What did you say, scumbag?"

"You heard me."

The cop shook his head. "You ain't never gonna learn, are you? Now I'm going to do a vehicle inspection. Put your headlights on."

"What the fuck—"

"Put the fucking headlights on. I'm not gonna ask you again."

The driver, mumbling to himself, put his lights on.

The cop walked around to the back of the car and smiled. "Oh, my. You got a taillight out, pal."

The driver jumped out of the car. "It can't be out. This is a brand-new fucking car, for chrissake." As he bent over to bang on the faulty taillight, his tight jacket rode up, revealing the handle of a gun.

The cop reacted by slamming the surprised man's head on the trunk and yanked the gun away. "Frankie," he yelled to his partner. "He's got a gun." The other officer rushed over and helped handcuff the driver.

Arberlaez, suddenly aware of the commotion outside the schoolyard, turned and saw his driver being arrested. He whispered something to his bodyguard and they began to walk out of the schoolyard toward the police officers.

Castillo, his hand still on his gun, started down the steps toward them, but stopped when he saw another police car enter the block with lights flashing. When Arberlaez saw the other car coming he stepped back into the crowd and sent his bodyguard to retrieve the keys.

As the last radio car was leaving the scene, a brick arced off the roof and struck the vehicle on the left rear fender. The only sign from the driver was a momentary flash of taillights as the car continued down the street.

While Arberlaez stopped by his car to talk to someone, Castillo ran for his own car. By the time the Lincoln, now driven by the bodyguard, was pulling away from the curb, Castillo was in a position to follow.

At 96th Street the Lincoln turned south onto the FDR Drive. At 72nd Street it exited. A few minutes later the vehicle pulled up in front of a high-rise apartment building on 74th Street off First Avenue.

Castillo pulled into a spot in front of a fire hydrant and watched. Arberlaez got out and said something to the bodyguard, who then drove away. As Arberlaez walked into the lobby, Castillo saw his chance. He jumped out of his car, darted up the street, and came into the lobby right behind Arberlaez. There was a doorman, but he was busy untangling the leashes of a tenant's three toy poodles and didn't see Castillo come in.

Castillo got on the elevator with Arberlaez. They were the only two in the car. Arberlaez pressed the tenth floor. Castillo pressed twenty-four, the top floor, and stepped back. Arberlaez's expensive cologne filled the elevator. He glanced at Castillo once, looking at his soiled army field jacket in disdain.

As the elevator approached the tenth floor, Arberlaez stood in front of the doors. Castillo slipped his gun out and jammed it into the back of Arberlaez's head. "When the doors open, don't get off," he said softly. He felt Arberlaez stiffen, but the man made no attempt to turn around.

"If this is a holdup," Arberlaez said in a calm, even voice, "I'll give you what you want. Put the gun away, there's no need for it."

Castillo jammed the gun barrel into Arberlaez's expensive razor-cut hair. "Listen, asshole, I'll decide what's needed."

The doors opened and closed and the elevator continued its climb to the twenty-fourth floor. "All right," Arberlaez said in a voice now tight with fear and rage. "Who are you and what do you want?"

Castillo tapped the back of Arberlaez's neck with the barrel. "Not yet."

The doors opened on twenty-four and Castillo shoved Arberlaez out. He looked down the hallway and saw a red exit light. "Come on," he said, pushing Arberlaez. "This way."

At the top of the staircase Castillo kicked the door open and shoved Arberlaez out onto the roof. A noisy, high-pitched ventilator whined, blotting out the street noises twenty-four floors below. As he pushed Arberlaez toward the back of the roof away from the street and the noisy ventilator, he noted with satisfaction that they were atop the highest building in the area. No one could look down on them.

"Okay," Castillo said. "This'll do."

Arberlaez turned, his face contorted with rage. "Enough of this shit. What do you want?"

"Information."

Arberlaez's eyes narrowed. "You a cop?"

"FBI."

Arberlaez snorted. "Bullshit. The FBI doesn't do this. You're either DEA or the city police."

Officer DOWN

Castillo grinned. "Hector, does it really matter?"

Arberlaez's eyes widened at the sound of his name. "You look vaguely familiar." He studied Castillo's face. "Do I know you?"

"No." At the time of the trial Castillo had been wearing a full beard and shoulder-length hair. There was no way Arberlaez could remember him.

"Don't strain yourself, Hector. All us cops look alike."

Now that he knew he was dealing with a policeman, Arberlaez relaxed. True, he'd never been treated like this before by a cop or anyone else, but it could have been worse. When the gun had been shoved into the back of his head, he'd been convinced it was a hit. "I won't talk to you unless you put the gun away." he said.

Castillo, standing a safe seven feet away, studied the man in front of him. They were about the same age, but Arberlaez had him by a good twenty pounds. And Arberlaez's thick neck was mute testimony that he hadn't risen to the top of the pile because he was a terrific bookkeeper. Castillo knew that in his earlier days Arberlaez had been a gang enforcer, and by all accounts, an especially brutal one. "Turn around and spread 'em," he said.

Arberlaez turned and put his hands against the wall of the elevator machine room. Castillo kicked Arberlaez's legs farther apart and patted him down. He quickly found a nine-millimeter in a shoulder holster. He pulled it out and tossed it behind a pile of empty tar cans. "Okay," Castillo said, holstering his weapon, "we can talk now."

Without warning, Arberlaez spun around and slashed at Castillo with a knife which, Castillo realized too late, Arberlaez had concealed in a scabbard attached to his left forearm. Castillo jumped back, but not soon enough. He felt hot sticky blood begin to flow where the knife had slashed through his field jacket. As he was back-pedaling, he tripped over the tar cans and fell onto his back. He tried to unholster his weapon, but Arberlaez lunged at him. Castillo, forming a V with his two thumbs, thrust his hands in front of him and stopped the downward movement of the knife. At the same time he kicked up into Arberlaez's exposed groin. Arberlaez's eyes bulged and his knees buckled. Castillo, still holding on to Arberlaez's wrist, twisted, sending Arberlaez crashing to the ground. Castillo scrambled to his feet, extended Arberlaez's knife arm, and delivered a sharp kick to the man's underarm. He heard a snap and the knife fell from the hand, now uselessly attached to a dislocated shoulder.

Castillo's carefully seasoned professionalism dissolved in an all-consuming rage. He grasped Arberlaez's expensive silk tie and started dragging the man toward the edge of the roof. Arberlaez, his eyes bulging, desperately clawed at the tarred roof with his one good hand, leaving a trail of broken fingernails and blood.

Castillo's only thought was to get Arberlaez to the edge. He felt a sharp pain in his side every time he tugged the heavy body, but the edge was getting closer and closer. There was no retaining wall and the bushes and concrete twenty-four floors below came into view. Finally they were at the precipice. Slowly, he forced Arberlaez's head, then his shoulder over the side. Arberlaez, almost unconscious from the tightened tie around his neck, was turning a dark reddish-purple. His eyes bulged as he got a glimpse of the ground far below. Castillo began to feel Arberlaez's dead weight lighten as the body teetered on the edge. *One more push.* He put his palm on Arberlaez's sweating brow and . . . stopped. As he looked into Arberlaez's fear-contorted face and the spittle-covered mouth open in a silent scream, the rushing in his ears began to subside. He yanked Arberlaez back just enough so that most of his weight was back on the roof.

Arberlaez, feeling the comforting roof under his back, loosened his death grip on Castillo's forearm and clawed his tie loose. *"Madre mia!"* he said, gasping for air. "Don't kill me. Please—"

Castillo's chest heaved from the exertion. "Listen, motherfucker, I'm going to ask you questions. You lie to me and you'd better hope you can fly. *Comprende?"*

Arberlaez nodded his head.

"There's something big coming out of Colombia. What do you know about it?"

"I don't know what you're talking—" Castillo nudged the body forward and Arberlaez felt himself teetering again. "I swear on my mother's grave. I don't know anything," he whispered hoarsely.

"What do you know about a splinter group of the Medellin cartel?"

"Nothing."

"Don't give me that bullshit. You're Colombian."

"I'm not in the cartels. I buy from many sources. Even if I did work for them, they would tell me nothing."

Castillo looked into the man's terrified eyes and believed him. Not even a cartel *jefe* would give up his life to protect the cartel and Arberlaez was just a couple of steps above a street-level dealer: a street-wise hoodlum who'd murdered and terrorized his way to the top. Clutching the man's lapels, Castillo was consumed with hatred for Arberlaez and what he stood for. For a fleeting moment he considered giving him that one last shove. It'll be over in a second, he thought, and one more scumbag will be gone. The thought passed and Castillo pulled the man back from the abyss.

Arberlaez sprawled on the floor and in a half daze pawed at his torn thousand-dollar suit with a hand stained with tar and blood. "You are a madman," he said, looking up at Castillo with eyes still wide with fright.

"You got that right, Hector. This conversation was just between you and me. If I hear you've spoken to *anyone* about this, I'll come back to finish what I started." He was confident that Arberlaez wouldn't tell anyone about what had happened. If for no other reason, his machismo wouldn't let him.

Arberlaez nodded. There was no doubt in his mind that this lunatic meant what he said.

Before Castillo left he retrieved Arberlaez's gun and stuck it in his pocket. In the elevator he examined his wound. It was bleeding a lot, but the gash wasn't deep. He stuffed a handkerchief in his shirt and zipped up his torn field jacket.

Back on the street a meter maid was just slipping a summons under his windshield wiper. The plump black woman cocked her head at him. "This your car?"

"Yeah."

"What you mean parking in front of a fire hydrant? Think you're a damn diplomat or somethin'?"

"I'm sorry." Castillo retrieved the summons from his windshield. "I had to say hello to a sick friend."

"Yeah, yeah," she said, making a beeline for a double-parked car up the block. "That's what they all say."

Chapter
14

8:00 A.M. WEDNESDAY, MARCH 27 • Following Lyle Petry's instructions, Ray Fleming waited in a shopping center parking lot near Springfield Boulevard and the entrance to the Long Island Expressway. At exactly eight A.M. a black Blazer pulled in behind him and honked. Fleming looked in his rearview mirror and saw Lyle Petry behind the wheel and a stranger sitting next to him.

Manny Botnick, sitting in the back seat, opened the door. "Get in, hotshot. Today we find out if you can use a shotgun."

Fleming, noting Botnick's eyes—puffy from lack of sleep—climbed into the back seat and tugged his friend's mustache. "I may not hit the target," he said, "but at least I'll be able to see it."

"Very funny." Botnick put his head back and closed his eyes. "I'm not used to this shit. Only farmers get up at this ungodly hour."

Petry turned in his seat. "Ray, meet Jimmy."

The well-tanned man, dressed in a camouflage suit, half turned and nodded.

Petry snapped the gear lever and the Blazer shot forward. "Take it easy," Jimmy said, as Petry gunned the powerful vehicle onto the eastbound entrance to the expressway. "You don't want to be stopped for speeding."

Petry laughed, but he slowed down. "Jimmy's one of my hunting buddies," he said to Fleming. "When we get there, you'll meet a couple more." He looked at Fleming through the rearview mirror. "Are you ready for some serious skeet shooting?"

"Sure. But like I told you, I've never shot skeet before."

"That sounds like a hustler's opening line if I ever heard one," Botnick mumbled.

"With your eyes it'll be a piece of cake," Petry said. "I'll give you a few pointers and you'll be shooting like a pro."

For the duration of the long ride the conversation was dominated by Botnick who, given the opportunity, was a nonstop talker. Jimmy grunted an occasional answer, but mostly smoked and stared out the window at the endless array of shopping malls and housing developments lining the edges of the expressway.

An hour later Petry turned off at Riverhead and headed north. At Route 25A he turned right. The North Fork was the most sparsely populated part of Long Island. But the frenzied, haphazard development that had blighted western Long Island was slowly creeping east. New housing developments and shopping malls were sprouting up, but there was still some open space left. Looking at the potato fields flanking the route, Fleming found it difficult to remember that they were only a couple of hours from midtown Manhattan.

Petry turned onto an unmarked dirt road. The potholes and ruts would have been rough going for a car, but the Blazer, with its large wheels and heavy-duty suspension, negotiated the road with little difficulty. About a mile into a stand of trees the road widened into an open clearing where two men, drinking coffee, stood next to a station wagon. Petry pulled in next to them.

A swarthy man with a neatly trimmed salt and pepper beard approached them. "Good morning, Lyle," he said with a thick Spanish accent.

Petry got out of the Blazer and nodded in acknowledgment. "Ray, say hello to Alvaro."

The man smiled and his white teeth gleamed against his dark skin. "My pleasure. I understand you are an excellent shot."

"Not with shotguns. I'm basically a pistol shooter."

The second man, a muscular black with a wide, friendly face, approached with a thermos in one hand and a sleeve of Styrofoam cups in the other. "I don't know about you guys, but I'm freezing my ass off." He handed a cup to Fleming. "Glen's the name. I want you to know this was not my idea. Outdoor shooting should only be done in seventy-and-above weather."

Jimmy held his cup as Glen poured. "You Southern boys got no blood," he said to Glen. "I don't know how the hell you made it through the Q course."

Just then, Petry bumped Jimmy, spilling hot coffee on his hand. Fleming, who'd seen it happen, wasn't sure if it was an accident or if Petry had done it on purpose.

"Christ," Jimmy yelled, wiping his hand on his jacket. "Watch it, Lyle!"

Petry smiled, but his eyes were cold. "Are we gonna shoot or are we gonna stand around here jawing all day?"

Jimmy blew softly on his burned hand and gave Petry a hard look. For a moment Fleming thought they might come to blows, but Jimmy threw the rest of the coffee on the ground and turned away. "Might as well," he said. "This coffee tastes like shit anyway."

The makeshift range consisted of seven stakes laid out in a rough semicircle. At each end of the semicircle was a trap machine with pull wires leading back to a plywood table.

Petry explained the setup to Fleming. "This is a real goatscrew operation but it approximates a skeet range. We have all the essentials: two trap machines and eight firing points laid out on a semicircle. You start at one point and move clockwise until you've fired from all eight points. Any questions?"

"Yeah. How the hell do I hit an eight-inch flying saucer?"

Glen pumped a round into the chamber. "Don't try to aim. Skeet isn't bull's-eye shooting; it's all instinct. Lead the bird and snap off the shot."

Petry led Fleming to a point behind the semicircle where the two pull wires met. "Stand here. We'll watch them shoot first."

The others took up positions on the semicircle. When everyone was in place, Jimmy, who was occupying the first position, yelled *"Pull."*

Petry yanked a wire sending a clay bird into the air. With a graceful fluid motion, Jimmy brought up his shotgun and pulled the trigger. The bird shattered.

"You powdered that sucker," Manny shouted.

Botnick, the next in line, yelled *"Pull."* Another bird glided across the front of the semicircle. Unlike Jimmy, Botnick's movements were more jerky. Some of his pellets chipped the clay, but it didn't break.

"You dusted it," Glen whooped. "No score."

As each man fired, Fleming began to see the different techniques. Botnick, an uncoordinated, clumsy shooter, hit only a handful of birds. Alvaro was better, but Jimmy and Glen were superb. Firing faster than Fleming thought possible they powdered every clay. Glen, who'd become bored with the ease of the contest, began to shoot from the hip. Jimmy, seeing what he was doing, did the same. Still, they hit every target.

"Don't pay attention to those hotshots," Petry said to Fleming. "They've been shooting skeet since they were shorter than a sawed-off shotgun. Come on, it's your turn."

Petry placed him at the six o'clock position of the semicircle. "Okay, Ray. Whenever you're ready."

Fleming took a deep breath and yelled *"Pull."*

Out of the corner of his eye he saw the clay rising from the left trap a lot faster than he'd anticipated. He raised the shotgun to his shoulder, sighted along the barrel, and squeezed the trigger. Nothing happened.

Botnick hooted. "Why don't you try it with the safety off?"

Fleming, feeling himself redden, snapped the safety off and yelled *"Pull."*

This time the bird came from the right. Off balance, he fired and saw the pellets fly harmlessly several feet behind the target.

"Lost bird," Glen yelled.

Petry stood close by Fleming's shoulder. "Remember to lead it," he whispered.

Fleming, angered and flustered by his unaccustomed clumsiness, took a deep breath and yelled *"Pull."* Again, the bird came from the right. This time he aimed a few feet in front of the clay disk and squeezed the trigger. The bird and the pellets collided in a midair powdered explosion.

Petry poked Fleming's back. "Way to go! Now you got the idea."

For the rest of the morning they took turns shooting. By eleven Fleming, Botnick, and Alvaro had had enough. As the other three continued to shoot, the contest between them grew more and more competitive. Soon they were doing things Fleming didn't think possible. Glen, with two shells loaded in his shotgun and another one in his teeth, called for three birds. With blinding speed he powdered the first two, and before the third clay hit the ground he'd loaded the last shell and powdered that one as well. Petry hit ten quick clays firing from the hip with his left hand. Just when Fleming thought he'd seen everything, Jimmy powdered three clays while firing between his legs. Fleming, whose training and inclination was to shoot slowly, was astonished by the accuracy and speed of the three men.

Around noon they stopped for lunch. Glen broke out a cooler filled with sandwiches and beer. He tossed a can to Alvaro. "You know what I hate about Colombia? There ain't a cold beer in the whole fucking country."

Alvaro, looking uncertain, glanced at Petry. Then he smiled. "The trouble with you Norteamericanos," he said, "is that you drink everything too cold."

Suddenly, Petry flung a can directly at Glen's head. "This one's *too* cold, dickhead."

With lightning reflexes, Glen's hand shot up and the can bounced away harmlessly. The big black's ready smile vanished and he glowered at Petry. "What would you like, sir?"

Petry smiled. "Let's try one not quite so cold."

Glen dug into the cooler and came up with another can. For a moment Fleming thought Glen was going to hurl it at Petry, but he bared his white teeth in a smile, shook the can, and gently tossed it to Petry. "I hope this is more to your liking."

Petry popped the top and the beer foamed out of the opening. "Yeah," he said, still staring at Glen. "Much better."

The moment of tension ended and normal conversation resumed. Although it was still March, it was a bright clear day and the afternoon sun, warm on Fleming's face, reminded him that springlike weather was rapidly approaching. With his belly full and a can of beer at his side, he rested his back against a tree and closed his eyes, glad to be alive and in the company of men who enjoyed shooting as much as he did. Even the sullen Jimmy, resting his head against a tree stump, seemed to enjoy the warming sun.

"Gentlemen," Alvaro said, breaking the magic of the moment, "what do you say to some handgun shooting?"

Fleming, now in his own element, felt more at ease. His shooting was in the groove and the only one who came close to his scores was Lyle Petry.

Alvaro studied Fleming's targets with admiration. "Excellent. Tell me, have you ever fired an automatic weapon?"

Fleming shook his head.

Alvaro looked at Petry. "I think we should give our young friend the opportunity. It will be interesting to see how he does."

Petry crushed a beer can and tossed it into a plastic garbage bag. "Why not?"

Jimmy lugged a duffel bag he'd retrieved from the back of the Blazer over to the table. He reached inside the bag and pulled out an Uzi submachine gun. "Now here's *real* firepower," he said, holding the weapon aloft.

Fleming stared at the menacing-looking weapon in amazement. "Aren't these things illegal?" he asked.

Jimmy looked at him curiously. "Only if they're rigged to fire automatic." He tossed the weapon to Petry.

"Come on," Petry said to Fleming, "let me show you how this thing works."

Even though they hadn't seen a house since they'd left the main road, and they were surrounded by trees, Fleming was certain there must be houses nearby. "Lyle, this is gonna make a racket. What if someone calls the cops—"

Petry pointed to a black cylinder attached to the end of the barrel. "A silencer."

Fleming nodded. He knew silencers were against the law, but he said nothing.

"We're just being considerate of the neighbors," Petry explained.

Botnick placed silhouette targets at the base of a high earthen mound that had been created as a bullet backstop. Petry stopped about twenty yards in front of the target and snapped a clip into the weapon. He crouched, and from the hip fired off three rapid bursts. When the smoke cleared, the center of the silhouette was shredded. He loaded another clip and handed the weapon to Fleming. "The safety is off," he winked, "so be careful."

The small dull-finished weapon looked more like a pistol than a submachine gun. Even with the folding stock extended it was only about two feet long and weighed no more than ten pounds. But in spite of its delicate look the weapon felt surprisingly sturdy in his hands.

Petry, standing behind Fleming, whispered instructions. "Lean into it a little, tuck the stock into your shoulder and let her go."

MICHAEL GRANT

Fleming pointed the weapon at the silhouette, pulled the trigger, and promptly emptied the entire clip. Surprised by the unexpected burst of fire, he'd jerked the weapon and only a few rounds struck the target. The others, climbing in a diagonal pattern to the right, slammed harmlessly into the mound.

"Whoa, Ray. Keep it down. It's not an antiaircraft weapon, for chrissake. Fire short bursts. It's easier to control."

"Hey, Lyle, this thing fired full automatic!"

"So?"

"Nothing." He was going to repeat that an automatic weapon was illegal, but he didn't want to sound like a jerk.

Petry loaded another magazine and handed the weapon back to Fleming. "Shoot again."

This time Fleming fired four short bursts and all the rounds smacked into the silhouette.

"Good. You have the idea. Let's all shoot."

Fleming turned and was startled to see that each of the others were holding Uzis.

Petry saw the look on Fleming's face and explained. "We like to trot these things out once in a while. It's more fun than skeet. Don't worry, no one can hear us, and we're miles from the nearest house. Manny," he called over his shoulder, "set up more targets."

After Botnick had placed fresh targets at the base of the mound, the six men lined up about thirty yards back and looked toward Petry. When he saw that everyone was ready, he yelled "Fire!"

A chill ran up Fleming's spine as all six Uzis fired simultaneously. The report, muffled by the silencer, didn't diminish the thrill of firing the weapon. For one accustomed to shooting pistols slowly and deliberately, firing an automatic weapon was an exhilarating experience. There was something primitively satisfying about aiming a weapon and watching a burst of bullets shred a target with no more exertion than the gentle squeeze of a trigger.

When the smoke cleared, Jimmy let out a rebel yell. "Look at that sucker!" He pointed at a gaping, jagged hole in the middle of his target.

**Officer
DOWN**

The worst target belonged to Botnick. He looked at Fleming sheepishly and shrugged. "I think I need a fucking cannon."

With each clip fired, Fleming grew more used to the weapon and his shooting improved. Petry and Alvaro, standing together and talking quietly, nodded approvingly.

It was almost four when they finally ran out of ammunition. "Okay, guys," Petry yelled, "what do you say we call it a day? Manny and Glen, police the brass while we clean the weapons."

Petry saw Fleming watching them pick up the expended brass. "This stuff is expensive to shoot," he explained. "We do our own reloads."

As they were getting ready to leave, Alvaro shook Fleming's hand. "It was a pleasure meeting you, Ray. I hope we can do this again sometime."

Alvaro left in the station wagon with Jimmy and Glen. Botnick and Fleming went back with Petry in the Blazer.

On the way into the city, Fleming, trying to sound casual, suggested they stop off at Chico's. The others readily agreed.

Fleming spotted Celeste as soon as they came in. It was only six-thirty, but the bar was already crowded. The three squeezed onto stools and ordered beers and burgers.

Celeste, who was alone behind the bar, had no time for idle conversation. She returned in a few minutes, slid the hamburgers in front of them, and rushed down to the other end of the bar to serve other customers. It made no difference to Petry and Botnick, who droned on about guns, women, and sports, but Fleming, who nodded at the appropriate times, wasn't paying attention. He was watching the dark-haired girl.

Petry finished his burger, had another beer and left. Ten minutes later, Botnick did the same. Fleming remained, but after an hour passed he began to get angry and embarrassed. Other than providing him with refills and a few snatches of conversation, Celeste ignored him.

By nine o'clock, the crowd had thinned and he'd had enough humiliation. He got up to leave, but Celeste came over and pushed him back down. "Don't go. I barely had a chance to say hello."

"You've been busy." In spite of himself the statement sounded like an accusation, but she seemed to take no notice.

"You're telling me. This is the first chance I've had to sit down all night. So how're you doing, Ray?"

Her smile dissipated his anger. "Good. We were shooting skeet today."

Celeste rolled her large dark eyes. "More shooting! Don't you guys ever get enough?"

"First time I've ever shot skeet."

"How did you do?"

"Pretty good. Lyle gave me a few pointers."

"Yeah, he's a great teacher."

Fleming studied her face to see if there was a double meaning in her statement, but he saw nothing. "Have you known Lyle long?" he asked.

"A few years."

"Where did you meet?"

"Right here."

"Chico's? It doesn't seem like his kind of place."

"The place is full of Colombians. He likes to practice his Spanish."

"Lyle speaks Spanish?"

"Yeah, he used to work in Colombia."

"No kidding. Doing what?"

"Exporting consultant. He speaks the language like a native."

"Are you Colombian?"

"Yeah, but I've lived here since I was six."

"That explains it. You don't have an accent."

Fleming, lost in thought, toyed with his glass. Finally he said, "Are you and Lyle—"

"No." The dark eyes studied him. "Lyle and I are just friends. Why?"

"I thought maybe you and me could go out sometime."

She flashed a smile. "Sure. When?"

"How about tomorrow night?"

"Can't. I'm working. How about the night after?"

"Okay, I'll call you."

The doors opened and five noisy men came in. "Celeste," one of them called out. *"Cerveza! Por favor."*

She mussed Fleming's curly hair. "Back to work."

Fleming drained his beer and left Celeste to tend the boisterous group.

Chapter
15

Ray Fleming left Chico's in a happy, euphoric mood. Too keyed up to go home, he took a cab back to Sunnyside and stopped off at a neighborhood bar. Over a couple of beers he reflected on the pleasant day he'd spent. He'd been in the company of men who liked doing what he liked and who were damn good at it. And he'd asked the most beautiful girl he'd ever seen for a date and she'd accepted. The world was perfect, except for . . . What? The truth was the day hadn't been *that* perfect. There was the business of the Uzis, and . . . and something else that he couldn't quite put his finger on. Underneath the joking and kidding, he'd sensed an undercurrent of tension and strained expectation from Petry and the others. On the other hand, maybe it was all in his imagination.

By the time he got home, it was after midnight. At the front door, he fumbled for his keys in the darkened doorway. Had he looked to his left, he might have seen the black Blazer, which had been follow-ing him since he'd left Chico's, parked up the block.

His father, hunched over the *Daily News*, sat at the table with a cup of tea in front of him and a cigarette dangling from his lips.

"Pop, you're not supposed to be smoking."

John Fleming glared at his son from under a pair of wild, unruly eyebrows. "I couldn't sleep. I've been nervous as a cat since that fool doctor told me to knock off the cigarettes."

"With good reason. You're in the beginning stages of emphysema. He said you—"

"Ack, what does he know? Next he'll have me out jogging, for Jesus' sake."

"Pop, you're only forty-seven. You make it sound like you're an old man."

"I am."

Ray studied his father under the harsh kitchen light. He was aging rapidly. His father had always been a bull of a man, never sick, never a complaint. But since the death of his wife two years ago, he seemed to have lost his grip on life. He'd always been interested in everything from politics to show business. But now he did little more than watch an occasional wildlife documentary on television and read the newspapers. Although he'd never admit it, the diagnosis of emphysema had badly frightened him.

"Raymond, do you want some tea?" the older Fleming asked.

Ray wanted a beer, but his father, who didn't drink, frowned on alcohol in the house. "Naw, I don't want anything."

John Fleming made an elaborate show of looking at the clock, raising and lowering his thick eyebrows as though he had difficulty in seeing the wall clock less than ten feet away.

"Were you driving your taxi all this time?"

"No. I was shooting skeet with some friends."

"You must have fired a fearful lot of bullets. You've been gone since seven this morning."

"We stopped off for something to eat."

"Were you with that Manny fellow?"

"Yeah."

His father said nothing, but the expression on his face clearly registered his disapproval. He sipped his tea and moved on to his favorite topic. "I thought you were going to go on the cops."

An old-fashioned Irishman, John Fleming saw the New York City Police Department as a ticket to a good, secure job. He'd never said so, but he'd been very proud when his son had passed the written exam. And he'd been just as silent when Ray told him he'd failed the medical.

Ray rolled his eyes. "I *am* going to be a cop, but they failed me on the back X-ray. I'm appealing the ruling, but these things take time."

"While you're waiting, why don't you go to college?" College was John Fleming's second road to economic salvation.

Fleming exhaled slowly. His father had a maddening way of asking the same questions over and over again, as though he hadn't heard the answers before. "That's why I'm driving a cab, Pop. I'm trying to get enough money together so I can go full time."

The senior Fleming studied his son from under his bushy eyebrows. "I don't see how you can save money when you spend a fortune on guns and bullets."

Ray Fleming fought back the anger he felt building within him. His father drove him crazy when he needled him this way. He never raised his voice; he never got angry. He just asked maddening questions and made annoying comments. The only thing that kept Ray from blowing up was the knowledge that his father only wanted what was best for him.

The son looked at his father's gray face and the anger dissipated. "Pop, I'm tired. I think I'll go to bed."

The senior Fleming went to the sink and, as he did every night,

Officer DOWN

rinsed his cup, dried it, and returned it to the cabinet. "I guess I'll go to bed too."

"Good night, Pop." Ray wanted to reach out and touch his father's arm, but he didn't. There was a genuine closeness between them, but it didn't extend to physical contact. "Do me a favor, Pop. Don't smoke anymore."

His father nodded and padded off to bed.

Ray went into his room and flipped on the TV. With the sound turned down he watched Arsenio Hall interviewing a rock musician decked out in chains and black leather. But his thoughts drifted back to the day's events once again. It probably didn't mean anything. Still . . .

He was going to wait until the morning, but he remembered his instructions. "Call anytime. I'll decide if it's important."

Reluctantly, he dialed the number.

"Hello," said a sleepy voice on the other end of the line.

"It's . . . it's Ray Town." Fleming felt foolish using his code name.

In his bedroom, Captain John Zakovitch sat up and turned on the tape recorder he kept hooked up to his telephone. "Yes, Ray. What is it?"

"It's probably nothing, but you said to call you if I heard anything about Colombia."

On the other end of the line Fleming heard a match being struck. "Give me twenty minutes. I'll meet you at the White Castle on Queens Boulevard."

Captain Zakovitch was on his fifth cigarette and Ray Fleming was polishing off a large bag of hamburgers by the time he finished recounting the day's events and answering the captain's many questions.

Zakovitch watched the young man rummage through the bag looking for another burger. "Still hungry?"

"Yeah, a little."

MICHAEL GRANT

"You've got some appetite."

Fleming grinned. "That's what my mother used to say—usually followed by a short prayer."

Zakovitch picked up the tape recorder and checked to see that there was enough tape. "Anything more to add, Ray?"

Fleming curled up a napkin and stuffed it in the bag. "Nope, that's it."

He rattled the cubes in his container and felt another pang of guilt. He hadn't told Captain Zakovitch about Chico's or Celeste. He reasoned she had nothing to do with the others and there was no point in bringing her into this. If it turned out later that she was involved, he could still tell Zakovitch.

He shook that troubling thought from his mind and said, "What do you think, Captain? Something going on with these guys or what?"

Zakovitch turned off the tape recorder and lit another cigarette. "Remember what I told you, Ray. Don't ask so—"

". . . many questions. I know, I know."

Fleming had heard it before. Since the day he'd been secretly sworn into the Police Department, he'd been hoping—expecting—to be involved in exciting undercover work. But all he'd done in the intervening three months was to hang around Blockmann's. His reports, which he called in daily to Captain Zakovitch, were all routine and boring. From the beginning Zakovitch had been vague about what he was supposed to do. He'd been told two things: Get to know Manny Botnick, and let it be known that he was looking for ways to make some easy money. That was it. In spite of Fleming's insistent questioning, Zakovitch wouldn't elaborate any more than that. In the beginning Fleming was convinced he'd been sent there to uncover a stolen firearms ring. But when he met Manny Botnick, a likable klutz who couldn't steal loose change from a blind man, he'd known that couldn't be the reason. But a noncommittal Zakovitch continued to accept his bland nothing-to-report reports without comment.

"But why shouldn't I ask questions? Shouldn't I know what's going down?"

"Going *down*?" Zakovitch picked a piece of tobacco off his tongue and flipped it out the window. "Ray, you sound like a TV cop show. But this isn't TV. It's for real. You're doing serious police work and I want you to take it seriously."

"I do, Captain, but I don't seem to be doing police work. All I do is hang around Blockmann's."

"That's what I want you to do. If you need to know more, I'll tell you."

Fleming flipped the rest of the ice cubes out the window and crushed the empty container. "Okay, you're the boss."

Zakovitch started the car. "I'm glad we agree on that. Let's get rid of the trash and I'll drive you home."

6:15 P.M. THURSDAY, MARCH 28 • It was just after six P.M. when Dan Morgan turned off the Brooklyn-Queens Expressway at the Metropolitan Avenue exit. Four blocks from the expressway he parked in front of a restaurant near the corner of Metropolitan and Dean Street.

The Greenpoint neighborhood, a small Polish enclave sandwiched between the Orthodox Jewish community of Williamsburg to the south and Maspeth to the north, featured stores where Polish was spoken and authentic ethnic food was plentiful.

John Zakovitch had called it a restaurant, but it was more a combination luncheonette-diner with steam-fogged front windows plastered with handwritten signs advertising the daily specials: today's was stuffed cabbage. When Morgan opened the door he was immediately assailed by warm, humid air heavy with the pungent smell of boiled cabbage and grilled kielbasa.

The captain, sitting in a corner booth, was halfway through a huge bowl of blood-red borscht. He looked up as Morgan slipped into the seat opposite him. "If you're hungry, Inspector, the borscht is very good." The craggy-faced captain scooped up a lethal dose of homemade horseradish and dropped it into his bowl. "Adds a little flavor."

Morgan, who had seen Zakovitch eat hot chili peppers as if they were marshmallows, shook his head. "Zak, your taste buds were cauterized years ago. You couldn't taste hot lead."

Zakovitch said something in Polish to a passing waiter. Moments later, the man returned and unceremoniously thrust a bowl of borscht and a steaming plate of pirogen in front of Morgan.

Zakovitch frowned as Morgan salted the borscht. "Do the Irish put salt on everything?"

"Yeah. I even salt pizza. Why did you want to meet here? I could have gone to your office."

Zakovitch pushed his empty bowl away and lit a cigarette. The ashtray was already filled with Zakovitch's unfiltered Camels. "I don't like too much traffic in and out of the office. Besides, this place has the best Polish food in the city."

Morgan inspected the surroundings. Every booth and counter seat was taken. It *must* be the food, he thought, looking at a flypaper strip hanging from the ceiling. The waiter deposited two steaming cups of mud black coffee and cleared away the empty plates in front of Zakovitch. When he'd gone, Morgan said, "What's up?"

Zakovitch squinted through the smoke. "One of my undercover people may have stumbled onto something about Colombia." He slid a manila envelope across the table. "Here's a copy of the debriefing."

Morgan, trying his best to look unconcerned, stuffed a pirog into his mouth. "Yeah? What's he say?"

"Nothing definite, but he went shooting with a few people who bear looking at. One, an American named Lyle Petry, speaks fluent Spanish. He used to work in Colombia. My UC says he's pretty good with firearms."

"What kind of firearms?"

Zakovitch stirred his black coffee. "The usual. Pistols, shotguns—Uzis with silencers."

Morgan, who was holding the milk pitcher, carefully lowered it to the table. "You do a background?"

"No record. But I don't have a good DOB. I can't even confirm if Lyle Petry is his real name."

"What about the others?"

"Couldn't. They only used first names." Zakovitch squinted through a blue haze. "There's something else. My UC's cover job is driving a cab. The owner of the cab company, an old friend of mine, told me he got a call from a man inquiring about my UC."

"What did the guy want?"

"He wanted to commend my UC for helping him carry his luggage up to his apartment."

"So?"

Zakovitch waved the smoke out of his eyes. "My UC never carried anyone's luggage."

"Did your UC tell Petry where he worked?"

"Yeah."

"Then Petry was checking up on him."

"Looks that way."

Zakovitch crushed the cigarette in the ashtray. "Inspector, the story about the State Department wasn't true, was it?"

Morgan smiled at the crafty old captain. Zakovitch had toiled in the shadowy world of intelligence long enough to recognize a con when he heard one. There was no point in continuing the charade. "No."

"Do you want to tell me what's going on?"

Morgan stared at the craggy face of his old friend. "I can't, Zak."

It was impossible to read the captain's face but Morgan could imagine what was going on behind those expressionless eyes. For more than a quarter of a century John Zakovitch had been at the center of every major intelligence operation in the department. But now he was an outsider; not one to be trusted. Once again Morgan began to have doubts about Cassidy's decision to exclude other cops. If they were going to find Puño Blanco, they'd need the help of people like John Zakovitch.

"Zak, what was said about Colombia?"

"Not much. A few remarks about the country. One of them, a man called Alvaro, had a Spanish accent. Another made a reference to being in Colombia."

"What's your undercover's opinion of them?"

"As far as he's concerned, they're a great bunch of guys."

"With Uzis? Sounds like a real fun bunch." Morgan stirred his coffee and tried to keep his tone conversational. "Zak, I have to talk to your undercover."

Captain Zakovitch's customary reserve eroded slightly. "Inspector, if you're working on something you can't tell me about, so be it. But when it involves one of my undercover people, that's something else. I have to know what's going on."

"Why?"

"He's not working out. I was getting ready to pull him when this came up."

Morgan's head shot up. "What's the matter with him?"

"Too cocky for undercover work. Thinks it's a game."

Morgan swore under his breath. "Didn't you know that when you hired him?" He realized too late the question had an accusatory ring to it.

"When you recruit them you never know. I interview them, I ask them questions, they give answers. But you don't really know how they're going to work out until they get into the street. I've had to drop some because they thought they were James Bond; others because they wouldn't recognize a KKK meeting if everyone was wearing bedsheets."

"Then why did you pick him?"

"He's an expert marksman. I needed someone with his skills to join a pistol club in lower Manhattan. Inspector, someday Ray is going to make a fine police officer. He's smart, idealistic, and aggressive. But aggression is the last thing I need in an undercover cop. This kind of assignment requires a unique temperament. He has to be smart, courageous—and paradoxically, passive. A good undercover cop has to have the patience to wait for things to happen to him. He can't force events."

"And your undercover lacks patience?"

Zakovitch nodded.

"How about some training? Maybe—"

"There's no way to train people who work for me. Their survival depends on their ignorance of police procedures and methods. They have to blend in, be one of the guys. It takes a special talent and I'm afraid my UC doesn't have it."

Morgan, who didn't like what he was hearing, changed the subject. "Who belongs to this pistol club?"

"Manny Botnick, one of the names on the list. He's been chasing radical causes since high school. He was with the JDL for a time, but they threw him out."

"Too crazy or not crazy enough?"

"Inept. The kind of kid who can't do anything right. Comes from money. I imagine Botnick's dabbling in radical causes is his way of proving to daddy that he's all grown up."

"Why are you interested in him?"

"Because he has a real knack for finding other loonies like himself. The majority of people who belong to gun clubs are upstanding citizens, but gun clubs also attract the lunatic fringe. Botnick's a lightning rod for screwballs like himself. If there are any wackos in that club, he'll find them."

"Sounds like a harmless asshole."

Zakovitch shook his head. "Don't underestimate him. True believers like Botnick are dangerous. If you present a cause to them in the proper light, they can be talked into doing some screwy things."

"He was one of the guys playing with the Uzis?"

"Yeah." Zakovitch smiled thinly. "But if it's any consolation to you, Inspector, my undercover tells me Botnick's a lousy shot."

"Not much consolation. You don't have to be Wyatt Earp to hit something with an Uzi. Does the undercover know about Botnick's background?"

"No. I simply told him to join the club, make friends with Botnick, and let it be known that he was looking for ways to make a fast buck."

"Why didn't you tell him about Botnick?"

"I wanted to neutralize his assertive tendencies. If he knew any more than that he might push too hard for information and that would make him vulnerable."

Morgan wasn't happy with Zakovitch's assessment of the undercover cop. If there was anything to the people he'd met, he'd be the link. If so, in spite of what Zakovitch said, he'd have to learn a lot fast. "Zak, I know you don't like it, but I have to talk to your man right away."

"You know that's out of the question, Inspector."

"Zak, I know the goddamn rules, but this is important."

The captain met Morgan's level gaze. "Inspector, if there's something going on, I have to know about it."

Morgan poured more milk into the muddy coffee, but it had little effect on the color. "What the hell is this? Black paint?"

Zakovitch, who refused to be distracted, said, "Uzis and Colombia spell drugs. I'm telling you, Inspector, my undercover isn't prepared for that kind of problem."

Morgan, angered by Zakovitch's obstinacy, and edgy because of the secrecy requirements dictated by Cassidy, snapped, "Zak, I don't give a shit if he's up to it or not. Set up a meeting."

Zakovitch didn't even blink. "I won't do that."

Morgan sighed and sat back. He knew he was about to travel down a one-way street from which there was no return, but he had no choice. "Captain," he said evenly, "I'm giving you a direct order. Set up a meeting."

"And if I don't?"

Morgan met Zakovitch's level gaze. "I'll have you transferred."

This time the captain did blink. Intelligence work was the only assignment he knew. He couldn't imagine doing anything else. Other than violently crushing his cigarette in the ashtray, there was no outward sign of emotion. "Inspector, you're not the same man I broke into the intelligence business twenty years ago."

Morgan refused to be swayed by the veiled appeal. "No one is. When can I see him?"

Captain Zakovitch sat back in his seat and suddenly looked a lot older. "Give me a number, I'll have him call you."

Morgan left the restaurant angered and disturbed. Keeping secrets and threatening old friends was a side to this investigation he hadn't bargained for.

Chapter
16

4:20 A.M. FRIDAY, MARCH 29 • The dream started. At first Dan Morgan merely uttered guttural sounds, but as the dream progressed to its frightening and inescapable climax, he began to thrash around in the bed. Finally, with a yell, he woke himself up. Unable to go back to sleep, he flipped on the TV and made coffee. By the time the sun came up, he'd finished the whole pot.

As he was going out the door, the telephone rang.

"Inspector Morgan?" the tentative voice asked.

"Yeah."

"Ray Fleming. Captain Zakovitch said you wanted to talk to me."

Morgan looked at his watch. "Yeah. What are you doing at ten this morning?"

Ten minutes after Morgan arrived at the office, Chris Liberti, wearing a navy blue suit and matching heels, came in waving a copy of the *New York Post* at him. "You read Charlie Thurman's column?"

Morgan rubbed his temples to soothe what was promising to be a world-class headache. Charlie Thurman, a cop-baiting rabble-rouser, wrote a daily human interest column that usually focused on people who'd allegedly been wrongfully arrested, beaten, or in some way mistreated by the police. "No. What does he say?"

"He's started a body count." She opened the newspaper and read from the column. " 'First a headquarters cop, then a cop in Queens, and now a cop from midtown Manhattan.' " Morgan groaned. "Wait," Liberti said. "It gets better." She read from the newspaper. " 'Could this be the beginning of an uprising by people fed up with the callous, inhuman justice dispensed by the local constabulary?' "

"What—?"

"Yeah." She threw the newspaper in the wastebasket. "This lunatic thinks the killings are part of a people's revolt. He warns the mayor and the police commissioner that if cops don't start respecting the rights of the people, the killings will escalate."

Morgan stopped rubbing his temples; it wasn't helping. "What an asshole. He's in left field, but even so, that kind of talk can have a bad effect on cops. Saying something like that now is like pouring gasoline on an open flame."

Liberti took a small metal box out of a shopping bag and placed it on her desk.

"What's that?" he asked.

"An air purifier." She crawled under her desk in search of an outlet and Morgan couldn't help getting a glimpse of her well-shaped legs. "If Castillo insists on smoking those crappy cigars," she said from under the table, "I need something to contain the fallout."

Morgan, ignoring the reproachful tone in her voice, got up and poured himself a cup of coffee. He had no intention of getting in the middle of the cigar wars. "I hear Tony Renzi has been grumbling about the department's lack of response to the killings," he said.

Liberti, who made it her business to stay abreast of NYPD politics, knew Renzi was the president of the PBA. She stood up and straightened her skirt. "The PBA could really muddy up the waters if they start a job action now," she said.

"That's what the PC is afraid of."

Liberti picked up a crude crayon drawing of two large rectangles from Morgan's desk. It showed two stick figures in a window and a big animal at the top of one of the rectangles. "What's this?"

"Something my son made in nursery school. It's supposed to be him, me, and King Kong at the Twin Towers."

"That's so adorable. Are you the one who looks scared?"

"Yeah."

"I'll bet he brings stuff like this home every day, huh?"

"I don't see him every day. My wife and I are separated."

Feeling as though she'd invaded his privacy, she quickly dropped the drawing on his desk. Before she could ask any more questions, Castillo came in and dropped a two-inch-thick pile of Spanish-language newspapers on the desk. Every morning he'd been skimming the papers, especially the classified ads, looking for anything out of the ordinary. He tossed a summons on Morgan's desk. "Can you take care of this?"

Morgan snapped up the summons. "A fire hydrant? For chrissake, Don. Don't do this. You're lucky they didn't tow your ass away."

Castillo poured a cup of coffee. "I know. It's a jungle out there."

Liberti fingered his windbreaker. "Hey, what happened to the fashionable field jacket?"

"In the cleaners. I spilled something on it." Castillo sat down and grabbed a copy of *El Diario* off the pile.

Morgan tossed the summons aside and said, "I might have some good news. One of our undercover cops has picked up some information about Colombia." He handed them copies of the undercover's debriefing report. "Read. Then we'll talk."

Liberti was the first one finished. "When do we talk to him?" she said.

Morgan looked at his watch. "In about an hour."

Castillo's eyebrows descended over his dark eyes. "Who's going to do the debriefing?" he asked.

"The three of us," Morgan said.

The DEA agent shook his head. "Not me."

"Why?"

"I don't want anyone to see my face."

Liberti grinned. "Donal, you're not all *that* bad-looking."

Castillo ignored her. "I do undercover work. The less people who know what I look like the better."

Liberti shook her head. "I don't believe you, Donal. We *all* have to be here. He may say something that may be relevant to only one of us. Put a bag over your head if it makes you feel any better, but you gotta be here."

"She's right," Morgan said. "You're here because of your expertise on the Medellin cartel and Colombia. We need you for the debriefing."

The DEA agent ripped the cellophane from a cigar. "All right," he mumbled.

Forty-five minutes later there was a knock on the outer office door. Morgan opened it and a good-looking young man with thick, curly black hair stuck his hand out. "Inspector Morgan? Ray Fleming."

Morgan led him into the inner office and introduced him to the others. At Castillo's insistence, it had been agreed that no last names would be used, nor even what agencies they represented.

Fleming sat down and Castillo offered him a cigar. "You smoke?" The young cop shook his head.

Liberti waved a cup. "Thank God. How about some coffee?"

"Sure."

"How do you take it?"

"Light, extra sugar."

155   **Officer DOWN**

While Liberti was pouring the coffee, Morgan watched Ray Fleming take in the room. The undercover cop was curious; that was good. But he was far too obvious. Fleming's head was swiveling like the last turkey in the barnyard on Thanksgiving morning. A good cop would have scoped out the room before he was in his seat.

If Fleming was trying to figure out what went on in this office, he was wasting his time. Thanks to Chris Liberti's paranoia, there was nothing visible to indicate what they did here. For the past fifteen minutes, she'd been scurrying about sanitizing the room.

Morgan waited until Liberti handed the coffee to Fleming, then he began. "Ray, I guess Captain Zakovitch explained why we want to talk to you?"

"Yeah. I might have some information about an investigation you're conducting. Inspector, can you tell me what this is all about?"

"No." Morgan saw the disappointed look in Fleming's eyes and added, "It's for your protection. Specific information might hamper your undercover attitude. Ray, how did you meet Lyle Petry?"

"I was introduced to him by Manny Botnick."

"How long have you known Botnick?"

"Three months."

"What's he look like?"

"Chunky, about five-seven. Curly brown hair, scraggly mustache."

Morgan looked at the others and knew they were thinking the same thing: Ray Fleming had described the man who had given the money to Dave Keel the night of the headquarters bombing.

He continued the questioning. "Have you ever been to Petry's home?"

"No, sir. I don't even know where he lives."

"Does he own a Blazer?"

"Yeah. I think so."

"Do you know the license plate number?"

"No. I don't."

"How about the state?" Liberti asked hopefully.

Fleming half turned to her. "Uh, no . . . I didn't notice. I'm sorry."

Morgan was beginning to see what Zakovitch was talking about.

MICHAEL GRANT

An undercover's main function was to listen, observe—and remember things like plate numbers. "You don't have to apologize," Morgan said, betraying none of the disappointment he felt. "We understand this is all new to you. We're probably going to ask you a lot of questions you won't know the answers to. Just try to remember the best you can."

Fleming nodded and sipped his coffee.

"Has Petry ever spoken Spanish in front of you?"

"No."

"Then how do you know he speaks Spanish?" Castillo asked.

Fleming cleared his throat. "Uh, I think Manny told me he speaks Spanish."

Morgan resumed. "Did Petry tell you he worked in Colombia?"

"No."

"Then who—?"

"Manny. I believe Manny told me that too."

"Your report says you met Petry at Blockmann's pistol range. Have you met with him anywhere else?"

"Yeah. We went to the bar down the street from Blockmann's once. I don't remember the name. Then we met at that country club on Long Island."

"Did Petry ever talk politics with you?"

"No, sir."

Morgan glanced at his notes. "Let's talk about the day you went shooting with Petry and the others. Do you know who owns that land?"

"No, I don't."

"Could you find the location again?"

"I'm not sure. I wasn't paying a lot of attention. I know it's way out on Long Island. Somewhere on the North Fork," he added weakly. The "I don't know"s and "I'm not sure" had drained some of the cockiness from the undercover cop.

Liberti spread out a road map of Long Island in front of Fleming. "Can you show us where you went on the map?"

Fleming peered at the map to get his bearings. "Let's see, we started here and went east on the LIE." His finger traced the red-

lined Long Island Expressway out to Riverhead. "We went north to
. . . 25A, I think. Then east again. We stopped somewhere around
. . . here." He circled an area encompassing a five-mile radius.
"We made a right turn onto a dirt road and went into the woods."

"What was the name of the road?" Liberti asked.

"I don't think there was a street sign. It was just a dirt road."

"What can you tell us about the men that were there that day?"
Morgan asked.

"One of them, Alvaro, looked and sounded Spanish. The others
just seemed regular guys. They're unbelievable with firearms, I know
that."

"Let's take the people one at a time," Castillo said. "Describe
Alvaro?"

"Let's see . . . short, dark complexion, beard sort of salt and
pepper. I'd guess late forties."

"How about Jimmy?"

"Early forties. About five-seven. Looks like he's in real good physical shape. Didn't say much, but he had some kind of a Southern
accent."

"Glen."

"Fair-skinned black . . . with red hair. The guys kidded him
about his red hair and green eyes. I'd say he was about the same age
as Jimmy."

"How tall?"

"About my height. Six feet."

Castillo continued the questioning. "What did they do with the
expended brass?"

"They picked it up. Lyle says they do their own reloading."

"Did you have anything to eat or drink?" Liberti asked.

"Beer and sandwiches."

"What did you do with the garbage?"

"Um, we tossed everything in a plastic bag."

"The targets too?"

"No. They put the targets and the expended brass in the station
wagon."

"What did they do with the plastic bag?" Morgan asked.

"I don't know. Lyle, Manny, and I left before the others."

Castillo spoke up. "Did any of these guys use words or phrases that were unfamiliar to you?"

Fleming thought for a moment. "Yeah, come to think of it, Lyle used the word goatscrew a lot."

Castillo sat forward in his seat. "In what context?"

"You know, like when something is all fucked up."

"Anything else?"

"Yeah. I think it was Jimmy who said something about a Q course. I never heard that before. Maybe it has something to do with skeet shooting."

"Ray, were you in the military?"

"No."

"If you had to guess, who would you say was the leader of the group?"

"Lyle. Definitely. He pretty much told everyone what to do."

"How about Alvaro?"

"Naw. He kind of stood apart from everyone except Lyle. They talked to each other a lot, though."

Liberti flipped through her copy of the debriefing. "You've told us about Botnick, Petry, Jimmy, Glen, and Alvaro. Are there any others whom you've met through Petry?"

Fleming stared into his cup. "Nope. That's it."

When Morgan saw that Castillo and Liberti had no more questions, he stood up. "Come on, Ray, I'll walk with you to the elevator."

In the hallway Morgan pushed the elevator button. "Ray, thanks again for stopping by. Keep in daily contact with Captain Zakovitch and report everything to him no matter how insignificant it may seem to you."

"Okay, Inspector. Hey, was I any help?"

Morgan wasn't encouraged by the exuberant tone in Fleming's voice. Undercover cops who tried too hard made mistakes and sometimes got hurt in the process. "It's hard to say, Ray. An investigation entails collecting and sorting hundreds of bits of information. Sometimes the pieces fit, sometimes they don't. It'll be a while before we know."

"Will I be working on the case with you?"

Morgan looked into Fleming's expectant face and fervently hoped not. Fleming had all the makings of a bull in a china shop. "It's too soon to say," he said. "By the way, do you know what to do if Petry, or one of the others, suggests you engage in criminal conduct?"

"Sure. Captain Zakovitch said I should go along with it and call him right away for further instructions."

Dan Morgan looked at the young undercover cop and wished he were someone with more experience. "I don't know if it will happen, Ray, but one of those men may feel you out to see if you'd be willing to do something illegal. Don't be too eager to say yes, but give the impression that you're open to suggestion."

The elevator arrived and Fleming stepped in. As the doors were closing, Fleming stuck his head out. "Inspector, what reason should I give for doing something illegal?"

"Money," Morgan said, as the doors were closing. "The common denominator of most dishonesty."

When Morgan came back into the office Liberti and Castillo were already discussing the debriefing.

Liberti looked up. "If Donal is right, we got trouble with a capital T."

Morgan perched on the edge of Castillo's desk. "What's the bad news?"

"Goatscrew," Castillo said. "You ever hear the term?"

"No."

"It means disorganized chaos. What some call snafu."

"Who uses it?"

"Special Forces."

"The Green Berets?"

"That's what the media call them, but Special Forces is the proper name."

"There must be others who say goatscrew."

"Maybe. But not Q course."

"What's that?"

"The six-month qualification course Special Forces gives at Camp McKall in North Carolina."

Morgan sagged as he suddenly realized what had disturbed him about that radio car ambush. The position of the Mustang and the actions of the three perps smacked of military precision. "So you think Petry and the others are ex–Special Forces people?" he asked.

"Sounds that way. And if it's true, we're in deep shit."

"Why?"

"Because I know how these guys operate. They're the last people in the world I'd want to have as an enemy."

"Exactly what is it that Special Forces do? I saw the movie, but I assumed it was a lot of John Wayne hype."

"It was. Special Forces are trained to work alone or in small teams. They're all cross-trained in small arms, explosives, and assassination techniques. One time I ran into an old friend in a bar in Honduras. He was a Special Forces sergeant. He was drunk as a skunk, which is probably the only reason why he told me the story. It happened back in 'Nam in sixty-eight. His A team was given the task of assassinating a Communist leader in a border village, a known VC stronghold. This sergeant and four others made a high-altitude insertion into rice paddies two miles from the village. Armed with nothing more than knives and twenty-twos with silencers, they slipped into the village. The official's house was surrounded by North Vietnamese regulars, but they got in and popped their target. The wife and kiddies were sleeping in the next room, but no one knew a thing until the next morning when his wife found him in bed staring up at the ceiling with three eyes."

Liberti shuddered. "Reminds me of the horse's head scene in *The Godfather.*"

Castillo smiled thinly. "That was Hollywood fiction. But I wouldn't put it past some of these gung-ho Special Forces guys to pull something like that off."

Liberti idly bobbed her tea bag. "I had one experience of Special Forces soldiers in action and it made a hell of an impression on me.

The base Provost at Fort Benning had invited me to watch a military exercise. For the grand finale a team of eight Special Forces soldiers, dressed in black Ninja-type outfits, attacked a farmhouse where a hostage was being held. First, a helicopter appeared over the building and then all hell broke loose. Three guys rappelled out of the chopper onto the roof as the men on the ground rushed the doors and windows. Using CAR-fifteens, flash-bang grenades, and C-four, they penetrated that house in less than six seconds. I was in a reviewing stand a hundred yards away, but even from that distance the voracity of the attack was awesome. Later, I got a chance to meet some of these guys and I was struck by their intensity and barely suppressed aggressiveness. We were sitting in a tent having doughnuts and coffee, but they were so . . . vigilant. It was almost as though they expected someone to attack the tent. They reminded me of thoroughbred race horses waiting for the starting gates to open." She shuddered. "Real scary."

She held the tea bag up and watched the liquid drip back into the cup. "Now I see how they've managed to murder three police officers without leaving a trace," she said softly.

Morgan was thinking the same thing. "Alvaro must be the Colombian contact for Puño Blanco," he said.

Castillo nodded. "Probably."

"I wonder how and where Alvaro and Petry would have met?" Liberti said to no one in particular.

"That's easy," Castillo said. "Special Forces are officially operating in Honduras and El Salvador, but I know they've run covert operations in other parts of Central and South America, including Colombia."

Morgan was staring at the map of Long Island and an idea came to him. It was a long shot, but worth a try. He drew a circle around the area on the map Fleming had indicated. "We gotta find that shooting range."

Liberti looked over his shoulder. "How?"

"A helicopter."

"It's worth a try, but we can't use a police helicopter. We'll have to rent one."

Castillo looked puzzled. "Even if you locate the site, what do you expect to find?"

"For openers," Morgan said, "maybe the garbage bag."

"So what?"

"Fingerprints."

"Fingerprints?" Castillo repeated. "That stuff's been out in the elements for a couple of days. Could you lift anything now?"

"Sure," Morgan said. He added in a less optimistic tone, "That is, with a little bit of luck and a lot of technology."

"The cans maybe," Liberti allowed, "but not Styrofoam cups."

Morgan scowled at her. "You can lift prints from Styrofoam."

"Nope. Too porous."

"I'm telling you—"

"Maybe there won't *be* a garbage bag," Castillo said, cutting off the argument.

Annoyed that he'd let Liberti get under his skin, Morgan snapped at Castillo. "You got a better suggestion?"

"You can request satellite reconnaissance if you want, but there's only one way to ID Petry."

"How?"

"Fleming has to do it for us. He's got to find out where Petry lives."

"Easier said than done," Morgan mumbled, remembering Zakovitch's assessment.

"How about the next time Fleming meets with Petry, we follow Petry," Liberti suggested.

"Too risky," Castillo said emphatically. "If Petry is ex–Special Forces, he'll spot a tail."

"What about telephoto surveillance?" Liberti suggested. "We can at least get a photograph of him. Maybe his license plate will lead us to where he lives."

"Better," Castillo conceded. "But we'll have to keep our distance."

"No problem," the FBI agent said confidently. "I'll get a low-light-level telephoto camera from my tech services people."

For the first time since this investigation had begun, Morgan was beginning to feel like a cop. At last they had a solid lead to work with. "I'll call Ray Fleming and tell him to let me know the next time he's going to meet Petry. When he does, we'll be ready."

Liberti, seeing the DEA agent deep in thought, said, "What's up, Donal?"

Castillo ground his cigar into an ashtray. "I don't know why, but I got a feeling Fleming wasn't telling us everything."

Chris Liberti picked up Castillo's still smoldering cigar as though it were a dead mouse and dropped it into a Styrofoam cup of water.

Morgan's newfound euphoria began to evaporate. "Why do you say that?"

"I don't know. Something ain't right."

Liberti fingered her large hoop earring. "Now that you mention it, something has been bothering me too and I think I know what it is. I have the impression Fleming genuinely likes this Petry guy." She looked from Castillo to Morgan. "Could he be getting too close to him? It *is* an occupational hazard of undercover work, you know."

"It's only because he's new at this game," Morgan said, trying to chase away the ghosts of doubt. "I just hope his powers of observation get a lot better than they've been."

Dan Morgan stood up. "I'm gonna run over to headquarters and tell Cassidy about Fleming."

Castillo stood up and started to stretch, but he suddenly stopped and rubbed his side.

"What's the matter," Liberti asked.

"Nothing. A cramp."

She snickered. "You get a cramp stretching, you must be in lousy shape."

"Probably. Listen, I'm heading uptown to talk to my old partner. I'll see you guys later."

Morgan looked at Liberti. "In the meantime, Chris, why don't you see what you can do about a helicopter."

. . .

MICHAEL GRANT

Before Morgan had a chance to sit down, the police commissioner shoved a copy of the *Daily News* in front of him. "Have you seen this?" he growled.

Morgan glanced down at the lead story headline on page three: THIRD COP KILLED IN FOURTEEN DAYS: PATTERN OR BUSINESS AS USUAL? "Yes, sir, but I haven't had a chance to read it."

"They haven't hit the target yet, but they've started snooping. I'm getting calls from nosy reporters wanting to know more about these murders. Fortunately, the MOs haven't been that similar so I've been able to fend them off. But I can't keep doing this. Sooner or later, some besotted reporter is going to sober up and put two and two together. I also got a call from Renzi. He wants to see me today. Just what I need," the commissioner said dryly. "I wish the hell I had a better idea of what the cops on the street are thinking. No one tells me a goddamn thing up here on the fourteenth floor."

Morgan remembered there was a Midtown South Precinct retirement racket tonight. He'd had no intention of going, but now he changed his mind. It would be a good opportunity to find out what the cops on the street were thinking.

"Sir, there's a precinct racket tonight. Maybe I can get a feel for the mood of the cops."

"Good idea. What else are you people doing?"

Morgan hesitated. He hadn't planned on mentioning Fleming until they could verify the UC's information, but he had little else to offer his frustrated police commissioner. "We've received information from one of our undercover cops, but," he added cautiously, "we don't know how good the information is."

"What is it?"

"He's been hanging around with some people who have Uzis. They've mentioned Colombia a few times."

"Sounds promising. What are you doing about it?"

"We're trying to verify the information."

"What else are you doing?" the commissioner added impatiently.

"We're running name checks of all known radicals living in the city with possible connections to South America."

"And?"

"It's slow going, sir. Intel alone has a list of over fifty names and the FBI has a couple of hundred—"

"Screw the FBI," Cassidy exploded. "To them anyone who ever attended a peace rally is a radical."

"I know." Morgan struggled to keep his own temper in check. "We're weeding out the peripheral people."

"Damn it, that'll take you weeks and you don't have that kind of time."

Dan Morgan knew that only too well. Since they'd started this investigation four days ago, they'd been drowning in paperwork generated by Chris Liberti's damn computer. Each name represented a possible lead and had to be checked out. It was a tedious but necessary task, because one of those names might lead to Puño Blanco.

Morgan, seeing an opening, decided to make another try for more manpower. "Sir, if I had use of the Joint Terrorist Task Force—"

"No," Cassidy bellowed. "And that's final."

Cassidy's tone told Morgan that he'd better not bring up that topic again.

Chapter
17

Donal Castillo sat on a stool at the far end of the bar listlessly watching a Ranger-Islander playoff game. A jukebox, pounding out a Tito Puente salsa number, drowned out the voice of the excited announcer, who was trying to explain the last flurry of penalties. But the music didn't seem to bother the other patrons, who cheered as players from both teams filed into the penalty boxes.

The door opened and a short black man came in. The sides of his head were shaven clean and all that remained was a two-inch island of hair on the top of his head. Except for a few strands of gray in his mustache, he could have passed for a teenager.

The man climbed up on the stool next to Castillo and glanced up at the TV screen. "Who's winning?" he asked.

"How the hell should I know," Castillo answered. "All they've done is fight for the last fifteen minutes."

The man's face broadened in a gaptoothed smile. "That's the trouble with you Cubans, man. All you know about ice is you put it in a glass."

Castillo grunted. "I like a game I can understand, like baseball."

"Baseball?" the man repeated. "For fags, man. They pay those dudes three mil a year and most of the time they sit on the sidelines nursing hemorrhoids and whatnot. Now that," he nodded toward the screen, "is a *real* game with *real* men. Look at that."

Both men watched as the camera zoomed in on yet another fight. A Ranger, stripped of his shirt, was sitting on an Islander's chest, pummeling him with his helmet.

Castillo turned to the man seated next to him. "How does a black dude like you get into hockey, anyway?"

The other man smiled balefully. "When that motherfucker Richards got me transferred to fucking Minnesota. That's how."

Castillo studied the man's haircut with evident distaste. "George, what the hell did you do to your hair? Looks like a dead beaver landed on your head."

George Albin, DEA agent and former partner of Don Castillo, shrugged. "It's what my people are wearing these days. You should talk. When you were working the campuses, you looked like fucking Cochise."

Albin rose off his stool and peered at the top of Castillo's head. "Speaking of Indians, it looks like you got scalped yourself, m'man."

Castillo scowled. "How long you been back in the city?" he asked, changing the subject.

" 'Bout a year. Took me nine months to get myself extracted from that godforsaken state and another nine months to thaw my black ass out." He poked Castillo. "Fucking Richards. When he dies, I'm gonna piss on his grave."

Castillo smiled. "Let's make sure we drink plenty of beer first."

"*Damn!* Why did that honkey have such a hard-on for us?"

Castillo's smile vanished. "Because we were good street agents. Something Richards wouldn't know anything about."

Albin grinned. "Yeah, but you gotta admit we did get into some crazy shit. That caper with the Mr. Softee truck was our undoing. Come to think of it, it was *your* idea to steal it. It was *your* idea to drive it through the fucking front window of that smoke shop. So how come *I* was the one exiled to Minnesota?"

"Because you're black?" Castillo deadpanned.

"Maybe, but truth is, you're the best agent the DEA's got. Wouldn't make no sense to transfer your ass to Siberia."

"So I went to Miami instead," Castillo said softly.

The playfulness went out of Albin. "Oh, yeah. I forgot. Hey, man, I was sorry to hear about Martinez."

"It happens." Castillo turned away and signaled the bartender for two beers.

Albin knew it was pointless asking Castillo about the circumstances surrounding Ralph Martinez's death. Donal Castillo seldom spoke about personal matters.

"How's Colombia?"

"Totally fucked up. Murder has become a cottage industry. *La compañía—*"

"Huh?"

"The cartel. They put out the word that they have a *trabajito*—a little job—and people apply for the position. They got a regular price structure: a hundred bucks for a lover, two thou for a government minister, more for a difficult target. Teenagers, who take most of the assignments, use motor bikes. One drives, the guy on the back is the trigger man. For a real important hit, the *compañía* may require a test killing to make sure the kids have the right stuff."

Albin scratched his head. "Man, and I thought New York was fucked up. So what are you doing here?"

"Chasing down a Colombian network that's setting up in the city, and I need to know what's been going on since I left. That's why I called you, Georgie. You always know what's happening."

"Don't pull my chain, Castillo. You know this city as well as I do."

"I've been away." Castillo slid a beer in front of Albin. "What's the latest rumors from the street?"

"The usual shit. I guess you heard about the three cops getting blown away?"

"Yeah. I saw it in the papers. What do you think?"

"I dunno. I got a few friends in the department. They're really pissed. They think the killings are connected, but they can't figure out why. If they knew that, they'd know who's doing it. I'll tell you, man, the uniformed cops in the street are *scared*. I know I'm keeping a low profile. I don't want some antsy cop blowing up my black ass before I get a chance to ID myself."

"Who do you think is behind it, George?"

"Beats the shit out of me. Any asshole with an automatic and a pocketful of crack thinks he's a drug baron. The fucking mutts on the street today don't need a real good reason for blowing away a cop."

"Where do the Colombians hang out these days?" Castillo asked, changing the subject.

"All over the place, man. Things have changed in this city. Used to be ethnics kept to themselves, but no more. Except for the chink gangs in Chinatown, everybody's everywhere. Coke and crack have blown this town wide open. Every cat and his brother is dealing Charlie."

"The Colombians gotta congregate somewhere."

"There's still some in Jackson Heights and Elmhurst, but not like it used to be. Who you looking for?"

Castillo used a napkin to wipe up a puddle in front of him. "I don't have any names yet."

"Good luck, m'man. You got your work cut out for you. You do a computer search yet?"

Castillo grunted. "Yeah, for all the good it'll do."

Albin nodded in agreement. The DEA administration, like most law enforcement agencies, had a great deal of faith in computer technology. But street agents knew it wasn't always as good as advertised. A lot of information in the computer banks was outdated or so generalized as to be useless. Agents were supposed to submit intelligence reports as to the whereabouts of high-profile dealers, locations, and suspected premises. But agents, afraid that making such information public would short-circuit their opportunities to make arrests, kept the important information to themselves. They reported the intelligence only after the arrest was made, insuring that the information was out of date and useless.

"This a DEA operation?" Albin asked.

Castillo made a face. "No. I'm working with the locals and the Bureau."

"I know a lot of guys in the PD. Who're you working with?"

Castillo's hooded eyes regarded Albin. "You wouldn't know them."

"Okay, okay. I can take a hint. I never asked. Any problems?"

Castillo studied his bottle. "I don't know yet. So far, they're really big on computers, briefings, and paper chases."

Albin looked into the intense black eyes of his old partner and saw more pain and anger than he'd remembered. Clearly, the death of Ralph Martinez had affected him. "Don, why don't you give up playing cops and robbers and go for a promotion? You got your shit together, man. We got too many guys like Richards who are just passing through on their way to another promotion. They don't stay long enough to learn the job like us street drones do. The agency needs guys like you."

Castillo shook his head. "George, I came into the DEA to lock up drug dealers. You don't do that riding a desk and shuffling papers."

Albin saw the intensity in Castillo's eyes and was genuinely concerned. "Hey, Donny, lighten up. You take things too seriously. You gotta remember one thing. This is a big fucking pageant and we all got roles to play. *We're* the good guys, and the dealers are the bad guys. Man, you know what I'm talking about. You've been to court. When you see the judge, and the defense attorney, and the prosecutor all making speeches at each other, don't you get the uncomfortable feeling that you're watching a fucking Broadway play? Donny, just don't take this shit too seriously."

Castillo lit a cigar and exhaled a thick cloud of acrid black smoke. "That's the only way to take this job. If you don't, you wind up dead."

Albin wrinkled his nose. *"Damn!* What are you *smoking?* Camel shit?"

"Not you, too?"

"Whaddaya mean?"

"Nothing." He pushed himself away from the bar and stood up. "George, thanks for meeting me." He tossed a card with a telephone number on it onto the bar. "If you hear anything about Colombians looking to do a deal, any kind of deal, with Americans, let me know."

Albin remained seated. "Sure, Don. If I hear anything, I'll call you."

He watched Castillo walk toward the door. Even his posture—broad shoulders, slightly hunched forward—suggested a man relentlessly stalking a prey. There was no question in Albin's mind that Castillo was pushing the envelope and was close to burnout. The question was how soon and what form it would take. Albin knew there were many kinds; he'd seen most of them firsthand. One was early retirement—a relatively benign form. Then there was booze—and sometimes drugs. But a more dangerous form of burnout manifested itself in what Albin called the Avenging Angel syndrome. Sometimes a man became so overwhelmed by what he saw that he was forced to reduce the conflict to its simplest terms: him against them. In this black and white world, laws and rules were seen as impediments to defeating the adversary. The avenging angel became a guided missile, seeking out his target to the exclusion of everything else. The only question was whether he would destroy himself before he destroyed someone else.

George Albin remembered the look in Castillo's eyes; he shuddered, and ordered another beer.

It was just after six P.M. by the time Chris Liberti got home. She was exhausted, but feeling very satisfied with herself. She'd spent a hectic day procuring a helicopter and, with the assistance of an FBI photo technician, had shot a series of flyover photographs of the area Fleming had identified.

It was almost seven-fifteen by the time she finished dinner—a huge Caesar salad and a glass of white wine—when the telephone rang.

She hit the Mute button and Jim Lehrer fell silent.

"Chris? Peter Blessing."

Chris sucked in her breath involuntarily. It had been almost two years since she'd heard that voice. "Peter. What a surprise. Where are you?"

"The Carlyle. I'm in town for a conference."

Her heart had begun to pound. "How'd you get my phone number?"

"I took a chance and called the New York office. You assigned here now?"

"Just temporarily."

"Anything exciting?"

"No. I'm helping the locals set up a computer network."

"I see. Chris, how about having dinner with me tonight?"

A knot in her stomach tightened. "I've just finished eating."

His laugh was still the same. "Have you learned to cook since I last saw you?"

In spite of her uneasiness she had to smile at the recollection. The first time she'd made dinner for him had been a disaster. The filet mignon came out looking like charred hockey pucks, the vegetables were cooked to a soggy pulp, and the dessert—some kind of French cream puffs—refused to inflate like the color photographs in the cookbook.

"Yes, I have." She eyed the remains of the Caesar salad. "As a matter of fact I've just made myself a wonderful dinner."

"Then how about dessert? I'd really like to see you," he said in a tone of voice that had more than once persuaded her to do something she hadn't wanted to do.

She twisted the telephone cord. "I don't think so, Peter. I—"

"Chris, I'm only in town for the night. Dessert and coffee. That's all."

She bit her lip. "No," she said more firmly. "I've got an early appointment tomorrow."

"Oh, I see." He sounded genuinely hurt. But, as she recalled, he never did handle rejection well.

After she hung up she refilled her glass, sat down on the couch, and recalled the first time she'd met Peter Blessing.

When she'd walked into the conference room of the U.S. attorney general's office and seen him, she'd thought he was the most beautiful man she'd ever met. Tall, with blond hair and dark green eyes, and dressed in a well-tailored three-piece suit, he looked as if he had stepped off the cover of *GQ*.

He stood up and shook her hand. "Agent Liberti, Peter Blessing. It seems we'll be working on this case for quite a while." Then, his green eyes gazing at her, he added, "I'm looking forward to it."

For the first time in her thirty-two years, Chris Liberti, the outspoken girl from Brooklyn, was speechless. She mumbled a reply and buried her face in her briefcase.

Later, she'd often wondered if she'd been attracted to him because he was so different from the boys and men she'd grown up with. Back in Brooklyn she'd known a lot of men named Pete, but none who called themselves Peter. Maybe the Roman numeral—III—at the end of his name had something to do with it. He'd graduated from Harvard Law in the top ten percent of his class, and although his father was a senior partner in a prestigious Boston law firm, to her delight Peter had chosen to go into public service.

During the long months of case preparation and the subsequent trial, they'd become friends, and eventually and inevitably, lovers. Soon, Peter began to talk about marriage, and for an idyllic while, it seemed very possible—until the weekend in Boston when she met his parents. They'd been very kind, actually too solicitous: Chris felt like a kid from the slums sent to the country for the weekend by the Fresh Air Fund. She had the uncomfortable feeling that his parents looked upon her as some sort of strange social experiment their son was dabbling in; interesting, but nothing to be taken seriously. What was more disturbing was that his mother, pencil thin, looked as though she'd never set foot in a kitchen in her life. On the other hand, *her* mother looked as though she'd never set foot *out* of the kitchen. There was no way these two could have anything in common, nor, she thought sadly, she and Peter.

That tension-filled weekend tilted their relationship subtly, but permanently, off its axis.

Her transfer to Atlanta offered a respite from the emotional pressures she was feeling. For a while there were the daily telephone calls and frequent weekend visits, but the distance between cities became too much of an obstacle and the affair quietly died out.

Now, staring at the muted TV and swirling a warm glass of chablis, those doubts, which she'd so successfully suppressed, resurfaced. Was it their vastly different backgrounds that had caused her to turn away or had she seen him as an impediment to her career?

From the day she'd walked through the doors of the FBI Academy at Quantico, she'd had just one goal: to rise to the top. Curious by nature and athletic by inclination, she'd been a natural. She graduated second in academics and fourth in physical training. In the intervening years she'd made the most out of every assignment offered to her. And now, if she, Dan Morgan, and Donal Castillo were successful in stopping Puño Blanco, her career aspirations would be assured.

"So why," she said aloud to the empty room, "do I feel so rotten?"

She pressed the Mute button and let MacNeill's question to the Secretary of Labor stop her from answering her own question.

Later that night, as she lay in bed staring at the ceiling, another strange, bewildering thought occurred to her. All the while she'd been thinking about Peter, she'd been comparing him to Dan Morgan. Dan didn't have the looks, the ambition, or certainly the wealth, but he had something that Peter Blessing couldn't buy with all his family's money: compassion and gentleness. She'd seen it the first day in the garment district office: a genuine sadness when he spoke about the deaths of those police officers. And she'd seen it when he talked about his son.

Before she dropped off to sleep, she had a thought that was both disturbing and pleasant: If given the chance, she'd willingly trade a million Peter Blessings for one Dan Morgan.

Chapter
18

The Grape n' Grain Bar and Grill, located a few convenient blocks from the Midtown South station house, was the cops' hangout of choice. It was the place where they assembled to celebrate promotions, transfers, and retirements and for the occasional bachelor party.

The food wasn't exceptional, but neither were the prices, and *that* was a real plus in an area of the city where food tabs resembled the national budgets of some third-world countries.

When the Midtown South cops threw a racket at the Grape n' Grain, they were chased upstairs so they wouldn't scare the regular diners. At the top of a rickety flight of stairs was a long narrow room dubbed the Holding Pen by a precinct wag. With its beer-stained rug, which had long since lost its color, and garish wallpaper that might have been stolen from an old New Orleans whorehouse, it wasn't much to look at. But it offered all the essential equipment. Half the length of the room was taken up by a ring-stained oak bar. The rest of the available space was crowded with round wooden folding tables. There was no space for dancing because there were only two pastimes acceptable to the cops using the room: stand at the bar and drink or sit at the tables and drink.

The reason for tonight's festivities was the retirement of Charlie Hultz, the precinct's administrative lieutenant. The room was packed to capacity not because of Charlie Hultz—the cops unanimously loathed the nit-picking, paper-pushing, pain-in-the-ass administrator —but because his retirement offered an excuse for cops to have a few drinks away from civilians, judges, lawyers, wives, and, now that female cops were attending these affairs, husbands.

Dan Morgan intentionally arrived at the Grape n' Grain late because he wanted to avoid the other bosses who were bound to ask probing questions about his sudden transfer to the PC's Office. Having attended these parties for the last twenty years, he'd noticed an interesting phenomenon: an inverse ratio existed between drunken cops and sober ranking officers. The reason for this phenomenon was understandable. Drunken cops sometimes did foolish things that were in violation of the department's *Patrol Guide*—if not the penal laws of New York State. So it was in a ranking officer's best interest, careerwise, not to be a witness to such transgressions.

It was just after two A.M. when Dan Morgan opened the door and walked into the smoke-filled Holding Pen. He immediately spotted Deputy Inspector Frank Statton, sitting alone at a table, looking very unhappy. The only reason Statton was still there was because as the new commanding officer he was expected to stick around and be one of the guys. Unfortunately, Statton, who'd spent most of his career in a string of uninteresting assignments in One Police Plaza, had never been one of the boys and never would be. When he looked up and saw Dan Morgan, he smiled for the first time all evening.

Someone shoved a beer bottle in Morgan's hand as he made his way across the crowded room shaking hands and trading quips with a dozen men. He sat down next to the deputy inspector. "How's the party going, Frank?"

"All right, I guess." Statton glanced at his watch and shook his head. "Jesus, it's only two o'clock. How long do you think I have to stay here?"

Morgan looked around the empty table. Frank Statton's half-finished glass of ginger ale was the only one on the table. "I'd say you've done your time."

Statton looked relieved. "Yeah? Ya think so?"

Morgan nodded.

Statton glanced around nervously. "I got a good scare a couple of minutes ago," he said in a confidential whisper. "I saw a few guys clearing a space around the tables at the other end of the room. I thought the sons of bitches were going to bring in a topless dancer again. I warned them last week. *No* goddamn topless dancers." He shook his head remembering the repercussions from a caper that had entered into the folklore of the precinct. A few years earlier a topless dancer had performed at a promotion party. Later in the evening, four drunken cops and an equally inebriated dancer had attempted to re-create Lady Godiva's ride—on Eighth Avenue with a mounted cop's horse.

"They're probably getting ready for the crap game," Morgan said.

That explanation made Frank Statton look even more uneasy. The new precinct commander regarded Morgan with sunken, hollow eyes. "You can't trust these crazy bastards. Jesus, Dan, you spent a *year* here. How'd you do it?"

Before Morgan could answer, the door was kicked open and a wild

178   MICHAEL
        GRANT

shrieking sound filled the smoke-filled, stagnant air. Standing in the doorway was Parnell O'Flaherty, resplendent in the kilt of the department's Emerald Society Pipe Band. The obese cop, looking like a Yugo in a plaid skirt, strode into the room to the skirl of bagpipes. Oblivious to the handful of napkins, stirrers, and bottle caps bouncing off his high black fur hat, he solemnly marched in half-step down the length of the bar, playing a tune recognizable only to himself.

Statton put his head in his hands. "Christ, I hate bagpipes. It has a real bad effect on drunken cops."

Just as O'Flaherty was nearing the end of the bar, Sal Petracco, O'Flaherty's radio car partner, lifted the piper's kilt and grabbed a handful of his left cheek. Startled, O'Flaherty squeezed the bag under his arm, and the music, dissolving into a discordant shriek, sounded like a flock of geese flying into a brick wall. O'Flaherty, spinning around to see who had violated him, slipped on the beer-wet floor and fell on his kilt with a resounding crash. Enraged, he came off the floor with fire in his eyes. "You ginny *bastard*," he howled.

Petracco, doubled over with laughter, didn't see O'Flaherty swing the bagpipes. The skin bag, whacking the side of Petracco's head, bleated like a sheep in extremis. Before either man could do any serious damage to the other, several cops pulled them apart.

Dan Morgan, who had jumped up to stop the fight, turned toward Frank Statton with a grin, but the inspector was gone.

"Hey, boss, how you doin'?"

It was David Sanchez and his eyes were bright and glassy.

"Pretty good, David. How'd you make out with the president in court?"

The young cop's face darkened. "It's all bullshit." Morgan noticed the young cop was slurring his words. "They let him cop to dis con. He walked with a twenty-five-dollar fine. Ain't that some shit? He tries to punch out *my* fuckin' lights and they call it dis con. There ain't no fuckin' justice in this city."

Jimmy Raven, a PBA delegate, slid up beside Morgan. "Hey,

boss," he said, leading Morgan away from the morose cop, "let me buy you a drink."

Little Marge O'Neil, dwarfed behind the big oak bar, stuck out a wet hand. "Inspector Morgan, good to see you, son. What are you having?"

Morgan held up his empty beer bottle. "Another one of these, Marge."

Born and raised in Hell's Kitchen, Marge O'Neil—purported to be the oldest barmaid in New York City—always tended bar for the precinct's rackets. Last year a precinct cop reported that his *grand-father* remembered being served by her when he was a rookie in 1927. Marge never denied the rumor.

She handed Morgan a dripping bottle. "It's good to see you, love. But you don't want to hang around too long." She nodded in the direction of the cops lining the bar. "This lot is getting ready to cut loose." She looked past Morgan. "I see Frank Statton hightailed it out of here. He's smarter than he looks."

Raven raised his glass in salute. "Thank God the hump finally took the hint and went home."

Morgan wrapped his wet bottle in a napkin. "You guys not getting along with him?"

"About as well as Saddam Hussein and the Kurds. I wish you were back here, boss."

Morgan was beginning to wish the same thing, but he said, "Once he gets used to the precinct, he'll calm down."

Raven made a face. "Inspector, I know you gotta back another boss, but let's face it. Frank Statton is a Plazanoid. He should be in command of a platoon of photocopy machines in One Police Plaza, not *real* cops."

Just then an argument broke out at the other end of the bar between a radio car team.

"Listen, schmuck," Linda Booth, a diminutive brunette said. "You're not bringing a thirteen-shot nine-millimeter into *my* radio car."

Jack Vincent, a thin, blond-haired kid with acne, steadied himself on the barstool. "Whaddaya mean *your* car?" he demanded.

"Watch my lips. N-O. The only one you'll manage to shoot with that thing is *me*."

"Bullshit, Linda. I'm a good shot. I always do better than you at the range."

"That's not saying much," a voice from the other end of the bar shouted. "She hasn't got the strength to hold the gun up for more than one round at a time."

She flicked her middle finger in the general direction of the voice. "Up yours, pal," she said, and renewed her attack on her partner, who was beginning to list to port. "What do you need all that fire-power for, anyway?"

"Don't you read the goddamn papers? Three cops have been killed. I wanna be able to protect myself. That a goddamn crime or what?"

At the mention of the murdered police officers, the room became silent. Tom Johanson, who at forty-seven was the oldest radio car cop in the precinct, leaned forward and looked down the bar toward Vincent. "Hey, Jack," he said. "I read the papers too. Those cops didn't have a chance to defend themselves. You can carry a Patriot missile if you want, but it ain't gonna protect you from a bomb or an assassin's bullet."

"Maybe so, but I want a little more firepower than the friggin' peashooters the department makes us carry."

A heavyset black cop with a wide grin put his hand on Vincent's shoulder. "Well, I don't want you backing me with a nine pointed at *my* ass, Jack. You're as jumpy as a Waterford crystal collector living in Southern California."

Vincent shrugged the hand off his shoulder. "Well, fuck you, then. The next time you get a gun run, I won't back you up."

Johanson stood up. The easygoing smile was gone. "Jack," he said evenly, "if I thought it wasn't the booze talking, I'd knock your ass right off that bar stool. I don't care what the *Patrol Guide* says and I don't care what the PC says. We *always* back each other up. Got that."

Vincent waved a hand in Johanson's direction. "Don't get your balls in an uproar. I know."

The tense silence was broken by Sal Petracco. "I hate to say it," he said, "but I think we could use a little music. Hey, O'Flaherty, play something on that sack o' banshees, will ya?"

O'Flaherty, who was sulking in the corner, looked up from his beer. "I won't play *shit* for you, greaseball."

Petracco looked toward the ceiling and sighed. *"Marone.* This donkey bastard is worse than my old lady. All right already, I'm sorry I grabbed yer ass."

"That's not what he's mad about." Vincent thumped the bar. "He wants you to do it again."

In the ensuing laughter, Morgan turned to Raven. "The troops jumpy about the murders?"

Raven rolled his eyes. "Yeah. A lot of them are beginning to pack heavy artillery. I just hope some poor civilian doesn't get pumped with thirty pounds of lead by mistake."

"What's the PBA think about all this?"

Raven trusted Morgan, but not enough to talk about a PBA-sponsored job action. "Let's just say that a lot of delegates are putting the screws to Renzi. They want to see some union action."

Morgan was expecting it, but he didn't like hearing Raven give voice to his own fears. "Carrying unauthorized weapons isn't the answer," he said.

"Boss, *I* know that and *you* know that, but try telling that to a cop who thinks he's a target every time he straps a radio car to his ass. These guys are scared and I don't blame them."

"Neither do I," Morgan said, studying his bottle.

He pushed the unfinished bottle away and stood up. He'd come here to find out what cops were thinking and he had. He waved to Marge and shook a few more hands as he headed for the exit. Suddenly a droning tone, sounding like an air raid siren, filled the air. At the other end of the bar O'Flaherty was warming up his bagpipes. A grinning Sal Petracco, friends with his partner again, put his arm around O'Flaherty's broad shoulders. "Hey, pardner," he said, "can you play any *real* songs on this octopus?"

"Like what?"

"I don't know. Somethin' good. How 'bout the theme from *The Godfather*?"

As Morgan went down the stairs, he heard the first strains of "Danny Boy" on the bagpipes and, for the first time all day, smiled.

Chapter
19

7:30 A.M. SATURDAY, MARCH 30 • After stopping at the FBI's Tech Services first, Chris Liberti came into the office waving a large white bag. "I found a terrific French bakery in Soho," she announced. "Their croissants are made with whole grain wheat. Wait'll you taste them."

Morgan tossed a folder aside. "What are you so happy about?"

"Just this." With a theatrical flourish, she pulled a set of photos from her briefcase and tossed a set to Morgan and Castillo. "Aerial reconnaissance: courtesy of the FBI."

Castillo squinted at the photos. "Anything look promising?"

"Yep. Three areas. I've circled them in red."

Morgan, impressed with the speed with which she'd gotten the helicopter and the photos, studied his set. They'd been taken from about three hundred feet and the resolution was excellent. The problem was the trees. The dirt roads were clear, but once the road ran into the tree line it was difficult to see what was under it. "You do good work," he said. "We gotta get out there right away. Can you and Don—"

"Can't," the DEA agent said, looking up from a photograph. "I'm meeting a CIA agent at Kennedy this afternoon for an update on Puño Blanco."

Morgan turned to Liberti. "Okay, it's you and me. Let's go." Just as they were leaving, Morgan received a forthwith telephone call from the PC's office. He rushed over to One Police Plaza and spent the rest of the morning and part of the afternoon waiting for the police commissioner to return from *his* forthwith to the mayor's office.

It was just after three P.M. when Tom Cassidy, his face flushed, stormed off the elevator. Morgan was shocked at the man's appearance. Cassidy looked tired, but his famous temper was intact. The commissioner snatched the stack of telephone messages offered to him by his secretary and brusquely waved Morgan into the office.

He sat down heavily and tossed the messages on the desk. "I just got the reaming of my life," he whispered hoarsely.

Morgan, thinking it best not to say anything, simply nodded.

Cassidy pointed a thick finger at his deputy inspector. "I told you time was a problem. Well, we might have run out of time."

Morgan sat forward. "Why?"

"Golden's murder may have been the final straw. Rebellion has started in the ranks. Last night a radio car team in the Seven-seven balked at responding to a gun run without a backup. The sergeant ordered them to go, and when they didn't, the duty captain sus-

185   **Officer DOWN**

pended them. When word of *that* got out, others started going sick. Last night's late tour was only fifty-one percent of minimum manning. Operations had to fly cops in from Queens to fill the void. Some smart-ass son of a bitch cop called a Queens councilman and told him the Police Department was stripping his borough. The councilman immediately called the mayor." As Cassidy related his story his face got redder and purple veins were jumping in his neck. "I've just spent the last hour explaining to the mayor why I left the borough of Queens without cops all night."

"Does the mayor know about Puño Blanco?" Morgan asked.

"Jesus, no. Even if Coffey said it was all right, I wouldn't tell that dumb bastard. If he knew about Puño Blanco, he'd have the governor calling out the goddamn National Guard."

Cassidy leaned forward and lowered his voice. "The mayor doesn't know the half of it. The night before another cop was suspended for carrying an unauthorized rifle in his radio car. Then four cops in the Three-oh responded to a report of shots fired and broke the doors down in three apartments looking for the gunman." Cassidy wrenched his tie loose. "It wasn't even a gun for chrissake. It was a couple of firecrackers."

He looked down at his desk and snatched up a message. Morgan noticed a half-finished pack of Tums on the desk. "Look at this. Renzi wants to see me about a matter of grave importance." He crumpled the message and threw it in his wastebasket. "Renzi's gotta be feeling the pressure."

"Think he'll cause a problem?"

"Damn right. I'm convinced the PBA isn't behind these sporadic incidents, but if another cop is killed, the PBA will pull a job action. I don't know what kind, but it's a certainty it'll screw up this city." Cassidy popped a Tums in his mouth. "If Renzi gets even a whiff of Puño Blanco, he'll go to the papers and blow the issue wide open."

"Renzi wouldn't do that. I'm sure he'd come to you first. Once you'd explained the need for secrecy, he'd go along with it."

"No he wouldn't. You're a good cop, Morgan, but you don't know a damn thing about politics. Renzi wouldn't have a choice. He's got a

186   MICHAEL
       GRANT

handful of ball-breaking delegates who would love to have his job. If they found out about Puño Blanco, and his knowledge of it, *they'd* expose it and make it look like Renzi was in the department's hip pocket. He couldn't get elected dog catcher after that. No, Renzi's stuck between a rock and a hard place. If the PBA finds out about Puño Blanco, it'll be headlines. What I said earlier about time constraints is now doubly true."

Morgan felt a dull throb starting in his temples. As if things weren't bad enough, he thought, now he had to worry about the PBA finding out about Puño Blanco before he could make an arrest.

Cassidy sat back and pinched the bridge of his nose. "Dan, if another cop is killed, I'm thinking of issuing a memo about Puño Blanco."

Morgan was caught off guard by the commissioner's about-face. "You can't do that," he blurted.

Cassidy tried a smile. "It seems I remember you sitting in that chair just about a week ago and telling me I *had* to tell them."

"I was wrong. I know that now. If we expose Puño Blanco's plans, they'll disappear. But the next time they pop up we may know nothing about it until it's too late."

Cassidy's red-rimmed eyes studied Morgan. "We don't know a damn thing about them now."

Morgan hesitated. He'd wanted to have the garbage bag in his hands and a confirmation of prints before he told the PC, but Cassidy needed some good news. "Sir, we may have a real lead on Puño Blanco." He told Cassidy about his plan to look for the garbage bag.

The news had a quieting effect on the commissioner. "So what's next?" he asked.

"Liberti and I are on our way out to Long Island to look for the site. If we find that bag, we may be able to lift prints."

Cassidy slammed his beefy hand on the desk. "Well, stop sitting around here and get going."

Morgan stood up. "Sir, about that memo—"

Cassidy scowled. "I'll rethink it."

As Morgan was going out the door, he heard Cassidy tell his

secretary to get Renzi on the telephone. Hearing the weariness in the voice, Morgan's dream of one day being the police commissioner suddenly seemed more like another nightmare.

Donal Castillo, who was sitting facing the door, saw the man come in and speak to the hostess. She pointed to Castillo's table and the DEA agent watched as the short, nondescript man with thick horn-rimmed glasses picked his way around chairs and carry-on bags. Dressed in a slightly baggy suit, he looked more like a harried businessman than an employee of the Central Intelligence Agency.

"Kenneth Harrison," he said, slipping into a banquette seat opposite Castillo.

Castillo returned the firm handshake. "What time does your connecting flight leave?"

"Thirty minutes."

"You want coffee?"

Harrison grimaced. "I've had all the airline coffee I can stomach for one day."

Castillo got right to the point of the meeting. "Anything new on Puño Blanco?"

Harrison took off his thick glasses and rubbed them with a napkin. Without the glasses his eyes were big and soft, like a child's. "Our analysts in Langley are almost certain that the people you're looking for are ex-military types."

"Why?"

"The cartels have a history of using ex-military assets. In the past the Medellin cartel has hired ex-SAS Brits and ex-Israeli commandos to train their enforcement units."

"No shit. Could any of them be involved with Puño Blanco?"

"Negative. We've been watching them very closely."

"We think we're on to some Special Forces people," Castillo said quietly.

Harrison didn't seem surprised by that revelation. "There are any number of highly qualified ex-military men willing to do anything for money. It stands to reason that Special Forces personnel are more than qualified for the assignment. Besides," he added, "renegade Special Forces people are nothing new. Since the early eighties, we've been tracking ex–Special Forces people who have used the southeast desert area of Arizona to train foreign terrorists in the use of explosives and weapons."

Castillo was surprised to hear that foreign terrorists were being trained on American soil. He wondered how much more the poker-faced man from the CIA knew. He suspected Harrison had been instructed to tell Castillo only what was absolutely necessary. It was typical of federal agencies like the CIA: ask questions, but provide as little information as possible.

Castillo leaned forward. "Harrison, the theories of a bunch of desk jockeys at Langley are interesting, but do you have anything more specific than that?"

Harrison carefully replaced his glasses. "I'm afraid I don't. As you know our operative's cover was blown. Since then the cartel has been taking extraordinary measures to prevent further infiltration. More than a few unfortunate souls have been murdered on the basis of mere suspicion."

Castillo suspected that the mild-mannered man sitting opposite him had, like himself, spent a lot of time in Colombia. But their professional interests were very different. To Castillo Colombia was narcotics, drug dealers, money, and supply lines. From his political perch Harrison saw the country in terms of a larger geopolitical picture. Castillo needed to know more about Harrison's view.

"I know a lot about the Medellin cartel," Castillo said. "But I don't have a good handle on how or why they've teamed up with terrorist organizations. How can they work together? Aren't their political philosophies incompatible?"

Harrison, delighted by the opportunity to explain political events in Colombia, leaned forward and rested his elbows on the table. "Ultimately they are," he said. "The cartels want a government cowed by corruption and fear, while the terrorists want to overthrow the existing government and see a new order created. But they've put ideology aside, because right now it's to their advantage to work together. At least for the time being.

Officer DOWN

"To appreciate the political climate in Colombia now, you have to understand something of what's happened in the past few years. The most spectacular example of narco-terrorism occurred in 1985 when M-19 guerrillas attacked the Palace of Justice in Bogotá and held three hundred people—including fifty Supreme Court judges—hostage. The army, angered because of the government's indecision, attacked the palace with tanks and troops. When the smoke cleared, over a hundred people were dead, including all the judges, and all the guerrillas. The Medellin drug cartel paid M-19 four million dollars for that job."

Castillo recalled reading about the incident, but it had happened before he'd gotten to Colombia. "What was the reason for the attack?" he asked.

"The court was preparing extradition proceedings against several important drug lords who wanted those records destroyed. As you know, the only thing these people are afraid of is extradition. They know that if they're extradited to the United States they're looking at long prison terms. These people are used to getting what they want. In the past few years alone, the cartel has been responsible for the assassinations of a presidential candidate, an attorney general, a minister of justice, fifty judges, a couple of damn good journalists, and God knows how many hundreds of cops and peasants who were killed because they were in the wrong place at the wrong time.

"Incidentally, exporting terrorism isn't without precedent. A few years ago the FBI arrested three Colombians in New York City who were in possession of electronic remote-control detonating devices. They'd been sent by the Medellin cartel to assassinate the mayor and the head of your New York office. Then in 1986 a Chicago gang called El Rukns was arrested. They were looking for a contract from the Libyan government. When they were apprehended, they had a lethal pile of weapons—grenades, rocket launchers, machine guns equipped with silencers, and handguns. Then in 1988 Yu Kikumura, a member of the Japanese Red Army Group, was arrested in New Jersey for carrying explosives. He was planning to blow up buildings in New York City on the anniversary of the U.S. raid on Libya."

Castillo remembered the cases, but hearing Harrison's summary, it occurred to him that narco-terrorism on American soil wasn't a new idea. It had been tried before; it just hadn't been successful.

Harrison continued. "Those were the few cases that hit the media, but the FBI—with our assistance," he added with a touch of smugness—"has interdicted a lot more that the public never heard about. The point is, Mr. Castillo, these drug lords have so much money, power, and autonomy in other parts of the world, that they believe they're invincible."

Castillo was impressed with the CIA agent's recital of events in Colombia. He was familiar with most of what Harrison had told him, but he hadn't thought of it in that context.

The CIA agent looked at his watch. "Time to go. As soon as we have more intelligence, we'll let you know."

Castillo put a restraining hand on the man's arm. "Harrison," he said in a low, even tone, "time is something we don't have. There are only three of us beating the bushes looking for these sons of bitches. We need something concrete."

The CIA agent nodded sympathetically. "I know what you're going through, Mr. Castillo. Believe me, we're doing all we can to unearth more information."

From the genuine concern in the man's eyes, Castillo was convinced more than ever that Harrison was, or had been, a field agent in Colombia. "Okay," he said, releasing his grip on Harrison's arm, "I think we understand each other."

It was well after five P.M. by the time Morgan and Liberti arrived at the North Fork of Long Island. They found the first two sites quickly, but neither site showed any sign of having been used as a firing range.

Morgan turned back on Route 25 and switched on his parking lights. "Goddammit, it's gonna be dark soon. I hope we find the other location while there's still light."

Minutes later, Liberti, referring to the photos and a map, pointed to a dirt road up ahead. "There. That might be it."

Morgan turned onto the road. Even at five miles an hour the vehicle's bottom scraped the rut-filled surface. It grew darker as they drove deeper into the trees and Morgan flipped on his headlights. "I don't know if this is it," he said.

"It's gotta be this one," she said, with more hope than confidence. Seconds later, she leaned forward. "Look! There's a clearing up ahead."

Morgan pulled into the open space and turned off the engine. "Chris, there's a couple of flashlights in the glove compartment. Let's make this fast. It's getting dark."

Fanning out, they moved in a slow semicircle away from each other. In the murky light Morgan thought he saw a small hill about twenty-five yards into the trees. As he got closer the dim shape took form. It was indeed a pile of earth bulldozed about fifteen feet high.

It had now become so dark he had to turn on his flashlight to see. He knelt down and, upon closer examination, saw pockmarks in the earth where the bullets had slammed into the dirt. They'd found the site!

Just then Liberti screamed. Morgan jumped up and looked toward the direction of the scream, but he saw nothing. Yanking his gun out, he began to run toward the sound. About fifteen feet into the tree line, he stepped into a depression, tripped over a fallen log, and slid head first into a pile of leaves. The gun and flashlight tumbled into the underbrush.

Cursing, he groped in the darkness and quickly found the flashlight. But it wouldn't light. Forgetting his gun, he stumbled to his feet and continued on. "Where are you," he called out.

"Over here. Oh, he's so cute."

Cute? "*Where* is over here? I can't see you."

"By the big tree," she said softly. "Quiet, or you'll scare him."

Him? "Will you shine the goddamn flashlight this way so I can see where you are?"

A light beam from about twenty-five yards to his right hit him in the face, temporarily blinding him.

"Jeez, Dan, what happened to you?"

"I fell running to help *you.*"

"*I* don't need any help," she said indignantly.

"You—" He tripped over another branch and fell headlong into a bush. "Will you get that light out of my eyes? I can't see where I'm going."

He struggled to his feet. "Why did you scream?"

"This little guy scared me." She turned the light beam on a raccoon warily eyeing her from a tree stump.

With the light turned away from him Morgan couldn't see anything and promptly walked into a tree.

The light beam was back on him. "You're not much of a woodsman are you, Dan?" She could barely suppress the mirth in her voice.

Morgan sat in a pile of leaves and gingerly felt his forehead. No blood, but he had a bump the size of a walnut. "You're not exactly Shena, Queen of the Jungle yourself. Scared by a raccoon, for chrissake."

She came forward and helped him to his feet. "Hey, I'm a city girl. The only wildlife I've ever seen were roaches, rats, and guys wearing gold chains. You okay?"

He brushed the leaves from his pants. "No. I lost my goddamn gun back there."

"Uh-oh."

"Yeah, but at least I found the mound."

"And I found the wooden table. The stakes they used for skeet shooting are still in the ground."

Morgan took the flashlight from her and shined it down on his slacks. Bloodied knees showed through two jagged holes.

"Jeez, are you okay?"

"Yeah. Did you find the plastic bag?"

"Not yet."

Morgan wanted to go back and find his gun, but they only had one flashlight between them. "Come on," he said. "We'll look for the bag first, then I'll go back for my gun."

By now total darkness had descended upon them. Liberti led the way back to the wooden bench and showed Morgan the stakes in the ground.

Morgan shined the flashlight around the clearing. "They must have eaten around here somewhere." The light flickered, dimmed, and went out.

"Great," Liberti mumbled in the darkness.

Morgan thumped the recalcitrant flashlight, but it refused to come back on.

"Typical city quality," Liberti went on. "Do you guys buy *all* your equipment from army surplus?"

"Do you mind if we don't discuss the relative merits of city and federal government budgets right now?"

"So what do we do now?"

"We have the car. We'll use the headlights."

Back in the car, Morgan slowly moved the vehicle forward and backward while they both peered intently into the path of the headlight beam.

"Maybe it's not here, Dan. Maybe they took it with them."

"Maybe." He turned the wheel to the right and inched the car forward. There, just at the outer fringe of the headlights' glare, lay a lumpy plastic bag. They sat in silence staring at it for a moment. "Son of a bitch," Morgan whispered. "There it is."

He dragged the bag over to the car and, in the light of the headlights, carefully undid the tie. "Bingo!" he said peering inside. "Beer cans and Styrofoam cups."

Liberti looked at her watch. "Great. It's getting late. Let's get this stuff back to the city."

Morgan retied the bag. "Not until I find my gun."

"How are you going to find your gun in the dark without a flashlight?"

"I'm not leaving until I find it," he said evenly.

"But you're not *going* to find it. It's too dark."

"Go sit in the car. I'll only be a few minutes."

Liberti got in the car and slammed the door. She'd be damned if she'd help the stubborn jerk find a gun at night in the middle of the black forest.

When he wasn't back in twenty minutes, her anger gave way to concern. Maybe he'd fallen and hurt himself again or, worse, gotten lost. What an idiot. What was he doing running in the woods at night, anyway? Then it hit her. It was *her* fault. He'd been running toward her because she'd screamed.

Feeling guilty, she got out of the car and listened. Except for the occasional sound of unseen animals scurrying through the woods—a sound that gave her goose bumps—it was absolutely still. She strained to hear him crashing through the woods. Nothing.

Then someone touched her shoulder and she screamed for the second time tonight.

"Quiet," he whispered. "It's only me."

She spun around. "Don't you *ever* do that again."

"I'm sorry. I didn't know you were so jumpy."

She couldn't see his face, but she knew he was grinning. "I'm not. It's these damn woods. They give me the creeps. Did you find it?"

"No. I'll have to wait for daybreak."

"Are you nuts? *I'm* not staying here all night."

"Fine. Then take the car and go back. I'll grab a train tomorrow."

"And what do I tell Castillo? That I left you wandering around the woods looking for your gun?"

"Don't tell him that."

She detected a note of real concern in his voice. "Oh, and why not?"

"Chris, this is embarrassing enough. I'd appreciate it if you wouldn't tell anyone else about this."

"It was an accident. What's the big deal?"

"You wouldn't understand."

"What's *that* supposed to mean? Because I'm a woman I don't know anything about the mysterious ways of men? So you lost your gun. Big deal. Buy a new one."

They stood no more than three feet from each other, but in the dark they couldn't see each other's face. Liberti began to giggle. "This is ridiculous. I never realized how hard it is to have an argument with someone you can't see. What are you doing, Dan, smiling or frowning?"

"Neither. I'm trying to figure the best way to handle this."

"I know what we're going to do. We'll find a motel and be back here at first light."

Morgan started to protest, but she opened the door and got in the car. "Not another word or I'll tell everyone you lost your little gun."

Chapter
20

The season had not yet begun and most of the motels were closed. After driving around for almost an hour, Dan Morgan and Chris Liberti pulled into the parking lot of the Spindrift Lodge. Even in season it was unlikely that the dilapidated, windblown motel attracted much of a tourist clientele.

Liberti got out of the car and inspected the building with folded arms. "Jeez, this joint makes the Bates Motel look like the Plaza.

Dan, if they've got stuffed birds in that office, I'm sleeping in the car."

Morgan pointed at a half-lit neon sign. "Well, at least it overlooks ——ENIC LONG ISLAND SOUND. Or so the sign says." He opened the trunk and took the plastic bag out.

"What are you going to do with *that?*" Liberti asked.

"This is staying with me. Murphy's Law is working overtime today. With my luck some son of a bitch will steal the car."

"Dan, you can't bring that into the motel office."

"Watch."

Inside, the dimly lit office smelled of mildew. There was no one behind the desk, but they heard a muffled TV in the next room. Morgan tapped the bell and an elderly man, wearing a greasy cap that stated "Life's a Beach," stuck his head through the curtain. "Yeah, what do you want?"

"Do you have a room?" Morgan asked.

"Course I got a room. I got a whole motel full of rooms. Want one?"

"That's why we're here."

The man flipped open the guest register and asked the question he loved to ask couples. "One room or two?"

"Two," Morgan said.

"One," Liberti said simultaneously.

The old man let out an airy cackle. "Make up your minds, folks."

"We're only going to be here a little while," Liberti whispered. "Why not one room?"

"Two," Morgan said emphatically.

The old man, wondering what kind of antics required *two* rooms, squinted suspiciously at Morgan. "We don't rent by the hour, bub. Stay ten minutes or the whole night; same price."

As Morgan signed the register the old man inspected his disheveled guest. "Been in a motor vehicle accident, bub?" He pronounced the word *vee-HIcle.*

"No." Morgan didn't elaborate. He had no intention of explaining anything to this old geezer.

The man, still looking Morgan over, spotted the garbage bag at his

MICHAEL GRANT

feet and his eyes narrowed. "Don't allow no trash in my rooms, bub. Dumpster's out back."

Morgan stared into the man's watery eyes. "It isn't trash, bub. It's my luggage." Behind him, he heard Chris suppress a giggle.

The old man's eyes fluttered. He'd seen a lot of crazy things in his time, but a garbage bag for luggage was a new one. "Rooms are on the second floor," he said, disappearing into the back room.

Standing outside her door, Liberti looked at her watch and poked Morgan in the ribs. "Hey, bub, it's only nine and I'm starving. What do you say we find a wonderful seafood restaurant, get something to eat, have a couple of drinks, and maybe even dance?"

Morgan looked into her twinkling eyes and for a moment she reminded him of Sarah. She had the same zany sense of playfulness. It had been a long day. He was tired, hungry, and he could certainly use a drink. But then he looked down at his torn slacks. "I don't think so, Chris. Unless there's a fairy godmother waiting for me in my room with a new pair of slacks, I'll have to pass."

"Yeah, I guess you're right. Give me the keys to the car. The North Fork is full of seafood restaurants. I'll bring us back some lobster, steamers, and beer How does that sound?"

"Sounds great. I could use a drink."

While Liberti was gone, Morgan took a shower and brushed more leaves and twigs out of his clothing. It was almost an hour before a chagrined Liberti returned.

"What a *burg*!" she announced. "Everything is shut tighter than a crab's ass. I'm afraid this is it." She held up a greasy bag. "Burgers from the local diner. However, I did manage to find a deli." She held up a six-pack.

"The most important part of the meal," he said, relieving her of the beer. "It's a mild night. We can eat out on the patio overlooking scenic Long Island Sound."

Liberti stepped out onto the tiny deck, which indeed did have a wonderful view of the sound. A full moon, just beginning to peek over the horizon, trained a thin strip of shimmering light across the water. "Hey!" she said. "This isn't half bad."

Morgan opened two cans and gave her one. "We'll have to drink out of the can. The last occupants apparently absconded with the crystal." Then in a more serious tone he said, "I'm sorry to do this to you, Chris. I—"

"No apology necessary, sir. It's not every day a girl gets to stay at a fancy seaside resort."

She was about to sit down, but Morgan cautioned her. "Don't sit on that chair. The leg's broken."

She slid into another chair and clanked cans with him. "That's what I hate about antiques. They're so delicate."

"Yeah. Hey, did you mean what you said earlier about dancing?"

She ran her hand through her hair. "Sure. I'm such a romantic. I love to dance, especially to something slow and dreamy. How about you?"

"Two left feet. Lucky for you I had torn slacks."

She looked into his eyes. In spite of his smile, there was a sadness, the same sadness she'd seen the first time she'd met him in the police commissioner's office. "Maybe," she said. "Maybe not."

Morgan tore open the bag of fries and started to dump ketchup on them. "Hey," Liberti pushed his hand away. "Go easy on that stuff."

"You don't like ketchup?"

"It's no good for you. Full of sodium."

"You a health nut?"

"You make it sound like a disease."

"It's been my experience that most health nuts are fanatics."

"Why? Because we want to stay healthy? You should pay a little more attention to yourself, Dan. Look at you. You're pale, probably in lousy shape, and you drink way too much coffee."

Morgan grinned at her. "I'll try to do better, mom."

Liberti grinned back and pointed a soggy fry at him. "See what you've done? You scratch a health nut and you get an evangelist. But seriously, Dan, the shooting must have taken a lot out of you."

His smile vanished. "How did you know about that?"

"I . . . heard," she said evasively.

"Did you check me out?" he demanded.

"Oh, come on, Dan. Are you going to tell me you haven't checked me out?"

"No. I—" He saw her right eyebrow go up. "Okay, I happened to talk to a friend in the Bureau and he mentioned a few things. That's all."

"I heard you were hurt pretty badly," she said quietly.

Morgan popped a fry into his mouth. "To paraphrase Mark Twain, the reports of my injuries were greatly exaggerated." He handed her a burger, dripping grease. "I hope your health-conscious stomach can handle this."

"How did it happen?" She tried to make the question sound conversational.

Morgan put his burger down and his eyes took on a faraway look. Since the incident he'd spent every waking moment forcing the memory of that night from his mind, but the mere mention of the event was enough to drag him back into that hallway, inhaling the pungent smell of stale urine, seeing the peeling walls, and feeling the grit of the dirty tiles under his shoes. "I don't know what happened," he said. "That's the problem."

He fell silent and Liberti thought he wasn't going to say any more, but he continued. "I was a captain in Manhattan North Detectives. I went with a sergeant and two detectives to serve a murder warrant on a man named Willie Lawrence. We had information that he was hiding in his sister's apartment. When we were in position at both ends of the hallway, one of our people called Willie and told him the police were on the way."

"Good move. If it works, it flushes the target. It's easier to take him outside the apartment."

Morgan's jaw knotted. "Yeah, but it didn't go exactly as planned. Willie came out, but he was using his two nieces as shields."

"Oh my God! How old were they?"

"Four and six. We couldn't shoot." Morgan stopped talking and stared out across the black water.

"What happened next?" she asked softly.

"Everything happened so fast it was all a blur. One of the detectives at the other end of the hallway—a kid named Fredericks—stepped out into the open. I don't know why he did that. I saw Lawrence point the gun at him and I yelled to distract Lawrence." A tightness constricted his throat and he stopped talking. He didn't want to go on, but in spite of his anguish it felt good to finally tell someone.

"I'm not sure what happened next," he continued. "There was a flurry of shots. Fredericks and I were hit. In the confusion the other guys grabbed Lawrence. It was over in seconds."

"Did you shoot at Lawrence?"

Morgan's voice was barely audible. "There was one round fired from my gun, but I don't remember firing it."

"What happened to Detective Fredericks?"

Morgan paled. "He died on the operating table."

Chris Liberti saw the agony in Morgan's eyes, but she asked the question anyway. "Whose bullet killed him?"

In a monotone Morgan recited the facts as though he'd memorized them. "Inconclusive. Lawrence and I were both firing thirty-eights. There was a total of four shots fired. Lawrence fired three and I fired one. One round struck Fredericks, another round lodged in the wall behind him, the third round lodged in the ceiling above Lawrence's head, and the fourth one hit me. All four rounds were distorted on impact and rendered useless for ballistics comparison. Because of the loose plaster in the wall and ceiling, they couldn't even plot the angle of entry."

She put her hand on his. "And you think you killed Officer Fredericks."

Morgan pulled his hand away. "I don't know. I wish to God I knew one way or the other."

She pulled her hand back self-consciously. "Was there an investigation?"

"Yeah. There was a full investigation and I was exonerated. The sergeant testified that Fredericks was hit with the first bullet fired by Lawrence. But all the shots were fired so quickly, I'm not so sure he'd be able to tell." Morgan's tone was ironic. "They even gave me a medal."

MICHAEL GRANT

"God, what an experience. Have you gotten any help for this, Dan?"

Morgan grunted. "I don't need help. This is something I have to work out for myself."

"That's crazy. You can't work out something like this because you suppress everything, and the only thing left is guilt."

Morgan managed a smile. "You sound like a shrink."

"I've had some experience with this sort of thing," she said quietly.

Morgan found himself studying her lovely face and looked away. "I hear you did some undercover work on the Mafia."

"Chicago." She ran her fingers through her hair. "Apparently I was too successful. The don's son fell in love with me. We'd almost wrapped up the investigation when someone blew the whistle on me. I was having dinner with a couple of crooked attorneys when he found me. I didn't know my cover had been blown. But when I saw the look in his eyes as he walked toward the table, I knew something was terribly wrong. Suddenly, without warning, he pulled a gun and started shooting. I don't know if it was because he was a terrible shot or he was blind with rage, but he missed me. My backups killed him."

Staring at this small attractive woman, Dan Morgan still found it hard to believe that she was an FBI agent. "Did you see a shrink?" he asked.

"Yes. I was in a real bad depression. I felt responsible." She smiled sadly. "Even Mafia guys can be nice when they're not breaking legs."

"Did the counseling work?"

"Yes, but it took a while. I'm still terribly sad that he had to die, but I no longer feel responsible for him."

Morgan dabbed a french fry in a puddle of ketchup. "I'll work it out too."

"Dan, don't try to work this out alone. It's too dangerous."

He looked up. "What do you mean?"

"I know what you're going through. You have all this guilt bottled up inside you. Until you learn that you're not responsible for every cop's life, you're not going to get over this shooting incident. As a matter of fact in your shaky frame of mind you could be a danger to yourself."

"How?"

"If you get into another shooting incident, you might hesitate— and that could cost you your life. You might even sacrifice your own life; purposely put yourself in the line of fire in order to expiate your guilt."

Morgan gazed out over the water. "You've spent too much time with the shrinks. I'll be okay."

They finished their meal in gloomy silence and when they were done, Liberti noticed Morgan kept glancing at his watch. She stuffed the wrappings in the bag and stood up. "I guess it's time to call it a night."

"Yeah, we gotta get up early. I'll pound on your wall when it's time."

At the door she said, "Don't worry about the gun, Dan. We'll find it."

"I know." He scratched the stubble on his chin. "Twenty-five years on the job and I never even lost a pencil. Now this."

Standing there in his torn slacks, he looked like a little boy who had lost his favorite toy. Without thinking, Liberti reached up and tousled his hair. "It'll be okay." Surprised and embarrassed by her behavior, she quickly closed the door behind her and went to her room.

Morgan opened another beer and went back out on the deck. Staring out at the inky black water he began to think about Sarah. When they were first married, they'd spent several weekends a year out at Montauk, just walking along the quiet, sandy beaches and discovering new restaurants. But then Danny was born, and they never seemed to find the time. How many times had he promised Sarah they'd come back here? But now he'd lost her and there would be no more weekends. He crumpled the empty can and violently threw it into the wastebasket.

Around four-thirty Chris Liberti awoke with a start. Was that a shout she'd heard or was she dreaming? Wrapping a blanket around her, she opened the patio sliding door and peeked out. The moon had risen high in the sky and a light breeze ruffled the mirrorlike water below.

Morgan, wrapped in a bedspread, was sitting in a chair staring out at the water.

"Dan, can't you sleep?"

He turned so abruptly she was afraid she'd awakened him.

"Huh? Oh, no. I don't sleep well in strange beds."

"I don't mind the bed, it's the smell I can't take. I think the last occupant slept with a sack of flounders. Dan, did you hear something a minute ago? Like a shout?"

Morgan shook his head.

"I must have been dreaming." She pulled the blanket tightly about her. "Can I come over?"

Morgan nodded and pushed a chair toward her with his foot. She climbed over the short wall separating the two decks and sat down. "Isn't this a beautiful night?" she said, tucking her legs under her and looking at the canopy of shimmering stars overhead. "I think us city folk miss a lot. You can't enjoy a night like this in a tenement."

"What part of Brooklyn?"

"Bensonhurst. How'd you—?"

"A wild guess."

"My accent? Funny, I don't hear it."

"Take my word for it." Morgan shook his head. "Bensonhurst! Half the wiseguys in the city come from Bensonhurst. Where did you get the idea to become an FBI agent?"

"In college. I was going to be a teacher, but the thought of being hassled by a bunch of screaming, runny-nosed kids for the rest of my life changed my mind. I wanted something different. Something exciting."

"So you chose the Bureau."

"Yep." She looked closely at him. In spite of the cool night air his forehead was bathed in perspiration. "Dan, are you all right?"

"Yeah." He wiped his forehead with the edge of the bedspread. "I forgot to open a window. The room was stuffy. Where have you worked?"

She ran her hand through her hair and it quickly bounced back into place. "I've been in the Bureau for twelve years. Did some time in Chicago, Atlanta, and Miami. In case you're wondering, I'm thirty-four."

Morgan caught himself staring at her thousand-watt smile. "You look a lot younger. Oops. Is that a sexist comment?"

"That's all right. I'll let it pass this time, bub."

"You like the Bureau?"

"I love it. I intend to be the first female ADIC in New York."

His eyebrows went up. "Assistant director-in-charge of the New York office. You don't kid around, do you?"

She tried to read the expression in his eyes. Was it admiration or incredulity? She decided the latter. "You don't like women in police work, do you?"

He was about to deny it, but instead he said, "No, I don't. Nothing personal, Chris, but I don't think women should work in a job where their lives are in jeopardy."

"You don't think women can take care of themselves?"

Morgan shuddered involuntarily. "There are a lot of people who can't take care of themselves. Men included."

"You been separated long?" she asked, changing the subject.

"Nine months."

"I'm sorry. Broken marriages seem to be an occupational hazard in police work."

Morgan heard the low rumble of a boat's engine. He looked out into the murky blackness and saw the boat's faint red and white running lights. "Yeah." Then he turned to look at her. "You married?"

"No."

"Ever come close?"

She wrapped her arms around her legs and rested her chin on her knees. "Once." She smiled sadly.

"What happened?"

"I'm not sure. I think my career got in the way."

"How could you let your career—" He stopped in midsentence as he thought about his own situation. Hadn't he let his career come between him and his wife? "You ever regret it?" he asked.

She gazed out into the inky blackness. "Yeah," she said softly. "Sometimes." Then she shook her head and her mood changed. "It's not easy being in the Bureau, Dan. We move around a lot. Besides, some guys are intimidated by what I do for a living."

Morgan hunched his shoulders inside the bedspread. The breeze had begun to blow harder. "I can understand that. A buddy of mine who sold computers was married to a cop. At dinner he'd tell her about the new computer line his company was bringing out and she'd talk about a robbery arrest she'd made. Pretty soon neither wanted to hear about the other's day and they ran out of things to talk about."

"Sounds like he felt inadequate."

Morgan shrugged. "Could be."

She studied him in the faint light. "You seem pretty secure, Dan. I don't think that would bother you."

He stood up and looked at the sky: There was a faint glow in the east. "It'll be dawn soon. Why don't you get some sleep?"

She stood up. "Okay." She was about to climb over the wall, but she stopped. "Dan, I'm worried about Ray Fleming."

"Why?"

"Working undercover is a lonely, scary business. He shouldn't have to do it alone."

"We have no choice. He's in the middle of it."

"But he needs the support of an experienced handler."

"You?"

"Captain Zakovitch."

"I'd like that, but it's impossible. You know what Coffey said."

"I don't care what he said. We can't let Ray hang out there all by himself."

He looked at her carefully. "What you're suggesting isn't going to enhance your chances of becoming an ADIC," he said.

"I don't care. Ray Fleming is more important than my career—and yours."

Morgan was stung by the remark. Since they'd begun this investigation, he'd had reservations about using Ray Fleming, especially if he was forced to keep Zakovitch out of the picture. He'd told himself that it was out of his hands. But was it? Or was he protecting his own career by hiding behind Coffey's ill-advised order?

"Just think about it, will you, Dan?"

"Okay," he said. "I'll think about it."

She climbed back over the wall. As she was going inside, she noticed that he'd sat down again and was staring out into the darkness. It seemed like only a half-hour later, he was pounding on the wall.

They drove back to the woods and Morgan quickly ran to the place where he'd dropped his gun. After feeling around the pile of leaves for a few minutes, he raised the gun triumphantly and shouted, "I got it!"

Chris Liberti, leaning against a tree, saw a bright smile that was in sharp contrast to the somber looks of last night. It suddenly occurred to her that she'd never really seen him smile before.

He came toward her brushing the dirt and debris from the gun. "I feel a hell of a lot better."

She picked a leaf off his shoulder. "You look a whole lot better, too. You should smile more often."

He holstered the gun and was suddenly all business. "Come on, let's get back to the city and see if this bag will give up some prints."

Chapter
21

7:45 A.M. SUNDAY, MARCH 31 • On the drive back into the city the question of who should examine the contents of the bag touched off an argument. Dan Morgan, justly proud of the NYPD lab's reputation, wanted to take it there. But Chris Liberti insisted that the Bureau's lab was better equipped to handle the technical difficulties involved in lifting prints from cups and cans that had been lying in a plastic bag for three days. Reluctantly, Morgan finally agreed when Liberti pointed out that the farther away the evidence was from the city, the less likely it was that a security leak would occur.

After dropping the bag at the FBI headquarters in Federal Plaza, Morgan and Liberti went back to the office.

Donal Castillo was just hanging up the telephone. "Well," he said, "did you find the trash bag?"

"Yeah." Morgan poured his first cup of coffee for the day. They'd been in such a hurry to get back to the city that they hadn't even stopped for breakfast.

Liberti dunked an herbal tea bag in a cup of hot water. "It's on its way to Washington. With a little bit of luck we should have the results by tomorrow."

The DEA agent, scrutinizing Morgan's ripped slacks and generally disheveled appearance, grinned. "What happened? You have to fight a grizzly bear for the bag or what?"

"It's a long story." Morgan lowered himself into a chair and suddenly realized how tired he was.

Castillo turned to Liberti and smiled lewdly. "You've been gone all night. You gonna tell me the long story?"

Liberti inhaled the spicy aroma of the tea. "Grow up, Castillo. What have you been doing since we've been gone?"

He told them about his meeting with the CIA agent. Then he said, "I've been calling some friends who might be able to get us access to the Special Forces personnel records."

"Any luck?"

"Yeah. I just got off the phone with an old army buddy, a major in CID. I didn't understand what the hell he was talking about— something about downloading and patching—but he said he'll be able to arrange for you to access their computer files, including Special Forces personnel records. You'll have to talk to him."

"Great!"

Morgan yawned and stood up. "Yeah, that sounds good." He didn't know what they were talking about, but he was too tired to care. "I don't know about you, Chris, but I'm beat. I'm going home and get some sleep."

Castillo picked up a message and waved it in the air. "Er, before you go, I've got some good news and some bad news."

Morgan sat down again. "Give me the good news first. I can use it."

"Ray Fleming called earlier. He's going to have a meeting with Petry today."

Morgan blinked and his eyes felt as though they had sandpaper in them. "What's the bad news?"

"He doesn't know what time."

Morgan wanted sleep, but his fatigue was forgotten at the thought of getting a look at Petry. He threw his crumpled cup in the basket. "All right, we'll need a vehicle, cameras—"

"I've already set everything up." Castillo turned to Liberti. "You weren't here, so—"

"No, no, that's all right." Liberti, almost giddy with exhaustion, was delighted that Castillo was going to take the photos. Since sunrise she'd been thinking of nothing but a comfortable bed that didn't smell of dead fish. "Should I come?" she asked halfheartedly.

"No," Morgan said. "Don and I can handle it."

"Besides," Castillo added, "this is just a photo op."

"What do you mean?" Morgan asked.

"If Petry is Special Forces, we're dealing with a pro. We don't want to let him know we're looking at him or he'll disappear."

"What if he vanishes anyway? All we'll have is a goddamn picture."

"What do you suggest?" Castillo asked.

"Follow him."

"You're nuts. He'll spot you in a minute. We get the pictures first, then—"

"Castillo, we haven't got the time to dick around with this guy. Three cops are dead."

"I can count," Castillo said evenly.

Liberti stood up. She was too exhausted to referee a fight between Morgan and Castillo. "Well, I'm going to call it a day. If you need me you know where to get me. By the way, I've set up an appointment to interview Amonti and Lopez tomorrow morning at the precinct. Boy," she mumbled, putting on her coat, "what a way to spend Easter Sunday."

Morgan's mouth fell open. *"Today's* Easter?"

Liberti picked up her bag. "Yeah, why? You got a date with the bunny?"

"Shit! I was supposed to help my son hunt for Easter eggs this morning." He looked at the clock; it was just after eleven. "Maybe it's not too late." He grabbed for his jacket.

"What if Fleming calls and you're not here?" Castillo asked.

Morgan slid back into his chair.

Chris Liberti saw the despair in Morgan's eyes and forgot her own exhaustion. "Go ahead, Dan," she said. "I'll stay with Donal."

Morgan was tempted by the offer, but he couldn't leave now. He was running this team and he belonged here. "No, I'll stay," he said. "Go home, Chris. We'll call you if we need you."

"But Dan—"

"For chrissake, will you go?"

Liberti looked to Castillo, who silently nodded for her to leave.

As soon as Liberti left, Morgan reached for the telephone.

"Sarah, it's me . . . No, I can't . . . Something's come up . . . it's a long story. Listen, can we talk about this some other time? Put Danny on the phone. Where is he? . . . When will he be back from church? All right, I'll call back then. Sarah, I'm really . . . Sarah . . . ?" Morgan slammed the telephone down.

Castillo, with his back to Morgan, quietly puffed on his cigar and pretended to read a report. Finally, he broke the strained silence. "Police work sucks, right?"

"Fucking A," Morgan said bitterly.

The waiter offered menus to the two men. "Can I interest you gentlemen in dessert?"

Lyle Petry waved the menu away. "Just espresso for me." He looked across the table at his companion. "How about you?"

The bearded man skimmed the dessert selections but found noth-

MICHAEL GRANT

ing to his liking. "Espresso and sambuca. Please don't forget the three coffee beans." He opened a silver case and offered a cigar to Petry. Petry didn't smoke, but he did enjoy the occasional good cigar, especially one from Cuba.

Petry exhaled and studied the glowing ash. "Why is it always three beans?"

"I don't remember, but it is good luck." Alvaro smiled.

The men waited in silence as the waiter delivered the coffee and a bottle of Sambuca. When he'd gone, Petry resumed their conversation. "Well, what do you think of the project so far?"

The Colombian poured the clear liquid into two cordial glasses. "I admire your style. With your usual thoroughness you have thought of everything." His smile vanished. Without it the dark face looked more menacing. "But I still say we should begin issuing communiqués telling them who we are."

Petry shook his head. "Not yet. We're dealing with the New York City Police Department, not a handful of scared-shit village officials."

Despite his efforts to appear in control, Alvaro couldn't quite hide his anxiety. "Then when?" he whispered. "The whole purpose of this project is to bring pressure to bear on the United States government to stop the extraditions. If they don't know *who* we are, and *why* we're doing this, then the whole exercise is pointless."

Even though no one was in hearing range, Petry lowered his voice. "The intent of the assassinations," he said, "is to create confusion, doubt, and fear in the police. If you've been reading the newspapers, you know that I've done that. But I want these cops to swing in the breeze a bit longer. Three of their own have been neutralized and they don't know who is doing this or why. I want them to think about that. After Trojan Horse the credibility of the NYPD will be finished and the city will be in turmoil."

Alvaro refused to be mollified by Petry's self-confident air. "My colleagues are getting impatient, Lyle." He didn't mention the veiled threats he'd received the last time he'd spoken to them. "They have already spent a great deal of money on this project and still there are no results."

Officer DOWN

Petry poured a generous amount of the sambuca into his cup and stirred it. "Your 'colleagues' have plenty of money, so don't cry on my shoulder, Alvaro. You guys don't understand the psychology of Americans. You're used to cowering illiterate, frightened peasants. One call to a village magistrate threatening to blow up his courthouse is enough to spring someone from jail. But a threat like that in this country is like a lightning rod. It'll attract every law enforcement agency for miles around." Petry saw the anger flashing in his companion's eyes and softened his tone. "We're right on schedule. Soon, I'll be ready for Trojan Horse. *Then* we tell them who we are."

The Colombian's smile was melancholy. "Trojan Horse. I suppose one never loses the military penchant for code names."

Petry crushed his cigar in the ashtray. "It has a double meaning," he said evenly. "The Trojan Horse is also the insignia for Special Forces."

Alvaro swirled the beans in the thick, clear liqueur and looked pensive. "Do you ever wonder what our lives would have been like if we—"

Petry angrily cut him off. "That's ancient history and I don't dwell in the past."

But there wasn't a day when he didn't think of the past. Petry had first met Alvaro when he'd been assigned to assist the Colombian army in a search-and-destroy campaign against the cocaine-processing factories in the mountains. Alvaro, then a colonel, was in charge and Petry was his counterpart. Alvaro and Petry did things in those mountains that changed the course of his life, but he didn't resent the dour-faced man sitting across from him. Always the pragmatist, Petry realized that he'd done what he'd done with his eyes open and there was no one else to blame but himself.

"By the way," he said, changing the subject, "you haven't told me what you think of the team I've assembled."

Alvaro frowned. "It's not an A team, I can tell you that. I have no problem with Jimmy and Glen. But Fleming and Botnick? You can't be serious. Botnick strikes me as being rather frivolous."

Petry chuckled. "He's an asshole, but he's perfect for this assignment. He *is* the Trojan Horse."

Alvaro shook his head. "I still don't understand how you could have trusted Manny to help plant that bomb."

"That was his test, Alvaro. And it was done under test conditions."

"What do you mean?"

"Glen was covering Jimmy from the shadows of the Municipal Building with a rifle and night scope."

"Did Manny know this?"

"No, but as it turns out, he handled that derelict very well."

"What if he'd panicked?"

"Glen had instructions to take him out."

Alvaro swirled the dregs in his espresso cup. "You leave nothing to chance, do you, Lyle."

The pale green eyes met the Colombian's. "Something the army taught me. Never go into anything without a backup plan and a suitable escape route."

"What about Fleming? True, he is an excellent marksman, but does he have what it takes for this operation? I would prefer another Jimmy or Glen."

"Alvaro, I have limited assets to work with. Ray Fleming's working out fine. So far he's shown he can handle stress and he's interested in making money—two important attributes."

"But will Fleming be able to carry out Trojan Horse?"

"He'll be well tested before then."

The Colombian's interest was piqued. "How?"

Petry smiled, but said nothing.

The Colombian stroked his beard nervously. "You don't trust anybody, do you."

"That's why I've lasted so long in this business."

Alvaro drained the last of the sambuca and signaled for the check.

Petry looked at his watch and stood up. "Gotta go, I'm running late."

"A date?"

"No." The half smile reappeared on Petry's face. "I'm going to meet Fleming. You could say I've got to see a man about a Trojan Horse."

Ray Fleming was engrossed in cleaning his field-stripped pistol and didn't notice Petry standing behind him.

"Not so much oil, it'll attract dirt."

Startled by the voice behind him, Fleming dropped a spring. Petry sat down across the table from him. "Why so jumpy?"

"I didn't know you were there." Fleming looked at the wall clock. "You're late."

"I got tied up."

Ray Fleming tried not to stare, but he couldn't help himself. He was curious to see if Petry, the man Inspector Morgan and the others were so interested in, looked any different from the man he'd met just eleven days ago.

Petry handed Fleming the slide mechanism. "How'd you do tonight?"

"Lousy. I couldn't hit shit."

Petry shrugged. "It happens. Come on, let's go to Chico's for a couple of beers. I'm buying."

"No," Fleming said almost too quickly, "I can't." Chico's was the last place he wanted to go tonight.

Petry rubbed some oil off a spring and handed it to Fleming. "Why not? Celeste is probably working."

Fleming struggled for an excuse. "I don't have time. I'm driving the graveyard shift tonight."

"Sounds pretty grim. But you have time for a beer. We'll go to that joint down the block."

They sat at the half-empty bar and ordered two beers. "Hey, how're you doing with Celeste?" Petry asked.

"Good. We've gone out a couple of times." He wasn't about to tell Lyle that he'd stayed in her apartment last night.

"I told you she was a great kid. Was I right?"

"Yeah."

"There's only one problem."

Fleming was suddenly alert. "What's that?"

"Well, it isn't just her. I guess she's no different than most women. They all like the finer things in life. And the finer things cost more than you can afford driving a cab."

"I don't think she's like that at all."

"No, not in the beginning. But they all get tired of the same old shit. Women like variety, excitement. Unfortunately, it all costs money. A woman as good-looking as Celeste can always find someone to give her that kind of life."

Fleming, recalling last night's long, incredible night of sex, didn't want to hear that. "I don't think she's like that," he said.

Petry grinned knowingly.

"All right," Fleming added quickly, "so maybe I don't know. But it doesn't make any difference. I can't afford to live the jet-set life."

Petry studied Fleming's reflection in the bar mirror. "Maybe you can."

"How? Money matches?"

"There's a good buck in that, but it's not steady. In spite of what Manny says it isn't easy finding pigeons like those two at the country club."

Petry downed his beer and ordered two more. Suddenly he swung his stool around and faced Fleming.

The look on Petry's face made Fleming uncomfortable. "What?"

Petry shook his head. "I'm trying to decide if I should tell you."

"Tell me what?" Fleming's heart sank. Lyle was going to tell him there was still something going on between him and Celeste.

"Ray, I'm going to tell you something. If you don't want to hear it, say so, and the conversation never happened. Okay?"

Fleming nodded.

"Robbery," Petry whispered.

Fleming, who'd been expecting to hear something about Celeste, was caught off guard. "What did you say?"

"I'm planning a robbery and I want you in on it."

Fleming felt the hairs on the back of his neck rise. After what

Inspector Morgan and Captain Zakovitch had told him, he was expecting something. But still, he was stunned by the casual manner in which Petry brought up the topic. "Lyle, you gotta be kidding!"

"Ray, I'm not talking about Willie Sutton shit. I know it sounds crazy, but a well-planned robbery is a lot easier than you think. You read the papers. Most of the time the bad guys get away."

"Maybe, but—"

"But nothing. You plan it right, no one gets hurt and you walk away with a bundle. Who loses? Only the insurance company."

Fleming, remembering Morgan's instructions, knew he should express some kind of interest, but it all sounded so crazy he wasn't sure how he should respond.

Petry looked at the confusion and disbelief in Fleming's face and was pleased. At least Fleming didn't try to cut off the conversation. As long as he was listening, Petry was confident he'd be able to talk him in to it.

"Ray, I'm planning something. If you want, you can be in on it."

"What would I have to do?"

"Drive the car."

"Is Manny part of this?"

Petry chuckled. "Are you kidding? He'd shoot himself in the foot. I've been watching you. You operate well under pressure. You're the kind of guy I need. If no one gets excited, no one gets hurt."

Since his conversation with Inspector Morgan, Fleming had been thinking about this moment. He'd even rehearsed how he would react and what he would say. But now that the time had come, his mind had gone blank.

Petry looked at him curiously. "Well?"

"This is really screwy."

"I know it sounds that way, but just think about what it will be like when you have some real money in your pocket. You can take Celeste to dinner in the Bahamas."

Fleming's mouth was dry. He took a long swallow of beer and the cold liquid soothed his dry throat. "Okay," he said finally. "I'll do it."

Petry smiled. "Ray, it'll be a piece of cake."

"When will we—"

"I'll let you know." Petry looked at his watch. "Hey, it's after eleven, you'd better get to the garage."

Outside on the street Petry put his arm around Fleming. "You need a lift?"

"No. I have my own car."

Petry climbed into his Blazer. "Take care, Ray. I'll be in touch."

Fleming stood on the sidewalk and waited for Petry to leave. As the Blazer pulled away, his eyes locked on the license plate and he memorized the number. It was his first official act as an undercover police officer. He felt a thrill at finally being involved in real police work. But he felt something else, something that puzzled him. Guilt.

At the other end of the block, four hundred feet away, Dan Morgan sat behind the wheel of a rented panel truck. "Are you getting him?" he whispered.

In the back of the darkened truck Donal Castillo adjusted the tripod-mounted camera. "Yeah. Two great head shots. I just wish this was a sniper rifle instead of a camera."

"How about the plate?"

"One second." As the Blazer pulled away from the curb, Castillo switched on his infrared spot illuminator and a high-output wavelength, aimed at the back of the vehicle, bathed the license plate in invisible light. Castillo brought the camera's lens into sharp focus and pressed the shutter. "Got it. New York registration JTN-405."

Morgan, watching the taillights of the Blazer receding down the street, was having a bout of "worst case scenarios." What if the plate was stolen? What if it was a phony? What if Petry dropped from sight? Morgan started the engine.

Castillo looked up from his camera. "Don't go yet. Wait until he clears the block."

"I'm gonna follow him."

"Don't," Castillo cautioned. "He's a pro. He'll spot you."

Morgan slipped away from the curb with his headlights off. "I'm a pro too."

From a discreet distance, Morgan followed the Blazer as it headed east, and then turned north on Sixth Avenue. This time of night was ideal for a tail. Traffic wasn't too heavy, but there were enough cars to hide behind. Despite his doubts about following Petry, Castillo got into the spirit of the chase and engaged in a steady stream of encouragement and advice from the back seat. "Slow down . . . Let that cab get in front of you . . . Watch that light . . ."

Notwithstanding Hollywood movies and detective novels, tailing a vehicle alone, especially on crowded city streets, is almost impossible. The need to stay far enough back from the subject vehicle to avoid detection also increases the chances of losing it. Traffic lights, spillbacks, and darting taxis were only some of the obstacles to be overcome. But an incessant flow of advice from Castillo was one obstacle more than Morgan was willing to bear. After six blocks of nonstop advice, Morgan shouted, "For chrissake, Castillo, will you shut the fuck up?"

The DEA agent stopped in midsentence and fell silent.

Now that Morgan could concentrate on the Blazer, he relaxed a little. "Look at him," he said confidently. "He has no idea he's being followed."

The DEA agent, peering over Morgan's shoulder, said nothing.

At 17th Street the Blazer turned left. Slowing down, Morgan turned into the block just in time to see the Blazer make another left on Seventh Avenue. Morgan sped down the block. As he turned onto Seventh Avenue, he saw the Blazer make another left into 16th Street.

"What the hell is he doing?" Morgan said in exasperation.

"Game's over," Castillo said in an I-told-you-so voice. "Break it off. He's doing ring-around-the-rosy. He'll keep circling the block until he's sure no one is behind him. If you keep following him you might as well turn on the lights and siren."

Disgusted, Morgan pulled into the curb at Seventh and 16th Street. "Damn it! If we had two cars, we could have bracketed him. With one car on Sixth and another on Seventh—"

"It wouldn't do any good," Castillo said, unscrewing the camera from the tripod. "He'll do the same thing three or four more times before he finally goes home. You oughta know it's impossible to tail someone who's looking for one. Like I said, we're dealing with a pro."

MICHAEL GRANT

Frustrated, Morgan sat in the darkened panel truck and watched the Blazer drive by him as it circled the block three more times. Each time the vehicle passed, he got a momentary glimpse of the driver's face. The blond-haired man looked totally unconcerned.

The Blazer didn't come back a fourth time.

"That's it," Castillo said. "He's gone."

Morgan slammed the truck in gear and screeched away from the curb.

Castillo grabbed for the sliding camera. "Where are we going?"

"Back to the office to run the plate."

"Waste of time," Castillo said.

Morgan looked at the DEA agent through the rearview mirror. "Why?"

"This guy's too sharp to drive a car with a traceable plate."

Morgan, remembering the unconcerned look on Petry's face, had to agree.

Chapter
22

7:30 A.M. MONDAY, APRIL 1 • Chris Liberti sat in the office of the commanding officer of the Midtown South Precinct, Dan Morgan's old office. While she was waiting for Officer Amonti to appear, she inspected the room for some mark of Morgan's tenure. But there was none. In large bureaucracies like the NYPD and the FBI, people came and went with such rapidity that they seldom had the opportunity to leave their stamp of individuality behind. Like so many inter-changeable modules they were plugged in and out as needed.

She'd already interviewed police officer Nelson Lopez, who had little to add to the written reports compiled the night of the chase. Although it had been eleven days since the event, Lopez had still not gotten over the fact that he'd almost been killed because of a traffic summons.

The door opened and a good-looking cop in his late twenties came in. His eyebrows shot up in pleasant surprise when he saw Chris Liberti sitting there. "Hey, all right," he said, flashing a wide grin. "I was expecting a bunch of serious guys in trench coats."

"I'm Chris Liberti," she said, offering her hand, but not smiling.

Amonti held her hand with both of his. "Hey, Chris, whaddaya say we continue this interview over a couple of cocktails?"

Liberti shoved him backward and he fell into a chair. "Can it, cowboy. With a line like that you couldn't talk me into going to heaven with you."

Amonti, interpreting her refusal as simply the initial step in the dance of courtship, wasn't deterred. "Okay," he said, sitting back. "Ask questions first, we'll talk later. Hey, a *paesano*! What part of Brooklyn?"

Liberti's right eyebrow arched. "What makes you think I come from Brooklyn?"

"Come on. With an accent like that from Scarsdale you ain't."

"Bensonhurst."

"Bay Ridge. Hey, I used to play ball against those guys. You know Carmine Turrinto or—"

"Officer Amonti, can we dispense with the neighborhood geneal-ogy? I've got a few questions I'd like to ask you."

Amonti flashed his best smile again. "Sure, Chris. But call me Tony."

Liberti sighed inwardly. "Okay, Tony, I'm interested in the car chase you were in. Why don't you tell me about it in your own words."

Amonti fingered a thick gold chain around his neck. "There's not a whole lot to say. Nelse and I saw a Mustang with an equipment violation and we went after it. Turned out to be a ten-sixteen and the chase was on."

"Did you get a good look at any of the occupants?"

"Naw. I only saw the guy looking out the back window."

"Would you be able to ID him if you saw him again?"

"Nope. Too far away to get a good look. He had blond hair, that's all I can tell you."

"What happened when you came around the corner?"

He leaned forward and both his hands moved in animation. *"Marone!* The shit hit the fan. We make the turn and there they are —three guys pointing guns at us. Good thing Nelse cut to the left. It knocked us on our asses, but it probably saved our lives."

"What'd you do next?"

"We rolled out of the car, ready to do battle, but they were gone. It was really weird. I mean, it isn't like they were running down the block or nothing. I mean they were *gone.*" He sat back. "That's it, babe."

This interview, Liberti realized, was not going well. As long as Amonti insisted on hiding behind his tough cop, macho image, she wouldn't learn any more than she'd already gotten from the written reports. "Tony," she said quietly, "were you scared?"

Amonti's eyes flared at the challenge to his masculinity. "Naw, I was just pissed I didn't get a chance to return fire."

"You ever been shot at before, Tony?"

"No."

"And you weren't scared? Even a little bit?"

Anger flashed in his eyes. "Hey, I said no. All right? Have *you* ever been shot at, *Agent* Liberti?"

"Yeah, I have."

The eyebrows went up. "No kidding. When?"

"A long time ago."

"Were you scared?"

"Shitless."

Amonti looked at her for several seconds, then his whole demeanor changed. "Yeah," he said quietly, almost to himself, "me too.

MICHAEL GRANT

When Nelse and me turned the corner and I saw those guns, my whole fucking life passed before my eyes." He looked up startled, as though he'd forgotten she was in the room. "But I was ready to do what I had to do," he added firmly.

"I know you were, Tony. That's what we get paid for."

He studied the floor. "Right."

Watching the officer, who suddenly looked so vulnerable, it occurred to her that he probably hadn't had the opportunity—or the desire—to express his fears to anyone. Inability to admit and talk about fear was a debilitating occupational hazard for police officers.

She touched his arm. "Tony, now that you and I don't have to con each other, I'd like to hear your real impressions of that night. Stuff that didn't appear in the reports."

"There's nothin' else to say."

"What were you thinking?"

Amonti tugged at his gold chain, lost in thought. Finally he said, "I remember feeling real uneasy when we went after that car."

"Why?"

"I've been in a few stolen car chases. Usually, when they know they're being chased, the people in the car go bonkers. You know what I mean? Heads bob, wide eyes stare back at you. Sometimes they throw shit out the window; sometimes they jump out of the moving car. It can be a lot of laughs . . ." He paused. "But this one was different. I could see three heads in the car, but from what I could tell, they weren't even a little bit excited. Not for nothin', Chris, but when you're in a stolen car and you're being chased by the cops, you gotta get a *little* hyper. Right? But that blond-haired guy just kept staring back at us through the rear window like he knew . . ." Amonti's voice trailed off.

"Like he knew what?"

Amonti's eyes reflected a mixture of fear and bewilderment. "Like he knew we weren't going to catch them." He fell silent as he relived the event. Then he continued. "I only got a glimpse of them when we came around the corner, but I'll never forget it. They were behind the Mustang, crouching in the two-handed combat stance, like they were at a friggin firing range or somethin'. I mean, these guys were so

. . . professional and so . . ." He shook the cobwebs of memory from his mind.

"And what?"

"I can't think of the word."

"Anything else, Tony?"

"Nope. That's it." Amonti toyed with his cap nervously. "These guys shot Joyce, then they tried to kill Nelse and me. Who the hell *are* these guys?"

"That's what we're trying to find out." She closed her notebook. "Thanks for talking to me, Tony."

At the door, he stopped and turned around. "Hey, I just remembered the word I was trying to think of before. Military." Liberti's heart sank. "There was a kind of, you know, military precision to everything they did."

Liberti remained in the office after Amonti had left and stared at her notebook. Over and over again, she circled the word "military" with her pen, as she recalled the mock assault on that farmhouse in Fort Benning. "Just what we need," she said to the empty office, "terrorists with military training."

While Chris Liberti was talking to Officer Amonti, Dan Morgan was on his way to the Police Academy. He'd been awakened early by one of his dreams and had spent the rest of the morning thinking about what Chris had said in the Spindrift Motel. He needed to find out more about the problems of undercover cops and Ronnie Izzary was the one who could tell him.

Inching the car along 20th Street—chronically constricted by a long line of double-parked police vehicles—he wondered for the hundredth time whose bright idea it was to build the busy Police Academy facility in such a congested part of Manhattan. The Academy building, in addition to housing the recruit school, was also home to the crime lab, the Manhattan South borough office, the 13th Precinct, and a handful of miscellaneous units. On a daily basis hundreds of vehicles converged on a building with a woefully inadequate parking garage capacity. As a result, the streets surrounding the Academy were clogged with illegally parked cars. In keeping with the schizophrenic nature of the city's bureaucracy, parking enforcement agents routinely swept the area and ticketed every city vehicle within a ten-square-block zone.

After squeezing into an illegal spot on Second Avenue, Morgan walked back to the Academy building. When he got off the elevator on the sixth floor, Sergeant Izzary was waiting for him.

The slight, wiry-haired sergeant's grin revealed a set of crooked teeth under a black bushy mustache. "You find a parking spot?" he asked.

"Yeah. It only took fifteen minutes."

Izzary looked impressed. "Not bad."

"I've done worse. Hey, Ronnie, thanks for meeting me on such short notice. You got time to talk?"

"Sure. I don't have a class for another hour. Let's go to the library. It's the quietest part of the building."

Izzary led Morgan to two seats near the windows facing Cabrini Hospital. "Well," he said, sinking into an imitation leather chair, "what did you want to talk about, boss?"

"Undercover work."

Izzary's smile faded, but returned quickly. "You thinking of going under, Inspector?"

"No, but I have a nephew who's being offered the opportunity and he wants to know what I think. I told him I didn't know a hell of a lot about it, but I'd look into it."

Izzary's black eyes studied Morgan. "So what do you want to know?"

"The personal side. How'd you cope with being under cover."

Izzary smiled deprecatingly. "As you know, boss, not real good."

Morgan remembered the first time he'd met Ronnie Izzary. Every transferred detective is accompanied by a thick personnel folder with complete records of previous commands, complaints, commendations and "attaboy" letters from the public. By perusing these folders a commander can get a pretty good thumbnail sketch of his newest subordinate. But the intense, newly promoted detective's folder contained nothing except the basic profile sheet prepared at the Police

Academy. Yet the date of appointment indicated that Ronald Izzary had been a police officer for three years.

In spite of the paucity of information in Izzary's file, the new detective's spectacular career was common knowledge to anyone who read the newspapers. For the past six weeks, the press had been headlining one of the most sensational trials in recent memory. Ronald Izzary, an undercover police officer, had infiltrated a Puerto Rican separatist group. At the end of the three years the FBI and the New York City Police Department—with the help of Izzary—had amassed enough evidence to arrest and indict thirteen people.

The nature of Izzary's assignment instantly thrust the young cop into the center of a storm of controversy. When charges of entrapment, the defense's initial courtroom strategy, failed, they alleged that Izzary had illegally taken part in crimes himself, that he'd taken money, and that he'd used drugs. For a while the defense strategy worked. Ronald Izzary and the District Attorney's Office, scrambling to refute the charges, seemed to be on trial, but the prosecutor successfully rebuffed these spurious allegations and the thirteen were finally convicted.

Moments after the verdict was read, the district attorney stood on the steps of the courthouse in lower Manhattan and praised Officer Ronald Izzary as a hero. But within hours of that statement, radical Spanish newspapers, denouncing Ronald Izzary as a traitor, were hitting the newsstands in the Hispanic sections of the city.

Morgan had had his doubts that the newly minted detective would be able to handle it, but he was pleasantly surprised by the former undercover's performance. For the first couple of months Izzary stayed on top of his cases, kept his paperwork in order, and made more than his share of arrests. Then Morgan began to notice the signs —red eyes after a weekend swing, an increase in sick days, and more frequent requests for emergency days off. When Morgan was certain, he called Izzary into his office and confronted him with his suspicions.

At first Izzary denied that he had a drinking problem, but as Morgan cited example after example of shoddy work and performance, the detective began to waver in his denials. Finally, he broke down and began to cry. He begged Morgan to give him another chance, but Morgan, who'd had drunks try to con him before, wasn't swayed by the detective's emotional appeal. He gave Izzary two choices: volunteer to go into the department's alcohol rehabilitation program or Morgan would do it for him.

Izzary cursed Morgan and stormed out of the office, but he did as he was told. The next day the orders came up temporarily transferring Detective Ronald Izzary to Health Services Division. Two months later, he returned to full duty. The first day back, he walked into Morgan's office. Without saying a word, he dropped a small white box on the desk and walked out. Inside was a gold medal of St. Jude, the saint of the impossible.

Now, sitting opposite Ronnie Izzary in the Police Academy library, Morgan fingered the medal through his shirt. "No, Ronnie, *you* coped with the assignment. The department failed you. They dropped you into a strange world and when they were finished, they yanked you out and expected you to go on as though nothing had happened."

Izzary's eyes roamed to the window and he studied the buildings across the street. "That's the way it was then, boss. But things are different now. That's one of the things I do at the Academy: counsel undercover cops who come out."

"What do you tell them?"

Idly, Izzary picked at his mustache. "Damn, there's so much. For instance, all the time I was under, I had indigestion. I thought it was all the cuchifritos and shit I was eating, but it wasn't. It was the result of a chronic case of stress." He turned away from the window and fixed Morgan with sad black eyes. "Boss, you're always afraid. Afraid you'll say the wrong thing, afraid you'll bump into someone from the old neighborhood, afraid you're not doing your job well enough. And there's no one to talk to. Sure, you've got a department supervisor who gives you advice and instructions, but after a while you begin to distrust him. You say, 'Who the fuck *is* this guy? What does he know? *He* ain't the one putting his ass on the line twenty-four hours a day. *I* am.' "

Izzary stopped talking as a handful of recruits, lugging large black equipment bags and dressed in the two-tone blue uniforms of the

Police Academy, came in. The group found a table near the door and immediately started quizzing each other on the provisions of the penal law.

Izzary continued. "When you think like that, your priorities get all fucked up. It got so I trusted the people I was hanging around with more than I trusted my supervisor. At least I knew where they were coming from. My supervisor? After a while I wasn't sure if he was looking out for my interests or the department's." Izzary shook his head. "It gets crazy, boss. You *know* they're bad people, but some of them were real good to me. One night my car broke down, so a guy gave me the keys to his new car. 'No problem,' he says. 'Bring it back when you get a chance.' Just like that. Another guy knew I liked the Mets. He had a cousin worked at Shea. He got me tickets right behind home plate."

Izzary blinked rapidly and focused his attention on the buildings across the street again. "I had an affair with one of the girls," he said softly. "She was one beautiful woman." He turned back to Morgan and smiled. "When you're under cover it can get real crazy. Toward the end I didn't know what the hell I was doing. I was doing my job, but it was getting harder and harder. When I was told that the DA was getting ready to make the bust, I freaked out. I jerked the department around for months, telling them that something big was developing. It was bullshit. Nothing was going on. I just didn't want it to end."

"What happened?" Morgan asked.

"My supervisor was smarter than I thought he was. He realized I'd been co-opted by the group and recommended ending the investigation. You know, for months after it was over I used to wake up in a cold sweat. I felt like a . . . a traitor. They were my friends and my testimony put them all behind bars." He shook his head to chase away the ghosts. "It's a schizophrenic world. Intellectually you know they're no fucking good, but still . . ." His voice trailed off.

He cleared his throat. "I didn't start hitting the juice until I got into your squad. During the trial I was too busy to think about anything. It's later, when you have time to think, that you begin to second-guess yourself."

While Izzary had been recounting his experiences, Morgan had been thinking of Fleming. If Izzary, a street-wise kid from Spanish Harlem, had these problems, how would a white, middle-class kid from Queens hold up?

Morgan, forcing these thoughts from his mind, slapped Izzary's knee. "Hey, buddy, thanks. I know it isn't easy talking about it."

"It's not, but it's good to talk. That's why I like counseling undercovers. It helps me get in touch with my own feelings. Even now, I still have some hostility toward the department for putting me in that situation. But I'm working it out."

While Morgan rode the crowded elevator to the main floor, it occurred to him that Ray Fleming should have been sitting with those other recruits instead of forcing himself into the confidence of Lyle Petry. It also occurred to him that he had the power to remove Fleming from the investigation. All he had to do was support Captain Zakovitch's recommendation to drop Fleming from the undercover assignment. But before he could dwell on the consequences of that possibility the doors opened and he was swept out into the busy lobby.

Sitting at his desk, less than a fifteen-minute drive from the Police Academy, Police Commissioner Cassidy scrawled his signature on the bottom of a letter and tossed it into his out-basket.

Reluctantly, he pressed the intercom. "Send Renzi in."

Anthony C. Renzi, dressed in a continental-cut suit, striped shirt and paisley tie, looked more like a Wall Street MBA than the president of the 22,000-member Patrolmen's Benevolent Association.

Watching the polished young man slip into a seat opposite him, Cassidy longed for the old days when PBA presidents were elected solely on the strength of ethnic heritage, personality, or the ability to hold drink. Negotiating skills and knowledge of spread sheets were unnecessary in those simpler days. Some PBA leaders might have been good cops, but most were inept politicians. They were certainly no match for wily police commissioners and slick city negotiators, who wined and dined—mostly wined—these political neophytes. By the time the party ended, the rank and file had a lousy contract, the city had extra money to spend on matters more important than police officers' salaries, and the hapless PBA president was left with heartburn, a hangover, and a tough, uphill fight for reelection.

How times had changed. In the past twenty years the Police Department, no longer an exclusive employment agency for the city's lower-class Irish and Italians, had been attracting a more diverse population. The ethnic mix was not only good for affirmative action, it indirectly benefited the police union members as well. Aspirants to the post of president could no longer rely simply on the votes of their "own kind." They were forced to campaign on more concrete issues —such as competency and integrity.

Cassidy envied his predecessors. They didn't have to deal with the likes of a Tony Renzi with his graduate degree in industrial relations. Renzi, a polished negotiator, didn't pound desks, curse, or threaten. He preferred to sit at the negotiating table with his patented pained expression, which he usually wore when he was taking some unsuspecting city contract negotiator to the cleaners. He'd used the pained expression so often, he'd developed a permanent funereal countenance.

Tony Renzi, Cassidy observed morosely, was wearing his pained expression now. "What can I do for you, Tony?"

"Commissioner, thanks for seeing me. I know how busy you are."

"I always have time for you and the PBA."

The stroking ritual ended, Renzi came directly to the purpose of his visit. "I'm sure you've been seeing what's in the newspapers. My membership is understandably concerned."

"Tony," Cassidy said evenly, "I'm as troubled as you are by these murders, but you know this city. Sometimes there's no rational explanation for the violence. I can assure you that the department is doing everything possible—"

"The department isn't doing enough," Renzi replied quietly.

Cassidy, straining to keep his temper in check, continued. "I've instructed the Chief of Detectives to assign more men to the case."

"I know that, sir."

There wasn't much that went on in the department—either officially or unofficially—that the president of the PBA didn't know about.

"Commissioner, the question everyone is asking is: Who's behind these murders? The FALN? A new terrorist group?"

Cassidy forced himself not to blink. "At this time we're not even sure they're related. The MOs aren't exactly the same and so far there's no evidence linking them. That's what we're trying to determine, Tony. We don't know who's doing this yet, but we will. We've had rashes of bombings and murders before in this city. Sooner or later we get them."

Renzi's pained expression grew more pronounced. "But cops weren't the target."

Cassidy studied the PBA president sitting opposite him and wondered how much he really knew. Obviously, he didn't know about the existence of Puño Blanco or he'd have come to this meeting with an army of TV cameras and reporters in tow. Cassidy knew Renzi's style, and decided he was on a fishing expedition. Still, Renzi was treading on dangerous ground and, somehow, Cassidy had to lead him away.

"Who says police officers are the target?" he asked Renzi.

"Commissioner, you know the pattern of terrorists as well as I do. They target embassies, airline offices, and banks for their protests. Then they send out communiqués explaining their actions." He leaned forward and Cassidy could smell his expensive cologne. "Someone blew up a cop at police headquarters, someone ambushed a cop in Queens, and someone shot a cop in Manhattan. But no one has come forward to take credit. So who are they? And what are they protesting?"

Cassidy felt a blowtorch ignite in his chest, but it would have been a tactical mistake to reach for the Tums with a watchful Tony Renzi sitting across from him. Obviously, the soft-line diplomatic approach, which was foreign to Cassidy's style, wasn't working. He decided a stronger approach was needed. "That's speculation on your part, Renzi, and that kind of idle talk could stampede the men into an ill-advised job action." He knew the PBA president was smart enough to pick up the implied warning in his tone.

Officer DOWN

"Sir, I'm fully aware of that and I don't raise the issue lightly. The point is three of my cops have been killed—"

Cassidy slammed his hand on the desk. "*Your* cops? Goddammit, they're *my* cops too." Cassidy was angry at himself for losing his temper, but it seemed to have a suppressing effect on Renzi.

"Sir"—Renzi's tone became more reasonable—"you and I have worked well together in the past. I know the welfare of the men is a top priority with you, unlike some commissioners before you. But there's a feeling in the ranks that something is going on and we're not being told about it. I have a few hothead delegates, especially in the ghetto precincts, who are making a lot of noise."

"What are they saying?"

Renzi adjusted his gold cufflinks. "That these murders are neither random nor unrelated; that cops are the target."

The blowtorch's flame intensified. Cassidy squeezed the arms of his chair and forced himself to ignore the pain. He needed something to keep Renzi at bay, and suddenly thought of it. It was a gamble, but if Renzi bought it, Cassidy would kill two birds with one stone: he'd give Dan Morgan a plausible cover assignment, and he hoped that the PBA would realize their commissioner was serious about these killings and back off. "Tony, right after that Queens shooting I assigned a deputy inspector to my office, but his assignment was kept low key. His job is to report directly to me about the progress of these investigations. He's also liaisoning with the Bureau, the DEA, and other federal agencies."

Renzi's expression didn't change. "That's good. Inspector Morgan is well respected."

Cassidy assumed a more reasonable tone. "Tony, I wasn't born the police commissioner. I was a cop for thirty-five years. I know what it's like on the street. You have my word that the full resources of the department are behind these investigations."

Cassidy stood up, signaling that the meeting was over. He put his arm around the PBA president and walked him to the door. "Tony, if we uncover any intelligence that the men need to know about, they'll be told."

Renzi, looking so pained Cassidy thought he might cry, said, "I

234   **MICHAEL GRANT**

hope so. If another cop is killed"—he paused for effect—"I can't take responsibility for the spontaneous actions of the men in the street."

Translation: The PBA had already made contingency plans for a job action. It was up to Cassidy to figure out what form it would take. Not that it mattered. Ticket blitzes, blue flu, and by-the-rulebook slowdowns had all been tried and had been successful. Looking at Renzi's gloomy expression, Cassidy shuddered to think what the PBA president would look like if he knew about the existence of Puño Blanco.

After Renzi left, Cassidy somberly stared at the calendar on his desk and contemplated the wrenching events since the headquarters bombing. In only eight months he was going to retire. In his thirty-five years in the department he'd managed to do what most police officers could only dream of: rise to the level of police commissioner in the greatest police department in the world. Furthermore, he was especially proud of the fact that during his tenure there had been no major scandals or crime waves.

Unlike so many soon-to-be retirees, who viewed the expanse of long workless days with trepidation, Cassidy was looking forward to polishing up his golf game. If he had the time and inclination, he might even lecture at John Jay College. But Puño Blanco could change all that. By merely agreeing to Coffey's requirement of silence, he'd put his entire career in jeopardy. If word of Puño Blanco —and the part he was playing in the conspiracy of silence—got out, he'd be finished and his career would be in ruins.

The thought of a wrecked career wasn't the only fuel feeding his ulcer. There was another more important consideration that he'd managed to suppress. Until now. What right did he have to keep the existence of Puño Blanco from his police officers? Puño Blanco had worked with a speed and efficiency that had both dismayed and saddened him. Since the first police officer had been killed by that bomb at police headquarters, he lived in constant dread of a notification that another police officer had been murdered. Even now he knew that his dreams of retirement would never be quite the same. On the golf course, preparing to make that six-foot putt, or in the evening, reading a good book with a glass of scotch at his side, he'd suddenly be reminded of those three police officers who had died, and he'd wonder, once again, if he'd done the right thing.

Cassidy winced as the knife buried deep in his gut twisted. He rummaged through his top drawer looking for a fresh pack of Tums. By the time he'd found them, he'd made up his mind. If one more cop was killed, he promised himself, he'd put out an order announcing the existence of Puño Blanco and to hell with his career. And to hell with Skip Coffey.

Chapter

23

6:00 P.M. MONDAY, APRIL 1 • *"Four-four Sector Charlie . . . respond to report of past burglary . . . 119 East 164 . . . apartment six north."*

Police Officer Bill Ivory keyed the mike. "Sector Charlie, ten-four." He turned to the driver. "What do you think, Tom, should we call for a backup?"

Tom Crowley, a man in his early thirties with a protruding belly that almost touched the steering wheel, chewed on his lip. Since the killings of Jeff Golden and Joyce Hauser, jumpy sector car teams throughout the city had become acutely aware of their vulnerability to attack. Now, each time they received a radio run, they had to wonder if it was legitimate or if they were being set up. Crowley knew that radio car teams were calling for backups with greater frequency, but that procedure made him uncomfortable. It was almost an admission that he couldn't take care of himself. "Naw," he said finally, "it's a quiet block. We'll just watch our asses."

They pulled up in front of the address and scanned the streets and rooftops before they got out. Satisfied that nothing was out of the ordinary, they moved quickly toward the relative safety of the hallway. Once inside, they drew their revolvers—something they didn't ordinarily do—and quietly climbed the stairs to the sixth floor. When they got to apartment 6N, they saw the handiwork of a junkie burglar's MO: the door had been kicked open, splintering the half-rotted doorjamb.

With guns at the ready, they stood on either side of the partially opened door. At Crowley's nod, Ivory banged on the door with his night stick. After a tense moment, a frail black woman peeked through the opening. "God bless you, officers, thank God you're here."

Relieved, if slightly embarrassed at their overly cautious behavior, they holstered their guns and went into the apartment. Ivory pulled out his memo book. "Name?"

"Norma Fletcher." The old woman dabbed at her eyes with a lace handkerchief. "I just returned from my sister's wake and I found this."

"Did she live here with you, Mrs. Fletcher?"

"Yes."

The two cops, glancing at each other, knew what had happened. Junkies read the obituaries looking for just this sort of opportunity. Sometimes the obit gave the deceased's address and the time of the wake and funeral. It didn't take a genius to figure out that no one would be home during those hours, making the home an attractive target.

The two cops looked around the trashed apartment. The burglar, in his frantic attempt to discover valuables, had dumped the contents of every drawer onto her shiny linoleum floor. Piles of clothing, photos—even her pots and pans—were strewn everywhere.

"What did they get?" Ivory asked.

"My TV. The only valuable I got left."

"How many times you been hit before?"

She sat down on the edge of the sofa. "Three times in two years."

"Time to move, Mrs. Fletcher."

She looked up at him with fear and resignation in her eyes. "Where am I going to go? My sister was my only living relative." Her eyes swept the violated apartment. "What's to become of me now?"

Ivory wrote the telephone numbers of several city agencies on a piece of paper and handed it to her. "Tomorrow, give them a call. They may be able to help."

She pointed at the door with a shaky, bony hand. "What am I going to do about that? I can't stay here without a lock on the door."

"Don't worry," Crowley assured her. "We'll get the super to fix it."

She scowled. "That no-account bum is always drunk. He don't fix nothin'."

Crowley smiled at the old lady's spunkiness. "Don't worry. It'll get fixed even if I have to do it myself."

After Crowley and Ivory took the report, they went to find the super. Mrs. Fletcher was right. They found the drunken man sleeping behind the boiler in the cellar. After considerable cajoling, culminating in the threat of arrest, he promised to fix the door. Before they left, Ivory reminded him they'd be back in half an hour to inspect his handiwork.

Back in the radio car, Ivory gave the disposition to Central. Then he sat back and rubbed his eyes. "Damn, all this tension is wearing me out. Every time I go to a job I feel like I'm going into combat."

Crowley scratched his chin. "I don't like it either, but what other choice we got?"

Before Ivory could answer, the radio crackled: *"Four-four Sector*

Charlie . . . report of a rape in progress . . . 360 East 153 . . . Caller states small child being raped at that address."

Crowley, the father of two small girls, snapped the car in gear. "That's a bad block. Request backup."

As the car lurched away from the curb with roof lights flashing and siren wailing, Police Officer Bill Ivory was talking to the dispatcher, asking for backup units.

As soon as the radio car turned the corner into 153rd Street, Crowley shut off the flashing roof lights and siren. Halfway down the block the vehicle screeched to a stop in front of an abandoned building. Tom Crowley was the first one out of the still rocking car. With gun drawn, he raced toward the entrance.

Ivory, not far behind, skidded to a stop. "Wait a sec," he shouted, "I forgot my flashlight."

Crowley, his mind preoccupied by the words of the radio dispatcher, *". . . rape in progress . . . caller states small child . . . ,"* didn't hear his partner, and hit the stoop stairs two at a time.

The buildings were supposed to be vacant, but junkies, who used them for sleeping accommodations and shooting galleries, had hacked away the concrete blocks in the windows and peeled away the sheet metal covering the entrances.

Out of the corner of his eye Crowley saw additional radio cars coming into the block from opposite ends and felt a sense of relief. Carefully avoiding the jagged edges of the metal door, he yanked it open.

Bill Ivory, running toward the stoop at full speed, was hurled backward into the street by the huge ball of fire.

Dan Morgan arrived at the scene within thirty minutes of the telephone notification. He'd been jolted when a sergeant from the commissioner's office called with the message that another bomb had gone off. But with a policeman's grim stoicism he'd forced himself to view this latest bombing as an opportunity to uncover better evidence. In his frustration and deepening anger, he counted on the axiom of policemen everywhere: all criminals make mistakes. Before Morgan hung up he'd instructed the sergeant to notify Liberti and Castillo.

A radio car and a row of hastily erected blue barricades blocked the entrance to the street, which was already clogged with police cars and fire trucks. After parking around the corner, Morgan pushed his way through the crowd, identified himself to the cops behind the barrier, and walked into 153rd Street, a block that typified the pervasive decay in the Bronx ghetto.

Interspersed among run-down tenements were a dozen abandoned buildings and a handful of empty lots where buildings had already been razed. The property had been fenced off, but the chain-link fencing had been ripped away and the lots were littered with abandoned cars, refrigerators, and bedsprings. Bricks and large chunks of concrete spilled into the street, reminding Morgan of the scenes of Baghdad he'd seen on the evening news.

As he drew closer to the confusion, the grim scene took on a more nightmarish cast. A dozen police- and fire radios tuned to different frequencies boomed unheeded messages into the night air, while emergency vehicles with red and yellow dome lights flashing cast eerie shadows on the hard, tense faces of the men intent on performing their unhappy tasks. On the street's asphalt surface thousands of bits of shattered glass sparkled like diamonds in the reflection of the revolving lights.

The sidewalks had been cleared of all pedestrians, forcing the curious to watch from doorways and windows. The more adventurous had climbed to the tops of the buildings to peer over crumbling parapets at the chaotic scene below. Catcalls and whistles rained down from above as teenagers, in a festive mood, viewed the excitement. In this neighborhood a diversion, any diversion, was welcome.

A teenager, one of a group of three standing in a doorway, said something and the others whooped in glee. But there was no humor in the shrill laughter. It was a taunting challenge aimed at a cluster of precinct cops who, talking in hushed tones, glanced uneasily into the street at the chalked outline of a body, a hat, and a flashlight—all that was left of the man who'd stood roll call with them less than three hours earlier.

A red-faced cop, hearing the taunt, spun around and snarled an obscenity. The boy gave the cop the finger. Before the others could react, the cop bounded up the stairs and grabbed the surprised teenager by the throat. A sergeant and two cops rushed up the steps and separated them. As the youths chanted "police brutality," the sergeant dragged the out-of-control cop over to a radio car and threw him into the back seat. The sergeant said something to the driver and the vehicle sped out of the block. The incident was immediately forgotten as the three teenagers, distracted by something else, ran into the building's hallway.

The stoop, protected by a rectangle of bright yellow crime scene tape, was the focal point of activity. Lit by large lights from a police Emergency Services truck, the building entrance took on the staged, artificial look of a movie set. Cops with cameras, clipboards and plastic bags swarmed over the stairs looking for microscopic clues in the pile of charred wood, twisted metal, and broken glass.

Morgan recognized Al Bryant, a precinct detective from the 44th Squad, making notes on a clipboard.

The black detective, completely bald except for small tufts of gray hair over his ears, looked up in surprise. "Inspector, you in the zone now?"

"The PC's office. You catching this one, Al? Dan Morgan asked him the dreaded question that all policemen asked at a time like this. "Who are the cops?"

"Tom Crowley and Bill Ivory."

Morgan exhaled, feeling a mixture of relief and sadness. He was thankful he didn't know them personally, but they were cops just like him. He stepped over a fire hose. "What've you got?"

"So far I got shit. At eighteen-thirty hours, Sector Charlie received a radio run to this building: rape in progress. Crowley was at the top of the stoop when it went off. He took the full impact of the explosion and died instantly. Ivory was blown into the street. He's still alive, but I hear he's in bad shape."

"Phony run?"

"Yeah. We searched the building. Nothing."

"Anything on the device?"

"Not yet." Bryant nodded toward the men on the stoop. "Arson/ Explosion is working on it."

"Witnesses?"

"One. He's at the station house."

Morgan felt a rush of excitement. *A witness!* Maybe these sons of bitches had made their first mistake.

The detective squinted up at the windows and rooftops above him. "Look at these fucking animals. There's gotta be a thousand people on this block. And only one guy admits to seeing anything. How could—" Bryant's head swiveled and his mouth dropped open as he watched a fire truck back across a bloodstain, leaving maroon tire marks on the street. "For chrissake, Dennis," he yelled to his partner, "protect that area, will you?"

"I've only got two hands," his partner snapped.

Bryant rushed into the street and motioned to a radio car to pull in front of the chalk markings.

Morgan, aware that he'd been purposely avoiding the scene, turned toward the stoop. At the top of the steps a detective, wearing a rumpled sport jacket, was on his hands and knees in front of the jagged metal door, examining something. "Hey, Tony," he yelled over his shoulder. "Take a look at this."

A second detective, nattily dressed in a three-piece suit, peered over his partner's shoulder.

The detective on the ground used his pen to point at a thin, half-inch length of monofilament line attached to the wooden doorjamb. Amid the debris it could have easily been overlooked by less experienced eyes. "Whaddaya think?"

Disregarding the broken glass and plaster chips, the well-dressed detective knelt down to get a better look. "Trip wire?"

"I think so."

"Get a picture. We'll bag it and send it to the lab."

"Professionals?" Morgan asked.

The detective, brushing the dirt from his trousers, looked up and saw the deputy inspector's shield pinned to Morgan's coat. He didn't know who Morgan was, but when someone wearing an inspector's shield asks a question, you answer. "Looks that way, boss."

Morgan squinted at the telltale wire. "Where do you learn this kind of stuff?"

The detective eyed the wire. "The military. You don't learn this shit at the Y. Trip wire was common in 'Nam. I used it myself. Look at that door. You don't have to be an expert to see where the charge was attached."

The detective was right. From the way the door was ripped open, it was clear that the charge had been attached to the back of the door at waist height.

"A professional plants his charge where he wants to do the most damage," the detective explained. "In 'Nam the VC had a great way to harass us. They attached light explosive charges to the bottom of trees and hooch doors. They weren't meant to kill—just blow someone's legs off. Not only does it scare the shit out of you, but it delays you while you take care of your legless buddies."

Morgan looked at the twisted metal door. "No harassment here."

"Nope. The scumbag who planted this wanted to kill someone." The detective looked Morgan in the eye. "What's going on, Inspector? Three cops killed. Now this. We got a fucking problem here or what?" Without waiting for an answer, he turned away to give instructions to the Crime Scene photographer.

Morgan's eyes swept the stoop and took in the carnage that had snuffed out a life in the blink of an eye. In the bright floodlights it wasn't difficult to trace the fine spray of blood, which started at the top of the stairs, increased in quantity, and ended in an ugly, coagulated puddle at the bottom, where another chalk outline of a body had been drawn. The sight of the blood and the faint smell of cordite in the air triggered a memory. Strobelike images of the hallway where he'd been shot flashed in his mind's eye. For the moment the remembered confusion—the gunfire and desperate shouts—were more real to him than the voices of the detectives standing less than ten feet away from him now. An unseen, cold hand clenched his gut and his vision began to blur. Unsteadily, he started down the stairs.

"Dan." Chris Liberti was standing in front of him. "I came as soon as I could."

From the way she was dressed it was apparent she hadn't taken the time to change. She was wearing a down vest over a well-worn jogging suit and sneakers. But even with her hair flattened with a sweatband, several cops were giving her appraising glances.

Morgan, glad to have something to do, took her aside and told her what he'd learned. While he spoke, he noticed that she didn't look at him. She listened, but like a good cop, her eyes moved constantly, taking in everything on the street.

"This turns the heat up on us," she said, echoing his own concern. "Cops are gonna start asking questions."

Morgan nodded glumly. "They already have."

"Any witnesses?"

"One."

"Great. Where is he?"

"The station house."

"Have you seen Castillo?" she asked.

"No. Come on," Morgan said, turning away, "there's nothing else we can do here. Let's see what the witness has to say."

As they were walking out of the block, Morgan saw six Hispanics standing in front of a liquor store. Donal Castillo, wearing his scruffy army field jacket, was standing in the middle of the group. Morgan was astonished by the transformation in the man. With his hunched shoulders and darting eyes, he looked nothing like the confident, cocky DEA agent Morgan had come to know.

The DEA agent stared at Morgan, but there was no sign of recognition in the hooded eyes. Still looking at Morgan, he said something to the others and they laughed.

As Morgan was driving toward the precinct station house, he said, "I saw Castillo on the street. He—"

"That field jacket is a nice touch," Liberti said. "He looked like a refugee from the Mariel boat lift."

Morgan felt the anger rising. "*You* saw him?"

"Sure."

"Why didn't you say something?"

"I didn't think you saw him and I didn't want to embarrass you."

"What the hell is *that* supposed to mean?" Before she could answer, Morgan turned into the precinct block and slammed on the brakes.

News media vehicles and TV transmission trucks were double- and triple-parked, blocking the entire street. "What the hell's going on?" he muttered.

She opened the door and got out. "Why don't you wait here. I'll find out." Before he could answer, she was out of the car and hurrying down the street.

A scowling captain came jogging up the block. Morgan recognized Ed Krug, one of the captains in his promotion class. Krug stuck his head in the car. "Dan, I didn't know that was you. I was going to chase you out of here." He straightened up and looked down the block toward the snarled traffic.

"Ed, what the hell's going on?"

The captain's chest heaved from the unfamiliar exertion of running. "What a fucking mess. If you're planning to go into the station house, forget it."

"Why?"

Although there was no one near them, Krug looked around furtively and lowered his voice. "The shit has hit the fan. This bombing was the last straw. The cops have started a job action. The late tour begins in a couple of hours and the borough is reporting that close to thirty percent of the troops have called in sick already. The press has gotten wind that the cops have started a job action and they've laid siege to the building."

Krug stood up to let a radio car pass. Then he continued. "I'll tell you, Dan, things have been getting real testy with the troops since these killings started. You change a cop's *meal* and you get an argument from him *and* the fucking PBA delegate. Last week the borough commander passed the word down: No more command disciplines or suspensions without his personal okay." Although the night air was chilly, Krug wiped his damp face with a soggy handkerchief. "He didn't want the PBA to have an excuse to start a job action in *his* borough. But it's started here anyway." He looked at Morgan wistfully. "Assigned to the PC's office, huh? Man, you don't know how lucky you are to be off the street."

Morgan was watching the TV crews light up the front of the station house in preparation for live coverage on the eleven o'clock news. "Yeah," he said. "Some guys have all the luck."

Less than five minutes later, a subdued Liberti was back. "The witness went home," she said quietly, "but I have his work address and telephone number."

Morgan nodded toward the turmoil down the street. "The job action has started." He started to say something else, but stopped when he saw the troubled look on her face. "What's up?"

Chris Liberti focused her attention on four solemn-faced police officers walking up the block toward them. "When I was in the squad room," she said in the same quiet voice, "they got the call from the hospital. The other police officer died five minutes ago."

Donal Castillo remained in the area and watched as the police vehicles, one by one, left the scene. Soon the last cop, who'd been assigned to block access to the street, stacked the barriers by the curb, and he too left.

Castillo zipped up his field jacket and walked into the block. As an undercover cop, he'd often been at the scene of street crimes both during and after the police had gone. Still, he was always astonished at the quick transformation that took place with the departure of the police. Young men and teenagers who felt compelled to demonstrate their manhood in front of the police by use of body language and tough talk quickly dropped the facade and returned to being themselves. Like forest animals after the hunter has passed, block residents, who for whatever reason didn't want to be seen by the police, came out of their apartments and into the street to verify that everything had indeed returned to normal. With the inquisitive cops gone, the street people dropped their guard. If Castillo was going to pick up information, this was the time to do it.

He entered a bodega situated almost opposite the bombing scene. The plate glass window, which had been cracked from the concussion of the explosion, had been hastily repaired with duct tape. Like most Spanish grocery stores, this one was short on space, but the owner made up for it by stacking everything—from Pampers to rat poison—right to the painted tin ceiling. A barrel-chested man with a thick black mustache was busy replenishing the beer stock. Watching cops investigating a bombing is thirsty work for the community.

Behind the counter a woman and a teenage girl, presumably the owner's wife and daughter, were stacking and dusting shelves. The only way for a bodega owner to survive economic disaster was to keep the overhead down, and the best way to do that was to employ family members. Age didn't matter; Castillo had seen them from nine to ninety behind the counter.

Castillo marveled at the resiliency of the bodega entrepreneur. He paid exorbitant rents to absentee landlords, and seldom qualified for insurance—and only then at usurious premiums. Bodegas opened at six in the morning and closed as late as the owner's courage would permit, seven days a week, fifty-two weeks a year. And for what? To eke out a living and hope that in the early morning hours some stoned junkie with a .357 Magnum didn't come into his store and blow him away for a register full of singles.

The man slipped the last can into the refrigerator and turned to Castillo. "Yes, what can I do for you?"

"*Cerveza.* Whatever's coldest."

The man slipped the can into a small bag and gave it to Castillo. The bag was a concession to the sensibilities of the police. Drinking alcohol in the street is not permitted, but when it's wrapped in a small brown bag, no one knows what's being drunk. The police and the community had long ago agreed to share this fiction.

Castillo popped the top and addressed the man in Spanish. "What happened outside?" he asked.

The bodega owner looked out the window and nervously wiped his hands on his apron. "There was an explosion. One cop died and they took the other away in a police car." He shook his head. "This block is getting crazy, man. Shootings, stabbings, and now this."

Castillo went to the door and peered across the street. A few people were milling about the stoop. An old man was pointing to the bloodstains at the foot of the stairs and shaking his head.

"Damn," Castillo said. "I thought Newark was bad. But ain't no one blowin' away the Law. Someone got a problem with the cops around here?"

"Probably the crackheads. Those buildings are supposed to be abandoned, but the junkies break in and live there. They shoot up" —he made an injection motion with his hand—"they sell all kind of drugs. Who knows what else they do in there. All the time, day and night, strangers driving through the block. A lot of them go into those buildings."

"Cops don't do nothin', huh?"

The bodega owner shrugged elaborately. "I call them. They come. They leave. The junkies come back."

Castillo turned toward the owner. "Why don't you get out?"

"Where would I go?" There was bitterness in his voice. "No one would buy this store from me."

Castillo turned his attention back to the stoop across the street. "Did the cops get anybody?"

"I don't know. A block like this, no one sees nothing. Last week a man was shot right in front of my store at ten in the morning. The cops came, they ask everybody, 'You see anything?' No. Nobody see nothing. I been robbed three times in eighteen months. The cops ask me can I identify the robber. I say yes."

"What happened?"

He shrugged. "They never catch the guy."

While Castillo had been talking to the bodega owner, two teenagers had entered the store and disappeared behind the high-stacked shelves. Suddenly, there was an explosion of breaking glass as a bottle of Lysol crashed against the rear wall.

As the owner ran to the back to investigate, one of the youths hopped over the counter. While he was rifling the register, the other stood guard with a sawed-off baseball bat. He brandished the weapon in Castillo's direction. "Stay the fuck out of this, man, or you get a busted head."

**Officer
DOWN**

Castillo looked into the teenager's bright, sparkling eyes and recognized the signs: he was high on angel dust. Putting his beer can on the counter, Castillo stepped between the boy and the door. He was about to draw his gun, when the owner and his family, huddled in the back of the store, moved directly into the line of fire.

The other youth, with the bills from the register stuffed into his jacket pockets, slid back over the counter. His feet caught a cigarette display, sending dozens of cigarette packs cascading onto the floor. He stood behind his accomplice and nervously licked his lips. "Come on, Hector," he said, peeking at Castillo with wide frightened eyes, "let's get the fuck out of here."

The teenager with the bat advanced tentatively toward Castillo. "*Maricón!*" he hissed. "Get out of my fucking way, man."

When he saw that Castillo wasn't going to move, he rushed the DEA agent and swung the bat. Castillo deftly sidestepped the charge and grabbed the youth's wrist. He whipped the arm forward and propelled the youth toward the door. Thrown off balance, the surprised teenager plunged head first through the plate glass door.

The second teen, seeing his partner lying on the sidewalk dazed and bleeding, fell to his knees and covered his head with his arms. "No, man. I didn't do nothin'."

Castillo grabbed him by the collar and jerked him to his feet. He pulled his right fist back to deliver a blow, but then he saw that the terrified youth was no more than fifteen. He opened his hand and slapped the boy's face until he was bleeding from the mouth and nose. Then he ripped the youth's jacket off and bills fluttered to the ground. When Castillo was satisfied that he'd recovered all the money, he turned the kid toward the door and with a solid kick to his back sent him sprawling out on to the sidewalk next to his bleeding partner. Without looking back they stumbled to their feet and stumbled down the street.

The frightened owner came forward slowly. "*Madre mia!* You see what I mean?"

Castillo nodded toward the door. "You got insurance for that?"

The man shook his head. "No more. These things happen too often." He knelt down and started picking up his money. "Thank you, sir, for your help. But it was a foolish thing to do. These kids are crazy. They kill you for a quarter."

Castillo heard the wail of a police siren in the distance and started for the door. He didn't want to be here when the police arrived. He opened the door and more shards of glass crashed to the floor. *"Tenga cuidado,"* he said to the bodega owner.

The frightened man looked up. "I'll be careful. *Gracias, mi amigo.*"

Chapter
24

7:10 A.M. TUESDAY, APRIL 2 • The next morning Castillo and Morgan came into the office together. Chris Liberti looked up from her computer. *"Qué pasó, señor?"* she asked Castillo. "What did you find out last night?"

He tossed a stack of Spanish newspapers on his desk and sat down. *"Nada.* No one saw nothin'."

"Would they tell you if they did?" she asked.

"Yeah. At least one bodega owner. Unfortunately, he didn't see anything. Except for that one witness, no one saw shit."

Morgan poured a cup of coffee and sat down. "Goddammit. *Someone* had to see something. It had to take time to plant that bomb."

Castillo put his scuffed Nikes on the desk. "Just a couple of minutes."

"It's gotta take longer than that."

"No it wouldn't. If the guy came prepared, that's all the time he'd need. Tape the device, set the trip, and go."

Morgan, irritated by the DEA agent's know-it-all attitude, was about to challenge him when he remembered what Cassidy had told him: Castillo had been a demolitions expert in the army.

"I wonder if this was the same guy who made the phone call in Queens?" Liberti asked.

"No." Morgan took a tape out of his briefcase. "A female made this call. I picked it up from Communications on my way here."

Liberti pulled a tape recorder out of her desk and inserted the tape. The sound quality was poor and she had to keep adjusting the volume. The 911 operator's voice was heard first.

"Police Operator Forty-seven. What is your emergency?"

The female voice was low and hesitant. *"I'd like to report . . . I mean . . . I saw a man drag a little girl into this building—"*

"What is the address?"

". . . I heard screams."

"The address. I need the address."

"What? Oh. East a hundred fifty-third Street. Three-sixty."

"Can you describe the perpetrator?"

"It was too dark. I . . . you'd better send someone quick. I think he's going to rape her."

"360 East 153rd Street. Is that correct?"

"Yes."

"May I have your name and a call-back number?"

"No . . . I . . ." The phone went dead.

The three stared intently at the tape recorder as though it might offer visual clues as well. Morgan got up and pressed the Stop button. "Comments? Impressions?"

"The call was made from the street," Castillo said. "I heard traffic noise in the background."

Liberti tapped a pencil against her cheek. "The voice was nervous, sort of mechanical—as if she was reading from a script."

Morgan summed it up. "So we have a white, nervous female who made the call from a street telephone."

"She's Hispanic," Castillo said firmly.

Morgan frowned. "I didn't hear that. Did you, Chris?"

Liberti rewound the tape and played it again. When it had ended, she said, "If she has an accent, I didn't hear it."

"Take my word for it," Castillo said. "She's Hispanic."

Morgan ejected the tape and handed it to Liberti. "Can you have a voice graph analysis done on this?"

"I think so. The sound is poor, but they can probably filter out the background noise. Dan, the Tech Services people had a hell of a time with that Queens tape. Maybe you could suggest that the PD purchase better quality tapes."

"I will," Morgan said dryly. "As soon as our budget equals the Bureau's." Morgan sat on the edge of Castillo's desk. "So what have we got?"

"There are at least two people in Puño Blanco—a female caller and a male bomber," Castillo offered.

"Not necessarily," Liberti interjected. "Maybe the woman planted the bomb."

Morgan shook his head. "Negative. I spoke to the Arson/Explosion detective on the scene. It was a professional job."

Liberti's right eyebrow arched. "There were plenty of women bomb makers in the sixties."

Morgan saw Castillo peel the cellophane from a cigar and quickly moved back to his own desk. "Attaching an alarm clock to four sticks of dynamite isn't the same as rigging a bomb with mercury switches and trip wires."

"You think a woman wouldn't know how to—"

"What the hell's the difference," Castillo said through a cloud of black smoke. "We know there are at least two people in the group."

"And professional," Morgan added morosely. "Five cops killed and we still don't have anything to go on." Morgan eyed the *Daily News* headline: POLICE JOB ACTION THREATENS TO PARALYZE CITY and a renewed sense of urgency gripped him. "We're running out of time, folks. Chris, are you staying on top of the lab people?"

"Sure. I've been calling them three times a day. The lab supervisor told me to get off his back. They're having a problem raising the prints, but he promised to call me the minute he gets results."

At the sound of the word "police" the three turned to the TV, which was tuned to a morning news program. The camera, panning the front of police headquarters, showed several dozen off-duty police officers carrying signs saying COPS AREN'T CANNON FODDER and COPS AREN'T HUMAN SACRIFICES.

A somber female reporter with straight blond hair stepped in front of the camera and said, "Off-duty police officers have been arriving at police headquarters since before seven this morning. Last night's tragic bombing and subsequent deaths of two policemen in the Bronx has apparently pushed the patience of the police to its breaking point. I've spoken to several officers, none of whom wish to be identified on camera, and they say they are no longer willing to be sitting ducks for the unknown assassins who have killed five of their own in the last three weeks."

The studio anchorman broke in. "Linda, what demands are they making?"

"First, they want the police commissioner to acknowledge that these killings are related, and second, they want drastic measures implemented to insure their safety."

"What would those measures be?"

"They want backups on every radio car run they respond to and they want to be authorized to carry automatic weapons in their radio cars."

"Linda, is this backup plan feasible?"

"No, Frank, it's not. The commanding officer of the department's Communications unit told me that they receive nearly nine million calls on nine-eleven annually. Those calls generate nearly four million radio car runs. As it is, the department barely has the resources to handle that volume. If they have to send two cars to each run, I'm told many calls will have to go unanswered."

"Linda, what about the issue of automatic weapons?"

"A high-ranking source in the department has told me that demand is untenable. Even if the department were willing to go along with it—and I'm told that it's definitely against such an idea—the logistics would be a nightmare. Each man and woman—all thirty thousand of them—would have to go to the range at Rodman's Neck to qualify in the use of the weapons. And that would take considerably more time than these demonstrators are willing to wait."

The video cut to the front steps of City Hall and showed Police Commissioner Thomas Cassidy hurrying grimly up the stairs. "Linda," the studio anchor said, "we've just gotten word that Commissioner Cassidy has been summoned to City Hall. Can you comment on that?"

"No, Frank, I can't. But I would assume that he's there to brief the mayor on the department's contingency plans to deal with this latest crisis."

Liberti turned the TV off as the station broke for a commercial.

"Heavy shit," Castillo said through a cloud of smoke.

"Yeah," Liberti said. "I guess it can't get any worse than this."

"Yes, it can."

Morgan and Liberti turned to the DEA agent. Castillo, carefully rotating his cigar to keep it burning evenly, said, "This job action means Puño Blanco may have completed the first phase of their operation."

Morgan felt his stomach knot. If Castillo was right, Puño Blanco was probably preparing for the main event right now. He suddenly felt claustrophobic. He had to do something, anything but hanging around the office listening to Liberti's goddamn computer cranking out more names. "I'm going to interview that witness," he said.

"I'll go with you," Liberti said.

Castillo looked at his watch. "I'm going out to the Island. I've got a date with a real estate lady."

.   .   .

It was almost two P.M. by the time Liberti and Morgan tracked down Angel Ortiz at his place of employment, a commercial building in midtown Manhattan. It took some doing to convince the suspicious building manager that Ortiz was not in trouble with the police, and he finally summoned the maintenance man to his office. At Morgan's insistence the nosy manager reluctantly left the three of them alone.

Angel Ortiz, wearing a well-ironed green maintenance uniform, was a stocky man in his early thirties. He looked up at Morgan. "Last night I told the police everything I know."

Morgan pushed a pile of papers aside and sat on the edge of the manager's cluttered desk. "I know. We'll try not to take up too much of your time. I understand you live on the next block from where the explosion occurred?"

"*Sí* . . . I mean, yes."

Liberti, who was occupying one of the two chairs in the tiny office, leaned forward. "Mr. Ortiz, would you be more comfortable speaking Spanish? We can get someone who—"

Ortiz's eyes flashed. "No. I can speak English."

Morgan groaned inwardly. The last thing he needed was a woman challenging his Latino witness's language ability. "I'm sure that won't be necessary," he said, more for her benefit than Ortiz's.

Liberti caught the cautionary message in Morgan's tone and bit her lip.

"Mr. Ortiz," Morgan continued, "where do you live in relationship to the building where the bombing occurred?"

"I live on the next block. The back of my apartment faces the back of that building." Ortiz took a pack of cigarettes out of his shirt pocket. Out of the corner of his eye, Morgan saw Liberti roll her eyes.

"Why don't you tell us what you saw?"

Ortiz sucked on the cigarette and smoke quickly filled the small room. "I just got home from work—"

"What time was that?"

"A little after six. I opened the window and I see this guy standing in the window of that building."

"What was he doing?"

"Nothing. Just standing there in the dark. Then he sticks his head

out and looks around real fast. Next thing, he jumps out the window."
Ortiz shook his head. "I seen a lot of crazy things go on in that
building; junkies selling and shooting up dope and stuff. But I never
seen no one jump out no window."

"How high is the window from the ground?"

"Maybe ten feet. He landed like a cat, you know? Just like that
dude in the Batman movie."

"Then what did he do?"

"He ran toward my building and disappeared into the cellar. "It
was really weird the way he did that without tripping over anything.
That yard is full of crap. I seen cops chasing junkies through there
and they're always falling on their asses." His grin faded when he
saw that Morgan wasn't amused. "Anyway, this guy ran through there
like he was floating or something. It was really weird."

Liberti leaned forward. "What floor do you live on, Mr. Ortiz?"
Ortiz exhaled smoke in her direction and she quickly sat back.

"The second."

"At that angle you must have gotten a good look at him."

"It was dark. And it happened real fast."

Morgan continued. "What was he wearing?"

"A black jacket and black pants."

"How tall?"

"Maybe six feet, but I ain't sure."

"Color?"

"White."

"You sure?"

"He was wearing a baseball hat, but I saw blond hair underneath."

"Did you see anyone else?"

Ortiz shook his head.

"Could you identify the man if you saw him or a photo of him?"

"The cops asked me that last night. I didn't get a real good look at
him."

Ortiz mistook the disappointment on Morgan's face for doubt.
"Hey, man," he said, crushing his cigarette into an ashtray. "I'm not
afraid to finger that dude. I got a kid and I'm fed up with the shit that
goes down in that neighborhood. If I could identify him I would."

Looking into Angel Ortiz's defiant eyes, Morgan believed him. He was exactly what a cop looked for in a witness: good powers of observation and lack of fear—two rare commodities in ghetto neighborhoods. There was only one thing wrong with Mr. Ortiz as a witness: he hadn't gotten a good look at the blond man, no doubt the same blond man Officer Amonti had seen looking at him from the rear window of the Mustang and the one Dan Morgan had seen driving the Blazer. The one who looked so cool, so calm. So professional.

Chapter
25

It was almost four-thirty by the time Castillo, dressed in a dark blue business suit, stepped into a real estate office on Main Street in Riverhead.

A heavyset woman, wearing oversize turquoise glasses, looked up. "Yes, may I help you?"

"Mrs. Goff?"

"That's me." Her predatory smile revealed a mouthful of capped teeth. "Please call me Goldie. And what can I do for you, Mr. . . . ?

"Moreno. I'm interested in leasing a large tract of land in this area. Do you think you could help me?"

She slipped her glasses off and squinted at him through mascara-ladened eyes. "Is this for yourself or do you represent a company, Mr. Moreno?"

"A company." He lowered his voice and winked. "I can't say any more than that. I'm sure you understand."

She leaned forward and her overpowering perfume stung the inside of his nose. "Oh, I do indeed," she said. "There are many, many large developers who are leasing or who have purchased outright land in our fair community. When the economy turns around, the land in this area will be worth a fortune. But I'm sure you already know that." When he didn't answer, she continued. "How much property are you looking for exactly?"

"That depends. But I'd say at least a couple of thousand acres." What the hell, he thought, as long as he was going to be a developer, he might as well go big time.

Goldie Goff's eyes widened and he could almost see dollar signs flashing in her dilated pupils. "Mr. Moreno, I'm sure we can accommodate you. Do you have a specific area in mind?"

"Yes. Do you have aerial maps?"

She led him to a back room where there was a wall-size aerial photograph of the area. He tapped the spot that Morgan and Liberti had identified as the location of the firing range. "Somewhere around here."

Mrs. Goff slipped her glasses off and squinted at the photo. "I'm afraid this area has only small parcels available. Nothing of the size you are looking for."

Castillo tapped the spot again. "That's too bad. We're really interested in that area."

Mrs. Goff chewed on the tip of her glasses with her expensive teeth. "It's funny you should be interested in that particular area. I sold two hundred acres at that very location just a few months ago."

Castillo knew that. He'd already been to the town hall and had read the deed recordings. That's how he knew she was the real estate agent of record. He also knew that the land had been sold to KTR Industries and he was hoping she could shed some light on who those letters represented. Castillo smiled knowingly. "Any chance you sold that land to KTR Industries?"

Her eyes widened. "Why, yes. How did you—"

"We in corporate acquisitions represent a very small community, Goldie. We often run into each other at auctions and conventions. The last time I ran into someone from KTR they said they were interested in the North Fork. Did you deal with Paul Webster? A blond-haired man about six feet—"

"No. A Mr. Nieves."

"A short man with a salt and pepper beard?"

"That's right. You know him?"

"Not very well. I only met him once. I'm terrible with names. Let me see . . . Carlos . . . ?"

"Antonio."

"Antonio Nieves. Right. It certainly is a small world, isn't it?"

"It certainly is."

"KTR specializes in strip malls. You must have done very well for yourself."

Goldie Goff's face sagged in disappointment. "I tried to talk him into more expen— suitable land, but he was quite adamant about that specific location."

Castill studied the map closely. That particular location was perfect for a firing range. There wasn't a house for miles around.

Goldie, who was also studying the map, said, "Seems like an awfully isolated place to build a strip mall."

"You never know," he said. "I'm sure he had his reasons."

"I guess so. Mr. Nieves certainly was secretive. I don't think he said more than twenty-five words to me the whole time I was with him."

Castillo saw that there was nothing more Goldie could offer him

MICHAEL GRANT

and he took his leave. But not before he promised the discouraged woman to return the next day to visit some promising sites.

When Morgan and Liberti got back from interviewing Ortiz, they'd spent the rest of the afternoon cross-checking names on Liberti's computer lists. The list was getting shorter, but it was still too long. It was almost eight o'clock by the time Morgan stood up and said, "That's it, Chris. Let's call it a day."

As they were going out the door, the telephone rang. Morgan picked it up. "Yeah?"

"Hey, Danny boy, what are you doin' for dinner?"

It was Hank Staiger, Morgan's DEA contact. He waved Liberti on and sat down. "Thanks for getting back to me so fast, you hump."

"Hey, you're lucky I'm calling you at all. I'm up to my ass in alligators here."

"You're breaking my heart."

"Hey, Morgan, you want to have dinner? Yes or no?"

"Where?"

"Downtown. Near the office."

Morgan jotted down the name and address and hung up. As he was locking the door, he muttered an oath. On the other side of the door Liberti's damn computer started chattering. And that meant one thing; more names to check.

Morgan got to the restaurant early and took the opportunity to call home to say goodnight to his son, whom he hadn't seen in over a week. But he was too late. Sarah coolly informed him that his son had already gone to bed. She was still furious at him for not showing up Easter morning and the strained conversation ended quickly.

Exasperated, he went into the bar and ordered a double scotch. He was halfway through his second drink when he spotted Hank Staiger coming toward him. Staiger, who had always been heavy, had gained even more weight since they'd last met, but there was no mistaking the flamboyant DEA agent's huge handlebar mustache.

Morgan took his drink and they followed the waiter to a table in the rear. As soon as they were seated, Staiger grabbed his throat dramatically with one hand and the waiter's arm with the other. "I need a drink," he whispered hoarsely. He looked at Morgan. "What are you drinking?"

"Scotch."

"Yeah, it's been that kind of a day." He released his viselike grip on the waiter's arm. "Make mine a double. I gotta catch up."

He picked up a breadstick and bit it in half. "So, Danny, how's your sperm count?"

Morgan grinned. "Hank, we haven't seen each other in over a year and the first thing you ask is how's my sperm count?"

"Jeez, I'm sorry." He reached a huge hand across the table. "How have you been, sir?"

"Fine."

Staiger's eyes narrowed. "You look like shit."

"Thanks."

"You lose some weight?"

"I don't think so."

"Maybe it's me." He patted his ample stomach. "I'm getting bigger, so I guess everyone looks smaller." The eyes narrowed again. "You *have* lost weight. You don't have cancer, do you?"

Morgan smiled at his irreverent friend. "If I did, you'd be the first to know."

"You okay from the shooting?"

"Yeah."

Staiger popped the rest of the breadstick into his mouth. "Police Combat Cross, huh? Some guys will do anything to get a medal." He leaned across the table and whispered, "Level with me, Danno, did you shoot yourself or what?"

"If I was going to shoot myself, Hank, I'd have aimed for the head or some other nonvital organ."

Staiger's hearty belly laugh caused a few heads to turn. "I'm glad to see your sense of humor has improved."

The waiter returned with the drinks. "Are you ready to order, gentlemen?"

Staiger looked at his watch and frowned. "Yeah, I guess we'd better. I gotta get back to the office."

MICHAEL GRANT

Morgan saw a chance to needle Staiger. "I thought you big bosses worked regular hours."

Staiger grunted and buried his face in the menu. After a cursory look, he handed it back to the waiter and said, "I want a big steak very rare." He looked up at the waiter to emphasize his point. "I want it so rare it'll moo when I stick my fork into it. Got it?"

"Yes, sir. Very rare."

Morgan ordered prime rib.

When the waiter had gone, Staiger raised his glass. "Here's to two old marriage-wrecked cops with nothing better to do than have dinner like a couple of fucking old maids."

Morgan touched his glass. "Hank, you always had a way with words."

Staiger shrugged modestly. "How long you separated, Danny?"

"Nine months."

Staiger attacked a butter patty with the end of a breadstick. "You don't mind if I delve into your private life, do you?"

"It's never stopped you before."

"Sarah is a great lady and you're not a bad guy. So what happened?"

Morgan took a drink and waited for the burning sensation in his throat to subside. "The usual. She thinks I care more for the job than I do for her." That wasn't the primary reason for their separation, but it was the only one he was willing to talk about.

"Is she right?"

That was a question Morgan had been asking himself since the separation and he still didn't know the answer. "I don't know. What are you up to?" he asked, trying to change the subject.

"The usual bullshit." The DEA agent looked glum. "Sometimes I think I should get out. It's not the same being a boss. I'm drowning in paperwork. I miss the action. Don't you?"

"Hank, I'm—" He stopped himself in time. He'd almost told his friend about his new assignment. "The paperwork gets in the way sometimes," he added quickly, "but there's still enough action to keep me interested."

Staiger looked doubtful. "Even as a boss?" He picked up another

Officer
DOWN

breadstick. When he saw that he had no more butter, he reached over and took Morgan's. "This shit's full of cholesterol. You don't need it." Without missing a beat he continued. "I don't think I should have taken this fucking promotion. I got a title, I'm making more money, but it sucks. The only action I get is trying to hit on the boss's secretary."

"Any luck?"

"Naw. She's in her twenties. She looks upon me as her *father*, for chrissake. Let's face it, Danno, us old guys have been put on waivers."

"What do you mean *us*? I'm only forty-five."

The DEA looked interested. "Danno, you getting any?"

"None of your business."

"You ain't getting shit, are you?"

"Can we change the subject?"

Staiger's eyes widened. "You don't wanna talk about sex? What else is there?"

"Donal Castillo."

"Okay, okay. The word is that he's good. In fact, one of the best. Apparently, Castillo is a man of many faces. The brass in Washington are real high on him. But—"

"But what?"

"The field supervisors who have to work with him don't share that opinion."

"Why?"

"They say he's a bit of a maverick; marches to his own drummer. Frankly, the field bosses I spoke to say he's a real pain in the ass. A good agent, but a pain in the ass. On the other hand, other agents like him. When he goes after something, he's like a guided missile."

Staiger finished his drink in one gulp and gently wiped the ends of his mustache with the napkin. "Did some undercover work for us in Miami and Colombia. They tell me he actually infiltrated the Medellin cartel. Now *that* took balls."

Morgan studied Staiger's big, friendly face. "I hear another 'but' in your tone. What's wrong with him?"

"He lost a partner in Miami and he took it pretty hard."

MICHAEL GRANT

"What happened?"

"I don't know the whole story. It seems Castillo and his partner were doing a UC operation on a Colombian-controlled Miami group. Someone fingered them as narcs. Castillo was warned in time; his partner wasn't."

"What happened to his partner?"

"We put every available agent into Miami and scoured the city for three days. Castillo was the one who found the body. I hear it was pretty gruesome. Those mothers play hardball."

"Is he married?"

"Only to the DEA."

The food arrived. Staiger lowered his ear to the plate and stabbed the meat with his knife. He looked up. "Hear that? The death rattle. I think I just killed it. Now *that's* rare!"

Morgan cut into his prime rib and tried to ignore his ghoulish friend.

Staiger skewered a bloody piece of meat on the end of his fork and waved it in the air. "Ya know, this reminds me of an autopsy I attended once. It was the first time we found out mules were swallowing condoms stuffed with cocaine. It was the damnedest thing. The X-ray looked like he'd swallowed a link of sausages. No shit. I was getting ready to call the FDA in on the case. When the doc cut him open my partner passed out. He thought the poor bastard had been attacked by giant intestinal worms. The mule had swallowed *fifteen* condoms. Do you believe that shit? Unfortunately, one of them broke and hot-loaded him to hell. What a way to go." He waved the bloody piece of meat at Morgan. "There's a moral to be learned here, Danno. *Never* use cheap condoms."

All the while Staiger told his story, Morgan nodded and grunted as though it were the most interesting dinner conversation he'd ever heard. He knew how Staiger's mind worked. Any sign of revulsion on the part of the listener only encouraged him to tell even grosser stories.

Staiger, peering across the table at his old friend, looked mildly disappointed at Morgan's lack of reaction. "Danno," he said, changing the subject, "why do you want to know about Castillo?"

"Can't tell you, old friend."

Staiger nodded. "Okay." He was enough of a professional not to pry further.

They spent the rest of dinner talking shop. After Staiger had finished polishing off a huge slice of apple pie topped with a double scoop of chocolate ice cream, Morgan signaled for the check. "I guess this is one advantage to being separated. I have time to have dinner with old friends."

"Who are you kidding, Dan? You never rushed home when you were married."

With a start—and a stab of guilt—Morgan realized his friend was right.

The waiter returned and Morgan signed his credit card voucher. Staiger popped an after-dinner mint in his mouth and pocketed Morgan's. "This shit's full of calories. It's not good for you."

When the waiter had gone, Morgan, concerned that he might have given away too much by his questions, said, "Hank, you're a smart son of a bitch. I don't want you putting two and two together from our conversation."

Staiger's eyes widened in amazement. "I won't. Swear to God. But if I do," he added slyly, "my lips are sealed."

On the way back to his apartment Dan Morgan reflected on the strange subculture of policemen. Despite their commonality of purpose, law-enforcement agencies harbored a deep distrust of each other. Because of this suspicion they often unwittingly conducted parallel investigations with embarrassing, if sometimes humorous, results.

More than once the police department and a federal agency had literally bumped into each other as streets full of speeding cars gave chase after the same fleeing suspect. At other times jubilant cops with suspect in tow had been met on the stairs by tardy, if breathless, federal agents waving a warrant for the same prisoner.

Fortunately for the public's safety, this official mistrust didn't always filter down to the cops and agents who worked in the streets.

MICHAEL GRANT

Friendships forged in damp cellars, in the backs of freezing surveillance trucks, and in smoke-filled gin mills, overrode the official interagency rivalries. So while paranoid bureaucratic administrators plotted their investigations behind closed doors, cops and agents sat over a couple of beers and freely exchanged the information they needed to get the job done.

But even in these informal settings there were unwritten rules. One was allowed to seek information without offering explanation and answers were provided without question. It was understood that secrets had to be kept and the need for confidentiality was respected. But that didn't stop cops, curious by nature, from drawing their own inferences from blandly worded queries. Nevertheless, Morgan was confident that even if Staiger guessed the reasons behind his questions, he'd never reveal his thoughts to anyone.

Back in his apartment he stayed awake watching TV until his eyes grew heavy with sleep. For a little added insurance, just before he went to bed, he drank a double scotch straight up, hoping to anesthetize himself from his dreams.

4:25 A.M. WEDNESDAY, APRIL 3 • Jimmy and Glen sat in a stolen car under the West Side Highway facing a hulking, rotting warehouse, a remnant of better days when the New York waterfront was the center of shipping commerce. In those days a variety of ships, from sparkling white ocean liners to rusting cargo freighters, sailed into the port of New York to disgorge everything from bluebloods in silk hats and furs to crates of bananas and tractors.

But that time had passed. The largest of the ocean liners, dinosaurs in the age of the Concorde, had been consigned to salvage yards, while smaller, more economically viable ships now sailed out of Miami and earned their keep by ferrying vacationers to and from the Caribbean Islands. The flotilla of rusting freighters had scattered to other ports of call in nearby Brooklyn and New Jersey.

The city, in its slow, plodding way, had been making plans to revitalize the waterfront, but the location Lyle Petry had chosen for this clandestine meeting wasn't even on the drawing board yet. He'd chosen it precisely because it was a deserted area, used primarily as a truck storage depot for neighboring warehouses.

Jimmy, impatiently drumming his fingers on his knee, sat up and nudged Glen. "Here they come," he whispered.

Glen, who'd been dozing, blinked the sleep out of his eyes and watched the dirty white panel truck pull into a space between two parked trailers.

Before he got out of the car, Jimmy glanced up and down the street. When he was satisfied no one was around, he opened the door. "Wait here," he said. "I'll check 'em out first."

A short, dark-skinned Hispanic stepped out of the panel truck and pulled his collar up around his neck to shield himself from the damp wind blowing off the Hudson River.

Jimmy walked up to him. "How's the weather in Philly tonight?" he asked.

Pepe Aruano's anxious expression collapsed into a nervous smile of broken and black teeth. For a moment he'd been afraid that the stranger approaching him was a policeman, but the scowling, dark-haired man had asked the right question.

The mysterious nature of this job had made Aruano uncomfortable, but the man with the salt and pepper beard, a fellow Colombian, had promised him and his cousin a lot of money to make the delivery. Aruano didn't know what was in the back of the truck, but he assumed it was narcotics. Back in Philadelphia, Aruano had been told that the man with the beard was connected to the Medellin cartel. If he and his cousin did a good job, the man had promised, he and his cousin would get other jobs. And that would mean more money to send home to his wife and seven children.

Now, Pepe Aruano's brow furrowed as he tried to remember the correct response to the question. His English wasn't very good and the sentence he had been instructed to say made no sense to him. "Hotter than hell in August," he said haltingly.

Jimmy nodded. "You're late. What happened?"

The look in the stranger's eyes frightened Aruano. He looked down at the ground and concentrated on a grease patch on the broken concrete. "I am sorry. I did not want to get caught speeding on the turnpike with . . ." He inclined his head toward the panel truck.

Jimmy looked into the front seat. "Who's that?"

"My cousin, Ralph. He can be trusted." As soon as he said it, he regretted it. It came out sounding like maybe he couldn't be trusted. But the stranger seemed to take no notice.

Jimmy turned and motioned toward Glen. "Okay, *amigo*," he said to Aruano. "Let's do it."

Glen pulled the car alongside of the truck and he and Jimmy watched as Aruano and his cousin transferred five boxes to the trunk of the car.

When they were done, Aruano slammed the trunk and nervously wiped his sweating hands on his tattered polyester slacks. "We go now." He nodded to his cousin, and the young man, who didn't speak a word of English, walked back toward the passenger side of the truck. Glen followed him.

Jimmy put his arm around Aruano as they walked toward the driver's side. "*Amigo*, you did a good job."

Aruano was uncomfortable with the stranger's arm around his shoulder, but all he said was, "Thank you."

Without warning, Jimmy's arm slid around to the front of Aruano's throat. A blade flashed in the darkness and Jimmy, with an upward thrust, buried the knife up to the hilt in Aruano's back. Jimmy felt the blade scrape against the backbone and twisted the handle sharply. The two hands tightly gripping his forearm relaxed and Aruano's paralyzed body slumped to the ground. Jimmy grabbed the man's hair and with one quick motion yanked the head back, exposing the throat, and deftly severed the carotid artery.

It had all happened so fast the terrified man had not had the opportunity to scream. Now, the horror on Aruano's face gave way to puzzlement. He looked up at Jimmy wide-eyed. He tried to mouth the word "why," but it came out a wet, gurgling sound.

On the other side of the truck, Aruano's cousin had opened the door just in time to see an arm go around Pepe's throat. He was about to yell a warning when something looped around his neck and he felt his body being jerked off the ground backward. Frantically, he

271 **Officer DOWN**

clawed at the thing that was choking him. Bright lights flashed before his eyes and his oxygen-starved lungs felt as though they were going to explode. Then everything went black.

Glen, who had thrown a loop of piano wire around the man's neck, had pivoted and pulled the man onto his back. He felt the body jerk in its death spasms, then become still. He gave one last tug on the wire and released the body.

Ignoring the stench of excrement hanging in the air, Glen bent over the lifeless body. Carefully avoiding the blood dripping from the thin, red line across the man's throat, he put two fingers on the carotid artery. Satisfied there was no pulse, he rose, coiled the wire and ran around to the other side of the vehicle.

Jimmy, wiping the bloody blade against his victim's jacket, looked around carefully to make sure they hadn't dropped anything. "Okay," he said calmly. "Let's go."

The ringing telephone shattered the only decent night's sleep Dan Morgan had had in a week. He groped for the phone and squinted at the clock radio. The red numerals showed 5:05. "Yeah?"

"Inspector Morgan? Detective Scott from the Chief of Detectives office. I got an order here says we're supposed to call you on all unusual homicides."

At the beginning of this investigation, Morgan had asked the PC to issue such an order. It was better to lose a little sleep than to miss out on a homicide that might lead to Puño Blanco. "Yeah." Morgan rubbed his eyes. "What've you got?"

" 'Bout ten minutes ago a Tenth Precinct sector car came across a double homicide over by the piers. One victim was stabbed to death. The other was strangled. Apparently by piano wire."

"Piano wire?" Morgan sat up and reached for a pad and pencil. "You got a perp?"

"Not at this time."

"Victims?"

"Two unidentified male Hispanics. The precinct also recovered a panel truck at the scene with Pennsylvania plates." The detective

MICHAEL GRANT

chuckled. "Jesus. *Piano* wire! Not too many guys get snuffed with piano wire around here."

That's exactly what Morgan had been thinking. After he hung up he called Castillo and told him to meet him at the scene. He was going to call Chris, but decided there was no point in all of them losing sleep.

Fifteen minutes later, Morgan drove up to the scene. Bright yellow evidence tape, defining the crime area, encompassed the space around the white panel truck and two tractor trailers. Pinning his shield on his chest, Morgan slipped under the tape and immediately spotted the distinctive silhouette of Solly Katz. At six feet seven inches, Katz had developed a permanent hunch from leaning down to talk to a much smaller world. If Solly Katz was the tallest cop Morgan knew, he was also the most melancholy. Ever since *Man of La Mancha* had come to Broadway, Solly Katz had been dubbed the "detective of the woeful countenance." Morgan had never met a more pessimistic man, nor a better detective.

"Solly, you catching this one?"

The detective turned around and his eyebrows went up. "Inspector Morgan, you in the borough?"

"The PC's office. I was just passing by."

"Ah, a friend in high places. Have you come to take me away from all this?"

Morgan grinned. "From what? Being a detective? The most exciting job in the Police Department?"

Katz raised one eyebrow in recognition of the sarcasm. "Inspector Morgan, I've been a second grader for over ten years. I'm fifty-six. I shouldn't have to schlep through blood and guts at five o'clock in the morning. Where did I go wrong?"

Morgan patted the detective's arm. "It's a dirty job, Solly, but someone's gotta do it."

Katz scratched his balding head. "Another hour and I'd have been off the clock. Now I'm going to be up the rest of the day trying to solve these two mysteries."

Morgan followed Katz's gaze. The two bodies, still in their original positions, were covered by plastic sheets. "Have you ID'd them?"

"No, sir. They got no wallets on them. Two John Does. Or is it *Juan* Does?" Katz's smile consisted of baring his front teeth and grimacing as though he were passing a kidney stone.

"Any motive?"

"It ain't robbery. They both got a little money in their pockets and one still has a watch and a ring."

"What do you think, Solly?"

Katz shrugged elaborately. "Me? I don't know what to think. But the ME said—"

"The ME was here already?" Usually it took hours for the medical examiner to show up at a homicide.

"I lucked out. He was at a suicide around the corner." Katz tried another smile. "We got so many homicides in this city we oughta assign an ME to each sector car."

"Next time I talk to the PC I'll recommend it. What's he say?"

Katz pointed to one of the bodies, which appeared to be floating in a copious sea of reddish-brown coagulated blood. "Very unusual. That one was stabbed in the back. Just once, but it severed the spinal column. The doc says that would instantly paralyze him. Then for the coup de grâce, the perp sliced through the carotid artery. The poor bastard died of shock due to massive loss of blood."

Morgan began to lose interest in the murders. It sounded like the murderer was some screwball with a medical background. "Were the cuts surgical?"

"Nope. But not the work of a slasher either. The doc says whoever did this knows how to use a knife."

"How about the other guy?"

"Garroted by a thin wire. Very exotic. I ain't never seen one of those before. But the ME has."

"Where?"

" 'Nam. He said those guys— Whaddaya call them? You know. The guys who used to take on battalions of gooks with Swiss Army knives and shit."

Morgan felt a knot in his stomach. "Green Berets," he said softly.

"Yeah, that's it. The doc said they used to do shit like that in Vietnam."

Morgan had turned his attention to the white panel truck. "What's in there."

"Not a thing. Even the glove compartment's empty."

Morgan suddenly had an idea. "Solly, call the Bomb Squad. Get the dog out here to sniff the truck."

"Whaaat . . . ?"

"It's a hunch, Solly. Indulge me. Okay?"

Katz grunted at the thought of adding more work to this bullshit double homicide. "Indulge. Is that a new word for Do it?"

"You got it. And don't let anyone near that truck until the dog has a go at it." He saw Castillo standing across the street smoking a cigar. "Get on it right away." Then he added, "Hey, Solly, you crack this one, you might make first grade."

"That'd be nice."

Morgan couldn't tell if Katz was smiling or having a gas attack.

He walked across the street and filled Castillo in. Fifteen minutes later, the Bomb Squad station wagon pulled up. A handler opened the back gate and a frisky black Labrador retriever jumped out.

Morgan and Castillo came across the street just in time to see the dog climb into the back of the panel truck. He circled the interior, sniffing every corner. Then he stepped back and sat down.

Morgan shivered involuntarily and it wasn't because of the damp night air. Bomb Squad dogs were trained to sit down when they smelled explosives. "Don," he said quietly, "the ordnance for the big event has been delivered."

Castillo dropped his cigar into a puddle and looked at Morgan with coal-black eyes. "Then they're going to do it soon."

Chapter
26

2:00 P.M. THURSDAY, APRIL 4 • Just three days after Ray Fleming had agreed to take part in the robbery, Petry called. "Ray, what are you doing now?"

"Nothing."

"Good. A money match has just materialized and I need a partner. You game?"

"Sure. When?"

"Right now. I'll pick you up in ten minutes. Queens Boulevard and Forty-third."

Ten minutes later, Petry pulled up to the corner. Fleming had been expecting the Blazer and was surprised to see Petry driving a tan Buick that apparently hadn't seen the inside of a car wash in months. He was also surprised to see Jimmy sitting in the back seat. Petry had said nothing about him coming.

Petry swung the door open. "Jump in."

Fleming slipped into the front seat and turned toward the man in the back. "You going to the match too, Jimmy?"

The man ignored Fleming and looked at Petry.

"There is no match," Petry said, easing the car away from the curb. "We're going to take down an armored car."

Fleming swallowed hard. *"Now?"* An image of Captain Zakovitch's stern face and his admonishment flashed in Fleming's mind: *As soon as you learn anything about this robbery, let me know.* "I mean we haven't talked about it or made plans or anything."

"*I* made the plans. Your part is simple. All you have to do is drive the car." He tossed Fleming a pair of latex gloves. "Put these on."

For the first time Fleming noticed that Petry was wearing a pair. He fumbled with the tight-fitting gloves and forced himself to concentrate. "Whose car is this?"

"You ask a hell of a lot of questions," Jimmy said from the back seat.

Petry shot Jimmy a withering glance in the rearview mirror. "It's stolen."

"Stolen! What if the police—"

"No problem. By the time the owner realizes his car is missing we'll be long gone."

Ray Fleming knew Morgan and Zakovitch had been displeased with his observations and intelligence gathering and he was determined to do better this time. He glanced out the window to get his bearings. After driving a circuitous route through the side streets of Queens, they arrived at College Point, an area Fleming wasn't familiar with. The streets they were driving through—mostly warehouses and concrete-mixing plants—all looked the same to him. He watched

Officer DOWN

for street signs, but most were missing. Finally he saw one, but Petry said something to him as they passed and he immediately forgot the name of the street. *Damn!* This was harder than he thought.

Petry pulled into a deserted street and stopped. "You drive." He slid over while Fleming walked around to the driver's side.

Fleming sat in the driver's seat and gripped the steering wheel tightly. The latex gloves were making his hands sweat.

Petry was watching him. "You okay, Ray?"

"Sure. I'm just . . . surprised, that's all. I thought we'd talk about it more. Go over some plans. Talk about who does what."

Petry chuckled. "You've been watching too many movies. We're not holding up Fort Knox, just a couple of old guys riding in an armored truck. Go to the corner and turn left."

Fleming, back on College Point Boulevard, wished he knew the area better. There were few landmarks and everything looked the same. He dreaded going back to Zakovitch and telling him he didn't know where they'd been. And Petry's directions didn't help. They made so many lefts and rights—even passing the same intersections several times—that Fleming was hopelessly confused.

Petry's voice broke his concentration. "Pull into the shopping center up ahead."

Fleming turned into a small L-shaped shopping center anchored on one end by a large supermarket. The rest of the building was occupied by a variety of small stores. Petry pointed to a parking spot and Fleming pulled in.

"See the bank?"

Fleming nodded. The bank, almost at the center of the L, was flanked by a dress shop and a jewelry store.

"In about five minutes an armored truck will come by for a pickup. It'll stop right in front. A driver and a guard will go in."

"Do they have guns?"

"Sure."

Fleming felt a rivulet of sweat trickle down his back.

"It'll be a piece of cake," Petry said. "A couple of guys making minimum wage won't be any trouble. Besides, we'll hit them so fast they won't have time to react. Now listen up. Timing is essential.

When they come out, a guard will open the back door. When you see that, start driving slowly toward the truck. When you see us jump them, speed up and be ready to pick us up. I'll toss the bags in the back window and we're outta here."

Fleming felt a cramp in his hand and realized he was squeezing the steering wheel. "Sounds simple enough."

"It is. When we leave, go past the supermarket and turn right. There's an exit at the far end of the parking lot. When we get onto the street, follow my directions. Any questions?"

Fleming blinked at the sound of a metallic click and looked in the rearview mirror. Jimmy had snapped a clip into an Uzi. "No," he answered. "No questions."

Petry's eyes swept the parking lot. "Okay, Jimmy, go."

Before he got out, Jimmy rolled the rear window down and stuffed the weapon into a black gym bag.

Watching Jimmy cross the parking lot, Fleming was amazed at how easily he blended in with the other shoppers. Not one of them would suspect the deadly contents of the bag he carelessly carried over his shoulder.

Petry slipped a 9mm Beretta from his shoulder holster. He checked the magazine, snapped the safety off, and slipped it back into his holster. "Okay, Ray." He opened the door and his eyes, alert, but amazingly serene, fixed Fleming. "It's the same as match shooting, buddy; concentrate, keep the pulse down, and the hand steady." He got out and disappeared into a pizza shop two doors away from the bank.

Alone in the car, Fleming tried to formulate a plan of action, but his mind, fogged by a rush of adrenaline, wasn't functioning properly. He should call Captain Zakovitch. But how? His eyes locked on a telephone booth less than twenty yards away. Was there time? Lyle had said five minutes, but how much time had passed since then? He cursed himself for not remembering to check his watch. He couldn't make the call anyway. Petry and Jimmy might reappear at any moment.

Maybe he could get someone to do it for him. A teenager on a skateboard was coming toward him and a mother, dragging a screaming child and an armful of groceries, was stopping at the car next to him. He could ask them . . . No. They'd think he was crazy.

Fleming drummed his fingertips on the steering wheel. The tightness he felt in his stomach both shamed and disgusted him. What the hell kind of cop would he make if he couldn't deal with pressure? His eyes went back to the telephone. It was so close. He took another look around. Neither Lyle nor Jimmy was in sight. "Fuck it," he said. He jumped out of the car and darted for the telephone. He fumbled through his pockets and came up with a quarter. He was about to deposit it when he looked up and froze. An armored truck had just turned into the parking lot. Slamming the telephone down, he sprinted back to the car just as Petry came out of the pizza shop eating a slice.

Safely back in the car, Fleming rested his head on the backrest. "Jesus! That was close," he said aloud, his eyes glued to Petry, who to the casual observer looked like a bored husband waiting for his wife to finish shopping.

Out of sight, in a hardware store four doors past the bank, Jimmy stood near the front window. He pretended to examine an electric drill, but he'd been watching Fleming's every move.

Fleming eyed the slow-moving truck and took some solace from its sheer massiveness. The squat, squarish vehicle with its thick windows and menacing gunports looked impenetrable. There was no way Lyle and Jimmy were going to get money from *that.*

The truck stopped and the driver, a young man with shoulder-length hair, and a gray-haired guard wheeling a dolly strolled into the bank. Petry casually tossed the remainder of the pizza into a wastebasket and wiped his mouth with a napkin. Fleming looked for Jimmy, but he was still nowhere to be seen.

Less than three minutes later the young guard, holding a gun at his side, came out followed by the older man pulling the dolly now piled high with canvas bags. The truck's back door swung open and the old man maneuvered the dolly into place. Mechanically, Fleming put the car in gear. Slowly, it inched forward. Clutching the steering wheel, he suddenly remembered the half-forgotten terror he'd felt as a child sitting in a darkened theater watching a horror movie. He knew something terrible was about to happen, but he was powerless to prevent it.

Neither guard saw Jimmy, who'd suddenly appeared, briskly walking along the outside of the truck. He swung the gym bag around to his chest and slipped his right hand inside. Petry, quickly glancing right and left, hopped toward the truck and pressed the Beretta to the young guard's throat. The man's eyes widened and his gun clattered to the pavement.

Fleming stepped on the gas and screeched to a halt alongside the truck. Before the car had stopped rocking, Petry was tossing canvas bags into the open rear window, while Jimmy nudged the frightened young guard into the rear of the truck with the barrel of the Uzi.

Fleming's anxiety began to ease. Lyle had been right. There was nothing to it. Everything was happening so quickly none of the shoppers was aware of what was going on.

Then he saw the old guard's hand move toward his holstered gun, and Fleming mouthed a silent no. Jimmy saw the movement at the same time and swung the barrel toward the man. The front of the guard's jacket exploded from the impact of the burst. Thrown against the heavy steel door, he clutched his stomach and crumpled to the pavement.

The Uzi's staccato burst ruptured the routine rhythm of the shopping center. Screaming women, clutching their children, dove into doorways and behind parked cars, while some men, with more curiosity than common sense, stuck their heads up to see what was happening.

Petry and Jimmy were in the car. "Go!" Petry shouted. "Let's get the fuck *out* of here!"

Fleming gunned the accelerator and the car shot forward. As he sped toward the supermarket, he glanced in the rearview mirror. A small crowd was beginning to gather and a man in a white apron was pointing toward them.

"Watch it!" Petry yelled.

Fleming's eyes flicked back to the windshield. He was bearing down on a woman pushing a shopping cart laden with grocery bags, with a young child in the baby seat. As he yanked the wheel to the left, the vehicle skidded out of control. Missing the woman by inches, he slammed into the side of a bread truck and glanced off. Frantically fighting the wheel, he regained control of the vehicle just in time to make the right turn at the end of the supermarket. As the car screeched into the turn both hubcaps flew off and caromed into a parked car.

"Straight ahead," Petry said in a quiet, steady voice.

Fleming saw the exit at the opposite end of the lot and stomped on the accelerator. When they got into the street, Petry said, "Okay. Slow down. Anyone following us?"

Jimmy, who'd been looking back the entire time, said, "We're clear."

"How's the car handling?" Petry asked Fleming.

"Okay."

"Make a left."

Fleming followed Petry's calm, monotone directions without question. Considering what had just happened, he was astonished at Petry's composure.

Careful to stay off main streets, they slowly made their way out of College Point. When they got to Roosevelt Avenue, Petry directed Fleming to the large commuter parking lot near Shea Stadium.

Jimmy, who'd stuffed the bank's canvas bags into an old suitcase, was the first one out of the car. He slung the gym bag over his shoulder, nodded to Petry and, without even looking at Fleming, walked away.

Petry glanced around the lot to make sure no one else was near. "Ray, get out of the car first, then give me your gloves."

Fleming had forgotten he was wearing them. He got out, tore the gloves off, and handed them to Petry, who stuffed them in his pocket.

"Come on, Ray, you look like you could use a drink."

They boarded the subway at Willett's Point. In an hour the rush hour would begin and the subway would become a pushing, swarming mass of people fighting to get home. But now, at three in the afternoon, the subway car was deserted—except for a homeless man at the other end curled up among an assortment of torn shopping bags.

Petry stretched his long legs out in the empty aisle and nudged Fleming with his elbow. "How you doing, ace?"

"You said there'd be no trouble."

"It couldn't be helped. No one expected that dumb bastard to go for his weapon."

Fleming looked out the window at the buildings passing by them in a blur. "You think he's dead?"

"Yeah."

Fleming felt numb. He'd never seen a man die. Swirling black dots obscured his vision, but he blinked them away. He thought of Captain Zakovitch. He had to call him, but first he had to get away from Petry.

Chico's was almost empty, but Petry led Fleming to the rear and signaled Celeste to bring them drinks. She came back with two beers. She took one look at Fleming and said, "What happened?"

Petry slid a beer toward Fleming. "Nothing. Leave us alone. Ray and I have to talk."

After she'd gone, Fleming took a gulp of beer and the cold liquid felt good in his parched throat.

"It's too bad it had to turn out this way, Ray, but it's done. The important thing now is to keep our mouths shut. There's no way the cops can trace this back to us. We're in the clear."

"What about Jimmy?"

"Don't worry about him."

The adrenaline that had been pumping through Fleming's veins since the holdup was quickly dissipating and he was suddenly exhausted. "Man," he said, slumping in his seat. "I feel like I could sleep for a week."

"It's been a rough afternoon, but you did good, Ray."

Fleming's head shot up. "Good? I almost ran a woman and her kid down. I crashed the car. I—"

"But you got us out. I knew you'd do okay. A guy who shoots the way you do pisses ice water. That's the kind of guy I like." Petry stood up. "I'll be right back."

A few minutes later he reappeared with Celeste, who was wearing her coat. She took Fleming's hand. "Come on, Ray. Let's go back to my place. You can rest there for a while."

Fleming remembered Captain Zakovitch. "No, I can't."

He stood up wearily. Celeste took his face in her hands and kissed him. "Come with me, hon. Just for a little while."

He looked into those beautiful, inviting dark eyes. He was so tired —too tired to talk to Zakovitch now. "Okay, but just for a little while."

Her apartment, located in a run-down tenement not far from Chico's, consisted of a kitchen, a living room, a bathroom, and one small bedroom. She had done her best to make the tiny apartment presentable, but the pressed curtains and highly polished linoleum couldn't conceal the cracked plaster and peeling ceiling paint of the decaying building.

She led him into the bedroom. A double bed and a dresser filled the tiny room. On top of the dresser a statue of the Virgin, next to which was a small vase filled with fresh flowers, competed for space with a dozen framed photographs. A votive candle bathed the room in a flickering, crimson light.

She pushed him down on the bed. "Get some rest. When you wake up, I'll make you something to eat."

"What time is it?"

"Four-thirty."

"I'll just take a short nap. Be sure and wake me at five. Okay?"

"Sure."

She pulled his shoes off and spread a blanket over him. The soft, comfortable bed smelled of her and he was asleep before she was out of the room.

Fleming's sleep was restless and troubled. His mind, fueled by guilt, conjured up terrifying visions. He was back behind the wheel, speeding toward the terrified woman. He tried to turn, but the car refused to respond. He stomped on the brake, but the car accelerated faster. Helpless, he gripped the wheel and braced for the impact. With the sickening sound of metal colliding with bone and flesh, the woman and baby flew up onto the hood. Her head smashed against

MICHAEL GRANT

the windshield, shattering it. Mouth agape, she clung to the hood and stared at him accusingly. Suddenly her hand reached through the broken window and she seized him by the throat. *"No . . . no—!"*

Celeste shook him. "Ray, wake up. It's okay."

Momentarily confused by the unfamiliar surroundings, he tried to rise, but she held him down. He looked toward the blackened window. "What time is it?"

"Nine."

"Nine!" He tried to get up but she pushed him down. "Celeste, I asked you to get me up at five. I gotta go."

She brushed back his damp hair. "Why? Baby, you needed the rest."

She was wearing a loose fitting terry-cloth robe and when she leaned forward it opened, revealing a glimpse of a smooth breast. She took his hand. "Ray, the other night was really wonderful." Smiling, she sat back, and with an easy shrug the robe fell away from her shoulders. The flickering candle, casting uneven, hypnotic shadows across the ceiling, augmented the surrealistic atmosphere. She leaned forward and kissed him gently. At this moment he didn't know if he was dreaming or awake, but it didn't matter. Nothing mattered except the two of them. The feel of her soft skin exorcised the demons haunting his mind. Time ceased and troubling thoughts of life and death dissolved in the warmth of her body.

After they'd made love, she rested her head on his chest and traced circles on his stomach with her long fingernail. But Ray Fleming, staring at the shimmering shadows on the ceiling, felt nothing. His sexual energies spent, his thoughts had once more returned to the events in the shopping mall parking lot. Since this afternoon—only six hours ago—he'd journeyed from the exciting, almost theatrical, world of cops and robbers to one where death and fear were real. He needed to talk to someone about what had happened.

"Celeste . . ."

She lifted her head and looked at him. "Yes?"

"Today . . ." He stopped, remembering Petry's admonishment: *Tell no one.* He stroked her silky hair. Right now she was the only one he trusted. Did Zakovitch and Morgan know what he was getting into? And if they did, why didn't they prepare him for it. "Today . . . Lyle and I . . . robbed an armored truck. A man was killed. We—"

"I know," she whispered into his chest.

He pushed her away and sat up. "You *knew!* How—"

"Lyle told me."

A throbbing pain attacked Fleming's temples. "What did he tell you?"

"Just that you were involved in something and a man was shot. I don't know any more and I don't want to."

She sat up and pulled the sheet around her protectively. "When you came in to Chico's today, you looked so awful. I made Lyle tell me."

Fleming felt a churning in his stomach. "Are you and Lyle—"

She shook her head. "I told you no. Ray, I've known Lyle for a long time and I know he's involved in a lot of bad things. That's one of the reasons we broke up. He used to disappear for months at a time, then he'd show up and expect us to continue as though nothing had happened. I couldn't deal with that."

Fleming dreaded asking the next question. "Do you know what he's involved in now?"

"No, and I don't care. What he does is his business."

Abruptly, he threw the sheet aside and scooped up his clothing. In the bathroom he splashed cold water on his face and examined himself in the mirror. "I gotta get away," he muttered to the sunken eyes staring back at him. "I gotta think this through."

When he came out, she was propped up in bed with a pillow behind her head.

"Where are you going, Ray?"

The dim candlelight made it difficult to see her face clearly. "Home. I gotta sort this out."

"Ray, don't do anything stupid."

"What's that supposed to mean?"

"I know you feel awful about what happened today, but don't go to the police. They'll put you in jail."

"You think I'm crazy? I won't do that."

"When will I see you?"

"I don't know. I'll call you."

He quickly closed the door behind him. He'd wanted to kiss her goodbye, but he was afraid that if he had, he wouldn't have left.

Fleming stopped under a streetlight and looked at his watch. He'd been walking the deserted streets of Sunnyside since he'd left Celeste's apartment partly because he thought better when he walked, and partly because he wanted to wait until his father had gone to bed.

When he got home it was after midnight. He paused at his father's door and listened to the soft snoring sounds. Satisfied, he went into the kitchen to turn off the light and saw the *Daily News* on the table.

Most people got their nightly news fix from the eleven o'clock news on TV, but not John Fleming. For as long as Ray Fleming could remember, his father's nightly ritual consisted of going to the drugstore on Queens Boulevard to pick up the early edition of the *News*.

Fleming groaned when he saw the front-page photo of the security guard lying in a pool of blood. The headline screamed: ARMORED TRUCK GUARD KILLED IN DARING DAYLIGHT HEIST.

Slowly, he sank into the chair and turned to page three. As he read the story his eyes locked on a sentence: *The guard, Thomas Martin, 60, a retired New York City policeman, was killed instantly by a blast from a submachine gun.* The print became blurry and he couldn't read the rest of the story. He closed the paper and stumbled to his room.

He lay in his bed staring at the ceiling, wondering what he was going to tell Captain Zakovitch. How could he explain being out of touch all this time? And once again he asked himself the question that had been nagging him since his first meeting with Morgan and the others: Should he tell them about Celeste?

More tired than he'd ever been, Fleming swung his legs over the side of the bed and reached for the telephone. He dialed the number and it rang several times. He was about to hang up when he heard the gravelly voice of Captain Zakovitch.

"Yes?"

Fleming cleared his throat. "I have to talk to you right away."

Captain Zakovitch, sitting at a table in an all-night cafeteria, studied Ray Fleming through a veil of smoke. He didn't like what he saw. Fleming, who had just finished telling his story, gulped down what was left of his black coffee. Zakovitch slid his untouched cup across the table. "You can have mine."

Fleming shook his head. "Captain, I wanted to call you before it happened . . . There wasn't time."

"I know. You did the right thing." Zakovitch didn't have the heart to tell him that trying to make a phone call under those circumstances was the worst thing he could possibly have done.

"I keep seeing that guard get shot . . ." Fleming shook his head to chase away the ghosts.

"Ray, understand something. This wasn't your fault. You did the best you could do under the circumstances."

Fleming, slumped in his chair, seemed to take little solace from the captain's words.

Zakovitch looked at the despondent undercover officer and was convinced, more than ever, that Ray Fleming didn't belong in the middle of—what? Thanks to Inspector Morgan, he had no idea what Fleming was involved in. Looking at Zakovitch's unruffled exterior it would have been impossible for anyone to guess the anger that was seething in him toward Dan Morgan. As soon as he was finished with Fleming, he promised himself he was going to call Morgan and get this straightened out once and for all. If necessary, he was prepared to take his objections all the way to the police commissioner's office, even if it meant the end of his career.

Zakovitch glanced down at his notes. Fleming's story had been disjointed and more than once, Zakovitch had had to go back over the chronology to get the story straight in his own mind.

"Ray, you said this happened around three o'clock. Tell me again where you've been since then."

Fleming licked his parched lips. "We dropped Jimmy off right after the holdup, then Lyle and I just kept driving around for hours. At one point we got something to eat, then we went to a bar somewhere in Brooklyn."

"Where did you eat?"

"I can't remember, Captain. Somewhere in Brooklyn. I don't know anything about Brooklyn."

"Were you in the Buick the whole time?"

Fleming hesitated. For a second he considered telling Zakovitch about Celeste. But how could he explain her now, at this late date? She had nothing to do with it, he told himself firmly. There's no need to involve her. "Yeah."

Zakovitch made a note. He had a lot more questions, but Fleming was in no shape to answer them tonight. He flipped his spiral notebook shut. "Okay, Ray, go home and get some sleep. Be at my office around eleven."

Zakovitch waited until Fleming left, then he went to the telephone and dialed Morgan's home number.

Chapter
27

3:15 A.M. FRIDAY, APRIL 5 • Morgan groped for the ringing telephone in the darkness. "Hello?"

"I know it's after three in the morning," Zakovitch said, "but I thought you should know. Ray Fleming took part in a robbery yesterday afternoon with Lyle Petry. A guard was killed."

Morgan rubbed the back of his neck and tried to clear his head. "Why wasn't I notified earlier?"

Zakovitch's voice was weary. "I just heard about it myself. I've just finished debriefing him."

"Where are you now?"

"An all-night cafeteria in Astoria. Corner of Steinway and Ditmars."

"Wait for me."

At that time of night Morgan had no difficulty with traffic. With the aid of a flashing dome light and judicious use of the siren, he weaved through the sparse traffic and arrived at the cafeteria in less than twenty minutes. Through the front window, yellowed with years of grease and smoke, he spotted Zakovitch sitting hunched over a cup of coffee with a cigarette dangling from his mouth.

Morgan was dying for a cup of coffee himself, but he didn't want to get involved in a dispute raging at the cashier's desk between the manager and a strung-out junkie who was claiming someone had poisoned his coffee.

Morgan slid into the seat opposite Zakovitch. "What happened?"

The captain ground his cigarette in the ashtray and promptly lit another one. "Yesterday afternoon Ray was supposed to go to a shooting match with Petry. When he got into the car, Petry told him they were going to take down an armored truck."

"Anyone else with them?"

"The man named Jimmy."

"Whose vehicle did they use?"

"Stolen."

"Prints? Witnesses?"

"Inspector, I just found out about this." The harsh neon lights overhead emphasized the deep lines in the captain's drawn face. "Besides, I'm in no position to call the squad for details."

"What time did this happen?"

"Around three in the afternoon."

"And you're just finding out about it *now*? Where the hell has Fleming been all this time?"

"With Petry," Zakovitch explained patiently. "He said he couldn't shake him. He called me as soon as he could."

Morgan, realizing he was taking out his frustrations on Zakovitch, altered the tone of his voice. "How's Fleming doing?"

"He's badly shaken. The guard who was killed was a retired cop." Zakovitch toyed with a pack of Camels. "Inspector, I don't know what's going on, but whatever it is, Ray Fleming can't be part of it."

"Why?"

"It's obvious from what happened yesterday that he's playing with the big guys. If you persist in using him, he's going to get hurt. He's in over his head. You can't jeopardize his life."

Stung by Zakovitch's words, Morgan lashed out. "I'm not jeopardizing anyone's life, Captain Zakovitch. Fleming wasn't drafted into this assignment. He knew what he was getting into."

Zakovitch shook his head. "He *thought* he did."

Morgan looked toward the sound of shouting. A uniformed cop, who'd come in to settle the dispute, had the junkie by the back of the neck and was rushing him toward the door to the accompaniment of jeers and catcalls from onlookers.

They both watched to make sure the cop didn't need their help. When Zakovitch was sure the officer had everything under control, he continued. "I'm going to make a recommendation that Fleming be terminated from the undercover program."

Morgan looked across the table at the ashen-faced captain and recalled, once again, his conversations with Chris Liberti and Ronnie Izzary. The more he thought about it, the more he was convinced that his team—and Ray Fleming—needed the expertise of someone like John Zakovitch. "Zak," he said evenly, "I'm going to tell you what Ray has stumbled in to."

Captain Zakovitch lit another Camel and sat back.

When Morgan finished, Zakovitch ground his cigarette in the ashtray. "Inspector," he said in a voice raspy with emotion, "I've dedicated my life to the Police Department, especially the Intelligence Division, and most especially to my undercover cops. In that time I've done my best to balance the needs of the department against the safety and welfare of my undercover officers. There have been times when I've put men's lives at risk, but at least *they* knew the risks, and *I* knew their capabilities." He lit another cigarette and Morgan noticed his hand was shaking. "You've put Ray Fleming, a man who's way over his head, into a difficult and dangerous situation, and that's an unforgivable breach of trust."

Morgan, smarting at the criticism, snapped, "Damn it, I don't want Ray Fleming in the middle of this either. I know he's over his head. If there was some way to insert an experienced officer in his place, I'd do it in a minute. But Ray Fleming is all we've got. Zak, these guys are pros. So far their only mistake has been Fleming, and I can't —I won't—correct *that* mistake. He's our only connection to Puño Blanco. We've *got* to shut these people down." Morgan sat back. "Zak, I need your cooperation and support. Do I have it?"

Zakovitch ground his cigarette into the overflowing ashtray and squinted at Morgan. After a moment he said, "All right, Inspector, you have it. But I want be kept informed of all developments."

"Done. As far as I'm concerned, you're part of the team."

Zakovitch looked at him curiously. "Are you going to tell the commissioner about me?"

Morgan exhaled slowly. He'd given a lot of thought to that question. By bringing Zakovitch into the operation, he'd violated Cassidy's direct order, but it didn't matter. The stakes were too high to worry about careers. "He doesn't need to know just yet," he answered.

Now he asked Zakovitch another question that had been on his mind. "Should we tell Ray Fleming what's he's involved in?"

While Morgan had been telling him about Puño Blanco, he'd been asking himself the same question. In most undercover operations the very nature of the criminal conduct being investigated is self-evident. But when it's not, it becomes a judgment call on the part of the controlling supervisor as to how much—if anything—he should tell the undercover about the people he's dealing with. There are several factors to consider. If it's important that the undercover officer gather physical evidence, then he has to be told so he can know what to look for. On the other hand, the personality of the undercover must be taken into account. Some police officers have no difficulty slipping in and out of their undercover roles, while others, unless they totally immerse themselves in their bogus identity, risk the chance of inadvertently exposing themselves.

Zakovitch realized it was unfair to call Ray Fleming a police officer. He'd received no training; he lacked the variety of experiences that tempered a police officer's judgment; and he'd never been exposed to the fear and violence of day-to-day police work. The sad truth was that Ray Fleming was nothing more than a paper police officer. The only step that he'd taken to become a member of the fraternity was to raise his right hand and take the oath of a police officer. But there was a lot more to being a cop than that. And yet, paradoxically, the very fact that he had none of these requisite skills might protect him in time of crisis. Remembering Fleming's foolhardy attempt to make that telephone call, he said, "No, Inspector. Right now, it's safer for him if he doesn't know." The weary captain looked at his watch and stood up. "Five o'clock. Time to go to work."

Dan Morgan remained at the table for a long time after Zakovitch had gone, wondering, among other things, if he'd made the right decision.

By the time Castillo arrived at the office, Morgan had already been on the telephone with the 109th Precinct detectives. Castillo had been in such a hurry, he'd cut himself shaving. Two red-stained pieces of toilet tissue clung to his face. Morgan wondered if the eccentric DEA agent used a straight razor.

Castillo plucked a piece of tissue from his chin and started the blood flowing again. "I read the story in the *Daily News*. Any leads for us?"

"Not yet. The squad found the getaway car in a parking lot near Shea Stadium. They're dusting for prints, but I doubt they'll find any. Fleming said they all wore rubber gloves."

"Where did they steal it?"

"A commuter parking lot in Mineola."

Castillo, pouring himself a cup of coffee, grunted. "Good move.

The owner wouldn't discover the loss until he arrived home that night. Plenty of time to use the car."

"I told Zakovitch," Morgan said quietly. "He knows everything."

Castillo, who was stirring his coffee with the eraser end of a pencil, stopped. "Cassidy's going to have your ass for breakfast."

"Fuck Cassidy—and Coffey," Morgan snapped.

Castillo tossed the wet pencil on the desk. "I'll be goddamned," he said, grinning. "I've been working with a closet boss-fighter all this time and I never knew."

"Not really. I hate doing this to Cassidy, but Coffey's got him by the short hairs. It doesn't matter what happens to me. We need all the help we can get."

Castillo put his Nikes on the desk. "Where's Chris?"

Morgan poured his fifth cup of the morning. "Federal Plaza. The lab results are in." He sat down and absentmindedly stirred his coffee. "There's something I don't get about all this. Why the hell would they do an armored truck?"

"On-the-job training," Castillo answered. "Petry needs to provide some OJT for Fleming."

Morgan looked at the wall map of the city. "OJT, huh? What else could they do?"

"Let me count the ways." Castillo ticked off the possibilities on his fingertips. "Blow up the Statue of Liberty, the Twin Towers, the Stock Exchange, St. Patrick's Cathedral." He saw the look of consternation on Morgan's face and added, "On the other hand, it wouldn't have to be anything as spectacular as all that. All Fleming has to prove is that he can handle the pressure for the main event."

"You think that armored car job was enough?"

Castillo snorted. "From what you told me, Fleming screwed up pretty badly. If I were Petry, I'd dump him."

Morgan nodded glumly. "That's what bothering me. Why doesn't Petry dump him?"

"Maybe he's planning to use Fleming as a sacrificial lamb."

Morgan felt a stab of guilt. "Jesus, I hope not." He drummed a pencil on the desk. "It just doesn't fit. Why would three pros be willing to work with a guy like Fleming who choked in the big game?"

Castillo regarded Morgan with his coal-black eyes. "There's another possibility: Petry's using Fleming as a diversion."

Morgan stopped drumming. "That would mean he knows Ray's a cop."

"It's possible. Fleming made a big mistake trying to make that phone call."

Morgan thought once again about the inexperienced cop and wished he had a more seasoned officer playing the role. "What can we do about it?"

"Right now? Not a hell of a lot. Tell Fleming to be extra careful. We'll have to wait for Petry to make his move."

Morgan looked back to the map. Now that the police job action had become daily headlines, that question of where the big attack would occur took on more urgency. "Any hunches about what the main event is going to be?" he asked Castillo.

The DEA agent smiled sardonically. "The Statue of Liberty, the Stock Exchange. Who knows? New York City offers an embarrassment of riches when it comes to spectacular targets for terrorists."

Morgan was growing increasingly uneasy with the matter-of-fact tone Castillo was using to discuss murder and sabotage in his city. All his life he'd gone up against criminals who were vicious, sadistic, and unpredictable. But he and his brother officers had taken them on one at a time. Although the number of criminals far outweighed the number of cops, the police prevailed because the criminals were disorganized and lacked the intelligence and motivation to use their superior numbers to advantage. Now Castillo was describing a cop's worst nightmare—an organized, awesomely equipped criminal element with enough motivation to take on the police in a fight to the death.

Morgan was brought out of his brooding when Chris Liberti came bursting through the door. "I've got some good news and some bad news," she said breathlessly.

"Why break the mood?" Morgan said glumly. "Let's start with the bad news."

"I've been researching KTR Industries, but it's going to take a lot more digging. So far the computer's traced the corporation to the Bahamas, then to a holding company in Venezuela, then another holding company in Panama. They're all shell companies. Even the IRS goes nuts trying to track down these Ping Pong companies. Most of them disappear in a blizzard of paper. I have a feeling we may never find out exactly who owns KTR Industries. But I'll keep looking."

"What's the good new?" Castillo asked.

"We have a hit and some promising prints. I just got off the phone with the lab boss in Washington. Incidentally, he wasn't too thrilled about rummaging through a sack of trash. But—"

"Who's the hit?" Morgan asked impatiently.

She withdrew photos from the envelope and passed them to Morgan and Castillo. "Glen A. Dickerson, male, black, forty-two. The photos aren't in color, but his pedigree says he has reddish hair and green eyes."

Castillo studied the photo. "What'd he get busted for?"

Liberti glanced at Dickerson's rap sheet. "This time? Three years armed robbery. Just got out eight months ago. Last known address was St. Louis."

"What about the other prints?" Morgan asked.

"Two good ones and three partials. Unfortunately, whoever these other guys are, they're not part of the nineteen million NCIC records in our files."

"That's it?" Morgan said in disgust. "The partials are useless. You need at least twelve points for a comparison."

She shook her head. "Not anymore. You haven't been keeping up with fingerprint technology. With enhanced imaging techniques our computers can make a positive ID on a lot less than that."

She sat down in front of the computer. "This shouldn't take long. With the help of Donal's CID contact, I've had all Special Forces personnel files, including fingerprints, downloaded into our mainframe in Washington. First we'll do a name check on Dickerson."

In response to her typed commands, a high-speed computer located in the bowels of the J. Edgar Hoover building in Washington

Officer DOWN

began to scan thousands of names. Within minutes the laser printer began spewing data. As soon as it stopped, Liberti ripped the pages out. "Bingo!" She read from the printout. "Dickerson went into the army in sixty-six and was assigned to the Fifth Special Forces Group from sixty-seven until he was dishonorably discharged in seventy-six."

Liberti tossed the printout to Morgan. "This calls for a fresh pot of coffee."

Morgan and Castillo exchanged looks. "Are *you* gonna make it?" Castillo asked. Since they'd been together, Liberti, who didn't drink coffee, had never made any.

"Yes, I'm going to make it," she said indignantly.

When she returned with a potful of water, Morgan asked, "What next?"

She poured water into the top of the coffee machine. "Do a print search. But that's gonna take a little longer. The computer is going to have to scan thousands of prints to come up with comparisons for the five we have."

"Did you run a name check on Petry?" Castillo asked.

Liberti's right eyebrow arched. "Yes, Donal. That was the *first* thing I did."

"Okay, okay."

Liberti sat down at the terminal. "With a little bit of luck, we should have results—"

"How about Fleming's prints?" Castillo asked.

Liberti sighed. "A set of his prints have been included in the database as well." She glowered at the two men. "Are there any *more* questions before I begin?"

Castillo shrugged. "Nope. Go for it."

Twenty minutes later, while Morgan and Castillo were drinking the worst coffee they'd ever had, the printer began to hum and they gathered around the terminal screen. The first message said: RE QUERY THIS DATE 5 APRIL 1991, TWO COMPARISONS ACQUIRED. NAMES TO FOLLOW.

"*Two* comparisons? That's it? So much for the wonders of image enhancement," Morgan muttered.

MICHAEL GRANT

A collective groan went up when they saw Ray Fleming's name appear on the screen. The second name was James T. Newell.

As soon as the printer finished typing Newell's personnel history and photo, Liberti ripped the pages out. "Newell," she said, scanning the pages, "joined Special Forces in June of sixty-six and was assigned to the Fifth Group as well. Dishonorably discharged in 1972."

"Why?" Castillo asked.

"Doesn't say. We'll have to dig into Mr. Newell's background for the particulars."

"How many people are there in Special Forces?" Morgan asked.

Castillo gingerly picked at the cut on his chin. "About five thousand in eight Special Forces Groups."

"Great! How are we going to find Petry in that crowd?"

"Deduction," Liberti announced. "We know Newell and Dickerson were in the Fifth Group together from sixty-seven to seventy-two. We'll concentrate on the people who were in that group during those years."

Morgan frowned. "Sounds like a lot of paperwork to wade through."

"It is," Liberti agreed. "And unfortunately computers won't be much help. It'll take a lot of hands-on work to dig out that information." She saw the gloomy looks on their faces and held up the grainy computer-generated photographs. "Hey, at least we've identified two targets."

Morgan studied the photos. Newell's dark, brooding eyes and thin, taut face was in sharp contrast to Dickerson's pleasant smile. Looking at the two faces Morgan was once again reminded that there was no such thing as a criminal type. Still he wondered, What kind of man would kill cops for money?

Castillo broke the silence. "We need Fleming to ID these photos for us," he said.

Morgan had the same thought. Moments later he had the young undercover cop on the telephone.

Chapter
28

Jimmy, sitting at the kitchen table in Petry's apartment, crushed a beer can and threw it into the trash. "Lyle, I'm telling you, Fleming's gotta go."

"He never made the call, Jimmy."

"Yeah, but he tried. You think he's a cop?"

Petry slid his can around in a puddle. "I don't know."

"Why don't you ask him who he was going to call?"

"No, I like it better this way. I know something he doesn't. In the unlikely event he is a cop, he can still fit into my plans."

Jimmy, impatient with complex issues, repeated his solution. "He's gotta go. I can't believe you let a couple of sorry-ass civilians like Fleming and Botnick in on this."

Petry glared at Jimmy. "Maybe I should put an ad in the classified section of the *Times*. 'Needed: ex-SF personnel for terrorist—' "

"Go ahead and joke, but the fact is, Fleming folded when the heat was on."

Petry tapped his can on the table. "I'll admit I'm disappointed—"

"Disappointed? Jesus H. Christ! In the past you'd never allow an asshole like Fleming to be anywhere near one of your projects. He panicked and almost got us killed yesterday."

Petry popped another can and slid it across the table to the angry man. Jimmy was right. He'd expected some jittery nerves, but the truth was Fleming hadn't performed well. "You've seen the plans," he said aloud. "I need him, Jimmy."

"Lyle, I'm telling you, this is going to be a goatscrew operation if—"

Petry slammed his hand on the table. "All right, you've had your say. Discussion's over. He stays." In a quieter tone he said, "Fleming fucked up yesterday. But I'm going to give him one more chance."

"What if he screws up again?"

"Then he goes," Petry said without hesitation.

Jimmy's angry eyes burned into Petry's. "And I want to be the one who takes him out."

Petry shrugged. "Suit yourself. In the meantime, I'm going to watch him very carefully. We're too close to wrapping up this project to let anything happen now." Petry looked at the wall clock and stood up. "I gotta go. I have a meeting with Alvaro."

Less than an hour later, Lyle Petry was standing in the vaulted vestibule of the Metropolitan Museum of Art, studying a thirteenth-

Officer DOWN

century coat of mail, when a voice behind him said, "Not very effective for jungle warfare, is it?"

Petry, examining the intricate metal scrollwork on the breastplate, answered, "But very effective for its time, Alvaro."

He turned to the bearded man. "Come on, I want to show you the Spanish sword collection. It's really something."

To an uninterested observer the two looked like any of the hundreds of tourists who wandered through the exhibits of the museum daily. A careful observer would have noted a pattern to their seemingly random meandering. They'd walk into a room, then quickly walk out again. In another room they'd seek a seat at the farthest corner and casually watch other patrons coming and going. But only a trained observer would have guessed the true purpose of their behavior: Lyle Petry and his Colombian associate were making sure no one was following them.

After a half-hour of this sitting and doubling back into rooms, Petry was satisfied that they weren't being followed. He led Alvaro to the wine bar and ordered two glasses of burgundy.

Alvaro sniffed the wine. "Well, Lyle. Why did you want to see me?"

From force of habit, Petry's restless eyes continued to inspect everyone who came into the sparsely occupied wine bar. "To give you an update. Fleming passed his first test."

"Really?" The Colombian looked doubtful. "With flying colors?"

"Close enough."

Alvaro, hearing the qualifying tone, turned his attention from the wine to Petry. "Is there a problem?"

"Maybe. Just before the armored car showed up, Fleming tried to make a phone call."

Alvaro paled. "Is he a policeman?"

"I'm not sure."

"What are you going to do about it?"

"Watch him carefully."

"But what if he's a policeman?"

Petry smiled confidently. "I can still use him."

Alvaro scowled. "You can't be so cavalier about this. If anything goes wrong—"

"Alvaro, you hired me to make sure nothing goes wrong. I'll handle it."

The exasperated Colombian said, "What would you have done if he was a policeman and he made a call to the authorities?"

"Then all bets would have been off. Jimmy and I would have waited to see if the cops showed up and then disappeared."

Alvaro slammed his glass on the table, causing a few heads to turn. "Lyle," he said in a voice barely above a whisper, "*nothing* must go wrong with this project."

Petry's voice was just as quiet, but the tone was rock-hard. "Don't tell me how to do my job."

The Colombian was the first to break eye contact. "All right. *When* will you get to the final phase of this project? "I'm getting a lot of pressure from—"

"Patience, Alvaro. I have one more test for Ray. If he passes that, I'm ready for Trojan Horse."

Alvaro viewed Petry's tranquil demeanor with irritation. He'd hired him for this assignment precisely because of his competence and icy coolness. Nevertheless, Petry's self-possessed disposition in the midst of all this was unnerving to the more emotional Colombian. Perhaps if Petry were exposed to the pressure he was getting from the leaders of Puño Blanco, he wouldn't be so calm. It made him feel better to think so, but he knew it wasn't true. All the time he'd been associated with Lyle Petry, both in the military and in their later dealings, he'd never seen Petry be anything but calm. It was almost unnatural.

"Lyle, I don't suppose you want to tell me about this next test?" Petry's silence answered his question. "Then tell me this: Do you plan to kill any more policemen?"

Petry looked pensive. "That depends on Ray. If he passes this next test, there won't be time."

Petry looked at his watch and stood up. He didn't like remaining in any one place too long. "I'll let you know when I have the results of his final exam." He slapped the nervous Colombian on the back and grinned. "*Cálmate,* Alvaro. Everything will be okay."

The two parted outside the wine bar, and Petry made his way to the Egyptian wing. Leisurely, he strolled through the maze of rooms containing the museum's impressive collection of jewelry and statuary of ancient Egypt, stopping occasionally to examine a display case. But he wasn't looking at the lifelike statues or the exquisitely hand-hammered jewelry. He was looking through the glass at the reflection of people behind him for a telltale sign of a familiar face or familiar clothing.

Forty minutes later, he left the museum.

Farther downtown from the museum, Dan Morgan was sitting in a luncheonette on West 36th Street. He pushed his pastrami sandwich aside and spread sixteen photos on the table. Scrupulously following the legal rules of a photo array, he wanted to be certain that the procedure was in strict compliance with the court's guidelines. It wouldn't do to lose the case because he'd shown only Dickerson's and Newell's photos to Fleming.

"Look at these, Ray. Take your time. Do you see anyone you recognize?"

Ray Fleming leaned forward and peered intently at the display in front of him. "Here," he pointed at one. "That's Glen."

"Recognize anyone else?"

Fleming scanned the photos and shook his head. "Nope. No one else."

Morgan scooped up the photos and spread sixteen more on the table. "Recognize anyone here?"

After a moment Fleming picked up one. "This is Jimmy. Inspector, where'd you get pictures of—"

"Do you see anyone else you recognize?"

Fleming turned his attention to the photos again. After a while he shook his head emphatically. "Nope."

Morgan scooped up the photos and returned them to an envelope.

MICHAEL
GRANT

As soon as he got back to the office, he'd prepare a report indicating that undercover police officer Raymond B. Fleming had identified photos number five and eleven: the photos of Glen A. Dickerson and James T. Newell.

That business out of the way, Morgan turned his attention to his two-inch-thick sandwich. All he'd eaten since three this morning was a stale bagel and a lot of strong coffee. "How're you holding up, Ray?" he asked through a mouthful of pastrami.

Fleming, toying with the pickle on his sandwich platter, shrugged. "Okay."

Morgan put his sandwich down and wiped his greasy fingers with a napkin. He'd been watching Fleming since they'd come into the restaurant fifteen minutes earlier, and he didn't like what he saw. The cocky, superconfident kid he'd opened the door to a week ago was gone. That didn't bother Morgan; uncontrolled cockiness was bound to get Ray Fleming into trouble. But he didn't like what he saw in its place. Fleming constantly worked his jaw muscles and the dark smudges under his eyes were mute testimony that he wasn't sleeping well. Zakovitch had said he was a big eater, but Fleming hadn't touched his sandwich.

"Eat up," Morgan said. "The pastrami in this joint is the best in the city."

"I'm not hungry."

Morgan stabbed a french fry with his fork. "Ray, that guard's death wasn't your fault."

Fleming was silent for a moment. Then he said, "I know. It's just that I feel so . . . useless. I'm a cop, but I'm not a cop. Inspector, I want to *do* something. I wanted to help that guard so bad . . ." His voice trailed off.

Morgan understood Fleming's anguish. "You ever see a man die before?" He was getting into a conversation he didn't want to have.

"No," Fleming said softly.

Morgan stared off into space. "It's never easy. Even when it's the bad guy. But it's part of a cop's job."

Fleming twisted his straw. "I just wish there was something I could have done."

There wasn't a day when Dan Morgan, remembering Detective Fredericks in that hallway, didn't say the same thing to himself. "I know, Ray. But there wasn't time, and there's nothing you can do about it now."

Fleming angrily threw the crumpled straw in an ashtray. "It shouldn't have happened," he said in exasperation. "Jimmy's a hothead, but Lyle . . . if that had been Lyle, he'd have found a way to take care of that guard without killing him."

Morgan, angered by Fleming's almost admiring tone, threw his fork down. "Ray," he said sharply, "get something straight. Lyle Petry is *not* one of the good guys."

Fleming turned to Morgan so quickly his elbow almost upset his Coke. He steadied the glass. "That's just it, Inspector. I don't know anything about Lyle. Who the hell *is* he?"

"Ray," he said quietly, "I'm not going to tell you who Lyle Petry is yet."

"But why—?"

Morgan put his hand up. "It's for your own protection. Captain Zakovitch and I have discussed it. It's important that you stay in your role. If Petry asks you to do what I think he will, your reaction is going to have to be totally and genuinely convincing."

Fleming nodded in acquiescence, but he didn't look happy.

Morgan took a different tack. "By the way, where's your cut from that robbery?"

Fleming was thrown off guard by the question. "Uh, I don't know."

"Have you asked for it?"

"No. That money's—"

"Illegal? Is that what you were going to say?"

"Well . . . yeah."

"To whom? Ray Fleming the cop or Ray Fleming the bad guy? Wouldn't Ray the bad guy want his cut?"

Fleming stared at his untouched Coke. "Yes."

"That's what I mean about staying in your role. It's important that you *think* like a guy who's involved with a couple of stickup men, and who's looking to do more of the same."

Fleming shook his head. "This is a hell of a lot more complicated than I thought," he mumbled.

"That's why I don't want you to know any more than you have to. Next time you see Petry, demand your money."

"Okay. I'm meeting him later. I'll ask him for it then."

Morgan could see that Fleming's head was spinning. He wasn't sure he should bring up the next topic, but he decided it was important enough to take the chance.

"Ray, there is one thing you could do now."

Fleming, eager to do something constructive, answered quickly. "Sure. What is it?"

"I'd like to get something with Petry's fingerprints on it."

Fleming looked perplexed. "I don't know anything about fingerprints. How would I do it?"

"Prints adhere best to any hard surface—a glass or a bottle, for example. If you could swipe something he'd touched, I might be able to lift his prints."

"Okay, I'll see what I can do."

"Good." Morgan remembered his earlier conversation with Castillo and added, "I'd like a print, but your safety is more important. Don't do anything to jeopardize that. Understand?"

"Yeah, I understand."

Morgan looked at his half-eaten sandwich and pushed it away; he wasn't hungry anymore. "I gotta be getting back." He stood up. "Keep in touch with Captain Zakovitch. Anything develops, let him know immediately."

Outside the restaurant, a cacophony of truck and taxi horns blared in a futile attempt to clear a path on 36th Street. Trucks, double-parked the entire length of the street, disgorged their cargos of cloth and finished clothing. The work of the garment district went on in spite of the protesting horns.

Morgan had put off asking this one last question. Indeed, he was afraid to ask it, but in fairness to Ray Fleming, he had to. "Ray," he said looking directly into the young man's troubled eyes, "Do you want out of this assignment? If you do, it's okay. No questions asked."

Officer DOWN

Fleming was distracted by a cabby and a truck driver who had gotten into a shoving match in the middle of the street. Other motorists, who didn't care about the fight, but who wanted to get out of the block, broke it up. "No, sir," he said, returning Morgan's gaze, "I want to see this through. That's why I became a cop."

Morgan, still standing outside the restaurant, watched Fleming walk away and tried to decide if he were pleased or disappointed with his answer.

Chapter
29

It was almost five P.M. when Fleming and Petry met in the bar down the street from Blockmann's. Except for a few regulars clustered at one end watching a baseball game, the bar was empty. Petry and Fleming sat at the far end, away from the TV.

Petry grinned at Fleming. "You want your money? Yesterday on the subway, I thought you'd never want anything to do with that robbery again."

"That was yesterday."

"And now?"

Fleming shrugged. "What's done is done. I want my share."

Petry elbowed Fleming. "What's the hurry? You planning on taking Celeste to some steamy tropical isle?"

Fleming forced a grin. "Maybe."

"Well, you gotta put it on hold for a while."

"Why?"

"The money's still hot, Ray. If we start spending it now, the serial numbers may make some bells ring. Let's give it a few months."

"A few *months*! Damn it, Lyle. You said I'd make some quick money."

"Take it easy. You need some dough, I'll lend it to you. No interest. How's that?"

Fleming feigned disappointment. "I guess I have no choice."

"I'm not holding out on you, Ray. But it's best I keep all the money with me for the time being. If it makes you feel any better, I'm holding Jimmy's share too."

"I said all right."

Petry squeezed the back of Fleming's neck. "What's up, pal? You seem jumpy."

Fleming shrugged the hand away. "Nothing."

"Problem with Celeste?"

"No. I told you I'm all right."

"Okay, okay. Order us a couple of more beers. I gotta take a leak."

Fleming waited for Petry to disappear into the men's room, then his eyes focused on Petry's empty bottle. If he were going to do something, he'd have to do it quickly. He resisted the impulse to grab it. He knew nothing about fingerprints except what he'd seen on TV cop shows, but he knew he shouldn't get his fingerprints on the bottle. He could use a handkerchief, but that would be too obvious. He looked toward the other end of the bar. The old bartender, intent on watching Dwight Gooden facing a three-two count with bases loaded, had his back to Fleming. Glancing quickly toward the men's room, he slid the bottle in front of him. He picked it up, holding the

MICHAEL GRANT

lip with his fingertips, and was about to slip it into his jacket when a voice shouted "Hey!"

Startled, he looked up. Gooden had fired an inside fastball to retire the side, and the bartender, flashing a toothy grin, was coming toward him.

"What are you gonna do, pal, steal the bottle for the deposit?"

Unnerved by the intrusion, Fleming banged the bottle against the edge of the bar and it slipped from his grasp.

"Oh, shit," the bartender muttered as the glass exploded across his tile floor.

Fleming heard a door slam behind him. Petry had come out of the men's room.

The bartender was leaning over the bar, shaking his head. "Jeez, look at the mess you made."

Fleming, afraid that the bartender was going to make an issue about stealing the bottle, said quickly, "Hey, forget about the goddamn bottle, okay? I'll clean it up. Just bring us two more beers."

The bartender eyed Fleming warily, wondering if he'd had too much to drink.

"Look, I'm *sorry*. All right? Just get the beer."

Petry slipped back onto his stool as the bartender turned away. He looked down at the broken glass. "What happened?"

"Nothing. I hit the bottle with my elbow and the old guy's having a shit fit."

Petry chuckled. "This place is a dump anyway. What's a little more broken glass?"

The bartender returned and slammed the two bottles down in front of them. Fleming felt his shirt sticking to his back. After what seemed like an eternity, the bartender picked though some bills from Fleming's pile and turned away without saying a word.

Petry watched the old man go back to his seat in front of the TV. "Touchy old bastard, isn't he?"

Fleming exhaled silently. "Yeah."

Petry turned back toward Fleming. "Ray," he said quietly, "how'd you like to make some real money?"

Fleming's nerves were stretched to the breaking point and he felt a strange mixture of euphoria and fear. His old cockiness returned. "Would I have to bury it in my back yard for a year?" he asked.

Petry laughed. "No. I promise this stuff will be as clean as a hound's tooth."

"What's the catch? I gotta kill someone?"

Petry's pale green eyes displayed no emotion. "Maybe," he said.

Fleming choked on his beer. "Lyle," he said, wiping a tear from his eye, "where do you come up with this shit? I keep waiting for Allen Funt to jump out of a closet and tell me I'm on *Candid Camera,* for chrissake."

Petry swept the money off the bar. "Come on, I don't want to talk about it here."

As they walked past the bartender, Fleming expected a snide remark about the bottle, but the old man, intent on watching Howard Johnson drill one into the upper deck, never saw them leave.

Petry weaved the Blazer eastward through the narrow streets of lower Manhattan and got on the northbound entrance to the FDR Drive.

"It's easier to talk here," he said, breaking the tense silence. "I got a confession to make, Ray. That armored truck robbery was a test."

Fleming's head swiveled toward Petry. "A test! For what?"

"To see if you had the balls to do what I'm going to ask you now."

Fleming's heart thumped. He looked out the window at the sparkling black water and the river's pristine silkiness had a calming effect on him. His eyes still on the water, he said, "Lyle, you lost me. I don't know what the hell you're talking about."

"Same rules as before, Ray. I'm going to offer you something. If you don't want to get involved, say so. Agreed?"

A tugboat silently knifed through the swift running current. A lone crew member, backlit by a hatchway, was smoking a cigarette and staring into the swift flowing water. "Okay," Fleming said, turning away from the boat, "let me hear it."

"I got a client who's gotten himself into some financial difficulties. He owns a warehouse in Brooklyn with a two-million-dollar insurance policy on it. If that warehouse is destroyed, his problems are over."

"You talking about a fire?"

Petry glanced at Fleming. "A bomb is much more thorough."

"You wanna blow up a fucking building?"

"Yep. Are you in? There's fifty thou in it for you." Petry's teeth gleamed in the darkness. "And it's all spendable right away."

"Before . . . you said something about someone dying. What did you mean?"

"When you use a bomb, you never know. We'll do our best to see that the building is empty, but there's always the possibility of collateral casualties. I just want to be upfront with you." He gave Fleming a curious look. "Do you think you could kill a man, Ray?"

"Christ! How should I know?"

Petry's eyes flicked back to the road. "You're right. You never know until the time comes."

Fleming's mind was racing. Was this the offer that Inspector Morgan spoke of? And if it was, did Morgan really expect him to say yes to blowing up a building?

"Well?" Petry asked.

Fleming looked out the window to his left. They were driving past some of the most expensive real estate in the city: Sutton Place. The closely packed multimillion-dollar town houses had a commanding view of the East River and the Queensborough Bridge. Fleming had been there many times with his cab to pick up silver-haired men in custom-fitted tuxedos and women in elegant, shimmering gowns. Long after they'd left his cab, the expensive essence of their perfume and cologne remained. What was fifty thousand dollars to them? But to someone like him, it was a fortune. For the first time in his life he was beginning to understand the seductiveness of easy money. He rubbed his temples to clear these distracting thoughts from his head. Lyle Petry wasn't offering this money to Ray Fleming, he was offering it to an undercover member of the New York City Police Department.

"Okay, Lyle. I'm in."

Petry lightly punched Fleming's arm. "Great! I knew I could count on you."

"When do we do it?"

"I'll let you know. I'm still working on the details."

Petry gunned the engine. "Where do you want me to drop you off? Blockmann's or your house?"

"Blockmann's," Fleming answered quickly. He didn't want Petry to know where he lived. But looking at the relaxed, smiling face, he had a feeling that Lyle Petry already knew where he lived. He fervently hoped Petry didn't know any more about him than that.

After Petry dropped Fleming off, Fleming rushed home to have dinner with his father. But he shouldn't have bothered. Dinner had not gone well. His father's needling about Ray's future had led to yet another heated argument. Ray, unwilling to endure the recriminating silence any longer, got up and began to clear the dishes.

John Fleming pushed the plate away and ran his hand over his mouth, a movement that meant he wanted a cigarette. Ray knew the old man smoked when he wasn't around, but Ray's constant carping had discouraged his father from smoking in front of him.

"What's your hurry?" the senior Fleming asked.

"I'm going to the movies." He had no intention of telling his father he was going to Chico's. That would have started another argument.

Ray had just loaded the dishwasher when the doorbell rang. He opened the door and was surprised to see Manny Botnick standing there.

The short man licked his lips nervously. "Hey, Ray. Can I come in?"

Fleming waved him in. "Sure. What's up?"

Botnick's eyes darted about. "Is your father home?" he whispered.

"Yeah."

"Who is it?" his father shouted from the kitchen.

"Manny," Fleming said. Silence. "Come on. Let's go to my room."

Botnick hadn't been to Fleming's home since the time he'd made the mistake of espousing his views on religion—"There is no God" and politics—"The left is the only hope of the free world"—to John Fleming. The senior Fleming's bushy eyebrows had begun high in the center of his forehead but, as Botnick continued his diatribe, the eyebrows sank lower and lower until the cobalt blue eyes were barely visible. Ray Fleming, seeing the unmistakable signs of growing rage, tried to interrupt Botnick, but his talkative friend was on a roll and couldn't be deterred. Finally, John Fleming, who'd had enough of this heretical ranting, rose and, like an Old Testament prophet, pointed a trembling finger at Botnick and pronounced, "Son, you're a Godless, Communist bastard and you'll rot in hell." Before the slack-jawed Botnick could utter a retort, the old man had disappeared into his room and slammed the door.

Botnick, clutching a black gym bag, sat down on the edge of Fleming's bed. Fleming reached for the bag. "Give me that. I'll just toss it—"

"No!" Botnick grasped the strap with both hands.

Fleming noticed that Botnick's droopy mustache was sagging from perspiration. "Okay. Don't blow a gasket. What've you got in there, gold?"

"Lyle sent me," Botnick said in a hoarse whisper.

"Lyle? Why?" Fleming's eyes went to the bag and a chill ran down his back. "Manny, what's in there?"

Botnick wiped his forehead with his sleeve. "A bomb," he said weakly.

Fleming took a step backward. "Jesus! You brought it *here*? Are you crazy?"

"It was Lyle's idea."

Fleming tore his eyes away from the bag. "Are you in this with Lyle?"

Botnick looked down at the bag on his lap. "Yeah. That's why I introduced you to him. He was looking for someone he could trust, someone he could—"

Fleming, enraged that Botnick would bring a bomb into his father's home, grabbed Botnick by the collar. "You dopey bastard—"

Botnick squeezed his eyes shut and clutched the bag tighter. "Ray, for chrissake, take it easy. This is a bomb."

Fleming let him go. "Can . . . can it go off now?"

"I don't know anything about these damn things. I'm just a delivery boy. Lyle says it's perfectly safe, but I've been shittin' bricks since he gave it to me."

Fleming paced the small room. "What the hell am *I* supposed to do with it?"

"Just keep it here. Lyle said he'll call you later." Botnick gingerly placed the bag on the floor at the foot of the bed. "It's safe. It won't go off," he said, not sounding at all convinced.

Caught off guard by the sudden turn of events, Fleming's mind raced as he tried to decide what to do next. He had to call Captain Zakovitch, but what if Lyle called him first and told him to plant the bomb?

Botnick slipped off the bed. "Ray, I gotta go."

Fleming was torn between anger and his responsibility to the Police Department. Furious at Botnick, he wanted nothing more than to smash that sad-sack face, but he held back. He needed information. He grabbed the shorter man by his jacket. "Manny," he said in a hoarse whisper, "you're not going anywhere until you tell me everything about Lyle Petry and you. What the fuck did you get me into?"

Botnick pulled away from Fleming's grasp. "Ray, I was only trying to help. Since I've met you, all you've talked about is finding a way to make a quick buck. Well, Lyle Petry is the way."

"How? By using my house as a bomb warehouse?"

"I didn't know he was going to do that. He said you knew all about it."

"Well, I fucking don't know all about it."

"I'm sorry. All right? Lyle's gonna call you tonight. He'll explain everything."

Botnick started to open the door, but Fleming slammed it shut with his hand. "Have you done this before?"

Botnick's eyes darted about. "Don't ask me that. Lyle told me never to discuss business with anyone."

Fleming took his hand away from the door. "We're friends. You can tell me."

"I can't."

"You afraid of Lyle?"

"You're damn right. Don't get me wrong. I like Lyle, but there's something about him that scares the hell out of me. You don't fuck with a guy like that."

Fleming studied Botnick's face to see if he was lying. He wasn't: the fear was evident in his eyes. He opened the door. There was no point in keeping Botnick hostage. Besides, he needed time to think about what to do next.

He put his arm around the little man. "I'm sorry I hassled you, Manny. It's just that . . . I didn't expect this."

Botnick, visibly relieved, straightened his jacket. "Hey, I understand. It scared the shit out of me too, but don't sweat it, Ray. Lyle knows what he's doing."

Fleming closed the front door on Botnick and turned. His father was standing in the hallway outside the kitchen. "What did *he* want?"

"Nothing. He just dropped off some gun magazines." Preoccupied, he started for his room.

"I thought you were going to the movies."

"I changed my mind." He looked at his watch and wondered if the bomb was set with a timer. He had to get it out of the house. But how? "I'm just going to watch some TV," he said, turning toward his room.

Back in his room he stared at the bomb. The innocent-looking bag had now taken on a more menacing appearance. He knelt down by it and started to unzip it, but suddenly pulled his hands back. What the hell am I doing? he thought. I don't know anything about bombs.

Unable to keep his eyes off the bag, he sat on the edge of the bed and reached for the telephone. The first thing he had to do was to get his father out of the house. With a shaking hand he dialed a number and a woman answered.

"Hello?"

"Hi, Aunt Mary. This is Ray."

"How are you, love?"

"Fine."

"I shouldn't even be talking to you," she said, trying to sound cross. "I'm only a few blocks away and I never see you."

"I'm sorry. It's just that I've been so busy."

"Don't give me that malarkey. How's your dad?"

"That's why I called, Aunt Mary."

"Is something wrong?"

"Nothing serious. It's just that he hardly ever leaves the house anymore. He spends too much time alone."

"Then for heaven's sake why doesn't the old fool come over and see me? I'm only a few minutes away."

"He's your brother, Aunt Mary. You know him better than I do."

"True. Lately, he needs a stick of dynamite up his arse to get him to do anything."

At the mention of dynamite, Fleming's eyes flicked to the black bag. "Maybe you could call him and invite him over."

"That's a good idea. I'll invite him to dinner Sunday. You too, if your busy social calendar permits."

"I was thinking about tonight, Aunt Mary."

"What? Now? Raymond, are you sure there's nothing wrong."

"Positive. It's just that he seems particularly down tonight. It'd be great if you could get him over to your place. Give him a cup of tea; talk about the old country."

"Child, the last thing John Fleming wants to talk about is Ireland. But leave it to me, I'll get the old goat over here if I have to come over and drag him by the heels. Put him on the phone."

"It'd be best if you called. Make it sound like it was your idea."

"Such intrigue. All right. Hang up and I'll call him. And Ray, you're a good son to think of your dad."

Fleming hung up. A moment later the telephone rang. He opened the door and listened. He couldn't make out the conversation, but he could tell by the sound of his father's voice that he wasn't pleased. A few minutes later his father shuffled down the hallway.

"Who was that?" Ray asked.

"Your Aunt Mary. The woman's daft. She's hearing noises in the apartment and she wants me to come over and find out what it is."

"The walk will do you good, Pop, and you can pick up the *News* on your way home. Say hello to Aunt Mary for me."

He waited for the sound of the front door to close and grabbed the telephone. He tried Captain Zakovitch first, but there was no answer. He dialed Inspector Morgan's number. It rang several times. He was beginning to think the Inspector wasn't home; then he heard Morgan's voice on the other end of the line.

"Hello."

"It's Ray."

"Yeah, Ray, what is it?"

"Inspector"—Fleming's eyes locked on the bag—"Manny Botnick just delivered a bomb to my house."

Chapter
30

For the better part of an hour Ray Fleming sat on the edge of the bed watching the gym bag, afraid to leave the room and afraid to stay in it. A brisk, unexpected knock at the back door made him jump. He opened it, half expecting to find Lyle Petry standing there. Instead, Inspector Morgan and the two who'd interviewed him pushed past him.

"We'd have been here sooner," Morgan said. "But we had to find another way in. Jimmy's out front watching the house."

Fleming, unnerved that his undercover role was intruding into his private life, slammed the door. "Inspector, working undercover is one thing, but having a bomb in my father's house is—"

"Where's the doorbell transformer?" Castillo interrupted.

"What? Oh, the cellar, I think."

"Chris, take the phone off the hook," Castillo said as he disappeared down the cellar stairs.

"Where's the bomb?" Morgan asked.

"Down the hall."

As Ray Fleming led them down the hall toward his bedroom, he saw Liberti take the telephone off the hook. "Why are you doing that?" he asked.

"Electrical impulses can detonate a device," she explained matter-of-factly.

The three of them crowded into Fleming's room and stared down at the black gym bag. Castillo, who'd come back from the cellar, pushed past them. He was carrying what looked like a doctor's black medical bag. He knelt down. "How'd it get here?" he asked.

"Manny brought it."

"Then it has to be pretty stable." He started to open the bag.

"Wait," Morgan said.

Castillo looked up impatiently.

"You can't fool with that thing here."

"Take it easy," Castillo said. "I just wanna take a look." Slowly, he unzipped the bag and shined a light inside. Involuntarily, the others took a step back. "Nothing too sophisticated," he said more to himself than to them. "Six sticks connected to a watch."

He stood up. "Pretty primitive, as a matter of fact. This is nothing like the other bombs they've used."

"Other bombs?" Fleming's eyes widened. "Has Lyle been involved with other bombs?"

"We don't have time to talk about it right now," Morgan snapped.

"Go to the front window and keep an eye on Jimmy. He's in a black Olds."

After Fleming left, Liberti said, "I wonder why Petry had it delivered here."

"Maybe it's another test," Morgan said, staring at the black bag on the floor.

"I say I disarm it right here," Castillo said.

Morgan's mouth dropped. "Are you nuts? What kind of damage would this cause if it went off?"

Castillo stared down into the bag and smiled grimly. "Enough to turn this house into a parking lot."

Morgan was astonished by the DEA agent's attitude. He was actually enjoying this. He turned to the FBI agent. "Chris, call the Bomb Squad. Tell them to meet us—"

Castillo put a restraining hand on Liberti. "You do that, Dan, and you blow the whole operation."

"Goddammit, I know that. But we're in the middle of a residential neighborhood. I can't risk all these lives."

"You're playing into Petry's hands," Castillo snapped. "This may be his last test for Ray. You call the Bomb Squad now, Petry and his people will disappear."

Everything the DEA agent said was true. Morgan was tired of getting whipsawed by Petry's feints and parries, but what choice did he have?

"Dan," Liberti said softly. "Petry's prints may be on it. You know the Bomb Squad's procedure. They'll take the bomb to Rodman's Neck and blow it up."

Morgan looked at Liberti in astonishment. "You too? I thought you had more sense."

"Damn it," she snapped, "sense has nothing to do with it. If we were using common sense, we'd be talking about this three hundred yards from here." She lowered her voice. "This is our first break. We gotta take advantage of it."

"Even if it's a bomb?"

Liberti nodded.

Morgan desperately sought a way to convince them that he was right. "What if it's a dud?" he said. "What if Petry comes back for it and finds it's been tampered with?"

"I can put it back together," Castillo said. "He'll never know."

"And how about you, Chris? Will you be able to clean up all traces of the silver nitrate?" A chemical used to lift latent finger-prints, silver nitrate, was notoriously messy and difficult to remove after application.

Doubt flickered in her eyes, but just as quickly vanished. "We gotta take that chance," she answered firmly.

Morgan threw out one last argument. "The Bomb Squad can get in here the same way we did. I can order them to leave the device intact. We can examine it once it's secured at Rodman's Neck."

Castillo shook his head. "You're assuming you have the time. Looking at this thing, I can't tell you when it's set to go. We have to do it here and now."

Morgan looked from Castillo to Liberti in frustration, and some-thing else—grudging admiration. They were both willing to risk their lives to learn more about Lyle Petry. So was he, but he didn't have the luxury of thinking only of himself. As a member of the New York City Police Department and the leader of this group, he was charged with providing for the safety and welfare of everyone in this city. And that included two foolhardy federal agents.

Regretfully, he looked down at the bag and wondered what intelli-gence it could yield. Suddenly, an image of the self-satisfied smile he'd seen on Petry's face as the man had driven past him four nights ago flashed into his mind's eye. Petry had had too much good fortune. He'd murdered five police officers and they still didn't even know his real name.

"Okay," he said quietly. "Let's do it."

Castillo picked up the bag carefully. "I checked out the cellar," he said. "This house was built over fifty years ago, when they still knew how to build houses. If the device goes, the foundation will absorb a lot of the shock waves."

Morgan put his hand on Castillo's arm. "You said it was a primi-tive device. Could it be booby-trapped?"

Castillo shrugged. "There are no guarantees in the boom business."

Morgan turned to Liberti. "Chris, go out the back way and wait—"

"Will you get *real*, Morgan?" Liberti's right eyebrow was arched. "*I'm* the one who's going to lift the fingerprints." Before he could respond, Liberti turned and followed Castillo out the door.

In the cellar Castillo slipped on rubber gloves. "I'll try not to mess up your print opportunity, Chris."

The FBI agent, sorting out her chemicals and brushes, laughed dryly. "Don't worry about me. Just do what you gotta do."

Morgan, holding a flashlight, squatted alongside Castillo.

After carefully inspecting the bag's lining for hidden wire, Castillo took out a razor knife and was about to start cutting the lining of the bag when Morgan stopped him. "What are you doing?"

"I'm gonna cut the bag away."

"You can't. Petry may pick it up."

Castillo muttered an oath. "You're right." He stared into the bag. "I hate to pick those sticks up. If it's booby-trapped, that's when it'll go." Cautiously, he put his hands into the bag and ran his fingers around the edges. "I don't feel anything. Well, here goes nothing." Slowly, he lifted the device out of the bag. In the glare of the flashlight the wrapped sticks of dynamite looked ugly and forbidding.

Using a magnifying glass, he carefully inspected the wires leading to the watch. Then, gingerly, he separated one wire from the others. He slipped a wire cutter onto a wire and looked up at Morgan with just a hint of a smile. "If I'm wrong," he said, "we're outta here."

The quiet metallic click of severed wire made Morgan blink.

Castillo exhaled slowly. "Wow," he whispered, "that's almost as good as getting laid."

Morgan grunted. "Is it still armed?"

"No." Castillo picked up the device and inspected it closely. With a puzzled expression he placed it back on the floor and cut a small slit in one of the sticks. A brown granular substance poured out into the palm of his hand. "Son of a bitch," he muttered.

"Looks like sand," Morgan said.

Castillo ran the grains through his fingertips. "It is."

Morgan ran his hand across his forehead and realized that his face, and Castillo's, were bathed in sweat. He stood up and stretched his cramped legs. "Son of a bitch. Another test."

Castillo threw the sand-filled sticks on the floor in disgust. "First the armored truck, now this. When is he going to get to the real thing?"

Morgan looked down at the device, which no longer looked menacing. "Only when he's sure Ray Fleming is one of them. Come on, Chris, it's your turn."

Ten minutes later, they watched Chris Liberti lift the last of the nine prints she'd found. "Okay, Don," she said, "it's all yours."

Castillo quickly reattached the wire and returned the sticks to the gym bag. He wiped as much of the silver nitrate off as he could, but some still remained.

Morgan looked at his watch. Twenty minutes had passed. "Chris, you want to get Ray?"

While Liberti went out to bring Fleming back, Morgan and Castillo returned to Fleming's bedroom where Castillo, at Morgan's suggestion, hooked up a self-activating tape recorder. If Petry called, they'd have a recording of his voice to compare against the calls made to 911.

Fleming came into the bedroom looking relieved. "A phony, huh? Why do you think—"

"When do you expect your father home?" Morgan asked.

Fleming looked at his watch. It was almost 10:45. "The *Daily News* truck doesn't deliver until eleven. He'll be home ten minutes after that."

"We think this is another test, but we don't know if it's over or just beginning. Don has hooked up a tape recorder to your phone. He'll show you how to use it later. If Petry calls and instructs you to deliver the device, go along with it. As soon as you get off the phone, call me. Got it?"

"Yeah. But what if—"

The telephone rang and the room grew silent. Liberti picked up the receiver and handed it to Fleming.

"Hello?"

"Ray, did you get the package?"

"Lyle. Yeah, I got it."

Morgan mouthed the words "pissed off."

Fleming nodded. "For chrissake, why'd you have a bomb delivered to my house."

"I'm sorry, Ray. I should have called you before Manny brought it over. Where is it now?"

"Right here where Manny left it. I'm afraid to touch the fucking thing."

Morgan nodded in approval. Fleming's acting was getting better.

"Well, you'll be rid of it soon," Petry said.

"When?"

"I'll be in touch. By the way, don't worry about the package. Just don't touch it and you'll have no problem."

Fleming hung up and told the others what Petry had said.

Morgan looked at his watch. It was just after eleven. "We'd better get out of here." He popped the tape out of the recorder and stuck it in his pocket.

After they left Fleming's house through the back door, they dropped the audio tape and prints at FBI headquarters. Liberti wouldn't leave until the tech supervisor promised her that they'd have the results before noon tomorrow. She'd also left detailed instructions that all good prints should be run through NCIC and the Department of Defense.

Chapter
31

7:45 A.M. SATURDAY, APRIL 6 • Chris Liberti was the last one into the office the next morning. In sharp contrast to her usual conservative dark skirts and jackets, she was wearing a calf-length denim skirt and a multicolored peasant blouse. It was a casual look that suited her, Morgan thought. Then it occurred to him: everything she wore suited her.

"Any news?" she asked.

Morgan looked at his watch. "It's only a quarter to eight," he said dryly. "Even the FBI isn't that efficient."

She dropped a bag on her desk. "I brought breakfast, guys."

Castillo ripped the bag open and peeked in. "What the hell is this?" he asked.

"Muffins made with whole grain, wheat germ, and a whole lot of other terrific things. I found this wonderful little health food bakery in the East Village. They have—" She stopped to watch Castillo sniffing the muffins. "What?"

"These things smell like they're made from seaweed."

"How would you know what they smell like? You smoke those putrid cigars. You couldn't smell cow crap if you were tap dancing in it."

"Maybe so," he said, bouncing one of the rock-hard muffins on the desk, "but I can smell these. Definitely seaweed. Pretty oily too. The seaweed probably came from Prince William Sound."

Ignoring Castillo, she turned to Morgan. "Would you like one?"

"You wouldn't have a bagel with a schmear in there, would you?"

"Afraid not." She dunked an herbal tea bag in a cup of hot water. "Hey, the hell with you guys. You wanna kill yourselves with cigars and cream cheese, be my guest."

Liberti ate her muffin while Castillo puffed on a cigar for breakfast. After a few bites she wrapped the muffin and stuffed it back in the bag.

Morgan stopped writing and looked up. "What's the matter? No good?"

"It's fine. I'm not hungry anymore, that's all."

"Come on, it stunk. Admit it."

"Well, it was a little . . . bland."

"Bland?"

"All right. It was lousy. But at least I try. If you guys—"

The telephone rang, interrupting the beginning of a health lecture. "Hello," she snapped. "Speaking." She tucked the telephone under her ear and started writing furiously. "Okay. Thanks a lot. I owe you one."

Gently, she put the telephone back on its cradle and jumped up. *"Yes!"* she shouted excitedly.

"Well?" Morgan and Castillo asked simultaneously.

"We got two positive IDs from the prints."

Castillo pulled his feet off the desk and a large cigar ash dropped onto his sweatshirt. He brushed at it, spreading a gray smudge across his chest. "What are the names?" he asked.

"Manny Botnick's name popped out of NCIC. No surprise there. But the Department of Defense files kicked out a Gerald L.—I wonder what that could stand for?—Parrish, male, white, forty-two."

She sat down at the computer and her fingers quickly typed a command. "Let's run Parrish's name through the Special Forces database."

Moments later, the screen displayed a profile summary. Liberti read it aloud. "Gerald *Lyle* Parrish, Captain, U.S. Army. Dishonorably discharged nine July eighty-three."

Morgan looked over her shoulder. "How about a photo?"

"Right." Liberti's fingers flew across the keyboard. "I'm asking for more details and a photo. It'll take a few minutes."

Eighteen minutes later, the fax machine and the printer began to chatter. Liberti tore the photo out of the fax and held it up. "Lyle Petry."

Morgan took the photo and studied it carefully. "It's him, all right." The fax reproduction wasn't very clear, but there was no mistaking the self-satisfied expression he'd seen the night he'd tried to follow Petry.

Castillo pulled the surveillance photos out of the drawer and compared them to the fax copy. "Goddamn," he whispered softly.

No one said anything, but they were all thinking the same thing. After searching for the elusive Lyle Petry for two weeks, they'd finally discovered who he was. The resulting emotions were a mixture of elation, satisfaction, and something else—impatience. Now that they knew who he was, they wanted it all: Lyle Petry, the bearded Hispanic, Dickerson, Newell. Puño Blanco.

Morgan broke the silence. "Chris," he said quietly, "would you call your contact in Defense and get complete files on all of them?"

Too excited to do much else, they spent the rest of the day waiting for Ray Fleming's call. Later that afternoon, Liberti received another call. "That was our tech services," she said, putting the telephone down. "Lyle Petry was the one who made the two phone calls to nine-eleven on that Queens cemetery job."

Morgan's eyes went to the photo of Petry pinned to the bulletin board and he was consumed with hatred for that calm, placid face. In a hoarse whisper he said, "We're gonna take this son of a bitch down."

It was almost eight o'clock that evening when Morgan stood up and stretched. "There's no point in all of us hanging around," he said. "Why don't you two go home. I'll call you if anything comes up."

Castillo and Liberti offered no argument. As they were getting ready to leave, the telephone rang. Morgan grabbed it.

It was Ray Fleming. "Inspector, Lyle just called. It's tonight."

Morgan pushed the speakerphone button and motioned Castillo and Liberti to sit down. "Where? When?"

"Twelve-thirty. I'm to go to 429 Columbia Street."

Morgan turned to look at the city map tacked to the wall. "In Brooklyn, near the piers?"

"Right. It's some kind of warehouse. I'm supposed to leave the bomb alongside a chain-link fence surrounding two propane storage tanks."

"Did he tell you to do anything with it?" Castillo asked.

"I'm to push the watch stem in. That won't do anything, will it?" The speaker box magnified the nervousness in his voice.

"No," Castillo said. "It doesn't do anything. He's just making it more realistic."

Morgan studied the city map. "Ray, be at the corner of Dean and Smith at midnight. It's only a few blocks from where you have to drop off the bomb. You'll get your final instructions then."

Morgan hung up and dialed the Brooklyn North Borough office.

"Lieutenant Bishop, Brooklyn North," a voice answered.

"Lieutenant, this is Deputy Inspector Morgan from the PC's office. I wonder if you could do me a favor?"

"Yes, sir." The lethargy went out of the voice. A favor from an inspector in the PC's office was an order, no matter how friendly the request sounded.

"We have a communication about a warehouse at 429 Columbia Street. I'd like you to find out who owns it. Get back to me right away." Morgan gave him a police headquarters telephone exchange that automatically call-forwarded everything to the garment center office.

Ten minutes later, the lieutenant called back. "That warehouse belongs to Tyler Foods," he said. "The warehouse is empty and the building has been up for sale for over a year."

"Thanks, Lieutenant."

Morgan hung up. "Petry was lying," he said to the others. "The building belongs to Tyler Foods, a major supermarket chain." He drummed a pencil on the desk. "Petry's sending Fleming to an abandoned warehouse with a dud bomb. Why?" Then it hit him: "He's going to retrieve the bomb," he said.

"Why?" Liberti asked.

"He not going to let something he made lie around in the streets, and more importantly, he'll be able to see if it was tampered with."

"Ohmygod," Liberti said. "You're right. The watch stem. It's a test to see if Fleming can follow instructions. We can't let Petry get his hands on it. He'll see the silver nitrate."

"How are we going to stop him?" Castillo asked with his customary pessimism.

Morgan looked at his watch. "We have almost four hours till the drop. I have an idea. Come on, I'll explain on the way."

Before they left, Morgan made a call to Captain Zakovitch.

A couple of minutes before midnight, Ray Fleming pulled into a parking spot at the corner of Dean and Smith. The streets were deserted. The chilly April night had kept everyone inside.

Moments later, he saw headlights approaching through his rearview mirror. A sudden thought panicked him. What if it was Petry? No, it couldn't be. How could he find him? He was blocks from the warehouse. As the car pulled in behind him he could see only one head. *Oh, shit. It is him!* He tried to think of an explanation. The other car's horn sounded, startling him. He got out.

Captain Zakovitch rolled the window down and smoke poured out. "You all set?" he asked.

"Yeah. Jesus, for a minute I thought you were Lyle."

Zakovitch's squinty eyes studied his undercover officer with professional interest. "How're are you doing, Ray?"

"Good. I was thrown when Manny brought that bomb to my house, but I'm okay now. I just wanna get on with it."

Zakovitch was encouraged by Fleming's tone—and body language. The earlier cockiness that had given way to nervousness had been replaced by a steady resoluteness. For the first time Zakovitch began to believe that Ray Fleming would be able to pull off this assignment. "Stay here until it's time," he said, lighting a cigarette. "Then leave the package exactly where you were told and get out of the area."

"Where should I go?"

"Home. We'll call you if we need you. Zakovitch remembered Morgan's explicit instructions and added, "Don't forget, Ray, it's supposed to be a live bomb, so don't throw it around. And don't forget to push the watch stem in."

At exactly twelve-thirty, Fleming turned into Columbia Street. About a hundred feet into the block he spotted the warehouse, a large white building to his right. He stopped in front of the propane tanks and glanced up and down the street. There was no traffic and no pedestrians. He got out, ran to the chain-link fence and, as Castillo had instructed, gently put the bag down. As he was pushing the watch stem in, a thought suddenly occurred to him: Why should he go to all this trouble to make believe he was handling a real bomb? As soon as he said it, the answer came to him: *Unless someone was watching him!* He felt the hair on the back of his neck rise and resisted the impulse to look around. He got back in the car and quickly drove away.

Had Fleming looked across the street to his left as he was leaving, he might have seen a lone figure standing in a darkened alley. Jimmy

MICHAEL GRANT

Newell waited until the car was gone, then started to step forward, but a movement across the street made him quickly step back into the shadows.

A bag lady, pushing a rusty shopping cart piled high with cardboard boxes and rags, was wending her way up the other side of the street. She drew abreast of the gym bag and stopped to peer at it, as if deciding whether she should take it or not. She started to push the cart forward, but stopped again. Glancing up and down, she shuffled over to the bag. Without looking inside, she tossed it on top of her pile and continued on her way.

Newell slipped a knife from his pocket. He started forward, but quickly stepped back to the safety of the darkened alley. A police car had turned into the street.

A uniformed Dan Morgan, driving a borrowed blue-and-white from the central motor pool, scanned both sides of the street. He thought he'd seen a movement in the alley to his left, but he couldn't be certain. When he was parallel with the bag lady, he stopped. "Better get home, old lady, before someone mugs you," he shouted.

Chris Liberti, pushing a wrinkled kerchief out of her eyes, glowered at Morgan. "Up yours, cop," she muttered.

Smiling, Morgan waited until Liberti had turned the corner, where Castillo was waiting for her. It'd take less than a minute to toss the cart into the trunk, and they'd be out of there.

When he was sure they'd had enough time, he continued down the block, glancing right and left. He saw nothing. Still, his cop's sixth sense told him someone was watching him.

After the police car turned off the street, Newell stepped out of the darkness. Muttering a curse, he hurried up the block in search of the bag lady.

Dan Morgan was waiting outside the motor pool facility when Castillo and Liberti drove up. He climbed into the back seat. "Any problems?"

Liberti turned around. She was still wearing the ridiculous house dress and raincoat she'd bought on Canal Street, but even in that rig

Officer DOWN

she managed to look feminine. "Just one sarcastic cop. I'm thinking of lodging a civilian complaint. How about you? Did you see anyone?"

"I thought I saw a movement in an alley across the street, but I'm not sure."

Morgan was feeling good about the success of their operation. "What do you say we go somewhere for a drink? I'm buying," he said.

"Ah," Liberti said, rubbing her hands together, "a little attitude adjustment. Just what I need."

At two in the morning it took some doing to find a bar in lower Manhattan that didn't look like they'd have to shoot their way out of. An hour later, they found one on Sixth Avenue. There weren't many customers, but those that were there stared at the unusually dressed trio as they came in. Liberti, wearing an ill-fitting raincoat, baggy stockings, and secondhand sneakers, looked like she didn't belong with Morgan, who was wearing a black trench coat over his uniform white shirt and black tie. Castillo, bringing up the rear, looked like a refugee in his rumpled field jacket.

Morgan threw some bills on the bar. "What are you guys having?"

Castillo and Morgan ordered beer, and Liberti ordered a martini, very dry.

"That doesn't sound too healthy to me," Morgan said.

"Will you stop? I'm not a health fanatic." She started to giggle.

"What's the matter?" Castillo asked.

"I was just thinking of the look on that bag lady's face when I said I wanted to rent her shopping cart. I think she was even more surprised when I brought it back."

Castillo snorted. "How're you going to explain a fifty-dollar fee for the rental of a bag lady's shopping cart on your expense voucher?"

Liberti looked pensive. "Hmm, I don't know, but it'll give the bean counters in Washington something to think about."

"Where's the bag?" Morgan asked.

"In the trunk."

Morgan handed Liberti her glass. "I would like to have hung

around to see who came for it. If it was Petry," he said, recalling that smiling face in the Blazer, "I'll guarantee he wasn't smiling."

Castillo swirled the liquid in his bottle and held it up in salute. "I'm beginning to really enjoy this assignment. Except for the bearded Hispanic, we've ID'd all the major players. Now it's time to hunt and stalk."

Chris Liberti, mildly disturbed by the intensity in the DEA agent's eyes, said, "Just don't forget that it was *my* computer that zeroed in on these guys."

Castillo clinked his bottle against her martini glass in silent acknowledgment.

"Before the self-congratulations get out of hand," Morgan interjected, "we still have a few problems to deal with. For instance, we don't know where or when the big event is going to take place." Concerned that he'd broken their rare optimistic mood, he added, "By the way, Zakovitch gave me some good news. He thinks Fleming's settling into this assignment."

Chris Liberti's smile was one of genuine relief. "I'll drink to that."

After the second round Morgan drained his bottle and said, "Let's call it a day. We have a lot to do tomorrow. Chris, when can we expect the personnel folders for Petry, Dickerson, and Newell?"

"First thing in the morning."

Outside, Morgan offered to give them a lift back to their cars, but Castillo and Liberti said they'd take a cab instead. The two waited for a taxi on Sixth Avenue for fifteen minutes, but at this time of night there were none to be had.

Liberti, tired of waiting, said, "Come on, Donal, let's take the subway. It'll be a lot faster."

They descended the steps into a dank subway station, smelling of stale urine. The token booth was closed, but there was a turnstile gate. Liberti tried to put a token in the slot, but there was something stuffed in the opening.

"Yo, it's broken," a voice said.

They turned and a tall, gangling man in his early twenties stepped out of the shadows. His watery eyes and half-open mouth spelled strung-out junkie. "You gotta use this gate."

Liberti saw that the lock had been broken, but she was too tired to care. She just wanted to go home and get some sleep.

As she started through the gate, the man grabbed her sleeve. "Yo. I works for the Transit Authority. Give me the token."

She started to hand it to him, but Castillo stopped her. "Don't give that asshole anything."

The man's eyes narrowed. "Yo, motherfucker, you best watch your mouth 'fore I bust you wide open."

Castillo, with just the hint of a smile, slowly unzipped his jacket and took a step back. "Whenever you're ready, asshole."

Liberti saw a strange look come into Castillo's face and it frightened her. "Donal, it's no big deal. Give him the tokens."

A knife appeared in the man's hand.

"Hey!" Liberti fought to keep her voice under control. "That's enough. I'm an FBI agent. Leave now, and there'll be no trouble."

The man, looking at her old clothes and cheap sneakers, grinned, revealing two missing teeth. "Bitch," he said. "If you're the FBI, I'm fuckin' Bernie Goetz."

Castillo heard a noise behind him. A second, heavier man emerged from the shadows. "Chris," he said quietly, "get out of the way."

The first man, drawing courage from the appearance of his accomplice, pointed the knife at Castillo. "Yo, you got a big mouth. Now I'm gonna cut your fuckin' heart out."

Liberti saw only a blur as Castillo's kick struck the man's wrist, breaking it and sending the knife clattering to the floor.

The man, looking at his limp wrist in disbelief, didn't see the next kick either. Castillo spun and delivered a roundhouse kick to the side of the man's face, slamming him against the gate. The distinctive snap of a breaking jaw echoed in the tiled station. Crouching, with both fists tightly clenched in front of him, Castillo moved in.

The man's eyes widened in terror. He backed up against the gate and tried to speak, but his jaw, hanging at an odd angle, refused to work properly. The best he could manage was a few garbled grunts.

The first straight-arm punch, delivered from the shoulder with precision and lightning speed, smashed into the man's nose, breaking it. The second punch, quickly following the first, struck his chest with a sickening thud. The man's eyes rolled back in his head, and he slumped to the floor.

When Castillo delivered the first kick, the second man had pulled a knife and started toward him. But in a matter of seconds, he saw his partner reduced to an unconscious, bleeding wreck and prudently decided to make a run for it.

Castillo caught him halfway up the stairs. Desperately, he kicked at Castillo and flailed at him with his knife, but Castillo grabbed his leg and yanked him back down the stairs, banging his head on each step. Fighting for his life, the man came off the floor slashing his knife in wide arcs. Castillo crouched and waited for his opportunity. Suddenly, his left hand darted out and he grasped the other man's knife hand in a viselike grip. Yanking the wrist forward, he spun and delivered an elbow into the man's rib cage, cracking several ribs. The man, gasping for air, slid onto the stairs, but Castillo was upon him.

"No, man!" the man screamed. "I didn't do nothin'."

Ignoring the plea for mercy, Castillo delivered a backhanded chop to the neck. The unconscious man rolled off the steps and sprawled across the floor.

Castillo, breathing hard, turned to look at Liberti, who stood open-mouthed holding a gun in one hand and her FBI credentials in the other. "You can put that away," he said, zipping up his field jacket. "He doesn't believe you."

"Are you *crazy*?" she shrieked when she found her voice. "Now we have to lock up these two."

"No we don't. They're just a couple of dirtbag junkies."

A train rumbled in the distance.

"We can't leave them here. Donal, they're not . . . dead are they?"

He looked down at the two unconscious bodies. "No, but they'll wish they were when they wake up."

It had all happened so fast, she didn't know what to do. They should arrest them, but then they'd have to explain what they were doing there. Castillo, making up her mind for her, took her arm and walked her through the gate. In the distance the incoming train lit up the track bed.

"Where did you learn that?" she asked.

"I was stationed in Japan for a couple of years. It gave me something to do in my spare time."

"You must have had a hell of a lot of spare time. What are we going to tell Morgan?"

"Nothing. It never happened."

"But—"

"Chris, we're not going to tell him. He'll only go ballistic."

Liberti nodded reluctantly. But at some time she knew she might have to tell Morgan about tonight. Not because of the fight, but because of the look she'd seen in Castillo's face. While he was taking those two apart, he was no longer a man. He'd become an unemotional, methodical machine capable of—what? She didn't know, but it made her wonder.

She was deep in thought and Castillo had to pull her away from the tracks as the train roared into the station in a swirl of wind and sound.

Chapter
32

7:30 A.M. SUNDAY, APRIL 7 • On her way in to the office the next morning Chris Liberti picked up the personnel folders for Petry, Newell, and Dickerson. Now they sat quietly, sifting through dozens of records, each documenting the rise and fall of three diverse military careers.

Morgan finished Petry's folder and threw it on the desk. "What a pile of crap," he said. "Must be a couple of dozen pages of data on Petry, but none of it useful to us."

Castillo looked up from Newell's folder and blew a line of blue cigar smoke into the air. "Like I said, we're not going to find Puño Blanco in a paper pile. They're out there in the street. *That's* where we'll find them."

Liberti, who was still angry at Castillo for his unnecessary behavior the night before, looked up. "Out on the *street?*" she asked in exasperation. "New York *City* streets? Eight-million-people-and-God-knows-how-many-miles-of *streets?* Exactly *where* in the street do you think they are, Donal?"

"I don't know, but we're not going to find them sitting on our asses in this office."

Reluctantly, Morgan had to agree with the DEA agent—at least partially. It was a certainty that they weren't going to find Puño Blanco in military dossiers. But they weren't going to find them in the miles of streets, either. "We're going to find Puño Blanco," he said aloud, "when Lyle Petry finally decides to bring Ray Fleming into his group."

Liberti closed the Dickerson file and threw it on the desk. "Dan, I have an idea. How about I set up an interview with Petry's old commanding officer? Maybe we can at least get an insight into Petry's thinking and personality."

"It wouldn't be a bad idea, but God knows where he's stationed, assuming he's still in the army. Besides, we don't have the time to jackass all over the country."

Liberti reached for the telephone. "Coffey said to call him directly if there was anything special I needed. Let's see if he meant it."

A few minutes later, after having explained the problem to the FBI Director, she hung up.

"What'd he say?" Castillo asked.

"He said he'd look into it and get back to me."

Castillo snorted. "Don't hold your breath."

Liberti rolled her eyes.

Castillo dug the knife deeper. "I'll get back to you ranks up there with The check's in the mail, and I promise I'll—"

She cut him off. ". . . I'll pull out. Yeah, yeah."

Two hours later the telephone rang and Liberti answered. Her eyebrows went up. "Yes, sir." She snatched a pencil and started scribbling notes. "Yes, sir. Thank you very much. We certainly appreciate it."

She put the telephone down gently and turned to Castillo triumphantly. "Oh, ye of little faith. That was Coffey." She read from her note pad. "Colonel Benjamin Thorne, U.S. Army Special Forces, will be arriving in New York at sixteen hundred hours today. He can be reached at the officers' billet on Governors Island. He is at your disposal."

Morgan was impressed. Cassidy had said they could get any assistance they required. But being a New York City cop who lived on a restricted budget and limited resources, he tended to think small. He reminded himself to start thinking big. When this case broke, he might be requiring the assistance of the entire federal government.

"Good," he said aloud. "I'm going downtown anyway. I'll interview him."

Dan Morgan, standing at the rail of the Governors Island ferry, stared at the brightly lit wall of high-rise buildings crowding the southern tip of Manhattan and wondered where Lyle Petry was at this moment. He didn't know, but if his meeting tonight with Petry's ex-CO was successful, he'd at least know more about who Lyle Petry was.

He followed a line of cars off the ferry and drove the short distance to the Officers' Club. Inside, the club's dimly lit, dark wood-paneled walls were decorated with military memorabilia from past wars.

He spotted the man he was looking for sitting alone at the far end of the bar. When he'd called Thorne and asked how he'd recognize him, the colonel's laughter had boomed over the telephone. "That's easy," he said. "I'll be the only black colonel there."

Morgan flashed his shield. "Colonel Thorne, Deputy Inspector Morgan."

Thorne stood up. A tall, dark-skinned black in his midfifties, he had the trim, athletic build of a man who worked out regularly. "What are you drinking?" he asked.

"A beer is fine."

Thorne ordered a beer and another bourbon and branch water for himself. When the drinks arrived, he handed the beer to Morgan. "Come on," he said. "Let's sit at a table."

Thorne studied Morgan with a humorous glint in his eye. "Inspector Morgan, you must have a lot of clout to have me ordered up here from North Carolina to talk to you on such short notice."

"I'm sorry if I inconvenienced you. It's just that—"

"No trouble at all," he said, waving his hand. "I have family in Brooklyn. Gives me a chance to visit." The congenial smile faded. "What did you want to talk to me about?"

"Captain Gerald Lyle Parrish."

The colonel's expression darkened. "*Ex*-Captain Parrish is not one of my favorite people."

Morgan, warming to the big colonel, leaned forward. "Then we have something in common. I don't like the son of a bitch either."

Thorne gave Morgan a curious look. "I was ordered to cooperate with you fully; hold nothing back. What do you want to know?"

"Why don't you just tell me about Parrish?"

Thorne sipped his bourbon as he gathered his thoughts. "We were stationed in Honduras at the time," he began. "Captain Parrish came into my unit in the fall of 1978. He was what we call a high speed–low drag type. He paid meticulous attention to detail and was outstanding both as an administrator and a field officer." Thorne chuckled. "Parrish would have made one hell of a used car salesman. He could—and did—talk his troops into doing things that a lesser officer would have had to order his men to do. He was in charge of a mobile training team tasked with providing FID training to—"

"Whoa! FID? You lost me."

"I'm sorry. FID—foreign internal defense. He was heading an MTT team whose mission was to train friendly forces in-country."

"What was Parrish's specialty?"

The colonel's slate gray eyes bored into Morgan's. "Demolitions and light weapons."

Morgan muttered an oath.

Thorne smiled. "I didn't think that would make your day. For the first year, he was the best damn officer I've ever had under my command. Then, we were assigned to—" Thorne, looking around, lowered his voice. "What I'm going to tell you now, I never said."

Morgan shook his head. "Understood."

"A year after Parrish arrived in my outfit, we moved into Colombia. We were tasked with assisting the Colombian Army in interdicting drug supply lines; searching out and destroying drug refineries deep in the mountains. No easy job. The country has more than one hundred thirty civilian armies, some of which are better equipped than our poorer NATO allies."

Thorne smiled and his eyes took on a faraway look. "Lyle Parrish was the best marksman I've ever seen. There are a lot of men who are good at shooting targets, but Parrish pissed ice water even when the targets were firing back.

"Inspector, anyone who watched the Persian Gulf war on CNN knows all about guided laser bombs. But back then, they were still in the development stages. A portable laser device was issued to my unit for field testing. It was perfect for our mission. Before the laser system, we'd find a drug factory in the mountains and call in an air strike. Problem was the tree canopy was so thick, the pilots often overflew the target. But now, all we had to do was train the laser beam on the site and the bombs would automatically be guided to the target." He smiled sardonically. "At least that's what the field manual said. Turns out it wasn't quite that simple. One day Parrish and his five-man team of nationals found a refinery. They climbed an adjoining hilltop where they'd be able to sight the laser onto the target. The current maximum distance for these devices is fifteen hundred meters. But then, it was a lot less. You had to get real close. Parrish set up the tripod and turned on the device, but it wouldn't work. While he was diddling with it, his team was spotted by the factory guards below. I was monitoring the operation at the base station. We were too far away to offer support, so I ordered Parrish off the hill."

"He didn't follow orders, did he?" Morgan interjected.

343 **Officer DOWN**

"No. Later, he told me his radio went out. Of course he was lying. The son of a bitch had turned it off. He finally got the laser working. The planes came in and blew the hell out of the factory, but by now, there were a couple of dozen men with automatic weapons swarming up the hill after Parrish and his team. It must have been one hell of a firefight. Later, we counted thirty bodies, including our people. Lyle Parrish, carrying the laser unit under his arm, was the only man to walk off that hill alive. His only wound was a machete slash to the arm. Out of ammo, he'd killed the last two men in hand-to-hand combat. I'd have put him in for a Silver Star, but we weren't supposed to be in Colombia."

"Sounds like the perfect warrior," Morgan said with a touch of admiration. And apprehension. "Any flaws in the man?"

Thorne absentmindedly played with his neatly trimmed mustache. "Just one. He was the most amoral and unemotional son of a bitch I've ever known." Thorne's eyes narrowed. "Inspector, sometimes there are things we have to do that we don't like to do. They may be legal, they may be moral, but still, they go against the grain. I've seen men struggle to do their duty under these circumstances, but not Lyle Parrish. He was absolutely coldblooded. You looked into those green eyes of his and you saw an iceberg. Maybe that's why he was so damned efficient. He never second-guessed himself."

"Where did he go wrong?"

"In those twelve months we worked closely with the Colombian Army. It was during that time that Parrish got involved with a handful of corrupt Colombian officers. Instead of destroying the factories, Parrish and the others started collecting protection money."

"Twelve months? Didn't you know what he was doing?"

If Thorne heard the accusatory tone in Morgan's question, he didn't let on. "You have to understand Special Forces operations, Inspector. We train our people to work alone. One Special Forces man assigned to a company of nationals is not unusual. In the field for months at a time, he's completely autonomous."

"When did you find out he'd gone bad?"

"About nine months into the operation, I started hearing rumors that Parrish was working with the drug cartels. I didn't believe it. He

MICHAEL GRANT

was too good an officer. But then, as reports from other reliable sources came in, I had no choice but to believe it."

"What'd you do?"

"I placed him under arrest."

"Did he do time?"

Thorne swirled the bourbon in his glass. "It seems the Colombian Army officers he was working with had friends in high places. What little evidence there was disappeared. The best I could manage was a dishonorable discharge for him. The son of a bitch didn't even do a day in the stockade," he said bitterly.

Listening to Thorne's description, Morgan began to understand why Petry had been so elusive. It wasn't luck. Glumly, Morgan wondered if he, Liberti, and Castillo were a match for him.

"Colonel, do the names James T. Newell and Glen A. Dickerson mean anything to you?"

Thorne shook his head. "No. Should they?"

"They're former Special Forces sergeants who worked with Parrish at one time."

"Must have been before my time. I remember the names of every soldier who ever served under me."

Morgan downed the rest of his beer. "Thanks, Colonel. You've been very helpful."

Thorne put his hand on Morgan's forearm. "I don't want to pry, but let me make a guess. Parrish, those two you mentioned, and maybe a few more, are the subjects of your investigation."

Morgan nodded, but didn't elaborate.

Thorne's eyes were now clouded with fury. "Inspector, there's nothing I hate more in this world than renegade Special Forces soldiers. Not only do they tarnish the reputation of the best goddamn fighting force in the world, they dishonor the memory of the men in Special Forces who have given their lives for their country."

The pressure increased on Morgan's arm. "I just wish there were a way for me and an A team to be assigned to your investigation. I can tell you this world ain't big enough for Lyle Parrish to hide in, if I'm looking for him."

Morgan, staring at the two Silver Stars and three Purple Heart ribbons pinned to the colonel's chest, wished there were a way to accept his offer. Instead, he said, "Colonel, in spite of what you've said about Parrish, I have a feeling you genuinely liked the man."

Thorne released his grip on Morgan. "I did. He was the best damn soldier I've ever seen." The colonel's eyes grew cold. "But because of what he became," he said harshly, "I wouldn't hesitate to put a round right between his fucking eyes."

Morgan stood up. "You know something, Colonel? You and I have something else in common. We're both members of organizations we're proud of. But human nature being what it is, there will always be a few renegade soldiers—and a few corrupt cops."

Colonel Benjamin Thorne rose to his full six-foot-three height and straightened his uniform. "Not if I have anything to say about it," he said.

Chapter
33

While Dan Morgan was talking to Colonel Thorne, Ray Fleming was firing the last of his fifty rounds. He lowered his sights and squinted toward the target in disgust. Lately, his shooting had been getting sloppy. He knew the reason, of course. Because of Petry, Inspector Morgan, and Celeste he was finding it hard to concentrate. He was debating whether or not to shoot another box, when Petry stepped up behind him.

"How's it going, Ray?"

Fleming turned and looked into the smiling face. He couldn't believe Petry's blasé attitude. He'd sent what Fleming thought was a live bomb to his house, but he was acting as though it was nothing more than a basket of fruit. Suppressing his anger he whispered, "How'd it go?"

A momentary flash of annoyance crossed Petry's face. "I don't want to talk about it here. Let's go down the block for a beer."

"No," Fleming said quickly. He didn't want to go there. He was still afraid the bartender might mention the bottle incident. "There's a joint a couple of blocks from here. Let's go there instead."

Petry looked curious. "What's wrong with the usual place?"

"I don't like the barkeep's attitude. Besides, this other joint has a couple of good jazz tunes on the jukebox."

He thought Petry was going to give him an argument, but he merely shrugged and said, "What the hell, a beer is a beer."

While Petry ordered, Fleming fed a handful of coins into the jukebox and punched up three vintage Barney Kessel tunes recorded in the fifties. As he climbed back on the bar stool next to Petry, Kessel launched into one of Fleming's favorites, "Sixty-four Bars on Wilshire." The up-tempo tune began with a short riff between the guitar and Shelly Mann on drums, and then broke into a tight unison run with guitar and sax.

Petry made a face. "You like that stuff?"

"Yeah. You don't?"

"I'm not much for music, but if I listen to anything, it's country." Petry grinned. "Give me a cold beer, a hot broad, and some good ol' country music anytime."

Fleming looked around to make sure no one was within earshot. "So, how'd it go?" he asked again.

There was that momentary look of irritation again. "Not good."

Fleming's mouth went dry. *Did Petry know about the tampering?* "I put it in the right place, didn't I?"

"Yeah, but it didn't go off."

"Shit. I don't have to do that again, do I?"

"No. My client got spooked and called the contract off."

Fleming was relieved. He didn't want to go through that again, even if it was a phony bomb. He remembered Morgan's advice and said, "So what about my money?"

"Sorry, buddy. Payment was only if the warehouse went up."

"Damn it, Lyle, *I'm* the one who risked my ass carrying that thing around the city. And you're saying I did it for nothing?"

Petry took an envelope out of his pocket and handed it to Fleming. "It's not the fifty thou I promised, but it'll pay you for your time."

Fleming hefted the thick envelope, wondering if he should count it. He decided not to and stuffed it in his pocket.

"Don't you want to know how much is in there?"

"I'm sure you did the right thing."

Petry looked at Fleming curiously. "You're okay, Ray." He studied his bottle pensively as if trying to make up his mind about something.

Fleming, watching him out of the corner of his eye, wondered if he were finally going to ask him the big question.

Petry picked at the label on the bottle. "Ray, I know we've done a couple of things that didn't turn out as planned, but I've seen enough of your style to know you have big *cojones*." He leaned close to Fleming and lowered his voice. "What we've done is peanuts compared to something I'm working on right now."

Fleming felt his heartbeat quicken. Should he take the bait now? No, he decided. He couldn't let Petry off that easily. "Lyle, so far *nothing* has gone right," he said heatedly. "Why should I risk my ass again? Fuck it. I don't want any more of your deals." He held his breath, afraid Petry would stand up and say, "Okay, I'll see you around." Instead, Petry regarded him with a look that was a mixture of curiosity and satisfaction.

"Ray, that's just the answer I wanted to hear. If you had jumped at the chance, I would have had some doubts about your judgment. You're right to think I don't know what the hell I'm doing. I have a confession to make. The shooting of the guard was unforeseen, but the bomb you planted was a dud."

Officer DOWN

"What—?"

"I needed to see if you could do it."

"Goddamn it, Lyle, I don't like being jerked around like this."

Petry put his hands up in supplication. "Don't get your ass in an uproar. You're right, but look at it from my perspective. This assignment requires all top-notch people. I had to be sure you fit in."

"Who are the other top-notch people?" he asked sarcastically. "Manny Botnick?"

"You don't have to know that yet."

"For chrissake, Lyle—"

"Are you in? Yes or no."

"How much?"

"A quarter of a million."

Fleming's eyebrows went up in genuine amazement. "Holy shit! Apiece?"

"Apiece."

"No more tests?"

"No more tests."

Fleming studied Petry's reflection in the mirror behind the bar. This is what he, Inspector Morgan and the others, had been waiting for. Had he played his role well enough to be accepted or was he about to say yes to another test? "Okay," he said. "I'm in. What do I have to do?"

"I'll explain fully at a meeting tomorrow night. But I'll tell you right up front, Ray. You may have to use your gun this time."

"You mean shoot someone?"

"That's exactly what I mean."

Fleming cursed Morgan. If only he knew what he was getting into, he'd know how to react better.

Petry saw the clouds of doubt forming in Fleming's eyes and said, "A quarter of a *million*, Ray."

"Okay. I said I'm in."

"Good. I'll pick you up in front of Blockmann's at six tomorrow night."

After he left Petry, Fleming followed Inspector Morgan's instructions and watched his rearview mirror to see if he was being tailed.

When he was certain he wasn't, he stopped at a telephone and called Morgan.

After he'd recounted what had transpired, Morgan asked, "Do you have any idea where this meeting is to be held or who'll be there?"

"No."

There was a pause on the other end of the line. Then Morgan said, "Come to the office at five tomorrow. I'll give you a final briefing then."

Fleming hung up and looked at his watch. He still had time to make his date with Celeste. He could use a pleasant diversion.

He arrived at Chico's just as she was getting off work. They went to a movie and got back to her apartment around midnight. He wanted to stay the night, but Celeste tried to beg off, saying she had to get up early the next morning. In the end his persistence finally won out. Later, he realized he'd made a mistake. They made love, but it wasn't like the last time. Celeste seemed preoccupied, and his mind was swirling with the latest development in the investigation. It was over quickly and they both promptly fell asleep.

Fleming woke the next morning and looked at the night table clock. It was after ten and Celeste was gone. He hadn't heard her leave. He went into the bathroom to take a shower, but there were no towels. He opened the bedroom closet to look for one, and something caught his eye. Pushed to the far end of the closet were several hangers containing men's clothing. Curious, he pulled the hangers apart and inspected the clothing. He recognized two sport jackets and a leather jacket. They belonged to Lyle. Confused and angry, he slammed the closet door shut. Unwilling to confront Celeste in this state, he dressed quickly and left the apartment.

He walked aimlessly through the streets of Elmhurst and tried to sort out what it all meant. Was she just allowing him to keep his clothing there or were they still lovers?

Captain Zakovitch, sitting in his sparsely furnished office, lit another cigarette and sat back to read the sixty-one pertaining to the recovery of the stolen car used in the armored car holdup. His eyes

Officer DOWN

stopped at the description and he reread the sentence. *"The above described vehicle was recovered in the Shea Stadium parking lot at 1630 hrs. this date."* Puzzled, he pulled out Fleming's debriefing and read it again. According to Fleming, he and Petry had driven around in that car for hours.

Zakovitch picked up the telephone and called the precinct desk officer. "Lieutenant, Captain Zakovitch from the Intelligence Division. Maybe you can clear up a matter for me about the car used in the armored car robbery? The sixty-one gives sixteen-thirty hours as the time of recovery. Could that be a mistake?"

"Let me check the voucher book" A moment later the desk officer was back on the telephone. "The time's right, Cap. The vehicle was recovered at four-thirty P.M."

Zakovitch put the telephone down, lit another cigarette, and dialed Dan Morgan's number.

It was just noon when Fleming got home. The telephone was ringing when he opened the door. It was Inspector Morgan.

"Ray, get over to the office right away."

Fleming didn't like the sharp tone in the inspector's voice. "Something up?"

"Get over here. We'll talk then."

When Fleming arrived at the office he was surprised to see a dour-faced Captain Zakovitch waiting with the others.

Liberti stood up. "How about a cup of coffee, Ray?"

Fleming nodded.

Morgan waited until Liberti handed him the coffee, then he said, "Ray, there's a discrepancy in your story about the armored car holdup that needs clearing up."

Fleming felt his stomach muscles tighten. "What's the problem?" His mouth had gone dry and he gulped the hot coffee.

"You said that you and Petry drove around in that car for several hours. Is that correct?"

"Yeah, a long time. That's why I couldn't call anyone."

Morgan's eyes bored into the young undercover officer. "That's impossible. The vehicle was recovered at four-thirty that afternoon."

Fleming felt a flush rising and his ears began to burn. He wanted to say something, but what could he say?

The painful silence was mercifully broken by Chris Liberti. "Ray," she said softly, "you lied. We have to know why."

Fleming's head was swimming. It had never occurred to him that they'd be able to find a discrepancy in the time. He tried to think of an excuse, but then he looked at the four grim faces staring at him and knew there was no point in making it worse. "I . . . there's something . . . someone I haven't told you about," he started tentatively.

Morgan fought back the anger rising in him. "Who?"

"Her name is Celeste Escobar. She's a barmaid at Chico's."

"What the hell is Chico's?" Morgan asked evenly.

"A bar Lyle hangs out in."

Castillo's sneakers came off the desk. "Petry hangs out in a bar called Chico's? You never told us that."

"I didn't think it was important."

"*You* didn't think it was important?" Morgan started out of his seat, but Liberti shoved him back down. Morgan, breathing hard, turned away. For a moment, while he was looking into Fleming's embarrassed face, he'd seen the face of Fredericks, just as he'd seen him in the hallway that night.

"How does Celeste fit into this?" Liberti asked.

Fleming cleared his throat. "She used to be Lyle's girlfriend."

"How long have you known this?"

"From the beginning." He heard Castillo mutter an oath in the background. "She said there wasn't anything between them now," he added quickly.

Castillo came out of his seat and stood over Fleming. "Hey, kid, are you banging this broad?" he asked.

Ray Fleming blinked rapidly. "I've . . . we've slept together."

"And that's where you were all that time after the holdup."

"It's not the way you think. I only went back there for a little while. I fell asleep . . . She was supposed to wake me . . ." His voice trailed off when he saw the look of disgust on Castillo's face.

A distressed Zakovitch had purposely remained silent while the three interrogated his undercover officer. But as he saw the mounting anguish in Fleming's face, a condition he felt partially responsible for, he felt compelled to come to the young officer's aid. "Ray," he said quietly, "why didn't you tell us about her before?"

"I . . . I didn't think she was involved and I didn't want to get her in trouble."

Morgan slammed his hand on the desk. "*You* didn't think she was involved? Who the fuck do you think you are? *I'm* the one who decides what's important. I told you that from the beginning."

Fleming stared at the floor and said nothing.

Liberti sat down next to Fleming. "Ray, what have you told her?"

He shook his head. "Nothing. She doesn't know who I am."

She looked relieved. "Do you know her birth date?"

"No."

"About how old is she?"

"I guess about twenty-five, twenty-six."

Even in his anger Morgan knew why she was asking these questions. She needed the information to run a name check on Celeste. "Chris," he said, forcing himself to remain calm, "play the tape of the nine-eleven rape call."

Liberti pushed the cassette into the tape recorder and punched the Play button. As Fleming listened to the female voice reporting the rape, he paled.

When the tape was finished, Morgan got up and punched the Stop button. "Well? Was that your girlfriend?"

"I . . . I think that's her."

"Are you sure?" Castillo pressed.

Fleming's face registered his turmoil. "I think so. The sound's not so hot, but—"

Morgan picked up a telephone that was connected to a tape recorder and handed it to Fleming. "We need a sampling of her voice for a voice analysis comparison. Call her."

Fleming looked at Morgan in panic. "Now?" The last thing he wanted to do was talk to Celeste. Especially in front of them.

"*Now*," Morgan bellowed.

With a shaky hand he dialed the number and prayed that she wasn't home.

She picked it up on the third ring. "Hello?"

"Hi, it's Ray."

"Baby, why'd you leave? I rushed home, but you were gone. I'm sorry about last night. I wasn't in the mood. Come over tomorrow night and I promise I'll make it up to you."

"I don't know if I can," he sputtered. "I'll call you. I gotta go."

Morgan, ignoring Fleming's discomfort, popped the tape out of the machine and tossed it to Liberti. "How quickly can you get a match on this?"

Liberti caught the tape and stood up. "Right away. I'll call as soon as I have results."

After she left, Castillo sat on the edge of the desk nearest Fleming. "Have you learned anything more about this meeting tonight?"

Fleming looked up. "No, sir."

Castillo's turned to Morgan. "Think we should wire him for this meeting?"

"No. They might search him."

Castillo turned back to Fleming. "Kid, we need as much information as you can get. Is Manny gonna be there?"

"I don't know."

"If he is, he's the weak link in this operation. Try to pump him for information."

"He's been pretty closemouth about Lyle."

"Does he drink?"

"Naw. A few beers and he's whacked."

"Good. Get him whacked. Drunks always shoot their mouths off."

Morgan looked at his watch. "You'd better be going."

Fleming stood up.

"And Ray"—Morgan's voice was steely—"you're a police officer. At that meeting tonight, observe, listen, and remember. Understood?"

"Yes, sir."

Then Morgan added, "Don is right. If you get the chance to go out with any of them, go. When you're finished, call. We'll be here."

Zakovitch, looking like a stricken father who has just discovered that his son is a drug addict, stood up. "Come on, Ray, you and I have a couple of things to talk about."

After Fleming left, Castillo lit up a cigar and studied the glowing ash. "You were pretty hard on the kid," he said.

An image of Fredericks's face popped into Morgan's head again. "He needed a kick in the ass. Besides, you were the one who said he should act like a cop."

"True. But scaring the shit out of him ain't the way to do it."

Morgan slammed his desk drawer shut. "*I'll* handle Fleming. If I need your advice, I'll ask."

Castillo shrugged. "You're the boss. What are we going to do about this girl, Celeste?"

"I'm writing a note to Chris asking her to run a name check on her when she gets back." Morgan looked at his watch. "Come on, it's time we were going too."

"Where?"

"Blockmann's. We're going to follow Petry when he picks up Fleming."

"Again? You remember what happened last time."

"I remember. But it's worth a try. The meeting might be at their safe house. Maybe we'll get a chance to tail one of the others."

"It won't work. Petry—"

"Don, I'm not going to sit here all night waiting for Fleming's call."

Castillo saw the determination in Morgan's face. "Okay," he said, chomping on his cigar. "Let's do it."

Chapter
34

Ray Fleming was surprised when Lyle Petry pulled up in front of Blockmann's in a taxi at exactly six o'clock. "I was expecting the Blazer," he said, climbing into the back seat.

"There's no place to park in this damn city. Penn Station," he said to the driver.

"We taking a train somewhere?"

Petry slapped Fleming's knee. "Questions. Always questions. Just sit back and enjoy the ride."

At the far end of the block, Morgan and Castillo, sitting in their rented van, were equally surprised by the arrival of the taxi.

"So much for the transmitter," Castillo mumbled as Morgan snapped the van into gear. Before they'd left the office, Morgan had insisted that they take a magnetic transmitter—another one of Liberti's toy's—with them.

The magnetic device, easily attached to the underside of a vehicle, can be useful in automobile surveillance. Using a portable radio direction finder to home in on the vehicle, it does away with the need to keep the vehicle in sight. There was one problem, as Castillo had been only too happy to point out: you have to get close enough to the vehicle to plant it. Morgan was aware of that, but he was hoping Petry might leave the vehicle unattended for a few minutes. Now, watching the cab make a left turn onto Church Street, he realized the transmitter was a moot point.

At six in the evening the streets of lower Manhattan were still clogged with rush hour traffic, a condition which Morgan viewed with mixed feelings. The crowded streets afforded him opportunity for cover, but they also increased the likelihood of his getting stuck in traffic. Skillfully, he weaved the van in and out of the paths of lumbering trucks and darting taxis, always maintaining the optimal distance. At 14th Street he had a close call. The light turned red and Morgan, to keep from losing the taxi, had to gun the van through the intersection to the sounds of protesting horns and fist-waving pedestrians.

At 33rd Street the taxi made a left. "Where the hell is he going?" Morgan muttered. "I can't believe he'd have a safe house in midtown Manhattan."

Castillo's eyes never left the taxi. "I'm not surprised by anything Petry does."

In the taxi, Petry leaned forward. "Pull into the side entrance," he instructed the driver.

The taxi pulled into the congested dropoff and pickup area in the transverse street between 33rd and 32nd. Petry slipped a few bills to the driver and jumped out. "Come on," he said to Fleming.

Walking quickly, they went to the front of the taxi waiting line and jumped into another cab. "Sixth and Fifty-third," Petry said, slamming the door.

Morgan and Castillo pulled up to the entrance of the transverse street just in time to see Petry and Fleming climb into another cab. "Shit!" Morgan muttered. With a squeal of screeching tires, he swung the van into the street.

Castillo, looking at the solid wall of taxis and pedestrians blocking their way, gripped the dashboard. "Where the hell are you going?"

"After that cab."

With a bouncing jolt the van catapulted onto the sidewalk. Pedestrians and redcaps scattered as Morgan gunned the engine and sped along the sidewalk. At the other end he drove off the curb with a jarring bounce, causing the low-hanging muffler to leave a trail of flying sparks.

At the end of the transverse street he screeched to a halt. Thirty-second Street was a solid wall of traffic. Inching into the traffic, they craned their necks looking for Petry's cab, but all they saw were identical yellow taxis all the way to Seventh Avenue. Morgan slammed his hands on the steering wheel in frustration.

"We lost them," Castillo said quietly.

"We'll drive around the block a couple of times," Morgan said halfheartedly. "Maybe we can—"

Someone thumped the side of the van. Morgan looked in his sideview mirror and saw a gray-haired traffic cop approaching. "Just what I need," he mumbled, rolling down the window. "Officer, I'm—"

The flushed-faced cop held on to the door handle to steady himself. "What are you? *Fucking nuts?*" he sputtered, trying to catch his breath. "Pull this piece of shit over to the side and give me your license and registration."

Morgan flashed his ID. The sight of a deputy inspector's shield had no affect on the enraged cop. "What's *that* supposed to mean?"

he said sarcastically. "Do deputy inspectors have the right to drive like *lunatics?* You almost ran over a dozen—"

"Officer," Morgan interrupted, "we're on a surveillance. We were trying to catch up to a cab."

The cop pushed his cap to the back of his head and looked toward Seventh Avenue. "Well, where is he?"

"We lost him."

His anger dissipated, the cop suddenly realized he'd been cussing out a deputy inspector. "I'm sorry," he said with the appropriate degree of respect in his voice, "it's just that—"

"No problem, Officer."

Morgan started to pull away, but the cop grabbed his arm and stuck his head into the window. "Inspector, could you do me a favor? I just ran two blocks to catch you and right now I got half the commuters in the city watching us. Could we make believe I'm giving you a summons?"

Morgan sympathized with the old cop's need to save face, but there wasn't time. "I'd like to help you, but we gotta go."

The cop wouldn't be deterred. "Then is it all right if I just chew you out?"

"Okay. I guess I have time for that. Be my guest."

The cop stood back and his face reddened. "And don't *ever* let me catch you driving like that again," he bellowed, pointing his finger at Morgan. "Now get the hell out of here."

Morgan, looking suitably chastised, pulled away to the applause and jeers of dozens of onlookers.

The cab pulled over at the corner of Sixth Avenue and 53rd Street. Petry and Fleming got out.

"Now what?" Fleming asked, rattled by all the subterfuge. "The Concorde?"

"Nope, we're here." Petry said, leading Fleming into the lobby of the New York Hilton.

The lobby was jammed with conventioneers. A chemical engineers convention was ending and an auto dealers convention was just beginning. It was easy to tell who was who: the auto dealers, clinking glasses and slapping backs, were in sharp contrast to the hung-over, sleep-deprived engineers waiting in the checkout lines.

Petry and Fleming got off the elevator at the fifteenth floor. Petry, Fleming noted, had apparently been here before. He led Fleming through a maze of corridors without even once glancing at the room number signs.

Petry slipped his key card into a door at the end of a corridor and motioned Fleming inside. It was a suite. To the left of the long hallway was a kitchen, and to the right a bathroom and a bedroom. Fleming heard subdued voices as he walked down the hallway. He stepped into the living room and stopped abruptly.

Manny Botnick stood up. "Hi, Ray. I'm glad you're with us."

Fleming looked past Botnick. A glum-looking Alvaro, sitting on the couch, waved. "Welcome, Ray."

Glen sat next to Alvaro. He smiled warmly and raised a clenched fist. "Okay, man," he mouthed.

Newell came out of the kitchen. "Has he been tossed?" he asked Petry.

"No."

Newell started to pat down Fleming, but Fleming pushed him away. "Hey, what the hell's going on?" he protested.

"It's okay," Botnick said. "We all got searched. Can't be too careful. Right, Lyle?"

Petry slid into a vacant chair. "Right, Manny."

When Newell finished his thorough patdown, Petry slapped Botnick on the knee. "Hey, Manny, how about getting us a couple of beers from the kitchen?"

"I gotta take a leak," Fleming said. "Where's the head?"

Dickerson pointed to a door off the living room.

Inside the bathroom, Fleming splashed some cold water on his face to clear his head. As he was drying his hands, he heard voices and put his ear to the door.

Petry was speaking to Dickerson. "Any problems with the truck?"

"It took some doing. You didn't want a major rental company, but I

Officer DOWN

found a little joint on East Tenth Street. He's only got a few trucks, but he has the kind we need."

"Good. You reserve it?"

"Affirmative. We got the truck from seventeen hundred hours tomorrow."

"How about the ladder?"

"Okay. I measured the back door. I can bolt a twelve-foot ladder to it."

Botnick's return ended the conversation. Fleming came out and sat down next to Petry.

"Okay," Petry said, waiting for everyone to settle in, "let's get to the briefback. You all know Ray." He squeezed Fleming's shoulder. "He's one of us now." Petry turned to Newell. "Are the Uzis, grenades, and explosives ready?"

"Cleaned and checked. We're ready to load the truck when Glen picks it up."

Petry opened his briefcase, took out a folder, and spread it out on the coffee table. Fleming concentrated on the map in front of him, a line drawing of First Avenue from 42nd Street to 48th Street.

"Okay," Petry said. "Listen up for your assignments." He pointed to a rectangle, representing the truck. "Manny, you'll drive the truck. Ray, you'll ride shotgun." He moved his finger north on First Avenue. "You'll drive up First Avenue. By the time you get to Forty-fifth Street, everything will be clear. Turn into Forty-fifth Street and park right here." He indicated a spot about ten feet off the corner directly alongside the building. "Glen will be waiting to pick you up with a car."

Botnick nervously picked at his mustache. "Do we have to set a timer?"

Fleming's head shot up. "A timer?"

"For the explosives," Petry said, his attention still on the map.

"What building is that?" Fleming asked.

Petry looked up and Fleming was startled by the complete absence of life in them: it was like looking into the eyes of a dead man. "The U.S. Mission to the United Nations," Petry said.

Fleming, keeping his facial expression neutral, nodded and looked back at the map.

"You don't have to set anything," Petry said to Botnick. "It'll be detonated remotely."

Fleming had dropped people off at the U.S. Mission in his taxi. "Isn't there a police booth outside that building?" he asked.

"That's right. Two booths with three to four cops in them," Petry said. "But they'll be neutralized before you get there."

Fleming couldn't believe he was hearing Petry talk about murdering police officers as calmly as one would discuss a picnic. He stole a glance at the others peering at the map to see their reactions. Glen and Jimmy peered at the map intently with somber, neutral faces. Botnick, picking at his mustache, licked his lips from time to time. And Alvaro, stroking his beard, simply looked tense.

Petry sat back. "Any questions?"

Newell glanced up at Fleming with a challenging look. "How about you?" he asked. "You always have a lot of questions."

Fleming shook his head. "Nope. I don't have to do much."

"I wouldn't say that," Petry corrected. "This is a good plan, but there's always the unexpected. If anyone tried to stop the truck, your job is to take him out."

"That shouldn't prove too difficult," Alvaro said, speaking for the first time. "Given Ray's proficiency with firearms."

"That's why I picked him," Petry said, standing up. "If there are no further questions, meeting's adjourned. "Jimmy, you and Glen leave first."

After they left. Petry put his arm around Fleming. "Well, what do you think?"

"Man, this is wild. Will it work?"

"Absolutely. First rule of planning a mission: keep it simple. This one couldn't be easier. Get in; plant the ordnance; and get out."

"But why the U.S. Mission?"

Petry dropped his arm. "Questions, questions. Don't worry about why, just think about what you'll be able to do with a quarter of a million." He looked at his watch. "Okay, you and Manny take off.

Ray, stay by the phone. I'll call you tomorrow with a time and a place to meet me."

After Fleming and Botnick left, Alvaro turned away from the window. "You have violated your own doctrine," he said to Petry. "This is not a simple mission; it's extremely complicated."

Petry snapped his briefcase shut. "Not when you understand it the way I do."

Alvaro opened the door. "You're the only one who does."

"I'm the only one who has to," Petry said, closing the door behind them.

Remembering Castillo's instructions, Fleming talked Botnick into stopping off for a drink. They found a small bar on East 65th Street where a jazz trio was playing.

While Fleming ordered the beer, Botnick watched the guitar player run through an up-tempo solo. "Hey, he's not half bad. What do you think of the drummer?"

Fleming was too preoccupied to appreciate the drummer's technique. He slid a bottle and a glass in front of Botnick. "Manny, what do you think of all this?"

Botnick poured his beer. "I try not to think about it." He turned back to the guitar player who was "trading fours" with the bass player. "Damn, he's really good."

Fleming started at the back of Botnick's head in resignation. There was no point in pressing him for information as long as there was a jazz group in the same room. He signaled the bartender for two more rounds.

By eleven-thirty Fleming and Botnick had moved to a table closer to the bandstand. Botnick's alcoholic tolerance both surprised and irritated Fleming. He'd lost count after their seventh beer, but Botnick showed no sign of getting drunk.

The combo took a break and Botnick took the opportunity to go to the men's room. Fleming was going to call Morgan, but the waiter said the telephone was in the vestibule of the men's room.

He looked down at his half-empty glass. Fortunately, the beer wasn't having an effect on him; it never did when he was under stress. But it had given him a world-class headache. He was trying to think of what else to do to Botnick, when he saw the little man stumbling back to the table. He was so drunk, he was bouncing off bar stools.

He flopped back into his chair and ran his hand over his mouth. "Jeez"—his voice was slurred—"I . . . don' know what happen' to me. I went to the john I was fine. Now . . . I'm all fucked up."

Fleming, suppressing a grin, knew what had happened to Botnick, because it had happened to him more than once. Sometimes he could drink for hours and not feel a thing. Then he'd get up and bang!—he was drunk. He didn't understand the phenomenon, but he was grateful nevertheless.

Over Botnick's feeble protests, Fleming ordered another round. As soon as the drinks came, Botnick grabbed the bottle, swigged from it, and slammed it on the table. He tried to focus on Fleming. "Jeez, Ray, you been drinking too much. You're all blurry." His chuckling brought on the hiccups.

Fleming, afraid Botnick was going to cause a scene, tugged at his sleeve. "Manny, this is a classy joint. The least you could do is drink out of the glass."

"Fuck 'em," Botnick growled. "I'm a man. I do what I want."

Fleming looked around uncomfortably. People were glancing their way. "Sure you are," he said.

Botnick leaned closer to Fleming's face and squinted, but it didn't do any good. The face was still a blur. "You don't believe I'm a real man, do you? Well, I am. I did things . . . you wouldn't believe."

Fleming leaned close to Botnick. "Try me," he whispered in his ear.

"I can't. Lyle said . . . tell . . . no one." He tried to pour beer into his glass, but most of it sloshed onto the table. Fleming blotted it up with his cocktail napkin. "I wasn't always a man," Botnick continued in a slurred voice. "I . . . screwed up a lot. Guess 'cause I was afraid or—what's that word my old man uses?—*inept*." Botnick snorted and hiccuped at the same time. "That's a big fucking word for a stupid, ignorant Jew."

"What'd you do?" Fleming prompted.

"Things . . . you wouldn't believe."

Fleming, glancing over Botnick's shoulder, saw that the trio was getting ready to come back. Once they started playing, he'd never get Botnick's attention. "Manny," he said in desperation, "I think you're full of shit."

Botnick's head came up. He tried to focus on Fleming with his sad eyes, now turned red. "Ray," he said quietly, "I helped Lyle . . . plant a bomb at police headquarters."

Fleming was jolted by the revelation. He didn't think the mild-mannered Botnick was capable of such an atrocity. "Why'd you do it, Manny?"

Botnick stared morosely at the tabletop. "Hey, who the fuck knows?" he said softly. "Lyle's a great guy. He's been a real friend to me. You too, Ray. You been a friend, too." Fleming felt a stab of guilt. "I know I can be a pain in the ass"—Botnick chuckled and burped at the same time—"lots of people have told me that. But you and Lyle, you guys have been real friends. You two are the first to accept *me*, warts and all. Ya know what I mean?"

It was obvious Manny hadn't wanted to help plant that bomb and Fleming had to know why he did it. "You could have said no."

Botnick scowled. "I couldn't say no to my friend."

"Why?"

"Because—" He stopped and thought about it. "I guess I didn't want Lyle to get mad at me."

Out of the corner of his eye, Fleming saw that the trio had returned to the bandstand and were looking over their music. Up until now he'd been afraid to ask direct questions, because he didn't want to raise suspicions. But he was running out of time. He hoped Botnick was too drunk to realize he was being interrogated. "Manny, this thing tonight . . . I mean it's really weird. Guns, explosives. Where the hell can they hide stuff like that?"

"I dunno."

"You ever been to Lyle's house?"

"Nope. Lyle's a fuckin' phantom. He pops up here . . . he disappears there."

"How about the other guys? Where do they live?"

"I don't know, but I dropped Glen off at Twenty-ninth and Third one time. I think he lives around there."

"No kidding. I got some steady customers over there," he lied. "You remember the address?"

"Naw. I dropped him at the corner. He was so fuckin' secretive, he didn't move until I drove off." Botnick chuckled. "But I saw him in the rearview mirror. He walked into Twenty-ninth Street." Botnick waved his glass in the air and sloshed beer onto his hand. "Glen's not a bad guy. It's Jimmy I don't like. The son'a bitch never smiles, but I get the feeling he's always laughing at me."

The band started up and Botnick turned, upsetting his glass with his elbow.

Fleming tossed some bills on the table. "Come on, Manny, it's time to go."

"Where we goin'? I haven't heard these guys yet."

"Manny, we've sat through two sets already."

"Really?" He turned and squinted at the band. "Did I like them?"

"You thought they were great." He helped Botnick to his feet and managed to get him out the door without upsetting any tables.

He poured Manny into a cab and gave the driver his address. As the cab pulled away, Fleming wished he could go home too. Right now he wished he'd never heard of Captain Zakovitch, Inspector Morgan, or Lyle Petry. But as he stepped into a taxi, he consoled himself with the thought that at least this time he had some good, solid information to offer.

Chapter
35

1:55 A.M. MONDAY, APRIL 8 • It was almost 1:45 A.M. by the time Ray Fleming had finished debriefing the team. On the advice of Captain Zakovitch, Morgan hadn't told Fleming about their plans. They still agreed the less Ray Fleming knew the better.

As soon as Fleming left, Morgan dialed Cassidy's private number. A duty captain answered.

"Captain, this is Deputy Inspector Morgan. I have to speak to the commissioner immediately."

"Inspector," the voice dripped sarcasm, "it's two in the morning. The commissioner isn't here."

Morgan, who had no time for officious palace guards, snapped, "Well, where is he?"

The voice at the other end of the line tightened. "I don't give that information to *anyone* over the telephone."

"Goddammit! Captain, check the special instructions log. I'm authorized to speak to the commissioner anytime."

The captain dropped the receiver on the desk. Morgan heard papers shuffling, then a mumbled "Oh, shit." The captain came back on the line. "I'm sorry, Inspector Morgan." The antagonism was gone from the voice. "The commissioner is in Albany."

"Get ahold of him and tell him to call me right away."

"What?" The captain wasn't accustomed to having a deputy inspector ordering the police commissioner to call *him*. He read the log entry one more time to make sure he'd read it correctly. It said: *Effective immediately and until further notice, calls from D.I. Daniel Morgan will be put through to me forthwith at any time of the day or night.*

The directive was clear. He couldn't get into trouble for following those instructions. "Okay, Inspector, I'll have the commissioner call you."

Morgan hung up and turned to Liberti and Castillo. "Botnick may have dropped Glen off at their safe house."

"There could be more than one," Castillo said.

"Yeah, but this one we can find. Chris, how many agents do you have at your disposal?"

"One call to Coffey, and I'll have as many as I want."

"Good. Get on the horn. We'll need a couple of agents to check the telephone company and Con Ed billing for every apartment on Twenty-ninth Street from Fifth Avenue to the East River."

Liberti looked puzzled. "What will they be looking for?"

"Apartments with minimum electric and telephone bills. The apartment that has both will be the one we're looking for."

"Okay. I'll also have them run name checks on Petry, Dickerson, and Newell. It probably won't do any good, but what the hell."

While Morgan had been talking to Liberti, Castillo had been thumbing through the Yellow Pages. "There's only one truck rental company on East Tenth Street," he said, jotting down the address.

Morgan poured two cups of coffee and handed one to Castillo. "We'll have to mark the roof of that truck so it can be surveilled from the air. We can't take a chance of losing it in traffic."

"Sounds good, but what will we use and how do we get to the truck?"

"Luminous paint." He looked at Castillo mischievously. "You any good at breaking and entering?"

Castillo opened his desk and took out a small leather pouch. "I just happen to own a set of lock picks."

Morgan looked at his watch. "I hope that garage isn't open all night."

Castillo read the Yellow Pages ad. "Open till midnight."

"Good." Morgan glanced at his notes. "I wonder what the hell that ladder is for?"

"That's what I was wondering," Castillo said. "Something doesn't add up. Uzis, grenades—Petry's too smart to take out those cops in the booth with automatic weapons. He'd use pistols with silencers or knives. Something's not right."

Liberti hung up. "I talked to Coffey. He's put twenty-five agents at our disposal, more if we need them. He'll notify the Secret Service to make sure the president and other high-profile dignitaries don't come into the city until this is finished."

Morgan studied the wall map glumly. "The United Nations is practically across the street from the U.S. Mission."

"Should we notify them?" Liberti asked.

Morgan could imagine the international incident if someone from the UN were blown up. "We can't," he said, turning away from the map. "We'd be literally telling the whole world."

Castillo said, "I agree."

"Yeah, but the PC doesn't know about this. He may see things differently."

As if on cue, the telephone rang. It was Commissioner Cassidy.

"What's up, Dan?"

"Puño Blanco is going to launch their attack tonight, sir."

"Tonight! That doesn't give us much time. What's their objective?"

"They're going to blow up the U.S. Mission."

"Good God Almighty! What have you done so far?"

Morgan told the commissioner about the notification to Coffey and his plans to find and mark the rental truck.

"Dan, I'm leaving for the city right now. I want you and the others in my office at nine sharp."

Morgan hung up and looked at his watch. They had only seven hours before they had to be in Cassidy's office. It didn't leave him much time. "Come on," he said to Castillo. "We have work to do. Chris, you stay here. As soon as your people come up with the address on Twenty-ninth Street, page us."

"Chris," Castillo whispered in her ear, "don't forget to pick up those items I requested."

"I won't," she answered with little enthusiasm.

Morgan and Castillo's first stop was a Department of Highways garage in lower Manhattan. A sleepy foreman was waiting for them. Morgan ID'd himself. "You Tony?"

The man scratched a day-old growth of beard. "Yeah. I got your stuff ready."

He looked at the two men curiously. Ten minutes earlier, he'd been awakened by a telephone call from the Assistant Commissioner of Highways himself, and told that someone named Morgan from the PD would be by to pick up a gallon of luminous paint and a brush. "Don't ask me why," the commissioner had added irritably. "I don't know either."

The foreman put the paint in Morgan's trunk. "What're you guys going to do with this?" he asked.

"Paint some white lines," Morgan said, slamming the trunk.

Ten minutes later, they drove past the garage on East 10th Street. The lights were still on.

"I thought they closed at midnight." Morgan said.

"That's what the ad said. Stop by that bar, I'll give them a call."

A few minutes later, Castillo, carrying a paper bag, got back into the car. "They are closed, but they're waiting for a tow truck to bring one of their vehicles back."

Morgan circled the block and pulled into a space by a fire hydrant.

"Here." Castillo took two containers of beer out of the bag and handed one to Morgan.

"I owe you one from the other night." He held his container up. "It's party time," he said gleefully.

Morgan studied the DEA agent's face in the dim light of the car's interior. "You really get off on this, don't you?"

"This is what it's all about, Dan. The paper chase is over. We're finally going to nail these motherfuckers to the wall."

Morgan couldn't understand the kind of rancor he saw in Donal Castillo's eyes. Like most cops he thoroughly enjoyed the heat of the chase, but he never personally hated the people he'd arrested—except for Willie Lawrence. Then he remembered what Hank Staiger had told him about Castillo's Miami experience. "Have you always had a personal hatred for drug dealers," he asked, "or just since Miami?"

Castillo turned in his seat and looked at Morgan with his coal black eyes. "You've been checking up on me."

"I heard. I'm sorry. It's tough losing a partner."

Castillo didn't take his eyes off Morgan. "Yeah," he said. "I guess you would know about that."

Morgan smiled grimly. "You been checking up on *me?*"

Castillo turned his attention to a passing pedestrian. "I heard about the shooting. At least you didn't work with that cop for fifteen months."

"Was he a friend?" Morgan wasn't sure he should have asked that question and was surprised when Castillo answered.

"Ralph Martinez was more than a friend. He was like an older brother. A lot of guys just go through the motions until it's time to collect their pension. Not Ralph. He was fifty-four, but he could run up stairs, over rooftops, and into alleys better than most rookies. The only thing he loved better than locking up drug dealers was his family. He had a wife and two beautiful daughters."

"What happened in Miami?"

There was a long silence. Morgan thought he'd broken the delicate connection between them, but after a moment Castillo continued. "We were working an undercover operation in Little Havana. Ralph and I were posing as monied guys from New York looking to set up a distribution network with one of the *mágicos*. They're called magicians," he explained in a bitter tone, "because they go from poverty to wealth in such a short time."

A car came down the block. Castillo stopped talking and his eyes checked out the vehicle's occupants. He waited for the car to leave the block, then he continued. "We were really pulling their chain—big Lincoln, expensive suits, plenty of flash money. We looked good." He stopped and stared into his half-finished container. "We were so close to making that bust. We were supposed to meet the main man on a Friday night to work out the details, but that morning I got a call from a *chivato*—a snitch. He told me someone had fingered Ralph and me. I called Ralph's house. Maria, his wife, said he hadn't been home all night. I alerted the office and we started looking for him. For three days we combed every inch of Miami. Nothing. Then I remembered a warehouse where we met these guys once. I went alone."

Castillo took a long drink. "I found Ralph hanging from a rafter. A longshoreman's hook had been shoved through the underside of his chin and they'd hung him up like that." Castillo's voice was flat and devoid of all emotion. "I've seen that technique used before. It's a slow, miserable way to die. You can't yell for help. Eventually, you drown in your own blood."

Morgan was about to say something, but he was distracted by flashing lights behind him. He looked in his sideview mirror and saw a tow truck with amber flashing lights coming down the block. "Here comes the truck," he said, breaking the somber silence.

Five minutes later, the lights in the garage went out. The last man out locked the door and left.

"Okay," Castillo said, "let's go to work."

They slipped into the hallway of an adjoining tenement, down into the cellar, and out into a back yard overgrown with weeds. Carefully stepping over old engine parts and spare tires, they came to a rusted steel door.

Morgan examined it for signs of an alarm. "What do you think?" he whispered.

Castillo played his flashlight on the rusty lock. "Looks like they don't use this door, but who knows?"

He laid the lock-pick set out on the ground. Morgan held the flashlight while he went to work on the lock. Less than a minute later, he looked up. "Get ready to run," he whispered, and pushed the door open. Instead of the expected alarm bell, they were greeted with a welcome silence.

There were no night lights on inside and the interior was completely dark. Castillo took a step into the room and suddenly stopped. "Shit!" he muttered.

Morgan, following close behind, bumped into him. "What's the matter?" he said.

Castillo shined his flashlight on the floor. "I stepped in shit."

The lyrics "meaner than a junkyard dog" suddenly jumped into Morgan's head and he slipped his gun from its holster. "You think there's a dog in here?" he said softly.

Castillo, who'd had more than one run-in with drug dealers' dogs, muttered an oath. "I don't think so," he said, trying to sound optimistic. "He would have barked when he heard us outside. Wouldn't he?"

"Not necessarily," Morgan muttered. "Dogs work in mysterious ways."

He was remembering an incident that had happened to him when he was a rookie. He'd climbed through the broken window of an apartment looking for a burglar. He didn't find one but, as he was heading through the darkened apartment, an enormous dog, looking

MICHAEL GRANT

like a cross between a grizzly bear and a werewolf, appeared out of the shadows. Until then, the dog had made no sound, but as Morgan slowly moved toward the front door, it bared its teeth, and a low, menacing rumble emanated from its massive chest. Morgan considered shooting the beast, but he'd concluded that six bullets would probably only aggravate it. For fifteen minutes he and the dog stared at each other. The dog watched impassively, until Morgan made a move for the door. Then the rumble began again. Ten minutes later, he was finally rescued by the animal's owner—a frail, eighty-year-old woman. From that time on, dogs had ceased to be Dan Morgan's best friend.

Morgan, who didn't have a flashlight, felt especially vulnerable standing in the darkened garage. "Don, shine the light around. If there's a dog here, maybe it'll flush him out."

Castillo played the light across the room, but there was no sign of a dog. Then Morgan, nervously glancing around, spotted a pair of eyes gleaming at him.

Keeping his voice low, he tapped Castillo on the shoulder. "To the right—between those two panel trucks."

Castillo trained the beam on the pair of eyes, and a cat, more frightened than they were, bolted under one of the trucks.

"Good thing it wasn't an attack cat," Morgan said, breaking the tension.

Now that the threat of a dog was gone, they returned to the reason they'd come. In the gloom, Morgan counted seven trucks of varying sizes. "Which one did they rent?" he asked in dismay.

"Do we have enough paint to do them all?"

"No." Morgan had a thought. "It has to be big enough to attach a twelve-foot ladder to the rear door."

Castillo played the light on the largest of the trucks. "Then it's gotta be this one."

"Okay, let's do it."

Five minutes later, they were back outside. Castillo carefully locked the door behind them. Morgan looked at his watch. It was after three. A wave of exhaustion came over him and he was reminded of those endless late tours he'd worked as a young cop. There was only one cure for late-tour fatigue. "Come on," he said to Castillo. "Let's get some coffee and head back to the office."

They were looking for an all-night restaurant when Morgan's pager beeped. Forgetting the coffee, he gunned the engine and headed uptown.

Liberti greeted them with freshly brewed coffee. "I checked out that room in the Hilton. It was registered to a Walter Quinn, who's been dead for eighteen months. They're using phony IDs."

"Yeah," Castillo added, "and you can bet they won't use that credit card again."

"Where's the safe house?" Morgan sipped the hot coffee. It was only slightly better than her first attempt, but it would have to do.

"Three-twenty-nine, apartment 4B. It was rented six months ago. The telephone has never been used for outgoing calls."

Morgan turned to Castillo, who looked as tired as Morgan felt. "Are you up to breaking into an apartment?"

"Nothing doing," Liberti said looking at the both of them. "Right now, you guys couldn't break into a piggy bank. Besides, the Bureau has people who can do that a hell of a lot better than you two."

Morgan found himself slumping in his chair and promptly got up. He was afraid that if he remained seated, he'd fall asleep. "Okay, tell them we'll need a wire—"

Liberti interrupted him. "I've made the arrangements. We've already set up a trap and trace on the line. Our tech services people are ready to go into the apartment as soon as they get the opportunity. I told them I want a wire on the telephone, a bug in every room, and a video camera, if possible."

Castillo, who was glad he didn't have to go anywhere for a while, said, "Good. Just make sure no one is home when they—"

"Donal," Liberti's right eyebrow was up, "the FBI taught you DEA guys everything you know about electronic surveillance."

Castillo's response was to peel the cellophane from one of his lethal cigars.

Liberti took a photo out of a folder on her desk. "Celeste Escobar," she said, holding it in front of her.

MICHAEL GRANT

Castillo took the photo from her and looked at it appraisingly. "That's one fine-looking woman."

Liberti peered over his shoulder. "I don't know. A little hard around the mouth if you ask me."

"How about a rap sheet?" Morgan asked.

"Yes, and very interesting, too." She read from the document. "Arrested in '86 and '88 for passing bad checks. In '84 she was arrested for prostitution."

Morgan shook his head. "Petry used her for bait to keep Ray interested. That son of a bitch thinks of everything."

Castillo, still looking at the photo, said, "She could keep me interested too."

Morgan felt his head clearing. The coffee was having the desired effect. "I think we've covered everything we can for the time being," he said. He looked at his watch; it was almost six. "We gotta be in the PC's office at nine. Why don't we all run home and freshen up? I'll meet you there."

Liberti, looking uneasy, opened a metal case. "Before you go, maybe you should take one of these." She held up a Glock 9mm semiautomatic.

"What the hell do I want that for?" Morgan said.

"It was my idea." Castillo took one of the Glocks from her. "I've seen the gun you use, Morgan. It won't do. A six-shooter firing a 148-grain bullet is okay for target practice, but that's it."

"What are we going to do with these," Morgan said. "Go to war?"

"Maybe. You heard Fleming. They're armed with Uzis. My weapon of choice would be a Heckler & Koch MP5 submachine gun, but they'd be too unwieldy for us." He patted the semiautomatic in his hand. "A sixteen-shot clip will have to do."

Morgan felt a rivulet of sweat trickle down his back. Castillo was talking as though it was a foregone conclusion that they'd be in a fire fight. He looked at Liberti. "What do you think?"

Liberti slipped the weapon into her shoulder bag. "A little overkill —you'll pardon the pun—couldn't hurt."

Morgan hefted the unfamiliar weapon, which felt very different from the Smith & Wesson he'd carried all his police life. He hoped he wouldn't have to use it, but staring down at the lethal weapon, he had to agree it would be a hell of a lot more effective than his thirty-eight.

"Okay," he said, exchanging holsters, "Let's get out of here. We have an appointment at nine o'clock."

At precisely nine o'clock, Commissioner Cassidy walked into the conference room followed by three uniformed ranking officers and two men in civilian clothes. The men in civies were Richard Coffey, the Director of the FBI, and Martin Prendagast, the Assistant Director in Charge of the New York Office. Finally, Morgan thought, we're bringing in the big guns. The others—Deputy Chief Bill Vogel, the grizzled commanding officer of the Special Operations Division; Inspector Mike Tully, the commanding officer of the Emergency Service Unit; and Captain Vinnie Ferrera, the commanding officer of the Firearms Unit—represented the police department's resources with the firepower and manpower they'd need to stop Petry.

Commissioner Cassidy's eyes swept the faces of the DEA agent and the FBI agent. He was shocked to see that they didn't look much better than Dan Morgan. Before the meeting, Cassidy had called Morgan into his office to caution him not to mention the name Puño Blanco at the upcoming briefing. The official story, which Cassidy and Coffey had previously agreed on, was that these unknown terrorists had been employed by the Libyan government. When Morgan had come into his office, Cassidy had been stunned by his deputy inspector's appearance. Now, looking at the three drawn and tired people, Cassidy realized what a burden he and Coffey had put on them. Nevertheless, he thought with pride, they'd accomplished their goal: they'd found Puño Blanco. The critical question was: could the combined resources of the New York City Police Department and the FBI stop them?

"All right," he said, sitting down, "let's get started. "Dan, everyone has been here since five this morning. I've briefed them on the threat and they've been working out our response."

378　　**MICHAEL GRANT**

Cassidy looked around the room. "I'm anxious to hear what you gentlemen have to say, but before we get into that, are there any questions for Inspector Morgan or the others?"

Captain Ferrera, the man in charge of the sharpshooters, spoke up first. "Dan, how many are in this group?"

"Five or six." Morgan wasn't sure Alvaro would take part in the attack.

"Are we dealing with bomb throwers or professionals?"

"Three are ex-Special Forces soldiers."

Ferrera winced.

Cassidy broke the tense silence. "It's been agreed that the FBI will have responsibility for the U.S. Mission's security. Our department will be responsible for everything that happens on the street. Skip, why don't you tell us about the Bureau's end of the operation first?"

Coffey nodded to Prendagast. The ADIC went to the wall map, an enlargement of a ten-square-block area surrounding the U.S. Mission. "The evacuation of the building has already begun," he said. "We're removing the staff a few at a time and replacing them with our people in order to maintain a semblance of normalcy. By three this afternoon, the only ones left in the building will be FBI agents."

Cassidy looked at Deputy Chief Vogel. "Bill, what about the cops in the booth?"

"SOD personnel, wearing flak jackets under their uniforms and armed with semiautomatic pistols, will replace the precinct cops at the change of tour at sixteen hundred hours today."

Cassidy was concerned about the safety of the men. "Those goddamn booths are made of plywood. Do we have time to reinforce them?"

"No, sir. I checked. We'd need to add several inches of steel. We simply don't have the time. Besides, if anyone is watching the Mission, they'd see what we were doing."

"He's right," Coffey added. "Tom, it's essential that everything look normal around the building."

Cassidy nodded. He understood the need, but he didn't like it.

"How about the helicopters?" Morgan asked.

Cassidy nodded. "You'll have two civilian helicopters with PD pilots at your disposal. Cassidy turned to his Firearms Unit commanding officer. "Captain, how are you going to protect those cops in the booth?"

Vinnie Ferrera went to the map. "We'll have five sharpshooter teams here, here, and here." He pointed to vantage points on nearby rooftops. "In addition, we'll have three of our best marksmen armed with automatic pistols secreted at the street level. There's no way anyone's going to get close to those booths," he said confidently.

Morgan, watching the efficient commander, reminded himself to talk to Ferrera about Ray Fleming. After this was over, Fleming, like any other new recruit, would be assigned to the Police Academy. But after his training, he'd have to be transferred somewhere, and Fleming, with his proficiency in firearms, would be a welcome addition to Ferrera's staff.

Cassidy was studying the map. "That truck will be coming up First Avenue," he said, addressing Inspector Tully. "How are you going to stop it? I don't want it getting north of Forty-second Street under any circumstances."

The commanding officer of the Emergency Service Unit took his turn at the map. "As soon as the truck crosses Forty-second Street, we'll seal off all traffic in a ten-square-block zone. Nothing will get in or out of the area. It'll take some close coordination," Tully continued, "but just before the truck arrives, we'll run three rows of tire razor ribbon across the avenue between Forty-second and Forty-third.

Cassidy was familiar with tire razor ribbon. They'd used it to secure a four-square-block frozen zone the last time Fidel Castro had stayed at the Cuban Mission. "That'll blow the tires, but it won't necessarily stop the vehicle," he said.

"That's correct, sir. We'll have a heavy-duty tow truck parked off the corner of Forty-third. If the truck continues to move, he'll ram it. Men armed with shotguns will be on both sides of the street, ready to neutralize anyone leaving the vehicle."

Morgan spoke up. "Wait a minute. The guy riding shotgun in that truck is my undercover man. *No* one is to fire at that truck."

"Then how are we going to stop it?" Cassidy asked.

"Botnick's going to be driving, sir. He's an amateur. As soon as he sees a show of force, he'll give up."

"Botnick's not going to be driving that truck."

All eyes turned to Don Castillo.

Morgan flushed. "That's not what Fleming—"

"I know what Fleming said," Castillo said, but it ain't gonna happen. Botnick *is* an amateur. That's why it's just occurred to me: Petry's not going to let an amateur drive a truck full of explosives."

"Well, who will drive it?" Cassidy asked.

"Newell or Dickerson."

"Are they the ex-Special Forces guys?" Ferrera asked.

"Yeah," Castillo answered. "And if one of them is driving that truck, he'll park it in the lobby of the Mission even if he has to drive it on wheel hubs."

Cassidy, already on edge, was distressed by this sudden introduction of new information. He glowered at Morgan. "What do you think?"

Morgan was caught off guard by Castillo's statement. "It's possible," he said. "Petry does like to make last-minute changes."

Cassidy's face was getting red. "Then that brings me back to my original question: *How* do we stop the truck?"

"Fleming."

Again, all eyes turned to Castillo.

"It makes sense," he said. "Fleming will be in the truck. Petry picked him because of his shooting skill, but he knows Fleming wouldn't be able to pull the trigger on a cop. He's gotta ride shotgun."

"So how does Fleming stop the truck?" Liberti asked.

"He kills the driver."

Cassidy, uncharacteristically at a loss for words, blanched, and the room became very quiet. The DEA agent's shocking suggestion had suddenly raised in his mind some foggy legal and moral issues concerning the use of deadly physical force. Yes, the truck was a deadly instrument, and technically a police officer could shoot the driver to prevent him from completing his act. But if the truck were

Officer DOWN

several blocks away, weren't there other alternatives that had to be considered first? And what of the moral implications? A police officer knows the day he straps on a gun that he may be called upon to take another's life. But never, in Cassidy's memory, had a police officer been instructed to take a life in such a premeditated fashion.

"Mr. Castillo," Cassidy said slowly, "the New York City Police Department is not in the habit of shooting people *except* as a last resort." He turned to his SOD commanding officer. "Give me some alternatives," he snapped.

Chief Vogel looked to his subordinates for support, but they were either intently studying the map or furiously writing notes. "I can't think of one, sir," he said quietly.

"Because there isn't any," Castillo said with finality. "You can't shoot at the truck because Fleming will be inside. He's the only logical choice to stop the driver."

An agitated Liberti drummed her glossy red nails on the table. "Donal, do you really think Ray is capable of doing that?"

Castillo regarded her with his black, hooded eyes. "Considering what's in the back of that truck, he'd better."

Cassidy's eyes roamed to the map as he envisioned tonight's scene. There would be more than fifty heavily armed police officers in civilian clothes within a three-square-block area. He could see the truck, tires blown, screeching and lurching up First Avenue toward the U.S. Mission. He could see police officers, one by one, popping up over the hoods of cars and opening up on the truck. He felt a hot knife-point in his gut. His sleeping ulcer had come to life.

"Very well," he said quietly. "Dan, inform officer Fleming he's to use whatever means necessary to stop that truck from crossing Forty-second Street."

For a moment Morgan met Chris Liberti's stunned eyes, but he quickly turned away. "Yes, sir. I'll tell him."

Cassidy stood up slowly. The lines etched in his face seemed to have deepened since the start of the meeting. "If there's nothing more, we have a lot of work to do between now and tonight. A temporary headquarters will be set up at the Thirty-fourth Street heliport. I want you all there by five o'clock."

Chapter
36

Less than fifteen minutes after they'd left the PC's office, Morgan, Liberti, and Castillo were waiting in their car at the corner of Third Avenue and 23rd Street for FBI agent George Niemann, the supervisor of the Technical Services Division. Niemann, wearing a nondescript workman's uniform, came around the corner and climbed into the back seat.

"How's it look, George?" Liberti asked.

"Not good, Chris. Except for a few minutes, Newell's been in the apartment since we've had it under surveillance."

Morgan, sitting behind the wheel, looked at the agent through the rearview mirror. "How do you know it was Newell?" he asked sharply.

"Chris gave us photos of all the subjects."

Liberti shrugged. "I figured everyone should know who the players are," she said.

"Yes, of course," Morgan mumbled, surprised that neither he nor Castillo had thought of it.

"Did you get in?" Castillo asked.

"Yeah. About an hour after we got there, Newell left. But he came right back. He must have gone out for a pack of smokes. I barely had time to set up a passive bug."

"What's in the apartment?" Morgan asked.

"No furniture. A few sealed boxes, but I didn't have a chance to look inside. I did see a duffel bag with a handful of Uzis. And, oh yeah, there were two tuxedos in the closet."

Morgan turned around in his seat. "Tuxedos?"

"Yeah. That was the only clothing in the closet."

"Did you see any explosives?" Castillo asked.

"Negative. They might be in those boxes, but I'm not sure."

"Who's watching the apartment now?" Liberti asked.

"We have six agents in and around the block." He looked at his watch and opened the door. "I gotta be getting back."

Castillo opened his door. "I'm going with you."

"Why?" Morgan asked, surprised that Castillo wanted to go with FBI agents.

"If we get a chance to get back in there, I might be able to disable the weapons and explosives."

"You think you can do that?"

"Depends on how much time I have and the sophistication of the explosives."

Liberti touched Niemann's arm. "George, keep in touch."

"I will. The PD has already set up their temporary headquarters. All our communications are being patched into their network."

Morgan watched the FBI agent and Castillo walk briskly up the avenue and drummed the steering wheel with his fingers. "That apartment sounds like a storage location. They're not going to meet there tonight."

Liberti nodded in agreement. "Should we attempt to follow Ray again?"

Morgan, remembering their earlier attempts, wasn't very optimistic. "Yeah, I guess we have to try," he said.

"That's what I thought. I've made arrangements for a dozen agents to surveil Petry when he shows up to meet Ray."

"Are they any good?"

"The best. And they've had plenty of practice. They spend most of their time surveilling KGB agents assigned to the Soviet Embassy. As soon as we find out where Petry is going to meet Ray, I'll set up the surveillance teams."

Morgan's pager beeped. "It's Fleming," he said, looking at the telephone number displayed. "Let's see what he's got to say."

Morgan called Fleming and told him to meet them at a restaurant on Lexington Avenue. It was almost eleven A.M. when Fleming slipped into the booth alongside Liberti.

She handed him a menu. "What are you going to have, Ray?"

"Nothing. I'm not hungry."

Liberti looked at the half-empty cups in front of her and Morgan and smiled weakly. "Neither are we."

"Well?" Morgan asked. "What time are you going to meet Petry?"

"Six o'clock. The southwest corner of Sixth and Fourteenth Street."

"Do you know where you're going?"

Fleming shook his head. "No. That's all he said."

Morgan jotted down a telephone number and slipped it to Fleming. "Memorize this and throw the paper away. If you get the opportunity to call us, use this number."

Fleming looked at the number. "Where is it?"

"It's a police temporary headquarters. The officer answering it will be instructed to answer 'Gotham Gunshop.' "

"We need whatever information you can give us," Liberti added. "But don't do anything to jeopardize your own safety."

"She's right," Morgan said. "Your safety is more important than information."

Fleming looked at his watch. "It's almost time. I'd better get going." As he started to slide out of the booth, Morgan stopped him. "Ray"—Morgan forced himself to meet the young undercover cop's tense gaze—"there's one more thing. We're pretty sure you'll be riding shotgun in that truck, but we're not so sure Botnick will be driving."

"Who will?"

"Probably Newell or Dickerson."

Fleming paled. He didn't want to be in that truck with either one of them. "Why won't Manny be driving?" His voice sounded hollow in his ears.

"It's too important an assignment. We don't think Petry will trust Botnick to carry it off." Morgan studied his coffee cup. "Newell and Dickerson are pros. They won't give up to a show of force as easily as Botnick. Ray, that truck can't get north of Forty-second Street."

Fleming's mouth felt as though there were cotton in it. "What do you want me to do?" he asked.

Morgan looked up. "Stop it."

"How the hell am *I* supposed to stop it?"

Morgan repeated the same deceptively bland phrase the police commissioner had used. "By whatever means necessary."

"You mean . . . *shoot* the driver?"

When Morgan didn't answer, Fleming looked to Liberti for support. "Chris, this is crazy. You guys got the whole Police Department out there and *I* have to shoot someone?"

Liberti put her hand on Fleming's arm. "Ray, there's no other way. We can't risk your safety by having someone on the street shoot at the truck. And that truck must be stopped."

Fleming's dismay turned to anger. "This is bullshit! I didn't become a cop to assassinate people. I—"

Morgan slammed his hand on the table. "Goddammit! *They* are the

386   MICHAEL
       GRANT

assassins. They've murdered five cops and they're planning to murder more. I said the truck is to be stopped and the driver neutralized. You do it any way you can."

"All right," Fleming said in a tight voice.

As he slid out of the booth, Liberti put her hand on his arm. "Ray, please be careful."

Fleming pulled his arm away. "Yeah," he said. "You too."

There was a long tense silence after the undercover cop had left the table. Finally, Liberti looked at her watch. "I'd better get going. I have to set up the surveillance people."

"Chris," Morgan said, "was there another way?"

Liberti saw the pain in his eyes and understood how he felt. When Castillo had first made the suggestion in the police commissioner's office, she'd been appalled. But the more she thought about it, the more sense it made. "No, Dan," she said finally. "I don't like it any better than you, but there is no other way."

Morgan nodded, but from the look on his face it was clear that he wasn't convinced. "Okay," he said. "I'll see you at the temporary headquarters at five."

She hesitated. "Dan, I won't be there."

Morgan looked up sharply. "What do you mean?"

"I'm going to be with the surveillance team."

"No, you're not. You're going to—"

"Dan, listen to me," she said softly. "I've been chasing Petry for two weeks now, but so far all I've seen are photos and reports. I wanna *see* this guy. I gotta do something . . . constructive. Can you understand that?"

He looked into her dark brown eyes and his mind was a jumble of confused emotions. He didn't know if he wanted her with him because he was afraid for her or because he didn't think she could do the job. But looking into her determined face, he knew he couldn't stop her. "Okay," he said finally. "But, damn it, be careful."

She patted his hand. "Sure, dad. I'll see you later."

"Wait." He jotted a telephone number down and handed it to her. "Captain Zakovitch. I want him in on the surveillance."

Liberti slipped the piece of paper into her purse. "Fine. We can use all the help we can get."

For a while after Liberti had gone, Morgan sat in the booth feeling useless. Castillo was on 29th Street waiting to break into an apartment and Liberti was planning a surveillance. His stomach had been churning all day, but he didn't know if it was fear or anxious anticipation. He wouldn't find out sitting here. He paid the bill and headed downtown to the 24th Street heliport.

Morgan drove under the elevated FDR Drive and parked alongside the temporary headquarters. The long blue and white trailer, with a thick umbilical cord of telephone and electrical lines running into its underbelly, was going to be the center of activity for the next several hours. Morgan was relieved that they finally had the assistance of every modern weapon and tool that the NYPD and the FBI could muster. Still, he couldn't shake the feeling that it might not be enough.

He climbed the steps and entered a world of state-of-the-art communications. The brightly lit trailer was compact, but utilized every inch of available space. Uniformed police officers from the Communications Division manned a bank of telephones with direct lines linked to all local, state, and federal agencies that might require emergency notification. At the other end of the trailer were five consoles, equipped with telephones and radio base stations. Each console had a hand-written sign indicating its particular function—*29th Street surv team; 23rd Street surv team; Aviation Unit; PC.* Morgan's eyes stopped at the last sign. It was marked *UC—Gotham Gunshop.* Morgan hoped that telephone would ring first. He had a nagging feeling Petry had one more trick up his sleeve.

The captain in charge of the temporary headquarters looked up quizzically from his desk. Morgan displayed his ID.

"Everything's shaping up, Inspector. The last of the phones are being patched in. We'll be fully operational within the hour."

A young cop, wearing the uniform of the Aviation Unit and an enormous handlebar mustache, looked up from his seat in front of the Aviation Unit console. "Pat Doyle," he said with a wide grin. "I'm the ground control liaison for your two choppers."

MICHAEL GRANT

"Good. Where are they?"

"One's parked outside, the other's at Floyd Bennett."

"Are they ready to go?"

The sunny smile disappeared. "Yeah, boss, but the weather forecast isn't good. They're predicting rain and possible thunderstorms."

Morgan's stomach knotted. They couldn't afford to lose sight of that truck. "They'll be able to fly, won't they?" he asked.

"You're in luck. You have two of the craziest pilots in the PD. They'll fly those birds unless the FAA orders them down. Even then, it'll be a tossup." He lowered his voice and looked around. "I'd be flying myself, but the CO grounded me for landing a chopper on a burning building last week. If the helo had gone up, it would have made a hell of an expensive barbecue."

Morgan grinned at the cocky pilot. "I presume it didn't."

"Naw. I rescued three people. The CO put me in for a commendation and grounded me the same day. Go figure."

Morgan looked at his watch. It was only one. He sat down with a cup of coffee and waited for the show to begin.

At 5:55 P.M. Chris Liberti was sitting in an FBI surveillance vehicle parked a hundred feet off the corner of Sixth Avenue and 14th Street watching Ray Fleming. More than a few passing females on their way home from work gave a second glance at the tall young man with the jet black curly hair. She'd told him to wear something distinctive. The red windbreaker he was zipping up was just the thing.

"Joe," she said to the man sitting next to her, "let's go over it one more time."

Agent Joseph Ingram glanced down at the clipboard on his lap. "We have chase cars covering both directions on Fourteenth Street. We have another unit half a block behind us covering Sixth Avenue northbound, and we have four people on foot, including Captain Zakovitch, covering the intersection."

For the past fifteen minutes, Chris Liberti had been watching the chain-smoking captain standing in a doorway near the northwest corner. In that time he must have smoked an entire pack of cigarettes. She was thankful that he hadn't been part of their team from the beginning.

Ingram looked up at the sound of car horns. The eastbound traffic on 14th Street was spillbacked onto Sixth Avenue. "I wish this wasn't the rush hour," he said. "We got all the bases covered, but look at that mess. If we get something like that between us and them, they're home free."

The heavy traffic had not escaped Liberti's notice. "I'm sure that's precisely why Petry has chosen this intersection and this location. As I told you earlier, Joe, this guy is a pro."

Ingram, a veteran of numerous elaborate surveillances, made a notation on his clipboard. "Yeah, well, so are we. There's no way—"

"Hold it." Liberti saw Fleming look toward the subway entrance, and tentatively head for the stairs. "Damn it," she said, yanking the door open, "he's going for the subway. Get on the radio. All foot surveillance people into the subway. *Now!*"

Glad that she'd had the foresight to wear flats instead of heels, she ran for the subway entrance at full speed. As she dodged pedestrians, she caught a glimpse of three agents and Zakovitch rushing down the subway stairs.

Fighting the rush hour crowd coming toward her, she pushed her way down to the lower level. She fumbled in her pocket through a pile of Kleenexes and found a token. As she jammed it into the turnstile, she looked up in time to see one of the agents run down the stairs leading to the uptown trains.

Like a fish swimming upstream, she waded through dozens of weary, and cranky, commuters. There were two trains on the platform. She caught a glimpse of Fleming's red windbreaker getting onto the local. The conductor announced the doors were closing. She was lunging for the closing doors, but out of the corner of her eye she saw Petry and Fleming step off the train. She stopped and quickly backed into the crowd. *Damn it. Petry was clearing the platform before he boarded the train!*

The doors closed and the train pulled out of the station. To her dismay she saw only Captain Zakovitch left on the platform. The other three agents were on the train.

Petry and Fleming quickly walked to the other side of the platform and boarded the express. Zakovitch, looking around for the other team members, spotted Liberti. She signaled him to stay off the train. There was no point in both of them jumping on and off. She boarded and positioned herself at the door connecting the cars. No matter what Petry did, one of them would be in a position to follow. She snatched her radio earpiece off and stuffed it in her purse. There were too many people around to use a radio. Besides, if Petry spotted the earpiece, he'd know instantly what it represented.

Above the heads in the next car she could see Fleming's curly black hair and Petry standing in the doorway. *Please stay on the train, you miserable son of a bitch,* she prayed.

The doors started to close. Petry pulled Fleming off. She groaned and looked away. A moment later, she looked up. *They were back on board.*

As the train pulled out of the station, she realized she was out of position. She could see them from her vantage point, but if they got off at the next stop, she was too far from the doors to get off with them. Slowly, she began to make her way through the crowd toward the doors. An elderly, well-dressed businessman engrossed in the *Wall Street Journal* and a heavyset woman, surrounded by shopping bags, occupied the two positions by the door.

She studied the two of them and made up her mind. She regretted what she was about to do, but she had no choice. Turning her back to the man, she slowly backed into him. Then she whirled. "You *pervert!*" she screamed at the startled man. "Keep your goddamn hands to yourself."

The man's face reddened. He started to protest his innocence, but she cut him off.

"A girl can't even ride the subway anymore," she shouted even louder.

Muttering apologies, the elderly man folded his newspaper and pushed past her into the crowd. He didn't stop until he'd gone into the adjoining car. Liberti backed into the vacated spot by the door and stoically acknowledged the sympathetic nods of the other female passengers.

The train was pulling into 34th Street. She knew she'd have only one opportunity to correctly guess Petry's intention. If she jumped on and off the train with them, she'd blow her cover.

The doors opened. Cautiously, she stuck her head out. Petry said something to Fleming. They got off and stood near the doors. She tried to read Petry's body language, but realized he was too much of a pro to give away his intent. She concentrated instead on Fleming. The young cop kept glancing at the doors. *Petry must have told him they were going to get back on the train!* She gambled and stayed on.

The doors started to close. Petry held it open and quickly glanced up and down the platform. At the last moment, he pushed Fleming inside as the doors closed behind them.

The train pulled into Times Square. This time she watched only Fleming. When they got off, he stood farther away from the doors. Liberti, taking a chance that she was reading him correctly, stepped off the train and stood in the crowd. As before, Petry waited by the doors, but this time he let them close without getting back on the train.

He and Fleming turned and quickly moved down the platform. Liberti, looking up at the bewildering array of train signs—EE, N, R, 1, 2, 3—hurried after them. She couldn't let them get too far in front of her. There were many trains coming into Times Square and Petry might board any one of them.

She followed them up a flight of stairs. As she got to the top, she heard a scream. Some teenagers had snatched a woman's purse and were running toward her. She pulled her shoulder bag close to her body and spun to avoid the snatching hands. They raced past her whooping and shouting. Regaining her balance, she turned to the last spot she'd seen Petry and Fleming. They were gone.

Chapter
37

Lyle Petry and Ray Fleming got off the crosstown shuttle at Grand Central Station and went upstairs into the lobby of the Grand Hyatt.

They stepped into an empty elevator and Fleming turned to Petry. "Damn, Lyle, you don't take any chances, do you?"

Petry punched the sixteenth floor. "You can't be too careful," he said.

The door opened and Petry quickly led him down the hallway to a room at the end of a corridor. Everyone was there except Newell. This time Dickerson frisked Fleming. He was apologetic, but his frisk was more thorough than Newell's.

Botnick, sitting on the couch next to Alvaro, was wearing a tuxedo. "Hey, Manny," Fleming said, trying to sound casual, "you going to a wedding or what?"

Still suffering the effects of a hangover, Botnick rubbed his temples. "Lyle told me to wear it."

Petry sat down on the couch. "Before we get started, anyone want a beer?"

Botnick was the only one who declined.

"Hey," Petry shouted into the next room, "how about a few beers out here."

A moment later, Celeste came out carrying a tray and Fleming's stomach knotted. Morgan had said that Celeste was part of Lyle's operation. But even after he'd heard her voice on that 911 tape, he'd deluded himself into thinking that Petry had forced her to make the call. She put the tray on the table and, avoiding eye contact with Fleming, sat down next to Petry.

Petry squeezed her knee. "Thanks, babe. All right," he said to the others, "listen up. This is the final briefing. First off"—he looked at each of them in turn—"the U.S. Mission is not the target."

Fleming tore his eyes away from Celeste and looked at the others. Only he and Botnick seemed to be surprised by this sudden change in plans. "Lyle," he said, "what . . . what about the truck, and—"

Petry looked amused. "We still have use for them." He spread a floor plan on the table. "This is the grand ballroom of the Knicker-bocker Hotel."

Fleming, not trusting himself to look at anyone else, riveted his attention on the boxes and rectangles that represented the grand ballroom. The Knickerbocker Hotel was the newest and most elegant hotel in the city. At its grand opening six months earlier, Fleming had driven people there in his cab and had worked its taxi stand since. The well-heeled people who stayed there were good tippers.

Petry continued. "Manny, you'll start things off. At exactly eight-fifteen you'll enter the hotel carrying that guitar case."

Botnick looked at the brand-new guitar case across the room. "What's in there?"

"C-four."

Botnick paled. "I have to carry *that* thing full of explosives?"

"It's perfectly safe. At eight twenty-five enter the grand ballroom and go to the bandstand."

"But I'm not working a gig there," Botnick protested.

"Doesn't matter. Tell the band leader there was some kind of mixup. At exactly eight thirty-five—and I mean exactly—flip that latch under the handle and get out of there."

Botnick's eyes went to the latch. "What'll that do, Lyle?"

"It'll set a timer." He saw the look on Botnick's face and added, "Don't worry, you'll have five minutes to get out of there before it goes off."

"Where do I go?"

"Leave the hotel and go home. I'll call you later."

Botnick looked relieved. "That's it? That's all I have to do?"

Petry grinned. "Yeah. Not bad for a night's work, huh?" He turned serious again. "The rest of us have a lot more to do. Ray, you'll be in the east corridor." He pointed at a corridor showing four exits leading from the ballroom to the kitchen. "As soon as you hear the explosion, set off four grenades. You'll also have an Uzi. Shoot anyone who tries to escape through those doors."

Fleming swallowed hard. "Lyle, after that explosion a lot of people will try to get out that way."

Petry looked at him curiously. "Exactly. That's why you'll set off the grenades. I want everyone to head for these exits at the west end of the ballroom." He pointed at four exits leading to the main corridor."

He turned to Dickerson. "Glen, you and Jimmy will be here with the Uzis." He indicated locations at either end of the corridor.

Dickerson, whose pleasant, jovial face was a mask of concentration, nodded. "Good crossing fields of fire, Lyle."

"Celeste and I will be here"—Petry pointed at a spot near the elevator bank—"to lob grenades at anyone who gets through your fire lanes."

Fleming felt physically ill. Looking at the floor plan, he could see Petry's plan was perfect. The people in the ballroom who survived the initial explosion would panic. Unable to get out through the kitchen exits, they'd be herded like cattle to their own destruction. No one would escape from that room alive.

"Any questions?" Petry asked.

Fleming heard himself ask, "Who'll be in the ballroom?"

Petry's pale green eyes were cold. "A few dozen of the top sports figures in America and a roomful of corporate execs with enough money to spring for the thousand-dollar-a-pop tickets."

Fleming slid down in his seat. For the moment, overwhelmed by the atrocity that Petry was planning, he forgot he was an undercover cop. Now he was just a twenty-one-year-old man, horrified by the thought of so many people about to be murdered. "Why?" he asked in a hoarse whisper.

Petry stood up. "That doesn't concern you." He looked down at Alvaro, who'd been intently listening to the briefing. "Are your communiqués ready?"

Alvaro patted his breast pocket. "They've been ready for a long time. Within fifteen minutes of the attack, I will have contacted the TV and news media."

Petry nodded. "All right, we have a lot to do between now and then. Glen, it's time to get the truck. Jimmy's waiting for you."

Fleming stood up. He had to get this change of plan to Morgan fast. "What time do you want me back here, Lyle?"

Petry gently pushed him back into his chair. "Hang around here until it's time to go."

Fleming fought back the panic that was threatening to overwhelm him. *He had to find an excuse to get out of the room.* An idea came to him. "Lyle, shouldn't I have a tux too?"

"I'm glad to see you're thinking, Ray."

"I'll go get one. There's gotta be a place around here where—"

"I already have one for you. Celeste picked it out. I think she knows your size." Petry sat back and flipped on CNN. "We've got some time. Relax."

Fleming stared at the screen and tried to concentrate on a segment

MICHAEL GRANT

about a drought in East Africa, but it was no use. He got up and went into the kitchen.

Celeste looked up when he came in. "Ray . . . I'm sorry."

He was ashamed to ask the question, but he had to know the answer. "Why, Celeste?"

"It was Lyle's idea. He wanted you for this thing. He thought . . . if I . . . I'd be a draw to keep your interest."

"Then you and Lyle—"

"We've been together for a long time. Look, Ray, I like you. I really do, but—"

She stopped. Fleming turned to see what she was looking at. Petry, finishing the knot in his bow tie, was standing in the door with a look of amusement on his face.

"Am I interrupting something?" he asked.

"No." Fleming tried to pass him, but Petry grabbed his arm. "Ray, let's clear the air. There was never anything between you and Celeste, at least as far as she was concerned. *I* told her to be nice to you. I'm sorry, but it had to be done."

Fleming jerked his arm away. "Lyle, I doubt you've ever been sorry about anything in your life."

Petry shrugged. "Listen, we have a job to do tonight. I don't want you mooning around. Pay attention to business."

"I can do my job."

Petry slapped him on the back. "Good. Now go into the bedroom and change. Your tux is laid out on the bed."

Fleming, feeling his world unraveling around him, stumbled into the bedroom and closed the door behind him. He'd been wrong about so many things—Lyle, Celeste, Manny. And Morgan had been right. The hard-nosed inspector had been right all along.

He took a deep breath. There was no point in wallowing in self-pity. He'd been a fool and he'd made some bad errors in judgment, but tonight was his chance to redeem himself. Petry, Celeste, and the others were the enemy and he wasn't going to forget that again. Ever.

As he started to unbutton his shirt, his eyes went to the telephone on the night table. Slowly, he sat down on the edge of the bed and stared at the instrument. He started to reach for it, but pulled his

Officer DOWN

hand back. *What if someone came in?* It didn't matter; he had to try. It was his only chance. Clearly, Petry wasn't going to let him out of his sight.

With a sweating hand, Fleming quietly lifted the receiver and quickly dialed the number Morgan had given him.

"Gotham Gunshop." Fleming recognized Captain Zakovitch's voice.

Before Fleming could speak, he heard Petry's soft voice behind him. "Ray, say one word and you're a dead man."

Fleming spun around. Petry was standing in the doorway pointing a gun at him. Fleming held the telephone out. "Take it easy, Lyle. I was only calling a gunshop."

Petry crossed the room in two strides and snatched the telephone from Fleming's hand. "Hello," he said.

"Yeah, Gotham Gunshop. What can I do for you?"

"I'm sorry," Petry said. "I seemed to have dialed a wrong number." He hung up and stepped back. "Not too smart, Ray. When you picked up the phone in here, a light lit up on the phone outside. Who were you calling?"

"I told you. A gunshop. I left a pistol in for an overhaul and I was calling to see if it was ready."

Petry's eyes were devoid of all emotion. "I don't believe you, Ray."

Celeste, her eyes wide with fright, appeared at the door. "What's the matter, Lyle?"

"Get out," Petry snapped. "This doesn't concern you."

A scowling Alvaro pushed Celeste aside. "Did he contact the police?" he asked in a voice constricted with fear.

With his eyes still on Fleming, Petry said, "No, but he took the bait. Ray, I'm really disappointed in you. You failed the last test."

Fleming's heart pounded in his chest. *"Police?* What the hell are you guys talking about? I told you I was calling a gunshop."

Petry regarded Fleming with a bemused smile. "Ray, you pick the oddest times to make phone calls. The day of the armored car holdup. Now this."

Fleming felt as though he'd been punched in the stomach. *Petry had seen him trying to use the phone that day!* He ran his fingers through his hair. "Lyle, where the hell did you get the idea that I'm a cop? Call the gunshop yourself. They'll tell you—"

"No. They may be able to trace the call. It's too late for verification. I'm curious, Ray. What are you? FBI? City police?"

Celeste grabbed Petry's arm. "Lyle, what are you going to do?"

Petry pulled away from her.

"Don't hurt him." Her voice cracked. "Tie him up. We'll be gone before—"

Petry turned his icy stare on her. "Get out of the room," he said softly.

She looked at Fleming and started to say something, but then she turned and ran from the room.

Alvaro slammed the door behind her. "Lyle, you must kill him."

Ray Fleming listened to Celeste pleading for his life and now Alvaro asking for his death with an odd sense of detachment. These people had the power of life and death over him, but he didn't feel fear or hatred toward them, just an all-consuming curiosity about his fate. And something else. Profound disappointment. It occurred to him that he'd never know what it was like to be a real police officer; to wear a uniform; to help an injured person; to make an arrest; even to write a ticket. He'd become a police officer because he wanted to help people, but now, he'd never get that chance.

Petry's face was a neutral mask as the gun in his hand came up ever so slowly. For the first time Fleming noticed that there was a silencer at the end of the barrel. Of course there would be; Petry thought of everything. He wouldn't risk the noise of a shot in a hotel room.

Fleming stared at Petry for a clue as to what he was going to do, but there was nothing in those glacial green eyes. No anger, no pity, not even the disappointment he professed to feel.

Fleming heard a soft *psst* and felt a sharp pain in his stomach. He'd fired thousands of bullets, but he'd never given a thought as to what it must be like to be shot. Surprisingly, the pain wasn't too bad.

Then he realized he was on his knees. He looked down at his shaking hands clutching his stomach. Dark red blood oozed between his fingers.

He looked up at Petry. The gun barrel came up another inch. With professional interest, Fleming calculated the angle. The gun was aimed at his forehead. A vision of his father, sitting at the kitchen table in his underwear, suddenly flashed into his mind. *Who was going to tell him to stop smoking now?*

Petry spoke. "Ray, remember that first match we had? I did throw away those last two rounds." He grinned. "You'll never see the day you could shoot better than me."

Without warning, Petry fired. The round struck Fleming in the center of his forehead. The undercover cop fell backward, knocking over an end table and a lamp.

Alvaro slumped against the wall. "What do we do now?" The Colombian was on the verge of panic. "The police may know of our plans."

"No they don't. Fleming said nothing on the phone."

"But he may have told them about the other plan."

"That's all right." He turned to look at the frightened Colombian. "I'm surprised at you, Alvaro. An old military man like you should realize the value of a feint. If the police know about the U.S. Mission, that's where they'll be—on the wrong side of town."

He slipped his gun back into his shoulder holster. "You'll take Fleming's place."

"*Me?* That's impossible. I have the communiqués to get out. I have a flight leaving—"

"Stuff it, Alvaro. I'm not going to let this turn into a goatscrew operation. You've seen the plans. I need someone to cover that corridor."

"But I—"

Petry fixed him with a challenging stare. "Scared?"

The Colombian's face contorted in indignation. "How dare you? I was in the military long before—"

Petry took another tux out of the closet and flung it at him. "Then get into this and stop the bullshit."

MICHAEL GRANT

Alvaro looked at the tux in disbelief. *"Another* tux? Then you knew . . ."

Petry shrugged. "Always make contingency plans. An old military man like you should know that."

The Colombian, seeing he had no choice, began to loosen his tie with shaking hands. He couldn't decide if he were more frightened of Petry or his superiors back in Colombia should this mission fail. "What about Botnick?" he said. "If the police should capture him leaving the hotel—"

"He won't be leaving the hotel," Petry said evenly. "There is no timer. When he flips that latch, he detonates himself."

Alvaro was suddenly gripped by a paralyzing fear. Petry was eliminating all witnesses: Fleming, Botnick, those two men who delivered the explosives . . . maybe him. "What surprises do you have in store for Glen and Jimmy?" he asked.

"None. They're professionals. I don't have to worry about them."

"And me?" He tried to sound confident, but the question came out in a hoarse whisper.

Petry smiled. "You're a professional, too. Aren't you?"

"Then from the beginning you planned to sacrifice Fleming and Botnick."

Petry looked down at Fleming's body. "Botnick, yes. Fleming . . . I wasn't sure." He looked at his watch. "Hurry up, Alvaro. It's almost time to go."

Chapter
38

Chris Liberti was sitting in the temporary headquarters trailer, telling Morgan about her failed surveillance of Petry, when Captain Zakovitch, who'd been monitoring the UC telephone, looked up. "Inspector, I just got a call."

Morgan rushed to the console. "Was it Fleming?"

"I don't know. At first there was no one on the line. I heard some muffled voices, then someone—it wasn't Ray—came on and said hello. When I said 'Gotham Gunshop,' he said he had the wrong number and hung up."

Liberti sat down heavily on the edge of the desk. "What do you think that means, Dan?"

"I don't know. Zak, is there a trace trap on that line?"

"Yes. They're running it now."

Donal Castillo, looking gloomier than usual, came into the trailer. "Did you get into the apartment?" Liberti asked.

Castillo scowled. "No. Newell's still there."

While Liberti was telling him about the aborted surveillance and the mysterious telephone call, a sergeant, wearing the leather uniformed jacket of the Highway Patrol Unit, stuck his head into the trailer. "Inspector Morgan?"

Morgan looked up. "Yeah?"

"Sergeant Graziano, Highway Four. I have five unmarked autos outside."

"Thanks, Sarge. Stand by outside. I'll let you know if I need them."

Morgan had ordered the vehicles in case they had to get someplace in a hurry. There was no better transportation available than Highway Patrol cops, who by temperament and training loved to drive fast.

The sergeant turned to leave, but he quickly jumped back into the trailer. *"Attention!"* he shouted.

Police Commissioner Thomas Cassidy came up the steps. "At ease," he said and went straight to Morgan. "Anything so far, Dan?"

"Yes, sir, but none of it good."

At five minutes after five, Glen Dickerson picked up the truck at the East 10th Street garage and drove it to a secluded spot on 14th Street near the FDR Drive.

Using a battery-powered drill, he made holes in the door for the ladder. To drill the last hole, he had to climb to the top of the door where his head was level with the roof. Had he not been intent on his work, he could easily have seen the freshly painted circle. A few minutes later, satisfied that the ladder was firmly secured to the door, he climbed back into the truck and headed uptown.

"Unit One to base," the voice boomed. The cop monitoring the safe-house console lowered the audio level. "The truck is on the scene."

Everyone in the trailer gathered around the speaker. Morgan snapped his fingers at the aviation liaison officer. "Doyle, get a chopper in the air. The truck is at Twenty-ninth and Lex. I want it kept under observation."

Doyle gave Morgan a thumbs-up sign. Moments later, there was a high-pitched whine outside as the helicopter lifted off.

"What's the latest on the weather?" Morgan asked.

Doyle shook his head. "Worsening."

Five minutes later, the FBI agent came back on the air. "Rabbit One to base. The two subjects are loading the truck with three boxes and a duffel bag. Be advised subjects are wearing tuxedos."

Morgan looked at Liberti and Castillo. "Those damn tuxes. What the hell's going on?"

"The truck is leaving the block. Should we follow?"

Morgan looked at Doyle. "Does the pilot have the truck in sight?"

Doyle nodded.

Morgan grabbed the mike. "Negative, Unit One. Keep the location under surveillance." He turned to Cassidy. "I don't want to risk being spotted with a ground surveillance," he explained.

"It's your show, Dan."

As an old street commander, it was a struggle for Cassidy not to take over the operation. But Morgan had taken it this far; it was only fair to let him take it the rest of the way.

Donal Castillo tore the cellophane from a cigar. "Things are getting curiouser and curiouser," he said softly.

Liberti moved to the other side of the cramped trailer to get away from the smoke. "You mean the tuxes?"

"That, and those boxes. From the description the agent gave me, it doesn't sound like explosives rigged and ready to go."

"Maybe they're going to do that somewhere else?" Liberti offered.

Castillo studied the cigar's ash. "Maybe. But where's Petry and Botnick?

"And Fleming," Morgan added glumly.

Doyle looked up from his console. "Inspector, the truck parked on East Fourteenth Street near the Drive. The pilot can't stay up there. They'll spot him."

Morgan keyed the mike. "Unit One, send one vehicle to the vicinity of East Fourteenth and the Drive. Keep the truck under surveillance and let me know the minute it moves."

Captain Zakovitch leaned over Morgan's shoulder. "Inspector, that call came from the Hyatt on Forty-second Street."

"What room?"

"Can't tell. All calls are routed through the central switchboard."

"Damn it. There's gotta be hundreds of rooms in that hotel." He turned to Liberti. "Chris, how many people do you have left?"

She consulted her clipboard. "Fifteen."

"Get ten of them over to the Hyatt right now. Stake out every entrance. I want to know as soon as they spot Petry or any of his people. Zak, you go too."

The captain from Intelligence already had his coat on and was heading for the door.

Morgan leaned over the officer monitoring the U.S. Mission console. "Anything?"

"No, sir. They just reported in. Everything's quiet."

Morgan looked at the wall clock. It was almost time. Where were they? Nothing was adding up. Dickerson and Newell were in the truck, and Botnick and Fleming, who were supposed to be in the truck, were nowhere to be found. He remembered all the changes Petry had made in the past and his stomach knotted. Was this another misdirection move? Was the real attack going to take place somewhere else?

Lyle Petry and Celeste Escobar, dressed in formal evening clothes, strolled out of the side entrance of the Hyatt and got into a cab. Fifty feet away, an FBI agent, sitting in his car with photos of Petry and the others taped to his dashboard, watched the revolving doors through a rain-pelted windshield. He was looking only for men, and didn't give the well-dressed couple a second glance.

Twenty minutes later, Petry and Celeste took the elevator to their room in the Knickerbocker Hotel. He went to the window and looked out. The desk clerk had been right. The street noise at the second floor was exceptionally loud. When he'd reserved the room earlier in the week, the clerk had recommended a room higher up. But Petry explained that his wife was afraid of heights. He checked his watch. Jimmy and Glen should be on their way by now.

Petry turned away from the window. "Where's our change of clothes?"

"In the closet," she said sullenly. "I brought the suitcase over this morning."

Celeste started for the bathroom, but Petry grabbed her arm. "What's the matter with you? You haven't said a word since we left the Hyatt."

She pulled away from him. "What do you think is the matter with me? Lyle, you didn't have to kill him."

"I had no choice."

"You're not even sure he was a cop."

"It didn't matter. I couldn't trust him after he made that call."

"So you killed him?"

"You'll get over it." He put his arms around her. "Think of the future. In a few hours we'll be on our way to Bogotá. After a couple of years there, we can go anywhere we want. Celeste, this is my last assignment. After tonight, I retire."

"I've heard that before."

"This time I mean it."

She tried to pull away, but his strong arms tightened around her waist. "Celeste, don't give me that holier-than-thou bullshit. You've been part of this operation from the beginning. Just because you didn't pull a trigger or set off a bomb doesn't mean you're not up to your neck in this. We have a job to do tonight and there's no time for self-pity. Pay attention to business."

406   **MICHAEL**
          GRANT

"I will."

He let her go and she went into the bathroom to fix her face.

"Unit Two to base. We're at Fourteenth and First. The truck is moving again. He turned right on First Avenue heading north."

Morgan looked up. "Doyle, get the chopper back up."

The cocky pilot looked uneasy. "It's raining pretty hard, boss."

Morgan was well aware of that. For the past ten minutes, he'd been listening to the rain drumming down on the trailer roof. "Can he go up?" he asked.

Doyle said something into the mike and there was a high-pitched whine as the helicopter's engine revved for a takeoff.

"Unit Two . . . Truck is at Sixteenth Street still heading north. The rain is really fouling up traffic. I'm afraid I may lose him. I need support out here ASAP."

Morgan keyed the mike. "Unit One. You copy?"

"Affirmative. Two teams on the way."

A loud thunderclap startled everyone in the trailer. Cassidy, who'd been pacing the narrow aisle, leaned over Doyle's shoulder and whispered, "Son, is that pilot in any danger up there?"

Doyle fingered his mustache, unsure what he should tell the commissioner. After a moment's hesitation, he said, "Lightning and wind are always a problem for a helicopter, sir."

The hesitation was all Cassidy needed to hear. He straightened up. "Bring him down," he said.

Morgan, who'd been studying the map, whirled. "Sir—"

Cassidy put his hand up. "No, Dan. I won't risk a man's life for a surveillance. Get more cars out there."

Morgan turned to Liberti in desperation. "Chris, what do you have left?"

Liberti consulted her clipboard. "The closest is two cars at the Hyatt. But they're—"

"Pull them off."

Morgan knew it could take them more than a half-hour to get to the truck, given the rain and the traffic, but he had no choice. Petry and the others had disappeared. The truck was his only link. As long as he could keep track of that vehicle, it would eventually lead to Petry.

"Unit Two . . ." The voice was high-pitched with excitement. "We've lost the truck. We're caught in a spillback at Twenty-third. Truck last seen heading north."

Morgan keyed the mike. "Other cars on the way, what is your location?"

"Unit Three . . . heading south at Thirty-fourth and Lex."

"Unit Four . . . we're at Twenty-eighth and Lex."

Morgan's eyes were glued on the map as he tried to imagine the progress of the truck up First Avenue. "All units cut over toward First Avenue. Now!"

"Unit Three . . . Negative. Thirty-fourth is a solid line of cars heading east."

"Unit Four . . . we have the same condition on Twenty-eighth Street. If we go into the block, we'll be stuck. Please advise."

Morgan heard the faint whomp-whomp sound of the helicopter coming in for a landing. It was his only hope. He turned to Cassidy. "Goddammit, sir, we've lost the truck. We *need* that chopper."

Cassidy ran his hand across his mouth. The sight of a helicopter crashing into the streets of midtown Manhattan flashed before his eyes. Then he saw the truck barreling into the U.S. Mission.

"Okay," he said, in a barely audible tone.

"Doyle," Morgan shouted, "I want both choppers in the air. Now! Have one run First, the other Third."

Outside, the pitch of the helicopter's engines increased as it reversed thrust and took off into the downpour.

Silently, everyone gathered around Doyle's console. "Can we hear what's going on?" Liberti asked.

Doyle flipped a switch and the pilot's voice was heard over the speaker.

"Goddamn, Doyle . . . it's like flying through a carwash. I can't see shit."

MICHAEL GRANT

Doyle winced and made a motion to turn the volume down, but Cassidy pushed his hand away. "Leave it alone, son. It's not the first time I've heard bad language."

"Bluebird Two to base . . . I'm on the scene."

Doyle keyed his mike. "Bluebird One is flying north on First Avenue. You sweep Third."

"Roger."

Doyle looked up at Morgan with pride. "You got two good people up there, boss. They'd fly those birds through the Midtown Tunnel if you asked them."

"Let's hope that won't be necessary," Cassidy said dryly.

A few minutes later, the pilot said, "Bluebird One to base . . . I'm at Fifty-seventh and no sign of the truck. There's dense cloud patches and visibility sucks. I'm going to sweep south on First Avenue at one-five-zero."

Doyle hopped in his seat. "Whoa! Bluebird One, you're in a helicopter, not a radio car."

"What's he talking about," Cassidy demanded.

"He going down to a hundred and fifty feet," Doyle explained. "Some buildings in that area are taller than that. He'll be flying between building lines."

Cassidy popped a Tums in his mouth and turned away.

Doyle put his hand over his mouth and whispered to Morgan. "Nine-eleven is really going to light up tonight. Wait'll the people on First Avenue get a load of a chopper whizzing past their windows. They'll think fucking King Kong is back in town."

"I have him," the calm voice of the pilot in Bluebird One said. "Heading north on First Avenue at Thirty-seventh Street."

There was an audible sigh of relief in the trailer. Cassidy, who had visions of two helicopters colliding in midair over Manhattan, put a hand on Doyle's shoulder. "Get that other helicopter out of there," he said.

"Notify Chief Vogel," Morgan said to the officer monitoring the U.S. Mission detail. "Tell him the truck is at Thirty-seventh Street." He looked at Liberti and Castillo. "Come on, let's go."

Officer DOWN

The three started to rush out of the trailer, but Cassidy's booming voice stopped them. "Where the hell do you think you're going?"

Morgan stopped at the door. "To the Mission."

"Like hell you are. There are more than enough cops there. I want you three right here so you can coordinate this thing."

Morgan threw his raincoat onto a folding chair, undecided if he were angry or relieved at Cassidy's order.

"Bluebird One to base . . . The truck just made a left on Fortieth . . . heading west."

Castillo hurled his cigar to the floor. "Goddammit! I knew it. That son of a bitch is going after another target."

Morgan ran to the wall map. "Where?"

A loud clap of thunder rattled the trailer.

"Oh, shit!" a voice said over the speaker on Doyle's console. All eyes in the trailer turned toward it.

"What's up, buddy?" Doyle asked.

There was no response, only the soft hiss of static. After an agonizingly silent moment, the pilot said, "Damn, that was close. A wind gust caught me. I almost landed in the reference section of the library."

Doyle fingered his handlebar mustache and chuckled nervously. "I hope your library card is current," he said.

Morgan slammed his hand on the wall map. "*Where* could they be going?"

Castillo squinted at the finely detailed map, which indicated all the important buildings and landmarks in the city, and began to recite. "Times Square, the theater district, the Port Authority Bus Terminal. If the truck heads south, there's always Madison Square Garden, Penn Station—"

Liberti, seeing the look on Morgan's face, pushed Castillo away from the map. "Knock it off, Donal. You sound like a tourist guide."

Morgan ran his fingers through his hair. Everything was coming apart. That son of a bitch, Petry, was going to outsmart them after all. He spoke into the mike. "All ground units be advised, the truck is heading west on Fortieth Street. Proceed to that general location as quickly as possible and look for that truck."

"Bluebird One to base. The truck has now turned north onto Eighth Avenue."

A frustrated Morgan, intently staring at the map, willed himself to predict the truck's destination, but it was no use. There were literally dozens of targets in that area.

"Bluebird One to base. I'm going upstairs. Heavy squall line just came off the Hudson. Visibility zero. Sorry, Doyle."

"No sweat. Can you hang around up there?"

"Affirmative. As soon as I get a hole, I'll go back down."

Morgan nervously paced the aisle. He was getting claustrophobia in the cramped trailer. He wanted to jump into one of those Highway Patrol cars parked outside and go look for them himself, but he knew it was futile. His only hope was the choppers. "Doyle," he said, "get that other chopper over to the West Side." He ignored Cassidy's sharp look. "As soon as there's a clearing, I want both of them to concentrate in that area."

Castillo lit up another cigar. "You'd better tell those people at the Mission to stay alert. There's nothing says the truck can't double back to the East Side."

Dickerson, edging past a double-parked taxi, turned right on 53rd Street. "How does it look, Jimmy?"

Newell squinted into the rain-obscured sideview mirror. "No one following us." He looked at his watch. "It's time. Head for the hotel."

Lyle Petry, holding a screwdriver, stepped out of his room and hurried down the corridor. He stopped in front of an emergency exit door leading out to a roof landing. When he was sure no one was coming, he carefully removed the screws from the alarm system's magnetic contact that was attached to the door. With the screws removed, the door contact stuck to the adjoining wall contact; the electrical circuit remained closed, but it was now possible to open the door without activating the alarm.

He stepped into an alcove and waited. A few minutes later, he heard a truck horn sound. Opening the door, he stepped out onto the roof landing and into the downpour.

Dickerson, who'd pulled the truck into the loading bay, had already flung the doors open and was halfway up the ladder when Petry stuck his head over the parapet. From the angle at which he was standing, a bank of spotlights shining down on the truck's rain-soaked roof obscured the painted circle.

Standing on the ladder, Dickerson passed the boxes from Newell to Petry. Newell, the last one up the ladder, slammed the truck's rear door closed.

"How'd it go?" Petry asked, as they slipped into his room.

Dickerson brushed the rain from his shoulders. "No problem. We took our time getting here. No one was following us, I'm sure of that."

Newell dried his wet head with a towel. "In all that rain, they couldn't have stayed with us anyway."

There was a knock at the door. Newell, slipping a gun out of a shoulder holster, tiptoed to the door and looked through the peep-hole. He stepped back and opened the door. Alvaro, looking like he'd been hit by a bucket of water, came in.

Petry smiled at the Colombian's disheveled appearance. "Any problem getting here?"

"I had to ride that filthy, smelly subway. And then I got soaked walking to the hotel."

Petry slapped him on the back. "After tonight you can take a limo any place you want."

Alvaro fell into an armchair and rested his head on the back. "I hope so," he said, wishing this night were over.

"Bluebird One to base. There's a break in the clouds. I'm going down to traverse the side streets."

"Bluebird Two to base. I'll run the avenues."

"Hey, fellas"—Doyle reminded them—"be careful. There're no traffic lights up there."

Doyle turned to Morgan and for the first time that night looked discouraged. "Spotting a truck in midtown at night is tough under the best of circumstances; it's like flying through a canyon. But with this wind and rain . . ." The sentence ended with a shrug.

Morgan resumed pacing in the cramped aisle. The worst-case scenario was coming about. Two professional terrorists, driving a truck loaded with explosives, were loose in the city, and he had no idea where they were.

"Bingo!" It was Bluebird One. "The truck is parked in a loading bay on the north side of Fifty-third between Seventh and Broadway."

Liberti fingered the spot on the map. "Must be the Knickerbocker Hotel."

Castillo snapped his fingers. "That's it. Tuxes, hotel. It's all falling into place."

Cassidy put a big hand on a police officer's shoulder. "Son," he said quietly, "get that hotel's security director on the phone."

A moment later, the cop handed the telephone to Morgan. "I have Mr. Landon on the line."

Morgan grabbed the telephone. "Landon, this is Inspector Morgan. Do you have any big events going on tonight?"

"Yeah, Inspector, we do. The First Annual Sports Night Dinner is being held in the Grand Ballroom."

"Who'll be there?"

"A whole crowd of people, including a couple of dozen top professional athletes and half of the corporate executives in the city."

Morgan put his hand over the receiver. "That's their target." He spoke into the telephone. "Landon, listen up. I'll be there as soon as I can. Have floor plans of the ballroom and the hotel ready for me when I get there."

Landon, hearing the strained tone in Morgan's voice, said, "Hey, boss. I'm a retired First Grader. Do I have a problem or what?"

"You sure do."

Morgan slammed the telephone down and looked at Cassidy. "We have to get over there."

Cassidy didn't want to see them all go, but he nodded and said, "Go ahead."

"Chris, you stay here. If—"

"Not on your life," Liberti said, slipping into a trench coat.

Morgan stopped at the door and turned around. There was no one in a command rank in the trailer he could give instructions to. In desperation he turned to the police commissioner. "Call Vogel. Tell him I need the sharpshooters and emergency service units at the hotel as quickly as he can get them there. And have the Bomb Squad respond with dogs."

In other circumstances Cassidy would have been outraged at a deputy inspector shouting orders at him, but he merely nodded and said, "Done. Get the hell out of here."

Chapter
39

Morgan, Castillo, and Liberti dashed across the rain-soaked parking lot and jumped into the nearest Highway Patrol vehicle. A rotund black cop took one look at them and tossed what was left of his coffee out the window. "Where to?" he asked.

Morgan slammed the door. "The Knickerbocker Hotel. How soon can you get there?"

The cop grinned. "If I have your permission to temporarily suspend the traffic regs, Inspector, no time at all."

"You got it." The cop jerked the gear lever and stomped on the accelerator. With squealing, smoking tires, the vehicle roared out of the parking lot toward 34th Street.

With the magnetic roof light flashing and the siren set on constant, the car weaved in and out of the rain-snarled traffic. The Highway Patrol cop made it most of the way across 34th Street by driving on the wrong side of the street. At each southbound intersection Morgan pressed his head against the windshield and looked for traffic coming from the right. The driver, his attention riveted to the traffic in front of him, punched through the intersection at Morgan's terse *"Go!"*

At Sixth Avenue a fender bender involving three taxis had caused a massive tie-up. Without hesitating, the Highway cop mounted the sidewalk, scattering startled pedestrians. Castillo, sitting in the back with Liberti, grabbed a door handle for support. "Jesus, Morgan," he muttered, "he must have gone to the same driving school you went to."

Three blocks from the hotel, Morgan switched off the lights and sirens. The car screeched to a halt at the front entrance. The trio were out of the car and banging through the revolving doors before it had stopped rocking.

Landon, who was waiting for them in the lobby, ushered them into the hotel manager's office. "This is Russell Odum, the manager," he said.

Odum, an impeccably dressed man in his late forties, had the prissy look of one who spends a great deal of his time running his finger across furniture looking for dust. "What seems to be the problem?" he asked.

Morgan swept a pile of papers off the manager's desk and spread out a floor plan of the ballroom. "How many people are in there now?"

Odum's face reddened. "Now just a minute. You can't come in here and—"

Castillo leaned across the desk and poked the manager's thin chest with his index finger. "Listen, asshole, someone is going to blow up your ballroom. Just answer the question."

Odum's face turned white. "Eig— eight hundred, not counting staff. I'll have to notify them at once."

He reached for the telephone, but Castillo slapped his hand away. "Don't do that."

"W— why?"

"You'll cause a panic."

"Well, I have to do *something*."

"Yeah, just sit there and stay out of this."

Morgan was still uneasy. They were assuming Petry and his people were in the hotel, but they couldn't be sure. He turned to the security director. "There's a loading dock on Fifty-third. Where does it lead?"

"That's not ours. It's next door to the hotel."

"What's next to the loading dock?"

"Our garage."

Morgan remembered the ladder. "How high is the roof there?"

"Maybe fifteen feet."

"That's it," Castillo said. "They'll use the ladder to get to the roof. Any doors leading to that roof?"

Landon consulted the building floor plan. "Yeah, one at the end of the corridor. But it's alarmed and I haven't received any reports of a violation."

Morgan grabbed the ballroom floor plans. "We're going up there now. Have one of your people check to see if that door has been tampered with. And alert all your guards. Have them report anyone, or anything, suspicious to you immediately."

At the door Castillo turned to the manager, who'd been listening to the conversation with bulging eyes and a slack mouth. "They'll be a lot of cops showing up here very soon. Why don't you just stay in your office."

In the elevator, Morgan, Castillo, and Liberti studied the floor plan. "Christ!" Morgan said. "The place is a labyrinth of corridors and stairwells."

Liberti was looking over his shoulder. "Yeah, but there's only two ways in and out of the ballroom. The east side exits lead to the kitchen and the west lead to a shopping promenade."

Castillo unsnapped the safety strap on his shoulder holster. "I'll take the kitchen exits," he said.

Liberti, watching Castillo slip additional clips into his jacket pocket, thought of that night on the subway and wondered if she should tell Morgan about it now. She looked into Castillo's eyes, but unlike that night in the subway, she saw only calm determination there. She was careful not to look at Morgan when she said, "Hey, guys, in a little while there's going to be a lot of cops swarming around here. Let's be careful. We don't want to shoot at each other."

Morgan stiffened as he remembered her warning to him that night in the Spindrift Motel. He busied himself adjusting the earpiece on his radio. The others did the same.

The doors opened onto a wide bustling promenade and Morgan looked upon the scene with dismay. He'd hoped that the lobby outside the Grand Ballroom would be quiet, but it was occupied by a couple of dozen shops and boutiques, all of them crowded with shoppers. "All right," he said. "Let's go to work. Chris, you cover the lobby. I'll check the stairwells."

Donal Castillo slipped into the ballroom. Dinner hadn't started yet. Most of the people stood around their tables chatting and craning their necks for a glimpse of famous athletes. Several faces looked familiar to him, but they were out of uniform and he couldn't put the names with the faces.

He worked his way through the crowd and went in the doors leading to the kitchen. Except for a few waiters scurrying about with water pitchers, nothing seemed out of place. He walked through the kitchen to see what was at the other end. The catering staff, busy assembling eight hundred appetizers, barely gave him a second glance. There was an exit at the far end which led to service elevators and a stairwell. Near the elevators he found a clothes hamper. He fished through it and exchanged his field jacket for the cleanest waiter's jacket he could find. He didn't have a bow tie, but it'd have to do. Satisfied that he knew the layout, he returned to the ballroom.

A tall black man with a huge neck approached him. Castillo knew he was a linebacker with the Giants, but he couldn't remember the name.

"Excuse me," the man said with a soft voice that belied his menacing stature, "do you think you could get some more ice for table fifteen?"

Castillo nodded. "Sure. Coming right up." He was about to relay the request to a passing waiter when he spotted Manny Botnick coming into the ballroom. The nervous little man, clutching a guitar case with two hands, was heading for the bandstand. Castillo's eyes went to the case and he knew: *That* was where the explosives were. Slowly, he began to make his way toward Botnick.

Manny Botnick, ignoring everyone in the ballroom, had only one thought on his mind: Get to the bandstand, flip the latch on the case, and get the hell out of there.

The band leader looked up as he approached. "Wrong room, buddy. I already got a guitar player."

Botnick looked at his watch. It was 8:20. Petry had told him to come into the ballroom at exactly 8:30, but Botnick, frightened by what was in the guitar case, wanted to be rid of it. A few minutes either way, he had reasoned, shouldn't make a whole lot of difference.

"Damn it," he said to the band leader. "That union hall is always screwing up my gigs. Hey, do you mind if I leave this here while I make a call?"

The band leader thumbed through his sheet music. "Be my guest."

Botnick, looking around for the best place to put the case down, saw a waiter making his way through the crowd. The man was wearing a waiter's uniform, but there was something odd about him. Botnick had played in enough hotels and had seen enough waiters to know what they should look like. What was different about this guy? It suddenly hit him: The tie! He wasn't wearing a tie. Just then, the oddly dressed waiter pushed a distinguished silver-haired man out of his way and Botnick knew: *He was a cop.*

Still clutching the guitar case he ran for the nearest exit. He crashed through the doors and found himself in the kitchen. Frantically, he looked for a way out. He spotted a red Exit sign at the far end of the kitchen and ran for it. It suddenly occurred to him he was still carrying the guitar case. He flung it onto a table filled with wineglasses and there was a resounding crash as a hundred glasses cascaded to the tiled floor.

As he reached the door he looked back. The waiter had come running into the kitchen. Botnick, puffing with exertion, slammed through the rear door and found himself in a hallway. He looked right and then left. He saw a stairwell and ran toward it.

Castillo had seen Botnick bolt for the exit, but he'd gotten tangled up in a group of autograph seekers surrounding a Mets pitcher. He got to the kitchen just in time to see Botnick run out the back door. He wanted to chase Botnick, but he had to secure the guitar case first. He scooped it up and looked for a safe place to store it. Just then, a chef's assistant, carrying a slab of filet mignon, stepped out of a walk-in freezer. Castillo pushed him aside and slid the case in the freezer. "I'm a police officer," he said, slamming the door. "There's a bomb in there. Everybody stay away from it."

Drawing his gun, he sprinted toward the back door and reached the hallway just in time to see the stairwell door closing. He pushed it open slowly and heard the sound of footsteps running down the stairs. He followed.

Castillo, who was in much better condition than Botnick, was catching up. Three landings below, Castillo could hear Botnick's labored breathing and knew he was just around the next corner. Grasping his gun with two hands, Castillo spun around the corner and flattened himself against the opposite wall. *"Police!"* he shouted.

Botnick, startled by Castillo's sudden appearance, lost his footing and started to slide down the stairs head first. Castillo put his gun up and started down after him.

Botnick, desperately flailing his arms, grabbed the railing and stopped his momentum. He awkwardly righted himself. Suddenly, he pulled out a gun and pointed it at Castillo.

The DEA agent, less than five feet away, was caught completely off guard. Instinctively, he slammed his body against the wall and

MICHAEL GRANT

pumped off three quick rounds. Botnick's body jerked, and rolled backward down the rest of the steps.

At the bottom of the stairwell, Castillo picked up Botnick's gun and examined it. "You asshole," he said aloud. "You forgot to take the safety off."

He keyed his mike. "Morgan, this is Castillo. Botnick is out of the game."

Standing in another stairwell, Morgan heard the transmission with a sense of relief. Moments before, the hotel security director had told him that the exit door on the second floor had indeed been tampered with. Now he knew they were in the hotel, but at least there was one less to worry about.

"Captain Ferrera to Morgan."

Morgan acknowledged the transmission. "Go ahead."

"I have fifteen men with me in the lobby and more on the way. Where do you want them?"

"I want every street exit covered. I'm in the northeast stairwell on the fifth floor. Meet me here with every available sharpshooter you have."

A few minutes later, Captain Ferrera and six police officers in civilian clothes came rushing up the stairs. "All the exits are covered," he said. "I left word in the lobby. As soon as the others arrive they'll sweep and secure the staircases."

"Good. Do you know what these people look like?"

The men nodded and Ferrera smiled grimly. "Since this morning all they've been doing is memorizing photos and cleaning weapons."

"Botnick has been taken out, but the others are somewhere in this hotel. Spread out. And be careful."

Morgan left Ferrera to assign his people and went back into the lobby where he found Liberti near the elevator bank.

"Anything yet?" she asked him.

"No. Ferrera's men are—"

He was interrupted by a breathless, excited voice on the radio. ". . . second floor . . . I'm in pursuit of . . . the black guy. He just ran into the . . . southwest stairwell."

There was a flurry of overlapping transmissions.

". . . on the way . . ."

"I'm on the sixth floor . . . coming down."

"Frank . . . I'm right behind you . . ."

"Should we go?" Liberti asked.

"No. He's got plenty of help. We'll stay here in case—"

He stopped when he heard the faint sound of automatic gunfire, followed by the distinct *pop, pop* of handguns. Morgan ran his hand across his forehead; his hand was soaking wet.

Liberti gave him a troubled look. "Dan, are you all right?"

"Yeah. I was just wondering where Fleming is."

Liberti had been wondering the same thing. "He'll be okay," she said, trying to sound more optimistic than she felt. "He has enough sense to stay out of the line of fire."

"Unless he's with Petry," Morgan said morosely. "We won't take that son of a bitch without a fight."

"We got him! We got him!" an excited voice shouted over the radio.

A moment later, the calm voice of Captain Ferrera came on the radio. "Dickerson is DOA, and we have a cop shot. Tony, have an RMP standing by for a hospital run. We're on our way down."

"Ten-four," a voice monitoring the radio in the lobby answered.

"Two down, two to go," Liberti whispered.

"Three, if Alvaro is with them. And we don't even know what he looks like. If—"

Morgan stopped to stare as a short, compact man, wearing a tux and carrying an overcoat over his arm, stepped off the elevator. "It's Newell," he whispered.

The man glanced at his watch and frowned.

"Let's get him," Liberti said, starting toward him.

Morgan grabbed her sleeve. "I'll go after him," he said with a dry mouth.

She pulled away. "I can take care of myself," she hissed.

"I know that, but someone has to stay here and look for Petry."

"Then you—"

"He's leaving. I don't have time to argue."

Newell began walking down the corridor at a leisurely pace, but as he got away from the shoppers, he quickened his step. At the end of the long hallway it intersected with another one. Newell had a choice of going left or right. He stopped as if to decide. Then, without warning he turned and made eye contact with Morgan, who'd been hurrying after him.

Caught off guard, Morgan stopped at the nearest door and fumbled in his pockets, pretending he was looking for his key. But he didn't fool Newell, who bolted down the left corridor.

Muttering an oath, Morgan drew his gun and ran after him. At the end of the corridor, he stopped and cautiously peered around the corner. Newell had run to the end, but he stopped when he realized it was a dead end. He threw aside his overcoat, which had been concealing an Uzi, and started back toward Morgan.

Morgan drew back and pressed himself against the wall. The gun in his hand was slippery. He wiped his palms on his trouser leg. He had to do something. Newell would be upon him in a moment. He dropped to the floor and, exposing only his gun hand and a small part of his face, peeked around the corner. Newell was less than twenty yards away.

"Police," Morgan shouted. "Drop your weapon. *Now!*"

Newell, unnerved by the disembodied voice, jumped back. His eyes darted about, seeking the source of the voice. But in the dimly lit corridor, he hadn't yet spotted Morgan's concealed position.

The ladies' room door to Newell's left opened and an elderly woman, wearing an evening gown, stepped out. He grabbed the startled woman and held her in front of him. Now that he had more time, he spotted Morgan. The Uzi barrel went to the woman's temple. "Put the gun down and step out where I can see you," he said.

Morgan hesitated.

"*Now!*" Newell shouted. "Or this lady loses her head."

The woman began to whimper. Morgan put the gun on the carpet and slowly got to his feet. His entire body was bathed in sweat. He stepped out into the open, but he stood close to the edge of the corner. "Give it up, Newell" he said. "The hotel is full of cops."

The mention of his name seemed to fluster Newell for an instant, but he quickly regained his composure. "Maybe so, but there's going to be one less cop to worry about."

As the Uzi's barrel swung toward him, Morgan saw everything in freeze-frame—the woman's bulging eyes; the menacing black hole at the end of the barrel; the dull look in Newell's eyes.

Suddenly, he was in the hallway of the tenement again. But this time he saw everything clearly. Lawrence, holding the two children in front of him, screamed, "Get away from me, cops." It was then that Fredericks stepped out into the open. Lawrence's gun swung toward the young cop, and Morgan, without thinking, stepped out into the line of fire. *"Lawrence!"* he shouted.

He'd hoped to distract him, but it didn't work. Lawrence never turned. Hoping to throw Lawrence's aim off, Morgan aimed at the ceiling above the man's head and fired. But Lawrence fired a split second earlier. Morgan saw Fredericks spin and slide down the wall. While Morgan was watching the cop fall, Lawrence whirled and fired at him. A sharp pain ran down his shoulder and everything went black.

Now, back in the hotel corridor, Dan Morgan blinked hard. He saw the woman's eyes roll up in her head, and he dove for the safety of the corner. The woman's falling body deflected Newell's aim and a half-dozen rounds chewed up the carpet where Morgan had been standing.

Morgan, grabbing for his gun, rolled twice, and came up squeezing the trigger as fast as he could. Newell, hit in the chest and stomach with three of the seven rounds fired, staggered backward and pressed the trigger. The magazine emptied into the wall, shattering a row of mirrors and an antique vase.

Morgan staggered to his feet and ran to the woman's side. Except for a good fright, she was unharmed. With a shaking hand, he keyed the mike. "This is Morgan," he said, breathing heavily. "Newell is DOA."

Standing together outside the ballroom Castillo and Liberti heard the transmission. Liberti exhaled sharply. "Thank God. That just leaves Petry."

424   MICHAEL
       GRANT

Castillo, who'd changed back into his field jacket, frowned. "What's the matter, Donal?"

"Where the hell *is* Petry?" He turned toward the elevator. "We have plenty of help up here. I'm going down to the second floor. We know they got in that way, he may try to get out that way too."

"I'll go with you." She was expecting an argument from him, but he said nothing and punched the Down elevator button.

When the gun fight between Dickerson and the police had taken place, Lyle Petry and Celeste had been standing in a clothing boutique opposite the ballroom. Petry was uneasy. It was almost eight-thirty and he hadn't seen Botnick go into the ballroom yet. Then Petry heard the gunfire and knew the operation was a bust. Taking Celeste by the arm, they'd calmly taken the elevator to the ground floor. When the doors opened, and he saw that the lobby was ringed with cops, they'd stayed on the elevator, got off at the second floor, and returned to their room.

Celeste was near hysteria. "Lyle, how are we going to get out of here? There are cops everywhere."

Petry yanked his bow tie off. "Get out of that evening dress," he said.

His original plan had been to stay in the room until the police had gone, but then he realized that they'd probably conduct a room-by-room search.

"How will we get out of here?" she asked.

"The same way Jimmy and Glen got in."

When they'd changed, Petry opened the door and peeked out. The hallway was deserted. "Okay," he said. "Let's go."

He stopped at the door, his eyes fixed on the box of grenades and automatic weapons lying on the bed. He didn't want to leave them, but it was best to travel light. A handgun, he decided, should be all he needed to break out. He slammed the door behind him.

Liberti and Castillo got off the elevator on the second floor and hurried toward the corridor leading to the emergency exit door. As they came around the corner, they saw a couple walking about twenty-five yards in front of them. At first Liberti barely gave them a second glance. After all, they were looking for men dressed in evening clothes. But then Liberti's eyes went to the woman's shoes. That's odd, she thought. She's wearing ordinary jeans, but she's got on a pair of sequined pumps, more suitable for an evening gown . . . She looked at the back of the man's blond head and an alarm bell went off. "Donal," she whispered, "it's Petry and Celeste."

Castillo slipped his gun out. The door leading to the roof was only ten yards away. He had to stop them before they got to that door. Once outside, they'd have the whole city to hide in.

Petry heard the approaching footsteps and whirled. He saw the gun in Castillo's hand and instinctively yanked Celeste in front of him.

"*Lyle*, what—?

He put his arm around her neck. "Don't worry, baby," he whispered confidently. "They won't shoot you."

Castillo reacted by violently shoving Liberti to the side as Petry's first shot whizzed past her ear. Then, without hesitating, he dropped into a combat stance and pumped six shots into the center of Celeste Escobar's chest. As he knew they would, the steel-jacketed, high-velocity bullets ripped through Celeste and into Petry.

Lyle Petry, caught completely by surprise by Castillo's unexpected action, staggered backward under Celeste's dead weight and fired off the remainder of his clip.

Castillo dove for the floor, but not quickly enough. Two rounds tore into his thigh. The impact spun him around and slammed him into the wall. Then the leg buckled. As he fell to the floor, he emptied his clip into Petry's chest. But it wasn't necessary. Castillo's first fusillade had mortally wounded the ex–Special Forces captain.

Liberti ran to Castillo's side and looked down at his blood-drenched leg. "Donal, I'll get an ambulance right away."

Castillo, grimacing, yanked his belt off. "Here, doc, tie this around my leg first. I think he hit an artery."

While she held the tourniquet firmly with one hand she fumbled for the radio with the other. "This is Liberti on the second floor in front of room two-one-six. We have an officer down. We need immediate medical attention."

Morgan came on the radio. "Did you get Petry?"

Liberti, overwhelmed by tension and fright, slumped against the wall next to Castillo and looked at the two sprawled bodies in front of her. "Affirmative," she said softly. "Petry and Celeste are dead."

Five minutes later, Morgan and Liberti stood with the PC in the hotel lobby and watched the paramedics wheel Castillo to the ambulance. "Did we get them all?" a stern Cassidy asked.

"All except for Alvaro," Morgan answered. "But we're not even sure he was here."

Had Morgan looked toward the elevator bank at that moment, he would have seen a man with a salt and pepper beard coming off the elevator with a shocked group of men and women in evening clothes.

The adrenaline still pumping through Morgan's veins made his eyes shine. "We haven't found Ray Fleming yet. I've ordered a room-by-room search of the Hyatt. Chris and I are going to go over there now—"

"Don't bother."

The three turned around.

An ashen-faced Captain Zakovitch, looking more gaunt than ever, was standing before them. "We found Ray Fleming."

Chapter
40

8:30 P.M. MONDAY, APRIL 22 • Donal Castillo was the last one to arrive at Rouen, a small French restaurant in the heart of Greenwich Village. Chris Liberti had decided they would have a farewell dinner before they went their separate ways, but it had taken two weeks to get all of them together. Castillo had been in the hospital, and Morgan, who'd taken an unexpected vacation, had just returned yesterday.

Castillo, hobbling on crutches, awkwardly slipped into the tight booth.

Liberti took the crutches and slipped them under the table. "You look like you're getting around on those things pretty good."

"I'd better. The doc says I'll be on them for at least two months."

"Not bad," Morgan said. "Considering you had a fractured femur and a severed artery."

Castillo took the menu from the waiter. "What are you guys having?" he asked.

"We ordered already. Dan is having duck and I'm having the sole. Donal, this is on me. Order anything you like."

Castillo studied the extensive menu, which was all in French. "Do you have a hamburger?" he asked the waiter.

Morgan elbowed Liberti. "You owe me a buck."

"We have steak tartare," the waiter said.

"What's that?"

"Freshly ground sirloin steak mixed with special herbs and topped with a raw egg."

Castillo handed the menu back to the waiter. "I'll have mine well done. Hold the egg."

"Sir," the flustered waiter said, "steak tartare isn't cooked."

"Why not?"

"Because . . . it's not supposed to be cooked."

Liberti's right eyebrow arched. "Hey, pal. He wants it well done minus the egg. You think the chef can handle that?"

"Very good, madam." The waiter turned on his heel and left.

Liberti shook her head in despair. "Donal, what am I going to do with you? I picked this place because I thought you'd order something other than a hamburger."

"I'm not much of a gourmet."

Liberti patted his hand. "I know. I know."

Morgan poured wine for Castillo. "What's the latest from Colombia?" he asked.

"I don't know who told what to who in Washington, but the day after the attack at the hotel, every available DEA agent was flown into Colombia for a full court press of the Medellin and Cali cartels. Then the State Department put the screws to the Colombian government. The word is we threatened to cut off aid. The resulting pressure on the cartels has them scrambling for their lives and property. The drug bosses, pissed about having so much attention drawn to them, put out a contract on everyone connected with Puño Blanco." Castillo managed a smile. "The Medellin cartel has a zero defects program for their management staff. For the past several days Puño Blanco members have been showing up in ditches and bombed cars. I think it's safe to say no one is going to suggest another terrorist attack on the U.S. any time soon."

"What about Alvaro?" Liberti asked. "Did you ever find out who he was?"

"Alvaro Gavis was an ex–army colonel."

Liberti perked up. "Did I hear the past tense?"

"Yeah. The people behind Puño Blanco didn't think much of Alvaro's results. We heard he caught a plane to Bogotá the night of the attack at the hotel. Two days later, they found him—I should say parts of him—on a dirt road outside Medellin. His dick was—" He looked at Liberti.

"Go ahead," Liberti said, shaking her head in resignation. "Say it."

Castillo reached for another roll. "His penis was stuffed in his mouth. The docs say that happened before he died."

The waiter arrived with the appetizers.

"Thank you for sharing that with us," Liberti said dryly. "It's done wonders for my appetite."

Castillo grunted. "How'd the cover story about Qaddafi go over?"

Liberti grinned. "Great! It explained the police murders and the assault on the hotel. Fortunately, no one in Puño Blanco lived to contradict the story. I hear Muammar has been sputtering denials since the story hit the paper."

Castillo picked up his glass. "Sure. He's scared shitless we'll bomb his tent again. Fuck 'im." He hoisted his glass in a toast. "I hope we do bomb his ass."

Liberti patted Castillo's hand. "Donal, you're such a humanitarian."

During dinner the conversation wandered from topic to topic, but none of it very important. Usually, when cops get together after the conclusion of a successful investigation, they never tire of talking about it, and with each retelling more and more outrageous embellishment is added. But that's to be expected. Cops have so few victories in their professional lives. But this night, as if by tacit agreement, no mention was made of the events that had occurred in the past several weeks. Their victory had been bittersweet. They'd stopped Puño Blanco, but it had cost Ray Fleming his life.

Finally, over dessert, the subject of the future came up.

"Where are you going next, Donal?" Liberti asked.

"Back to Colombia. You know how law enforcement works. You can only apply the heat for so long. Eventually you run out of money and manpower and business returns to normal. Someone has to be there to break their balls when things quiet down."

Liberti turned to Morgan, who'd been very quiet during dinner. "How about you, Dan?"

"Cassidy promoted me to full inspector."

"That's great. Where will you be assigned?"

"I don't know yet," he said vaguely. "I have a lot of lost time coming to me. I'm still on vacation. How about you?"

"The FBI Academy. I'm going to teach a terrorism course."

"Is that what you want?"

"Yep. It's a good career move for me. A year or so there, then back to the streets as a supervisor."

Morgan smiled. "Still on your way to the New York ADIC job."

"Sure," she said defiantly. "Why not?"

"The first time you told me that I thought you were nuts. But I was wrong. You'll make it and you'll be good at it."

"Well, thank you, sir."

Castillo looked at his watch. "Hey, I gotta get out of here. I got a plane to catch."

Liberti looked at him in surprise. "Tonight? You're still on crutches. Why don't you take some time off?"

Castillo scowled. "And do what? Fish? I'd be bored out of my mind. Hand me those crutches."

Morgan and Liberti helped Castillo out to the street and Morgan hailed a cab. Castillo opened the door and threw the crutches inside. Then he turned. A man not given to displaying his emotion, he looked decidedly uncomfortable. A sudden breeze ruffled his hair and he patted the sparse hairs back into place. "You two are wasted in the wrong departments," he said quietly. "You oughta be in the DEA."

"Wow!" Liberti said. *Two* compliments in the same night from you guys." She put her hand to her chest. "Be still my heart." Then, self-consciously, she stepped forward and kissed him on the cheek. "Here"—she slipped a small brightly wrapped package into his hand —"this is for you."

"What is it?"

"A whaddayacallit. A thing to clip the end of the cigar. Jeez, Donal, I hated it when you spit those things out."

Castillo slipped the package into his pocket. "I'll try to remember to use it."

Morgan stepped forward and put his hand out. "I can't say it's been fun, but it's been a hell of an experience working with you. Take care of yourself, Don."

Castillo's handshake was firm. "I always do," he said.

Liberti and Morgan watched the taxi pull away from the curb.

"A strange man," she said.

"We're all driven by demons," Morgan replied. "We just react to them in different ways."

Liberti looked up into his eyes. In the street light his blue eyes were a darker shade. "Come on, Morgan," she said, taking his arm. "I'll buy you a drink."

They found a small cafe a couple of blocks away. They descended a flight of stairs and stepped into a darkened grottolike room. Once they were seated, their eyes grew accustomed to the dim light and they saw that there were only a few people at the bar. They were the only ones seated at the handful of tables.

MICHAEL GRANT

As the waitress was putting their drinks down, a spotlight came on over the piano and a man wearing a tuxedo that might have fit him twenty years ago heaved himself up onto the bandstand.

He attempted an arpeggio that ended badly in a logjam of fingers halfway up the keyboard. "Enough of that." He cranked the mike closer to him and the amplifier whistled from the feedback. "Hey," he shouted in his best Las Vegas lounge voice, "is everyone having a good time?"

From the bar came the sound of a lone person clapping. It was the bartender.

"What do you say we liven up this joint?" the piano player said, launching into a vigorous—if not quite accurate—rendition of "New York, New York."

"Get a load of the rug on that guy," Liberti whispered. "It looks like the Howard Cosell model, only two sizes too small."

When Morgan didn't answer, she turned to him and saw that he was deep in thought. "Thinking of Ray?" she said quietly.

Morgan nodded.

For most of the evening he'd been thinking about the night he'd gone to Ray Fleming's wake. Unlike most police officers' wakes, there had been no cluster of cops standing at the back of the room, trying to carry on strained conversations while they waited for a decent interval of time to pass so they could retire to the nearest gin mill. Except for Zakovitch, Liberti, Castillo, and Morgan, Ray Fleming hadn't been a cop long enough to know other cops. Instead the room was filled with neighbors, friends, and relatives.

When Morgan came in he saw Fleming's father talking to the Police Department chaplain and went straight to the coffin. Ray Fleming was laid out in the dress blue uniform he'd never gotten the opportunity to wear. Pinned above his shield was one decoration: a gold edged green bar containing twelve blue stars—the Medal of Honor, the highest award the Police Department could offer.

Morgan looked down into Ray Fleming's placid face and tried to recall a prayer, but the only thing that came to mind were the words of a Whittier poem:

Officer DOWN

For of all sad words of tongue or pen,
The saddest are these: "It might have been!"

He rose and introduced himself to John Fleming. "I'm Inspector Dan Morgan," he said. "I worked with your son."

The gray-haired man appeared slightly dazed, but his handshake was firm. "Thank you for coming. You know, I still can't get it into my head that my son was a policeman." His eyes wandered to the casket. "We had more than a few rows over that. I was afraid he'd spend the rest of his life driving that damn cab."

"Ray was only a police officer for a short time, Mr. Fleming, but I want you to know he sacrificed his life to save an awful lot of lives, many of them police officers."

Fleming's gaze came back to Morgan. "Captain Zakovitch came to see me after . . . after Ray's death. He explained some of it to me."

"Then you know you can be very proud of your son."

"I am."

Morgan studied the stern face. Except for an added brightness in the eyes, there was no emotion in the heavily lined face. John Fleming reminded Morgan of his own father. They were both old-school Irishmen who adhered to the stoic rule, Display no emotion. Perhaps, Morgan thought, that was why the Irish made good cops. From early on, children of men like John Fleming and Morgan's father were taught to keep their emotions in check—an important prerequisite in police work.

A woman joined them and John Fleming introduced her as his sister.

"Are you a policeman, too?" she asked.

"Yes. As I told your brother, I worked with Ray. He was a fine police officer."

"Thank you. Earlier, that nice Miss Liberti and a Mr. Castillo stopped by. They said so many wonderful things about Ray."

With slightly trembling fingers, she took a pack of cigarettes out of her handbag. "Do you smoke, Inspector Morgan?"

"No, I don't."

She offered the pack to her brother. John Fleming was about to take a cigarette, but he pulled his hand back. "I'm not supposed to be smoking," he said gruffly. "Don't be offering me a cigarette, Mary."

His sister's tart response was interrupted by the chaplain, who announced that the recital of the rosary was about to begin. As the group droned the opening of the Our Father, Morgan slipped out the door.

After the funeral the next day, he'd driven straight to a friend's cabin in the Catskills where he'd spent most of two weeks walking in the woods and thinking about his options.

"You don't blame yourself for his death, do you?"

Chris Liberti's question brought him back to the present.

"What? Oh, no, I don't. I've been doing a lot of thinking since Ray's death. It took me a while to figure it out, but you were right when you said that I can't take on the responsibility for everyone's life."

She looked into his pensive face. "After my problem in Chicago I attended a stress seminar. The shrink said living through a life-threatening situation is an emotionally draining experience. You can become overwhelmed by self-doubts and guilt."

She was thinking about the turbulent, sleepless night she'd experienced after the hotel attack. They'd finally tied up all the loose ends and she'd returned to her apartment exhausted. But once in bed, she couldn't sleep. She kept seeing the shocked, horrified expression on Celeste Escobar's face when Castillo shot her.

All night she tossed and turned, pondering the legal and moral implications of what Castillo had done. Celeste was part of Petry's group and deserved to be punished. But she was unarmed. All of Liberti's moral instincts and legal training told her it was wrong to shoot an unarmed person.

Her first inclination had been to go to Morgan and tell him what had happened. But that wouldn't have been fair to him. He had enough problems. Of course there were always her own superiors . . .

As the early morning light began to filter through her bedroom

435 **Officer DOWN**

curtains, the moral and legal issues that had been keeping her awake all night began to seem naive and foolish. She and Castillo had not been in a classroom exercise. This had been no mock shooting, no role-play situation where, after it was over, everyone could debate endlessly about the appropriateness of a given response. No. In that hotel corridor they had been in a life-and-death situation with only seconds to make the correct decision.

Slowly, in those early morning hours she'd begun to clarify in her mind exactly what had happened and why. Petry was an excellent marksman. At that distance he would certainly have killed both her and Castillo. Fortunately for her, Castillo had made the correct choice for them. In that moment she realized she owed her life to Donal Castillo.

As she lay in bed with tears coursing down her face, she contemplated one final thought that both terrified and astonished her: she knew with a certainty that she wouldn't have been able to do what Donal Castillo had done, even if it meant her life.

"Sometimes I wonder why we do it," Morgan said.

Liberti shook the cobwebs from her mind. "I wonder how *long* we can do it? The shrink said we have a finite amount of emotional currency to pay for these events. Each time we're confronted by a life-threatening or traumatic experience, we pay out more currency. Soon there's nothing left."

"I may have reached that point, Chris."

She looked at him sharply. "Are you getting out?"

"I don't know. But I do know I can get out if I want to. I don't have anything to prove to myself or anyone else."

She slid her hand on top of his. "Enough of this gloomy stuff. Let's talk about more pleasant things. What do you say tomorrow night you come to my place for dinner? For dessert I'll microwave us some espresso."

"Hey, little lady, do you have any requests?"

Chris Liberti looked up at the piano player and realized he was addressing her. "I have a request," she said under her breath, "but I don't think the piano would fit."

"Show tunes, movies, Broadway plays," his voice boomed over the sound system. "What'll it be?"

She saw it was useless to ignore him. "Anything, as long as it's quiet," she said, hoping he'd take the hint and leave them alone.

"I don't think I know how that goes." He looked toward the bar and winked. "Maybe you could hum a few bars for me."

Again, the sound of the clapping bartender.

"I don't believe this," she said, putting her head in her hands. "I'm trying to seduce you and I'm being heckled by this Las Vegas dropout."

The piano player loosened his tie and opened his collar, revealing several thick gold chains tangled up in his hairy gray chest. In a poor imitation of Tony Bennett he began to sing: "Hello, young lovers whoever you are . . ."

Morgan waited until he was sure they wouldn't be bothered again. Then he said, "I thought you didn't cook."

"I don't. I figured you could bring the beer and we'd eat Chinese."

Morgan laughed.

"Hey, don't laugh. I may not be able to cook, but I set a mean table. Whaddaya say, Dan?"

"I don't know, Chris."

She heard the hesitancy in his voice and withdrew her hand from his. "Your wife?"

He nodded. "Yeah. We separated because of 'another man.' But it wasn't the usual triangle; my *ego* was the third party. After I got shot I had something I needed to prove to myself. Now that I've done that, I want her back."

Chris Liberti, suddenly feeling self-conscious, inched away from him. "Lucky woman. Will she have you?"

"I think so." He looked into Chris Liberti's soft brown eyes. "I'm sorry, Chris. Another time, other circumstances—"

"Hey, it probably wouldn't have worked out anyway. We'd argue all the time about which was better, the Bureau or the PD."

"The PD, of course—"

"See what I mean?"

"Hey, it's about that time, gang," the piano player announced. "The evening is drawing to a close and it's time to put your dreams away for another day." He played the opening chords of "Goodnight, Sweetheart."

"My God!" she said. "I haven't heard that since my high school prom." With a sad smile, she took Morgan's hand. "Come on," she said, pulling him to his feet. "Let's have one last dance."

E p i l o g u e

In June 1991, just two months after Donal Castillo returned to Colombia to continue his personal war against drugs, the Colombian Constitutional Assembly voted in a new constitution with a clause banning extradition.

Within hours of that vote, Pablo Escobar, the billionaire head of the Medellin cartel, and several of his associates surrendered to the authorities.